Lena, the sea and me

MARIA PARR

Translated from Norwegian by Guy Puzey

WALKER BOOKS

NORLA
NORWEGIAN LITERATURE ABROAD

This translation has been published with the financial support
of NORLA, Norwegian Literature Abroad

This is a work of fiction. Names, characters, places and incidents are either the
product of the author's imagination or, if real, used fictitiously. All statements,
activities, stunts, descriptions, information and material of any other kind
contained herein are included for entertainment purposes only and should
not be relied on for accuracy or replicated, as they may result in injury.

First published in Great Britain 2020 by Walker Books Ltd
87 Vauxhall Walk, London SE11 5HJ

2 4 6 8 10 9 7 5 3 1

Text © 2017 Det Norske Samlaget, Oslo
Originally published as *Keeperen og havet* by Det Norske Samlaget, Oslo
Published in arrangement with Hagen Agency, Oslo
English language translation © 2020 Guy Puzey
Cover and interior illustrations © 2020 Lara Paulussen

The right of Maria Parr, Guy Puzey and Lara Paulussen to be identified as
author, translator and illustrator respectively of this work has been asserted by
them in accordance with the Copyright, Designs and Patents Act 1988

This book has been typeset in Berkeley Oldstyle

Printed and bound in Great Britain by CPI Group (UK) Ltd, Croydon, CR0 4YY

British Library Cataloguing in Publication Data: a catalogue record
for this book is available from the British Library

ISBN 978-1-4063-8340-9

www.walker.co.uk

MIX
Paper from
responsible sources
FSC
www.fsc.org   FSC® C020471

Contents

Part One

Saltwater summer

CHAPTER ONE

Jumping from the breakwater

*T*he back door slammed shut, making our whole house shake. Then there followed an almighty crash, and somebody shouting "Oh, fishcakes!"

I stumbled out of my attic bedroom onto the landing, still half asleep. The rest of my family were already standing there with unbrushed hair and confused expressions. Minda, my big sister, only had one eye open. Dad looked like he hadn't worked out yet if he was a man or a duvet.

"Bang!" shouted my little sister, Krølla.

"What on earth was that?" asked Magnus, my big brother.

"Either there's been some kind of natural disaster," said Mum, "or Lena Lid's back from her holidays."

It wasn't a natural disaster. When I got to the bottom of the stairs, Lena, my best friend and dear neighbour, was standing there in the corridor.

"Hi, Trille," she sighed.

"Hi. What's that you've got there?"

"It's your present."

I rubbed my eyes. "Thank you. What is it?"

"A pile of sticks and broken glass, obviously! But it *was* a ship in a bottle."

Lena looked miserable.

"Maybe it can be fixed?" I suggested.

"Fixed?" said Lena. "It was supposed to be the best present ever. It can't be fixed! I really don't know how they managed to get that ship inside the bottle, Trille. The masts and sails were all up and were way wider than the neck."

Mum helped us clean up the shipwreck. She wanted to throw it away, but I gathered up all the bits of glass and wood in an ice-cream tub and put it in my room. It was a present, after all.

Lena sat down at our breakfast table. She looked different, and I had to check carefully several times to see what had changed. She'd had her hair cut and got some multicoloured braid things put in her hair. She'd got a suntan too. As for me, I felt a bit too much like my normal self, sitting there in the same old shorts I'd been wearing when she'd left. Our family hardly ever goes on holiday, or at least not abroad. We've got our farm and everything to look after. But Lena, that lucky sausage, she'd just spent two long weeks on Crete with her mum and her stepdad, Isak.

She'd drunk smoothies with little umbrellas in them, she told me while I ate my liver paste on bread. And she'd slept under only one sheet and swum in the warm sea. There were hundreds of little shops there, with millions of cool things she could get with her pocket money. Like that bottle. She'd had chips for dinner every day. And it was so hot around lunchtime on Crete that it was almost like standing next to a Midsummer bonfire the whole time.

"Smoking haddocks, you should've seen what it was like, Trille!"

"Yes," I said, carrying on munching.

It was annoying never having been to the Mediterranean. But I had something exciting to tell Lena too. I waited anxiously for her to ask if anything new had happened back here in Norway. But she didn't. On Crete there was a speedboat she'd taken to a little island, she told me, and her mum had tried being dragged along behind it with some kind of balloon in the air.

"Anyway, did I tell you how hot it was?" she asked.

I nodded. Lena went on about a stray dog called Porto, who might have had rabies, about some girls she'd played with – who hardly dared to do any balancing games at all – and about having pancakes for breakfast.

Eventually I couldn't wait any longer.

"I jumped off the highest part of the breakwater."

Lena finally stopped talking. She squinted at me suspiciously. "You're joking."

I shook my head. My neighbour got up. I could

quite clearly tell that this was one of those things she'd have to see before she could believe it. And see it she would!

"Thanks for the food," I called to Mum, who was somewhere in the kitchen, with my mouth full. Then I grabbed my towel from where it was hanging on the banisters.

The L-shaped breakwater in Mathildewick Cove is made of massive rocks and has a swimming area in the crook of its arm. In the winter, the storms blow in fine sand, which we use to make sandcastles and other fortifications. But when Lena went on holiday that summer, I'd been allowed to go with Minda and Magnus and their friends to the outside of the breakwater, where it's highest and the water below is deep and cold. It was almost like the beginning of a new life.

Lena's the champion of Mathildewick Cove when it comes to jumping off tall things. Nobody has less fear in their stomach. Or less sense in their head, as Magnus says. But even Lena's never jumped from the breakwater. She doesn't float very well.

"Throwing Lena into the fjord is more or less like dropping an anchor," says Grandpa.

It was quite a big deal that there was something I could jump from that she couldn't. I could tell that Lena wasn't best pleased.

There I was on the highest rock on the breakwater. It was the crack of dawn, and it was only sixteen degrees in the air.

"Are you sure you're psyched up enough for this?" Lena asked me seriously.

She was leaning over one of the other rocks, wearing her jacket and a Mediterranean scarf. I nodded. I'd jumped in the water lots of times while she'd been away. But it had always been at high tide. Now the tide was out, and it was further to jump. I could see the bottom. The wind buffeted my swimming shorts. For a moment I wondered whether it was really worth it. But then I saw Lena, back from Crete, leaning over the rock and not believing I could do it.

I closed my eyes and took a deep breath. One. Two. THREE!

Ker-splash! came the sound as I hit the water, and then *sworlsh* as the bubbling surface closed over my head. The first time I'd gone down into the deep like this, I'd thought I was going to drown. Now I knew that all I had to do was thrash my legs about like crazy and hold my breath.

"*Phuh!*" I puffed as I shot back through the surface of the water and into the summer morning air.

Lena had climbed up onto the highest rock and was looking down at me sceptically. I smiled triumphantly. I'd shown her this time!

Next thing I knew, Lena was putting one foot in front of the other and slapping her hands against her face to psych herself up.

"*Ay-ay-aaaaaaaaaah!*" she howled.

Then she flew through the air in her jeans, jumper, jacket, scarf and trainers.

Ker-splash!

* * *

It was only as she leapt from the breakwater that Lena properly landed home from her holidays. Talking about smoothies on Crete doesn't quite have the same shine to it when you've almost drowned

21

in Mathildewick Cove. She resurfaced after what seemed an endlessly long time, and then disappeared again with a *bloop*.

If Grandpa hadn't come along with his fishing gaff, I don't know how it all would've ended. He used the long pole with the hook on its end to pull Lena ashore like a giant fish, while she coughed and flailed about worse than ever.

"I did actually drown for a moment," Lena said afterwards. "I saw an enormous light."

We'd drunk two mugs of Isak's special red-hot July cocoa, but Lena was still shaking like a lawnmower left running.

"Pfft," I said. "You can't drown and still be alive. It was just the sun. That's what it looks like from underwater."

"You don't know what I saw! The sea in Mathildewick Cove is colder than iced tea. The people on Crete would seriously die if they went swimming here!"

I didn't say anything. It was where we'd always swum.

"Well," Lena went on, "never in my life am I going to jump from that breakwater again. Been there, done that."

She tilted her head back happily, downing the last few gulps of her cocoa.

CHAPTER TWO

The crowd at Hilltop Jon's farm

When Mum heard about us jumping in the water, she gave each of us a formidably large bucket.

"Anybody who's big enough to jump from the breakwater is big enough to start helping out a bit more. Don't come home until you've picked enough bilberries to fill these right up," she ordered.

Lena looked at the buckets in horror. "I'm not part of your family, Kari."

"Shall I remind you of that next time we're having pancakes with bilberry jam here and you suddenly pop round?" Mum asked her.

I could see that Lena was thinking about

answering back, but even she wouldn't dare to defy Mum. My mother's as strict as an old headmistress these days. Magnus secretly calls her "the Dictator". Lena says it's hardly surprising that Mum is so strict. She thinks things in the Danielsen Yttergård family are completely out of control. Minda and Magnus slam the doors so hard that our house is permanently trembling. And Krølla goes on and on so much that sometimes we could do with helmets to shield our heads.

"And then there's you, a lazy so-and-so always drifting off in your own world and never clearing away your plate after dinner. It's no wonder Kari has to sort you lot out. It's just a shame that innocent people have to suffer when all they've done wrong is live in the house next door."

As for Lena, she's pleased she can relax with her own peaceful family. Things have calmed down at their house since she and her mum got Isak. He potters around with his ruffled hair and never gets cross. I wonder if he's so calm because he's a doctor. Maybe he's so used to illness and drama that living with Lena is no stress at all. Sometimes Lena calls him "Dad", but when she does, she says it quickly and seems a bit embarrassed, almost as if she's afraid he'll disappear if he hears that word.

* * *

By the time we reached the forest where the bilberries grow, up behind Hilltop Jon's farm, we'd walked off the cold from our swim. Lena stuck her head down into her bucket.

"Child labour!" she yelled with all her might. "There's an echo in here, Trille," she added. "Kari might as well have given us a whole bathtub to fill up."

I sat down by a bilberry bush and started to pluck the berries off the stalks. The sun's rays sneaked their way between a thousand leaves, making a polka dot pattern on my T-shirt. Lena sat a short distance away, throwing pine cones.

For a brief moment, everything was lovely and quiet, like a summer's day ought to be, until she said, "One measly little brother, Trille. Is that too much to ask, do you think? Honestly?"

My best friend isn't a person who wishes for things. She just decides how things are going to be.

And two years ago, as soon as her mum had married Isak, Lena had made up her mind that they were going to have a baby, and that it was going to be a brother.

"It'll take a little while," she'd told Grandpa and me, "but soon I'll have a brother, who'll cry, poo, and look like me."

Lena was positively certain about it, and Grandpa and I were so used to things turning out as Lena wanted that we'd practically taken this brother for granted straight away. But now two long years had passed. Lena and I were about to start our last year at primary school, and there was still no sign of so much as one of that brother's little toes over in the house next door.

"Babies don't just turn up when you want them to," I said. "Mum told me."

"What does your mum mean by that? You've got so many brothers and sisters that you can't move without crashing into somebody whenever you enter or leave a room."

I kept on picking berries. After a while, Lena ran out of pine cones to throw, so she started pulling up clumps of moss instead. She laid them neatly in her bucket, and when it was almost full, she started picking berries with me.

"Lena," I sighed.

"One full bucket in no time at all. You should do the same, Trille. Nobody will notice."

"Yes, they will," I said. "They'll notice when they start taking the berries out and cleaning them."

"Yes, but I won't be there then," Lena assured me. "Shh, what was that?"

Desperate whimpers suddenly pierced the quiet summer air of the forest. We spun round and peered through the trees. We couldn't see anything to start with, but then the whimpering came again.

"It's a dog!" Lena shouted, rushing towards it. "It's got its lead stuck! Poor thing."

Imagine finding a dog in the middle of the forest! It would've been one thing finding Labben or Aiko or Brandy, or one of the other dogs from the local area, but it wasn't any of them. It was a brand new dog that neither Lena nor I had seen before. He had brown fur that shone beautifully in the sun, and he was looking at us with sad eyes.

"I think it's a sign," Lena said solemnly as we carefully freed him. "I think this is a dog that's come here to Mathildewick Cove to stay. In that case, I can always wait another year for a brother. We might even have too much on our hands as it is now…"

I looked at the dog's long lead. "Somebody owns him, Lena."

Lena didn't answer.

"Come on, boy!" she called.

Then she ran out of the forest and through the knee-high grass of Hilltop Jon's field – running backwards for a bit and then turning again – all the while laughing at her new playmate. Lena was well suited to having a dog.

But her joy didn't last long. At Hilltop Jon's farm was a massive white van with a whole bunch of people standing around it.

"Haas!" they all shouted.

The dog raced off, dragging Lena, who fell right over into a big, muddy tyre track and lost hold of the dog's lead. When she got back up, she looked like something the dog had left behind. For several seconds she stood glowering at the people below, her arms sticking rigidly out from her sides. Then she marched on down.

"You don't take very good care of your dog!" she told them furiously.

The people stared at us, clearly terrified, especially of muck-covered Lena. I moved towards them nervously. At the back of the group I saw a girl who looked almost like sunshine. She had a cloud of blonde curls around her head, and she smiled shyly as she scratched the dog behind his ears.

Then they started speaking in English. I'm much better at English than Lena. She can't see why she should have to learn English when she can already speak Norwegian. Although now she's been to Crete, perhaps she can see the point of it.

Before I could say anything, she'd beaten me to it.

"The dog was stucked in a tree!" Lena didn't know you say "stuck" in English.

"Ah! Thank you, thank you!" said a man who appeared to be the father of the family.

Lena stared at him angrily. She looked extremely dangerous as she stood there, dripping with mud.

"The ferry is that way!" she told them bluntly, pointing. "Come on, Trille."

I felt embarrassed. I smiled at the girl with the blonde curly hair, and followed Lena.

"Pickled herring, these tourists," she fumed, speaking in Norwegian again. "Always getting in a jam. Imagine being so lost that you end up driving all the way up here. They should have hazard lights stuck on them, the whole lot."

CHAPTER THREE

The message in a bottle

*L*ena said that she'd had enough of dry land, so the next day we decided to launch a message in a bottle. We used to send out loads of messages in bottles. This summer we'd only launched a couple: once from the ferry across the fjord, and another time from the breakwater. But Mathildewick Cove seemed to reel the bottles back in. They always ended up drifting onto one of the beaches by our house, and then people made fun of us. A proper message in a bottle was supposed to reach Shetland or Iceland. Or Crete, of course.

We'd got ourselves ready to leave at five o'clock in

the morning. Grandpa was going all the way out to the small island of Kobbholmen to pull in a fishing line that had been out overnight, and he was letting us come too.

"Can't it go any faster, this boat of yours?" Lena asked as soon as we'd put out to sea. "When I went to Crete, I went on a speedboat that—"

"When you went to Crete indeed, you little madam!" said Grandpa. "Do you think this is just any old boat?"

He struck his fist against the side of the cabin.

I don't think there's anybody more fond of their boat than Grandpa. His boat's called *Troll*. Grandpa's always had her.

"Can't you at least get an engine with a bit more horsepower for this old *Troll* of yours?" Lena moaned. "It's going to take us all day to get far enough out."

"I've got all day," Grandpa replied.

I sat down on the deck. Imagine if our bottle really did manage to cross the sea. We'd written a message in English with our names, where we lived, and a telephone number. We'd even put in a picture of ourselves. If somebody in another country found it, maybe they'd invite us to visit them.

"People from other countries are really cool," said Lena. "When I went to Crete…"

Grandpa and I exchanged a look and rolled our eyes.

"That's it. I can't be bothered sitting around here like a sea snail all day," Lena suddenly said behind me. Then she threw the bottle overboard with all the strength she could muster.

"Lena!" I shouted angrily. "We've only just come out onto the fjord."

My best friend gazed mournfully at the bottle. It bobbed up and down a little in the water and started gently drifting back inland in the breeze.

"Maybe I should jump in and get it back," she suggested.

"No, thank you, Lena Lid," said Grandpa. "I need my fishing gaff for other things today."

Lena flung herself down dramatically on the deck next to me. "Am I seriously going to be held hostage on this boat for the rest of the day? Have we got any biscuits?"

*

We chugged along the shores of the fjord until the
sea opened up ahead of us. Out there, the swell
rocked us like a great lullaby, and all the noise from
the shore was left behind. My frustration about the
bottle disappeared.

"Shetland's straight that way," I told Lena,
pointing to where the ocean met the sky. "And
there's Kobbholmen."

The small, dark island lay all alone amidst
the blue water. All that stood there was a lonely
lighthouse.

"Is the island deserted?" Lena asked.

"Well, it is these days," said Grandpa. "But people
used to live there in the past."

Lena and I looked at the little island and the
peaceful lighthouse. Imagine living there, in
the middle of the sea. As we came closer, we
could see a house and a shed too. Small patches
of grass came into view among the dark rocks.
Grandpa stood still for a time. He was looking at
Kobbholmen as well.

"You know, your grandmother grew up out here,

Trille," he said after a while.

"Huh?"

Grandpa nodded and began to manoeuvre the boat towards a buoy that was swaying in the sea a short distance away.

"You have a grandmother?" Lena asked, astonished. "Where have you been keeping her?"

"She's dead," I said. "She died when Dad was little."

"Oh."

Lena didn't say any more. She just stared at the lighthouse, deep in thought.

Grandpa moved calmly as he prepared to draw in the fishing line, as he'd done so many times before. He doesn't speak about my grandmother very often. But we always take two bunches of flowers when we go to the churchyard cemetery. One for Auntie Granny's grave, and one for Granny's. My real granny's grave has a small round gravestone that looks different from the others. At the bottom, it says: *Sadly missed.*

I kept looking at Kobbholmen. It was as if a

light had started shining around the island and the lighthouse. To think that my grandmother had grown up there. Had her father been the lighthouse keeper?

"Look out," said Grandpa as he started the winch.

The machine screeched and shook a little, then it started reeling in the line. Line fishing is an adventure. You never know what you'll find hanging on the hooks, and Grandpa always catches some fish. Nobody knows the fishing grounds around here better than he does. Once, when he was young, he caught a halibut that was bigger than he was: I've seen a picture of it. I dream of that happening again. That's why I always lean right over the side of the boat when we reel in the line. Grandpa lets me. He's not so strict when we're out at sea. The only thing he looks out for is that we don't fall against the winch, as that's how Uncle Tor lost half a finger when he was little. Dad's always nagging Grandpa to install an emergency stop button on the winch. It's supposed to be a requirement, Dad says. But nobody gets to tell

Grandpa what to do at sea. If somebody tries to tell him what to do with his boat, there's no way he'll do it.

"It's better to teach the young ones to be careful," he says, in answer to Dad.

Lena and I leant as far as we dared over the side of the boat, telling Grandpa every time we saw a fish approaching the surface. About halfway along the line, we saw something big and slippery writhing in the dark water.

"It's a megafish!" Lena yelled. "Oh, holy mackerel. It's a megafish, Lars. Reel her in!"

An enormous cod smacked onto the deck. Lena howled with delight and started jumping up and down like a yo-yo.

"Next time you come," said Grandpa, "we'll try a halibut line." He laughed and rubbed his hands together. "Then the little lass from next door will see a real fish! That's if you can be bothered to come on this old *Troll* again."

"Bothered?" Lena put one foot on the cod, as if it were a dragon she'd just slain. "Actually, I may very well become a fisherwoman when I'm older," she said.

"Aren't you going to be a goalkeeper?" I asked as I fetched Grandpa's knife.

"Yes, but I've got to have something to fall back on when I hang up my gloves."

*　*　*

We didn't see the message in a bottle on our way back, and we had plenty of time to look for it, as Grandpa wanted to set a herring net before we returned to shore.

"Mark my words, Trille," said Lena. "Soon somebody will be calling from Spain wanting to speak to us!"

But nobody did call from Spain. Something else happened altogether. And it happened that very same evening.

I was lying on the sofa, reading, when the doorbell rang. I heard Krølla running for her life so she'd get to open the door, and I was quite stunned when she yelled that there was somebody to see me. Who could it be? Lena never rings the doorbell.

When I reached the door, I was struck speechless. The dog from the forest was sniffing inquisitively at my socks, and there, on the bottom step, stood the sunshine girl.

"I found this," she said cautiously, passing me the bottle.

CHAPTER FOUR

Birgit

"What do you mean 'moved here'?" Lena whispered as she stared sceptically at the girl standing in our garden.

"The family with the dog have moved here! They're from the Netherlands, and they're renting Hilltop Jon's house!"

"Is that allowed?"

"Of course it is. Hilltop Jon lives at the retirement home now. Come on!"

I dragged Lena with me down into the garden. "This is Lena," I announced eagerly in English.

"Hi. I'm Birgit," the girl said, clearing her throat slightly, and politely reaching out to shake Lena's hand.

"Huh?" said Lena sharply. She seemed a bit rattled.

"Her name's Birgit!" I said.

I hoped Lena might jump at the chance to use the English she'd recently learnt on Crete to say something welcoming, but clearly not. She stared glumly at the dog instead. He gave her a friendly sniff, like all animals do when they meet Lena. I squirmed in the embarrassing silence.

"Ehm, do you want to build a floating thing with us tomorrow?" I eventually blurted out.

Lena stiffened beside me.

"Floating thing?" Birgit asked, slightly puzzled.

One evening earlier in the summer, while we were sitting on the balcony, drinking some coffee and having a snack, Dad and Uncle Tor had started chatting about when they were young and had built a raft that they sailed all the way across the fjord to town. They probably hadn't meant for Lena and me to overhear, as Dad's face took on a concerned expression when he realized that we were listening. They quickly moved on to talk about something else. But it was too late. If Dad and Uncle Tor could cross the fjord on a home-made raft, then so could Lena and I. Since then, we'd been secretly gathering flotsam and jetsam all summer, and hiding it in the old boat shed.

Now I stood there in the garden, trying to explain to Birgit what a raft was in English. The problem was that I couldn't remember the word "raft". I looked helplessly at Lena a couple of times, but she just stared fiercely back.

"It's a thing that … ehm … you float on it on the sea … ehm; it's a…"

"A raft," Lena said eventually, as if she couldn't stand listening to me fumbling any more.

Birgit lit up. I pointed down across the fields to the old boat shed, so she'd understand where our stockpile was.

"OK," she said, a little nervously. "Haas, *kom hier!*"

Then off she went, vanishing through the hole in the hedge and up onto the road, taking her curly blonde hair and everything else with her.

Lena shot off across the garden like a soldier into battle. I ran after her.

"Has something happened?" asked Lena's mum, Ylva, as we came storming into the living room.

"Yes!" I shouted. "A girl's moved here, and she's the same age as us."

Ylva pushed her glasses up and stared at me. "A new girl?" She clearly couldn't believe it. "Will she be in your class?"

I nodded enthusiastically. It was a miracle.

"So now you won't be the only girl in your class, Lena!" Ylva said, all excited. "That'll be a nice change."

Lena looked like she'd taken a cream pie to the face.

"A nice change?" she roared. "I couldn't care less about a nice change! It was Trille and me who were supposed to build the ... you know what, Trille. And it was a secret."

Ylva raised her eyebrows in suspicion. "What kind of secret?"

"Nothing," Lena said hastily.

"Nothing?"

"That's right. But anyway, it was me and Trille who were going to do it. Not some curlyhead from the Nuttylands who we don't even know!"

"I was only trying to be kind," I said.

"You're always trying to be kind, you are, like some kind of archangel! You're so kind that it makes me sick!" Lena shouted.

I stared at her, not believing what I was hearing.

"Lena Lid!" It's not very often that Ylva raises her voice. "Do you remember the day we moved to Mathildewick Cove?"

"No," Lena said stubbornly.

"Let me remind you, then," said a stern Ylva. "No more than an hour after we'd arrived, the doorbell rang. There was a *kind* boy at the door, wondering if you wanted to come out and play. Do you remember who it was?"

Lena closed her mouth and glanced quickly at me.

"Exactly," said her mum. "Now say sorry, and say it straight away."

For a long moment, it was as if Lena had been switched to silent.

"Sorry," she eventually muttered. It sounded like she'd had to drag the word out of her appendix.

"I'm sorry too," I said quickly. I knew I really

shouldn't have told an outsider about our secret raft plan, but why did Lena always have to be so difficult?

"That blasted bottle," Lena mumbled. "Is Mathildewick magnetic or something?"

"Still, it was somebody from another country who found it," I said, trying to cheer her up.

In return, I got a sofa cushion in the face.

As I shuffled off back home that evening, I had to stop and look out at the fjord. The flat sea was like a mirror below the evening sky. I felt an unfamiliar tingling at the bottom of my stomach. Might Birgit actually show up?

CHAPTER FIVE

An angel in the boat shed

*B*efore we went down to the beach the next day, Lena did some research on the Netherlands. In other words, she asked Isak, the cleverest person in Mathildewick Cove.

"Jiminy Monkfish, I don't need any books or Internet since that guy moved in. All I have to do is type in a search query and click on his belly button."

She gave me a short lecture while we organized our assembled junk and waited for Birgit. There are loads of people in the Netherlands, Lena told me, and large parts of the country are below sea level.

"Below sea level?"

"Yes, but they've built dykes to stop the water

seeping in and flooding everything. Isak says it's a nice country. Plus they're extremely good at football."

That football fact had clearly made Lena look at the situation in a more positive light. She's the goalie in our football team. When she stands in goal, yelling out orders, she's in her element. As for me, I'm starting to get tired of football. I'm no good at it. Everybody in our class plays, but sometimes I think I should just give up.

When Birgit finally peered round the boat shed door, Lena immediately started talking about football. She bombarded her with questions, but Birgit couldn't answer a single one of them.

"Sorry. I'm not really that interested in football," she apologized.

Lena stood speechless behind our collection of junk, brandishing a hammer. I was afraid the situation might get out of control, so I clapped my hands.

"Let's get building."

* * *

It was strange having somebody new involved in our project. I hardly dared to look at Birgit. It was almost like having an angel in the boat shed. When she lifted up a plank of wood, she did it carefully, as if she'd never done it before. Maybe she hadn't? Lena grappled with various pieces of driftwood and nails at a furious pace. The things Lena makes are rarely very pretty, but she usually manages to put them together, one way or another. I started to feel irritated that she wasn't showing the quiet Dutch girl more consideration.

Eventually Birgit mainly just watched. Did she think we were totally weird? I'd never thought that the things Lena and I do are strange. But now that thought was buzzing around my head the whole time. Did we seem childish?

"Lena," I whispered when we went out to fetch some more plastic drums. "Shouldn't we try to involve her a bit more?"

Lena looked at me as if I'd asked her to conjure up a town hall out of thin air. When she went back into the boat shed, she escorted Birgit up into the open loft and gave her a sheet, as well as Krølla's box of paints that she'd somehow got hold of.

"You can paint the sail," she explained, and then climbed back down. "Pass me the hammer, Trille."

* * *

Although Birgit was painting up in the loft and we were downstairs putting the raft together, we found out a lot more about her that morning. Birgit's father was an author and was going to spend a year writing. Her mother was an architect, but she wanted to try something else for a while. They'd been dreaming for ages of living on a small farm in Norway. Birgit's two elder brothers would be going back to the Netherlands when school started. They were at high school.

Word of the Dutch girl's arrival had rushed through the cove like a gale, and when we went up to my house to eat lunch, one person after another seemed to casually drop by. Lena's mum came to buy some eggs, and my older siblings, who were always pretending not to care about anything these days, spent a long time searching for various items in the kitchen cupboards. Mum even put out the chocolate spread, despite the fact it wasn't Saturday. I could feel the pride growing inside me. I was the one who'd found Birgit!

Eventually, Lena said "Ah-heeeem!" and nodded in the direction of the boat shed.

*

We did the last bit of joining in the sunshine out on
the foreshore. Birgit sat on a rock, watching. Was it
really stupid making a raft? I don't normally make
mistakes when hammering and so on, but that day I
hurt my thumb twice. Luckily I managed to act as if
nothing had happened.

When we'd finished, Birgit fetched the sail and
rolled it out. Lena and I were speechless. She'd
painted the sea and the sky, as well as the sun, and
at the top she'd painted Lena and me as a couple
of pirates. It was the best-looking thing made by
somebody my age that I'd ever seen.

"Wow!" I said. "That's fantastic."

I stuck out my arms in amazement and turned
towards Lena. She was gawking like a fish too, but
then she slammed her mouth shut.

"Is it waterproof?" she asked, sticking to the
practicalities.

CHAPTER SIX

The launch – and a wretched big brother

"They'll be calling us for dinner soon,"
Lena grumbled. She seemed in a rush as
she grabbed the raft from underneath and dug in
her heels.

It didn't budge one centimetre. I pushed as hard
as I could from behind. Birgit took hold of it on one
side, but it was no use.

"Push from the back with Trille," Lena ordered.
"Push hard."

Birgit carefully nudged the raft next to me.

"Come on, heave, for crying out trout!" Lena yelled.

I looked angrily at her. Getting angry helped.

It made us stronger, both Lena and me. The raft scraped across the stones.

As soon as it got some water beneath it, the raft let go of the ground and started gently and nimbly swaying on the waves. Cautiously, we climbed aboard, one by one.

Everything was fine for a couple of seconds, but then we felt something give way. I moved over a little so we wouldn't capsize.

"Help!" Birgit whispered, grabbing on to the mast.

First there was some bubbling around the boards, then the water started washing across the wood and wrapping mercilessly around our calves, until eventually the whole raft hit the sandy bottom with a sigh.

There we stood. All that was left sticking out of the water was half of ourselves, half the mast, and the sail floating on the surface and turning to watercolours.

"Wood's no good," said Lena from behind clenched teeth.

Then we heard laughter from the shore.

Whenever I make a house of cards and it collapses, or I make a raft and it sinks, Magnus appears like a genie from a bottle. I don't think I've ever once fallen off my bike without him seeing it. There he was now, leaning against the wall of the boat shed and slapping his thigh.

"Don't tell me that's supposed to be a raft. Don't say it! I'll die laughing," he said in between hiccups.

Lena jumped off. Our vessel rose from the bottom and almost floated up to the surface.

"Can't you see it's a submarine, you onion brain?" she shouted.

Then Magnus laughed so much he could hardly breathe.

Really? I thought. He's almost sixteen. Can't he find other things to laugh at than his younger brother? I felt embarrassed and looked at Birgit.

"I swear," Lena muttered. "I swear that by sunrise tomorrow, this idiot-proof raft will be afloat, and we'll be halfway to town."

When Lena swears something, it's going to happen. After dinner, we were back in the boat shed, making improvements. Birgit had gone home.

"It wouldn't have been safe enough even for just

two people," I said when we'd managed to flip the raft over and had started to attach another layer of polystyrene foam.

Lena didn't answer. She just swung her hammer so hard that I was glad I wasn't a nail.

* * *

When I went back inside that evening, my head was a mess from spending the day in the boat shed, but there was a full symphony at home, as usual. Minda and Mum were arguing tooth and nail about some trip or other that Minda clearly wasn't being allowed to go on, Krølla was playing her recorder, and Magnus was sitting on a chair wearing ear defenders. He chuckled when he saw me.

I slipped out through the door and down to Grandpa's flat. When you're in there, the rest of my family are only a distant muffled noise. You can hear the clock ticking and the cat purring. It's almost like another world.

But that day the racket had spread into the basement too. I stopped halfway down the stairs when I heard Dad's angry voice.

"When will you get it into your stubborn head?

55

You don't stand a chance in that boiler suit," he shouted.

"Uggh," Grandpa replied.

"Don't you 'uggh' me," said Dad. "We're worried about you!"

"Uggh," said Grandpa again. "If that's all you've got to worry about, then I hardly feel sorry for you."

I kept quiet as a mouse on the stairs so they wouldn't hear me.

"I've got a house full of half-crazy teenagers, but you're the worst of all!" Dad shouted. "And you're seventy-eight years old!"

"Precisely," said Grandpa. "Seventy-eight and old enough to make up my own mind. Get out of the way, lad."

I heard Dad's angry pacing and the clatter of Grandpa doing the washing up.

"Dad...," my father began again, in a softer tone.

But Grandpa cut him off. "Up you get, now, Reidar. You're making my plants wilt with all your shouting."

Then Dad came stomping up the stairs. He didn't even say hello as he went past.

"Were you arguing?" I asked anxiously when I got down to Grandpa.

"Uggh," Grandpa replied. "Your father wants me to start wearing some kind of massive survival suit when I'm out at sea." He wiped the worktop roughly with a cloth. "I've been wearing a simple boiler suit my whole life, and I'm not about to start staggering around like an astronaut on my own boat."

"But…"

"People shouldn't worry so much about an old duffer like me. It doesn't matter much any more, anyway."

"Doesn't matter? I don't want you to drown," I said.

"I'm not planning on drowning, Trille! I can look after myself. That's what I've always done."

He threw the cloth into the sink and found me some biscuits.

"If I started wearing a survival suit, then your father would want me to wear a life jacket on top, and if I wore a life jacket on top, then he'd want to tie inflatable rings to my hands. And if I had inflatable rings tied to my hands, then he would soon decide that I shouldn't be out at sea at all. Then I would definitely die."

I saw Grandpa in my mind's eye, wearing a survival suit with a life jacket and inflatable rings. On dry land.

"Doesn't Dad realize that you can look after yourself?"

Grandpa drummed his fingers on the table, as if the agitation from the argument had to get out somehow.

"He's always been scared that something might happen to me."

"Why?"

Grandpa sighed. "Well, I was all the children had left, you know, after we lost Inger."

Now he was talking about my grandmother again. I pictured the island and the lighthouse, and suddenly I had so many questions. But I didn't really know how to start.

"Did she have curly hair?" I eventually asked.

Grandpa looked at me in astonishment, and then laughed a little.

"Curly hair? No, she didn't. But she was the only

girl with short hair. Beat that, if you can. Anyway. What have you been up to all day? I can smell secret projects from miles away."

So I told Grandpa about the raft and Birgit and Lena. He's not the sort to tell or put a stop to crucial operations.

CHAPTER SEVEN

Do ferries have to give way?

The wind came plunging down from the mountains, making small, choppy waves on the sea. It was the crack of dawn. We peeped out from behind the wall of the boat shed to see Grandpa and *Troll* just leaving the pier and setting off out to sea. For the first time, I felt a slight twinge inside. What if Grandpa really was too old now to fend for himself out there? Should I start going with him more often?

Birgit had her chin buried in the collar of her jacket. She looked nervous.

"It's a bit windy," I said.

Lena narrowed her eyes as she licked her forefinger and lifted it into the air.

"The wind's blowing straight towards town."

She'd taken the paddles from my punctured rubber dinghy. And three life jackets. There was nothing more to discuss. Soon we were each sitting on a fish box on board the raft. The sail was hoisted. You could see Lena's head and mine at the top. The rest was a blur of watercolours. The raft looked sturdy in some ways, and wobbly in others. But the most important thing was that we were afloat. In just a few seconds we were out of the shallows and past the drop-off, where the water suddenly gets much deeper.

Lena and I paddled. Birgit held on tightly to the mast. I wished I could find a way to make her feel safe, but before I could think of anything, Lena started singing pirate songs. A little smile flashed across Birgit's face. It was so nice that I missed a paddle stroke.

Water kept on washing over our feet, and the raft was rocking more than was comfortable. A little voice inside told me that this wasn't the smartest thing we'd ever done. But Lena was right about one thing: the wind was certainly in our favour, blowing along the fjord and towards town. And it was too late to turn back. All we could do was keep a steady course and focus on our target. Dad and Uncle Tor had done it. I gulped and gave Birgit a smile of encouragement.

"Are you OK?"

"Mhm," she mumbled, just barely nodding.

"Ahoy!" yelled Lena. "There's the ferry. Good thing we didn't set off ten minutes later, or we'd have been smashed to pieces."

The ferry doesn't exactly go at breakneck speed. In fact, Lena and I have discussed many times how you'd have to search pretty far and wide to find anything as absurdly slow as that ferry. Lena's sure that it goes slow on purpose, just so that Dad – Able Seaman Yttergård – has time to have a coffee on each trip between selling the tickets. But today it looked different.

"Have they put on an extra engine or something?" Lena asked.

The ferry grew from being the size of a toy boat to the size of a ferry in a bafflingly short time. It almost felt like it was aiming for us. I paddled as powerfully as I could. On the other side of the raft, Lena was paddling so quickly that anybody would have thought she was trying to make some kind of seawater eggnog.

"Aren't big boats supposed to give way to small ones?" she shouted furiously.

I let out a desperate groan. "It's the other way round, Lena!"

Birgit's face was completely white.

The ferry's massive bow started to look like the maw of a monster. I was sure this was going to end in disaster, and I began waving my arms desperately. At the last moment, the ferry blasted its horn and veered out of the way. Thank goodness!

"Holy halibut, they shouldn't be sleeping at the wheel up there! It would've been quite a scandal if they'd run over us!" Lena bellowed.

She shook her fist and was so furious that I realized she must have been really scared too.

But we weren't out of danger yet. The ferry's wake was bigger than our raft could stand. The first wave swept right over our entire craft, washing two of our

fish boxes into the sea. The second one made the
raft tilt so much we almost lost our balance. And the
third was so powerful that Lena slid with a scream
into the water. When I threw myself across the raft
to rescue her, yet another wave came and tipped me
into the sea as well.

"We're shipwrecked!" Lena shouted from inside
her enormous life jacket.

She kicked and struggled to get back on board.
With Birgit's help, she eventually managed it, but
her lips had already turned blue by then. Luckily her
rage kicked in.

"Son of a sea bass, I'm going to crush that ferry the
next time I see it," she said, shivering. "I'm going to—"

"Can you help me first?" I shouted.

I'd never been in the sea fully dressed before.
Even though I was wearing a life jacket, it felt like
the ocean was dragging me down, trying to pull me
under into the darkness below. I was frightened and
kept kicking away in the cold water.

Birgit and Lena tried to spread their weight so
we wouldn't tip over too much when I pulled myself
aboard. Something was creaking perilously in this

raft we'd designed. One of the pieces of polystyrene came loose, and then another. The whole thing was disintegrating! I was left clinging on between one of the floating fish boxes and the crumbling raft, and I was just about to start panicking when we realized that the ferry had stopped.

Shivering and speechless, we saw they were sending out one of their lifeboats. Lena groaned as she hid her face behind her hands.

"If that's your dad coming to fish us out, then I think I'd prefer to stay here and drown!"

* * *

Of course it was Dad. Oh, how he shouted at us! He was like a football coach from town. Halfway through the worst volley, he put his arms around me and hugged me so tightly I thought I would suffocate. But then he started again. We could have drowned! Or got hypothermia! Were we planning on growing up and behaving like normal people sometime soon? And had we considered that the ferry was full of cars and passengers going to work? Now the whole timetable was a gigantic mess because we'd been thrashing about like befuddled seagull chicks straight in the path of the ferry. In the middle of the fjord!

But when he realized that there were three of us, he was completely derailed. Dad hadn't been at home when Birgit had visited.

"Have you taken a hostage?" he asked.

"Yes," Lena grumbled. "She's from the Netherlands. We were taking her back."

CHAPTER EIGHT

The day on Kobbholmen

Birgit kept her distance after that. We later found out it was because her parents thought we must be trouble. They were probably right. The story of the shipwrecked raft quickly spread all across the area, and for the first time in my life, I felt ashamed. To think that I'd invited Birgit to join in with something so stupid! What a muttonhead I'd been! I looked up towards Hillside and wondered what she was doing. The summer holidays were almost over. I should've been running around from morning until evening enjoying the last of my freedom. Instead I felt bored. It was as if Mathildewick Cove had become too small.

"You're all wound up, Trille," Mum said desperately one afternoon. "Go out and get some fresh air."

Out, out, out. We always had to go out. Couldn't she make some toasted buns and play a game with me instead? I walked down to the sea, feeling cross.

Ever since I was little, I've gone to Grandpa's boat shed to help him with things. We disentangle nets, prepare lines, and clean fish. Soon I'll know how to do most things by myself. Grandpa's passing his knowledge down to me. Sometimes when I coil a rope or put the knife in its place on the beam, I feel that I've done it just like Grandpa. The old men at the shop call me Mini-Lars. I probably take after Grandpa more than I take after my dad.

So I plonked myself on an upside-down fish tub in the boat shed. Grandpa glanced at me and pretended not to hear me sighing.

"I promised that little lass from next door we'd set a halibut line before the summer was over. Maybe we could do it tomorrow?" he suggested, digging out a large box of tangled fishing line.

I shrugged and lifted up one of the hooks.

Cool summer rain began to dance on the boat shed roof. I heard Dad shouting something in the distance, and Minda answering. Grandpa worked away calmly next to me with his big, tanned hands.

"Have you always been like you are now, Grandpa?"

Grandpa briefly shook a tangled piece of line, and a hook came loose. He put it in a wooden box.

"Old, grey-haired and fond of fish?"

"No…"

We sorted out a few more hooks. I shifted nervously.

"Have you always been so … content?" I eventually asked.

Grandpa looked at me, a little surprised. "Mm, yes. Except for getting in the odd bit of trouble in my youth."

"Trouble?"

"Well, you know the sort of thing. A bit of ants in my pants and some argy-bargy. Just ask Thunderclap Kåre."

He laughed, but I wondered what Thunderclap Kåre had to do with anything.

"But I've been really lucky. I'm healthy, I've got a family, I have a boat and plenty of time on my hands."

He shook the tangled line patiently.

"But Granny died," I blurted out.

Grandpa stowed away another hook.

"Yes." His hands stopped. I held my breath. "But I was lucky to be married to her first. That was the luckiest part of all, Trille lad."

He stowed the last hook in the box.

"Make sure you bring Lena tomorrow."

I nodded.

* * *

The sky was light blue and hazy when we put out to sea the next day. There wasn't a puff of wind in the air, the seabirds sailed silently above us, and it was as calm as I'd ever seen it out by Kobbholmen. Even Lena was quiet, as hook after hook of shiny herring bait plopped into the water and vanished into the darkness below.

"Those halibut are going to have a first-class meal down there now," she cackled as the last bit of herring disappeared from sight. "Delicious but deadly."

I could see that Grandpa was laughing inside. He likes being around Lena.

I peered through the haze at the lighthouse and the dark island. Lena did the same. Then suddenly she asked, "Can we go ashore?"

Grandpa threw the fishing buoy overboard and spat at it for luck, as fishermen have always done here. "Well, I was thinking we could do some fishing while we wait," he said.

"How many freezers have you got?" Lena said. "Don't they ever get full?"

Grandpa took off his cap and scratched his head. "You certainly have a way with words, Lena Lid. Maybe we will pay a visit to Kobbholmen, then."

* * *

As soon as I set foot on the old pier, my whole body began to tingle. A brand new place to explore! Lena and I set off towards the centre of the island. There were concrete steps and old railings everywhere. Our hands were drawn to the black rocks, warmed by the sun. We ran like crazy and climbed like mad.

71

"Hey, those look like eggs," said Lena when we'd scrambled up one of the highest crags and were looking down at a small bay full of round, grey boulders.

It was a bit hard to get down there, but we were soon on the beach, crouching and patting the smooth rocks. Only the sea could make something that smooth. All the edges and chipped parts had been ground away. I imagined how the roaring waves had washed over the shore right here, knocking and rolling the boulders against one another over thousands of years. I felt warm and happy as I sat down on one of the biggest ones and stared out to sea. Pink thrift flowers waved in the faint breeze, and the white lighthouse towered over us.

"Are you coming, then?" said Lena.

We went over to the old house. The windows were hidden behind great wooden boards, and the door was locked. How long was it since people had made coffee, had a nap, or done the dishes inside those walls? Lena managed to find an opening in the shed, behind a rotten plank of wood. It was dark and silent inside, with only narrow bands of light coming in.

She knocked on the woodwork as she inspected the whole room, and I suddenly noticed that she had grown taller. When she stood on her tiptoes, she could reach the ceiling. Lena's always been a bit shorter than me, but now she wasn't any more. What if the others in my class had grown just as much over the summer, and I was the only one who was exactly the same height as before? I took a nervous step in the dark. It was only gossip, but Lena had heard that Kai-Tommy's voice was changing.

"They used to keep chickens in here," said Lena, pointing behind some wire netting.

"Hmm," I said, remembering something Dad had said one Sunday at home when he was making chicken fricassee: "This used to be your grandmother's favourite dish, Trille. Chicken fricassee and home-made redcurrant squash."

When we got back to the lighthouse, I saw the two redcurrant bushes in a warm spot next to the steps.

And up on the steps themselves was Grandpa.

He'd kicked off his clogs and rolled up the trouser legs on his boiler suit, his white shins reflecting the sunlight.

Lena let out a shriek and covered her eyes. "I'm snow-blind!"

"Oh, be quiet, you!" Grandpa tossed us our packed lunches. He looked happy as he wiggled his toes.

"I definitely could've lived here," said Lena, plonking herself down on the bottom step.

"Oh, it's good on Kobbholmen today, but my, how the wind can blow out here."

"So was Trille's granny actually a lighthouse keeper?" Lena fished out a piece of bread as big as her face.

"No, her father was the lighthouse keeper," said Grandpa.

"Was she living out here when you fell in love with her?" Lena went on.

I glanced up at Grandpa. Was he getting fed up with all these questions about Granny? No. He looked happy.

"Well, I'd say she was living here when she fell in love with me!"

"*Pfft*," said Lena. "You're just boasting."

Then Grandpa told her gruffly that he had once been young and handsome too, whether we believed it or not.

"But I wanted to be an ocean-going mariner and sail to Shanghai and Liverpool and Baltimore. I wasn't about to fritter my time away in Mathildewick Cove and get married. Not on your nelly!"

He shook his head. "You two should've seen the long queue of girls I've turned down in my life!"

"Yes, I'd like to have seen that," Lena said drily. "Was Trille's granny in that queue too?"

Grandpa smiled and looked out to sea.

"Yes and no," he murmured.

A gentle breeze began to rustle softly through the grass around the steps.

"We'd better get in the boat, young 'uns!"

* * *

"How do you know where to put these fishing lines, anyway?" Lena asked as we approached the buoy.

Grandpa laughed. Nobody will ever share the secrets of how to find their best fishing spots!

"Inger," he said. "She was the one who showed me

the best places out here. Goodness knows I could've kept close to the shore, fishing for kelp cod with Thunderclap Kåre and Co., but that wouldn't have been as much fun. Can you reach the buoy, Trille?"

We didn't catch any halibut, but a whole heap of tusk and cod. Grandpa looked strong as he hooked them with his fishing gaff and pulled them onto the boat. Maybe I wasn't as much like Grandpa as I'd thought, I wondered, feeling sad in a strange and new way. Girls weren't going to be queuing up anywhere near me.

* * *

That evening, I cycled to the churchyard alone. Lena's often tried to scare me off from going there. She tells me about ghosts and grave robbers and Satanists and goodness knows what else. But I've always liked it there. This time it felt especially good to open the gate and walk in under the cool trees. My head was pounding from too much sun and sea.

I walked past Auntie Granny's grave and over to the small, round gravestone on the other side of the churchyard. *Inger Yttergård*, it said in gold writing. *Born 6 May 1933, died 22 November 1968.*

What was she like, I wondered, this lady who had been married to Grandpa? Mum had told me that she'd died of cancer. My heart felt crushed when I thought about it. Grandpa had lost her, and so had Dad. Long before I was here. Is it possible to miss somebody you've never met? I patted the smooth stone, and suddenly my fingertips remembered something. I took a step backwards and looked at the gravestone again, which I'd always thought was a little odd.

It was a boulder from Kobbholmen.

Part Two

Autumn uproar

CHAPTER NINE

Kai-Tommy's voice

*A*utumn was on its way. From my window, I could see *Troll* chugging cheerily out across a greyish-blue late August fjord. The school bell was about to start controlling my life, but Grandpa could carry on like before: fishing, drinking coffee and having a peaceful time.

As I turned away from the window and lifted up my satchel, I realized that I was looking forward to school a bit after all. Today I would get to see Birgit again. For the first time in my life, I spent a long time standing in front of the wardrobe, pondering what to wear. I didn't think any of my clothes were especially cool. I pinched some of the hair wax that Magnus keeps in the bathroom.

Usually Mum gets up before me, but that morning, on the first day back at school, she was still sleeping.

"Is she ill?" Magnus asked as he rummaged in the fridge.

"She's just tired," said Dad. There was a wrinkle on his brow.

I made my packed lunch as quick as the wind and leapt into my boots so I could walk with Minda and Magnus to their bus stop.

"Minda, did you notice that Dad was worried?" I scurried along beside her.

"Dad's always worried."

"But Mum usually comes to say goodbye and tell us to have a good day," I said.

Minda stopped. "Have you ever thought that Mum isn't just there to get up and say goodbye to you, Trille? Maybe she'd like to have a lie-in for once. Maybe she's got her own life to get on with!"

I opened my mouth to say something.

"And if you don't stop wearing those boots to

school soon, there'll be no hope for your social life," she finished and ran off to the bus.

I watched her go. What was wrong with wearing wellies to school? It was raining, after all! Then somebody grabbed my hood, almost strangling me.

"Why hello, you little gnome. Ready for our last year at primary? We're going to rule the school," said Lena, grinning.

Luckily, she was wearing wellies too.

Our cove is a bit out of the way, so it's a fair distance to walk to school. The first thing we come to is the road that leads up to Hillside, and after that there's quite a long stretch with the sea on one side and thick spruce forest on the other. I've lost count of the times Lena's disappeared up into the forest and frightened me out of my wits by jumping out at me further on. But today she walked with me all the way. We didn't see Birgit.

"Did you know that Ellisiv's bought this place?" Lena said as we passed the lone red cottage on the road between the forest and the ferry landing.

"Yes, Mum told me."

"Maybe we should start walking to school with our teacher."

Lena looked like she wasn't sure whether her suggestion was a good or bad idea. She's very fond of Ellisiv.

The ferry landing was deserted, and the little shop wasn't open yet. The local teenagers normally hang out there in the afternoons. They ride their mopeds and sit around on the tables.

"Sitting there and gaping at the ferry is enough to kill anybody's soul," Lena said once. "Just look at Magnus."

It wasn't exactly a nice thing to say about my elder brother. But she had a point.

Kai-Tommy was hanging over his handlebars as we entered the school playground, and he shouted something at us. His voice was deep like a grown man's, but it broke at the end, and the last words sounded like seagulls screeching.

"His voice *is* changing." Lena was impressed and shocked at the same time.

"Are you two hard of hearing?" he asked, skidding

to a stop in front of us. He was wearing new black trainers, and a cap and hoodie instead of a bike helmet.

"I didn't catch what you said because of your new voice," Lena said frankly.

Kai-Tommy jumped off his bike. "I said: have you seen Birgit?"

Huh? Had Kai-Tommy met Birgit?

He had. It turned out he and Halvor had spent a great deal of time with Birgit over the past few days. They'd been swimming at the ferry landing, and they'd even been to visit her up at Hillside. It took all my strength not to let my jaw drop. I was the one who'd found Birgit first! Why on earth would she spend time with Kai-Tommy and Halvor? They were the two biggest idiots in the whole school!

Lena told Kai-Tommy that we hadn't seen Birgit since the great shipwreck a couple of weeks ago.

"We were at death's door, and Trille's dad was so furious that I think she took fright."

Did Lena always have to blabber away like that? I didn't want Kai-Tommy to know anything. Not about Birgit, not about me, and certainly not about Dad.

*

What a terrible start to everything. Lena stayed there talking with Kai-Tommy, probably because he'd got such a wacky voice. I shuffled off inside, looking like an idiot in my boots. It was silent and deserted in the corridor outside the classrooms. Schoolbags were strewn everywhere. The last remains of the summer ran off me. I put my back against the wall and slid down. By now Grandpa would be somewhere out at sea. And I was stuck here.

"Are you all right?"

I hadn't seen her amidst all the bags. It was almost like she was hiding. Birgit. She was even speaking Norwegian now.

"Erm, yes," I said, blushing. "And you?"

She shrugged slightly. I don't know precisely what I'd been expecting, but when Kai-Tommy said they'd been hanging out with her, I'd assumed that she would probably be all stupid and arrogant now. But she was exactly the same. A cautious smile and a soft voice. Was it possible to be like that and yet still be friends with Kai-Tommy?

*

By the time the bell rang, the crazy morning had got better. I'd spoken with Birgit for quite a while. I'd told her about Ellisiv and about the school and our class. Birgit asked if we'd made any more rafts, which I flatly denied. Then she smiled, and my head went all fuzzy.

CHAPTER TEN

Lena and I go for music lessons

*O*n Tuesday, it was time for our music lessons to start up again. We'd been having them for the past two years: Lena was learning the keyboard and I was learning the piano. I'd explained to Mum that I'd prefer to play the drums, but for some reason or another that appeared to be out of the question.

"I have a feeling that I might have a talent for the drums," I told Lena.

Our lessons were one after the other this year too.

"You don't have a talent for the piano, anyway," she

replied, whirling the plastic bag with her keyboard book in it around her head like a sledgehammer.

"I'm better than you," I mumbled.

My best friend is absolutely terrible at the keyboard. Ylva loves music and plays all kinds of instruments, but Lena hasn't inherited a single gram of musicality. Sometimes when I've been listening to Lena mangling a song on the keyboard, I think that father of hers, who did a runner before she was born, must have been completely tone-deaf. But I haven't told Lena, of course. I think Ylva harbours a hope as deep as the forest that her daughter's got a musical side hidden away somewhere. She's very keen for Lena to learn the keyboard, anyway.

Mr Rognstad, our teacher, doesn't show much understanding of people who can't play. It's as if he thinks our lack of talent is on purpose. Lena behaves very strangely when she's having her keyboard lesson. She looks at the floor and turns into a little jellyfish mumbling "yes" or "OK" and nothing else, no matter how unfair he's being. Lena, who always speaks straight from the heart! I can't get my head around it.

"I'm going to give up this year," Lena said now.

"What about your skis?" I asked. Ylva had promised her new skis for Christmas if she kept up the lessons for another year.

"Ugh, there'll probably be just as little snow this year as there was last year. I hate music lessons. I can't keep on doing things I hate."

"I can't stop. Mum says—"

"Trille." Lena paused. "Have you ever thought that maybe sometimes you're right and your mum's wrong?"

I sank into my jacket collar and shook my head. But now Lena mentioned it, it struck me that there were a whole host of things Mum had said and done recently that I didn't agree with at all.

"Do you think my mum's been a bit strange recently?" I asked.

"Strange? She's totally cuckoo, Trille."

"What do you think is wrong with her, then?"

"The menopause."

It was as if Lena had been waiting for me to ask about Mum.

"Is that an illness?"

"Not exactly an illness."

It depended on how you looked at it, according to Lena. Some call it The Change. All women have to go through it when they reach the age where they can't have children any more. Their bodies change and start to become like old ladies' bodies. But before they finish changing, there's a lot of sweating and nerves and miserable stuff.

"Some of them become fat, and others just feel fed up. I think your mum's got both sides of it."

I was shocked. Poor Mum!

"In that case, I think it's best I choose another time to stop learning the piano," I said.

"That's probably wise," said Lena. "But I can stop. My mum's from a different generation than yours."

And then we'd arrived. Lena slowly opened the door to the music school corridor.

"I hope Kai-Tommy's still before me, like last year."

Kai-Tommy's even worse than Lena. For a while, when Lena and he were more enemies than ever, she had insisted on arriving for her music lesson a quarter of an hour early, so she could stand in the corridor and take joy in all the slip-ups and sighs coming from inside.

But today there was a surprise. Fantastic piano music was flowing out from behind the closed classroom door.

"That's definitely not Kai-Tommy," Lena declared. She listened to the piano trills, clearly downhearted. Maybe that's Mr Rognstad himself playing," she said hopefully.

Then the door opened, and out came Birgit.

"Hi!" she said, smiling in surprise. She was carrying a pile of notes under her arm.

I felt warm, then cold, then warm again. Could she play the piano too?

"See you next week, Birgit," said a happy Mr Rognstad. Then he turned towards Lena and seemed to deflate a little. "Back again this year, Miss Lid?"

I could see that Lena was about to give one of her typical replies, but then she closed her mouth. I don't know which of them sighed loudest as they disappeared into the classroom.

*   *   *

"How was it?" I asked Lena on the way home.

She had looked even gloomier than usual when she'd finished her lesson.

"All right."

My lesson had been just all right too. But now it was going to be another kettle of fish. I couldn't keep playing like a porpoise if Birgit might be listening. Just think, now I could chat with her in the corridor every Tuesday. I could teach her Norwegian words.

"Maybe we should ask Birgit if she'd like to go with us next time," I said.

Lena kicked a stone, which shot off an endless distance down the road. "Didn't I tell you that I'm going to stop going, you sea cucumber?"

But the next Tuesday, Lena was waiting with her keyboard bag once again.

"Weren't you going to give up?" I asked her, surprised.

"Do you think I can afford my own skis?" she snapped, glancing over at the junction of Hilltop Jon's road, where Birgit stood waiting.

CHAPTER ELEVEN

The new football coach

*T*hanks to Birgit, my music lessons were going much better than I'd thought. But football was ten times worse.

"You're kidding," Lena mumbled as we arrived at our training session. She propped her bike against the fence by the side of the pitch. "Where's Axel?"

Our old football coach – the one who'd discovered Lena's goalkeeping ability, and who was the nicest man in the world – was nowhere to be seen. Instead, Kai-Tommy's dad was standing there.

"Why would he bother to train us?" Lena whispered. "We're rubbish."

*

When he was young, Ivar, Kai-Tommy's dad, used to play in the first division. Kai-Tommy tells that to anybody with ears to listen. Kai-Tommy's big brother is also a real football talent. He plays for a junior team in town and has started training with their first team now and then. He's the one their father's been focusing on all these years. On the rare occasions he'd turned up at our matches, he didn't act like the other parents, cheering and jumping up and down however well we were playing. No, he kept totally silent with his eyes picking up everything. Kai-Tommy worked like a slave on the pitch then, and shouted twice as much at the rest of us when we were being useless, especially at me.

After one such match, when Kai-Tommy had snarled at me that I belonged at under-tens level and was a disgrace to the team, Lena had explained a couple of things on the way home.

"Kai-Tommy's got a major inferiority complex when it comes to football, Trille."

"What do you mean, an inferiority complex?" I asked angrily. I hated Kai-Tommy so much right then that steam was practically coming out of my ears. He'd almost made me cry!

"In Kai-Tommy's family, football is the most important thing in the world. His brother's really good, but Kai-Tommy's nothing special."

"He's the best in our team," I said harshly.

"*Pfft,*" said Lena. "When he shouts and yells, then everybody thinks that. And he shoots hard. But he's got poor technical abilities."

Technical abilities? Where did Lena pick up all these words?

"But…" I began.

"Kai-Tommy's an average player, Trille. And you can bet that doesn't impress his dad."

Lena didn't say any more after that. But it made it easier to put up with all Kai-Tommy's nonsense. When he shouted something angrily at me, all I had to think was that he had an inferiority complex. And poor technical abilities too.

But now, at the training session that day, I could tell things were going to be different. Kai-Tommy's father stood in the middle of the pitch, in a black tracksuit, rolling a ball under one foot. He looked lethal. Kai-Tommy swept back his fringe, making sure he looked good. I realized this inferiority complex was going to come out at every single training session now.

"I bet it's Axel's girlfriend who's made him stop coaching, so he can go with her to the cafe every single day instead," Lena grumbled.

We don't like our old coach's girlfriend. She's so pretty that Lena thinks it's made her crabby, and she doesn't know a thing about football, or about Axel really. We pictured Axel sitting in a deep cafe armchair in town, while we were hopelessly stuck at the training session.

"Oh well," said Lena, pulling on her goalkeeper's gloves. Clearly she wasn't about to let the change of coach get in the way of her plans.

All the boys from our class were there, as well as some from the class below. Kai-Tommy's father hooked up the ball with his hands. He had shiny black hair, and was very slim for a dad. Then he started talking.

"We're going to have certain expectations of each one of you now. Next year, many of you will start playing in town, and if you want to make your mark, we're going to have to start thinking long-term. That means training three times a week, and nobody gets to stay home without a good reason."

I gulped.

"Gulliver, Halvor's dad, will be the assistant coach. He'll take care of the practical side of things. So if you've got any questions…"

Lena and I exchanged glances. Kai-Tommy's dad *and* Halvor's dad? This was some kind of plot!

"Who normally plays in goal?"

My jaw dropped. How could he possibly not know? Everybody in the area knew that Lena was the goalie in our team. She stepped into the circle wearing her goalkeeper's gloves and looked up defiantly at the man in the black tracksuit.

"Me."

"Just you?"

The others shuffled nervously, and then Halvor stepped into the circle.

"I used to stand in goal sometimes, and when Lena's ill…" He quickly glanced at her, almost as if he was slightly scared.

Halvor, our new assistant coach's son and Kai-Tommy's best friend, must have grown about twenty centimetres over the summer. His long arms hung down on each side, goalkeeper-like. Lena had grown a bit too, but she was just as skinny as before. And her mum couldn't be further from being an assistant coach. I'm not sure Ylva even knows the rules of football.

I wonder if it was at that moment, standing in the circle with Halvor, that Lena realized things were going to change.

I don't want to remember the rest of that training session. We had to run until our mouths tasted of blood, and I ended up last in almost all the drills. Never had I felt so out of place. Both Lena and Halvor were being tried out in goal, but I wasn't paying attention.

By the time we went home, Lena had grazes on both her elbows, gravel on her face, and she was so tired that she got off her bike for the last hill. She didn't say a word until we were about to go our separate ways to our own houses. Then she looked out across the fjord, and at Grandpa moseying up from by the old boat sheds.

"Don't stop coming, Trille."

I couldn't even answer her. The only thing I was thinking about was getting out of my wretched football kit and into the shower.

"See you tomorrow," was all I said.

Then off I went.

CHAPTER TWELVE

The salt lick

*L*ena didn't ask about football again. She went alone to the next training session. I stood at the window and watched her cycle off without looking back. For two seconds, I felt like scrambling after her, but then I remembered about Kai-Tommy's dad and shuddered. I couldn't go through that again.

"Have you stopped playing football?" Dad asked.

I squirmed. I didn't really want to say I'd stopped. All the boys around here play football, after all.

"I'm taking a break," I mumbled.

Dad isn't usually one to let me avoid doing

things. But that day it was as if his thoughts were somewhere else.

"Well, if you're not going to football training, you can keep fit by lending your father a hand," he said. "I was going to take up a new salt lick for the sheep."

Was he joking? Our salt licks are ten kilo blocks of salt that give the sheep all sorts of minerals they need, but this one had to go all the way up to the Cliff. It would take the whole afternoon. I was about to say something about child labour, like Lena usually does, but then I saw the furrow in his brow. Mum was lying asleep on the sofa, and the kitchen looked like a disaster zone.

"OK," I said, heading out to the barn.

The Cliff is at the end of an endless mountain slope that starts down by the sea and is steep all the way up. I was breathing heavily long before I came close to Hilltop Jon's farm. But then it was as if I found my second wind. What if Birgit was home when I went past?

Hillside had been in a pretty bad state the last

few years that Hilltop Jon and his horse, Molly, lived there. Tiles were missing from the roof of the barn, the paint was flaking off the walls, and there were clumps of long grass sticking out of all the berry plants. Now I narrowed my eyes as I stopped for a moment. The infield was green and freshly mown. Herbs and vegetables were growing in a row of planters. The roof of the barn was as leakproof as a rain jacket, and the walls were newly painted.

A smell of freshly baked bread came drifting out of the kitchen window. It hardly looked like the sort of disaster zone I was used to at home, I thought with dismay.

"Hi!" Birgit's father, the author, climbed down from a ladder on the far side of the house. "Trille, isn't it?"

I nodded, and then suddenly remembered that this man must hold me responsible for almost drowning his daughter.

"Are you looking for Birgit?"

I blushed and shook my head. I felt it was impossible to explain all about the salt lick in

English, so I just patted the bag and said, "For the sheep."

And then I sped off.

The track was slippery after all the rain of the past few days, but as long as I stepped on the rocks, it was fine. Small birch branches and alder twigs smacked me in the face. Dad should have been up here ages ago to clear the track with his clippers. Why hadn't he done it this year? All my life, I'd thought that parents could do anything. But now I was starting to doubt it. Things were in a complete state at home. It was all wrinkles and mess and sleeping and arguing.

I clenched my teeth and tried to think about nice things, but the salt lick rubbed hard against my back, and the hill was making my thighs ache.

"Trille?"

"Aaaah!"

Birgit and Haas suddenly appeared ahead of me.

"Going up the mountain?" she asked.

I nodded.

"Mushrooms," said Birgit, opening a large basket.

A yellow glow came from inside.

Wasn't it lethal to eat mushrooms? That's what I'd learnt ever since I was little. You could die or get kidney stones just from swallowing a tiny piece of the wrong sort.

I don't exactly know how it happened, but Birgit put down her basket and came up the mountain with me. The warm September sun shone down on us, the track became drier, and the salt lick felt lighter. Neither of us said very much. She'd clearly been up there before. There's a visitors' book tucked into the small cairn that Minda and Dad made at the top, and her name was written there several times. Now she wanted to know the names of everything we could see. I strung up the salt lick and flopped myself down at the resting place by the cairn. Dad always points out places and tells me about them when we're up there. Oh, shear my sheep, if only I'd paid more attention! I told Birgit the names of the islands and mountains I was sure about.

"And that small one, all the way out there," I said

finally, "that's Kobbholmen. My grandmother lived there when she was little."

That made an impression on Birgit. Imagine having a grandmother who came from the sea. Grandpa was on his way out with *Troll*, probably going to set a net. Birgit looked at the tiny dot of a boat and wondered how I knew it was him.

I shrugged. "Is it true there aren't many hills in the Netherlands?"

It was. But there were other beautiful things. As the sun played cat and mouse with the clouds, Birgit told me in a mixture of English and Norwegian about her life there and the friends she'd left behind.

"Do you miss it?" I asked boldly.

She shrugged and smiled. She was used to missing places, she explained. "We travel so much."

Haas was lying down by my feet, looking at me curiously now and then.

"He's wondering where Lena is," Birgit said, laughing.

The dog opened his eyes wide when we mentioned her name. Lena takes chickens tobogganing, rides cattle, says "boo" to horses, and puts kittens in the dirty laundry to scare her mother. And yet I don't know of a single animal that doesn't like her.

"Lena's at football training," I mumbled, gulping down my guilty conscience.

And she really had been training. She'd trained so hard that she was still completely furious when I popped in to see her later that evening.

"I hate gravel pitches," she roared.

She was sitting on the kitchen table. She'd had a shower and was fiery red. Isak was cleaning the cuts on her knees and listening patiently to her as she shouted.

"Why can't we get an artificial grass pitch in this stupid place, like everybody else has? Ow!"

I sat down on a chair and asked her tentatively how it had gone.

Lena snarled. "I hate boys, I hate coaches, and I hate gravel. What have you been up to, then?"

I told her about the salt lick, but I couldn't bring myself to tell her all the rest. That I'd been for a walk with Birgit, that I'd been invited into her house afterwards and eaten fried chanterelle mushrooms on sourdough bread. That it was the best thing I'd tasted in all my life. And that I was slightly scared of dying of kidney failure, but it would almost have been worth it.

CHAPTER THIRTEEN

The girls of the class

"*Y*ou're each going to choose a book," Ellisiv said as she looked at us. "And then you're going to give a presentation on the book and the author."

I felt a weight like a stone in my stomach. Speaking in front of the class is my worst nightmare.

"What's a gifted child like you got to worry about?" Lena usually says when I tell her about my fear.

It was Auntie Granny who always called me that. "You're such a gifted child, Trille," she used to say. "You'll go far." Lena thinks it's an excellent expression.

Nobody in the world has ever called Lena a gifted

child. She's good at PE and break time. If you ask her, everything else at school's a pain in the neck. Maths is the worst. She and Andreas spend half of our maths lessons out in a group study room with their own teacher. Lena's tried to explain to both Ylva and Ellisiv that it's pointless to get somebody to try and teach her maths like that. She's going to be a goalie and will never have any need for all those sums. But it's no use. Ylva and Ellisiv are dead set on Lena learning maths, just like every other person. I don't understand why they worry. Lena will manage fine.

I laid my head down heavily on the desk and stared at my wet trainers.

"You're going to work in groups," I heard Ellisiv say, and I squeezed my eyes tightly shut. If I had to work with Kai-Tommy or Halvor, I might as well run away to sea.

"Trille, Lena and Birgit. You can go and sit in the library..."

My heart skipped a whole stack of beats. I gathered my books up all in a fluster.

"Look, there go the three girls of the class," Kai-Tommy muttered as I passed.

Halvor and a few others sniggered, but I pretended not to hear them. They weren't the ones getting to be in a group with Birgit.

Our library isn't big. I often go in the evenings with Mum, and I've read most of what they've got. Now Lena lay down on the sofa there, banging the heels of her wellies together with such force the noise filled the whole room. Birgit and I each sat on a chair and put our notebooks on the table. The three of us had hardly been alone together since the raft-wreck.

"Let's pick *Emil and the Great Escape*," Lena said. She'd clearly made up her mind already. "I've got the film of that one."

"Ehm, isn't it a bit childish?" I said, with a cough.

"No. It's pretty short too," said Lena.

I looked at Birgit. She rarely said very much in class, but she seemed a bit more relaxed now.

"Sure, let's pick that one," she said.

She'd read the book in Dutch when she was younger. It would be a good way to improve her Norwegian, since she already knew the story. Besides, she'd learnt about Astrid Lindgren, the author, for a school project a few years ago, and we thought we could include a bit about her other books too.

"Fine by me," said Lena. "But I want to do the bit about *Emil and the Great Escape*—"

"Because you've got the film," I said, finishing her sentence for her.

* * *

On weekdays, Lena and I are always the first ones home. When we get there, we rummage through all the cupboards in both our houses for something to keep us alive until dinner. Dad's started hiding his favourite biscuits in the sock drawer in his bedroom. On that particular day, there was a fruit bowl with some old grapes in our kitchen, so we sat down there.

"What a mess," Lena sighed, tidying up the newspapers on the table so she could get to the tablet lying underneath. "Are things completely out of control here?"

I looked around. It really was pretty chaotic in our house at the moment.

"Do you lot expect Kari to go round like a bin

lady, tidying up after you? In the middle of The Change? It's not easy, you know. I asked Isak."

I was about to remind Lena that I'd carried a massive salt lick all the way up to the Cliff the day before, but instead I opened the dishwasher and started emptying it. Birgit was going to come down when she'd had her dinner. The house couldn't look like this then!

"Smoking haddocks, we should make a film about *Emil and the Great Escape*," said Lena. "Ellisiv would be blown away. Then you wouldn't have to speak, Trille."

She said it in a perfectly normal way, as if it were the most natural thing in the world that standing in front of the whole class made me panic. I wrung out the cloth that was in the sink. It smelt foul.

"Did you know this?" Lena asked. She was using the tablet, swiping her fingers eagerly across the screen. "In the seventies, there was a TV series of *Emil*, but they didn't show the whole thing here in Norway. They were scared that children would start hoisting each other up flagpoles, like Emil does with his little sister, Ida."

She munched the old grapes as she read on. "What a load of rubbish! We've got to have that in our presentation. Actually, how about we…"

I pictured little Ida at the top of the flagpole. Sometimes I just know what Lena's thinking.

"Who are you planning to hoist up?" I asked, chucking the stinky cloth in with the laundry.

Lena closed the cover on the tablet.

"It will have to be whoever's lightest. Shall we go and pick up Krølla from her after-school club?"

CHAPTER FOURTEEN

Krølla at half mast

trictly speaking, we should have waited until Birgit arrived to start our book project, but we had to get this particular scene filmed while our parents were still at work. That much was clear even to me. I quickly fetched my bike, and we sped off to school. Krølla hates her after-school club. Every day she asks Mum if she can go home with Lena and me instead. For some reason or another, Mum thinks that's completely out of the question.

It wasn't hard to persuade Krølla to be part of Lena's film stunt. Before we knew it, she'd gone and found her red dress, so she would look like little Ida.

"You'll end up in two pieces if we tie that thing around your waist," Lena said, peering at the thin cord on the flagpole. "We'll need to use Magnus's climbing harness."

It was probably around then that I realized this was a bad idea. Magnus's property is sacred, but Lena's never worried about that.

"He never uses it anyway!" she said.

The harness was far too big for Krølla, so Lena immediately adjusted every single strap. My brother was going to go berserk, but at least Krølla was secure in the harness. Lena fixed her to the flagpole rope with a carabiner.

"We have to get this done before Magnus comes home," I said. "Are you all right, Krølla?"

She put on her sunglasses and gave the thumbs up.

"Take one. Action!" Lena shouted from over on the lawn, filming with her mobile phone camera.

That Emil must have been strong! It was hard work hoisting Krølla. I sent a thought to the top of the flagpole, hoping that the hole the rope went through could bear the load. With every pull, Krølla came

117

closer to the sky. She clucked away happily up there. I was struggling and sweating, but trying my best to stay cool. This video was going to be shown to the whole class, after all!

Krølla was only a couple of metres from the top when somebody coughed behind us.

It was Birgit and Haas. Why did she always suddenly appear like that? I gave such a start I lost my grip for a brief second. Krølla slid down the flagpole with a wail, Haas barked, and Birgit put her hand to her mouth. Miraculously, Krølla came to a stop just over halfway up the pole.

"Are you all right?" I shouted, trembling.

"I'm stuck!"

Lena looked accusingly at Birgit. "We were in the middle of filming a scene here!"

"Sorry," Birgit whispered.

The problem now was that we couldn't get Krølla up or down. She'd got herself stuck on a hook. No matter how much we jiggled and tugged, she wouldn't budge.

"Perfect," I sighed, as I saw the school bus stopping up the road.

The high school pupils were glued to the bus windows, examining the scene in our garden. I could see from Minda's face a hundred metres away that she was mortified.

"What's wrong with you?" she snarled furiously as she threw down her bag.

"I can see all the way to Mariannelund!" Krølla shouted bravely, trying to quote from the story about Emil and Ida.

Then Magnus saw the harness. "Seriously?!"

"We're only borrowing it," Lena said calmly. "Safety's our top priority."

Magnus was about to blow his top, but Minda stopped him. "Can't you for once try thinking about other people instead of yourself and your stupid stuff? We've got to get her down!"

My brother and sister tried jiggling the cord too, but Krølla was truly stuck, strung up there like a dried fish in the north wind. Magnus went to fetch a ladder, and just as he came back with it, the door to the basement flat opened and out came Grandpa. He's always having an afternoon nap when we come home from school. Now he screwed up his eyes as he looked at each one of us and then up at the flagpole. He was holding the telephone.

"Vera Johansen just phoned to see if I was dead."

"Huh?" I blurted out.

Grandpa scratched his chin drowsily. "Yes, since our flag was flying at half-mast," he explained. "So I told her I was only having a nap, which I was."

I glanced nervously at Birgit. If she didn't already think we were completely off our trolleys, she certainly would now. Why couldn't we just for once have a normal afternoon in the cove?

The ladder was no use – it was too unstable. Grandpa thought we'd have to use the tractor bucket to lift somebody up. Krølla sighed. She was starting to get bored now.

Mum came home from work at the worst moment imaginable. Grandpa was driving the tractor and concentrating on getting the bucket the right distance from the flagpole, while Minda was doing the best she could to cling on up there. Magnus was hanging on to the side of the tractor, giving directions. On the ground, a terrified girl from the Netherlands was trying to calm her barking dog, while Lena was standing on the table in the garden, wearing the world's largest grin as she filmed the whole scene from the perfect angle. I was holding the flag rope tightly, hoping that my little sister dangling up there was enough of a dramatic sight to stop Mum from noticing the deep ditches dug by the tractor tyres right across the flower bed and half the lawn.

"What in heaven's name is going on here?" Mum shouted.

"Trille and Lena have to do a book presentation," Magnus explained.

And Krølla's never going to be allowed to stop going to her after-school club, I thought to myself.

CHAPTER FIFTEEN

Mum goes to the doctor

It was that afternoon I decided to have a chat with Mum. Secretly, I'd been keeping an eye on her for several weeks to see if Lena's theory about The Change was true. After all, how could Lena be so sure that's what it was? What if it was something else? Mothers can get ill. My own grandmother had died young. She had been a mother too, just as much as my mum. It's not right for things like that to happen. Every time I thought about it, it was almost as if I couldn't breathe. The more I kept an eye out, the more worried I felt. Was Mum a bit fatter? She had more grey hair now, anyway, and she slept and slept, night and day.

There was nobody I could ask either. Dad had wrinkles on his brow and was getting worked up about the slightest things, while Minda just interrupted me in an annoyed way if I tried to ask her. Plus I couldn't bring myself to talk to Grandpa about it. What would he know about the menopause?

But that day, when Mum started crying just because Krølla was hanging from a flagpole, unharmed and perfectly fine, I couldn't leave it any longer.

So when evening came and everything had calmed down, I made some warm cocoa for her and sat down next to where she was lying on the sofa.

"Oh, thank you, Trille!" she said, clearly surprised, and sat up.

There had been a bit of bedlam and commotion after the business with the flagpole, but now the house was quiet.

"Mum. Don't you think you should go to the doctor to get your menopause checked out?"

"What?"

I wished Lena was there to explain, but she wasn't.

"Well, your body's changing, and you're getting a bit fat and fed up," I said glumly. "And it's probably just the menopause, but—"

Mum choked on her cocoa, sending it splattering halfway across the living-room table.

"Fat?" she shouted.

I gulped. "Well, maybe not exactly fat, but…"

Mum looked at me. "What is it, Trille?"

I poked at the sofa cushion. "What if it's something dangerous? What if you have cancer?" I eventually said, under my breath.

"Are you worried about that?"

All I could do was nod, as there was a lump in my throat now.

"Oh, Trille!" Mum stroked my hair. "I'll be turning forty-five next spring. I'm not young any more."

Wasn't she trying to make me feel better? Saying that she was old didn't help! Old people get cancer all the time.

"I haven't got as much energy as I used to. So maybe I feel a bit tired and cross when I've got a lot on my plate. And fat too."

She prodded one of the bulges on her stomach.

"Just a bit softer," I lied.

Mum snorted with laughter. "But that's the way it is with the menopause. It's nothing serious."

I thought about all her sleeping and bossiness. Was it really nothing bad?

"Would you feel better about it if I went to the doctor to check everything's all right?" Mum asked eventually.

I nodded.

"Then that's what I'll do first thing tomorrow, my darling Trille. Now, go and fetch some buns from the freezer, and we'll make ourselves even softer."

I felt as light as a feather that evening. I should have told Mum before that I was worried about her. She was only too happy to talk about it!

* * *

But the next afternoon, everything was as bad as it had been before. Mum's face looked all strange, and she asked the whole family to sit round the kitchen table.

"I've been to see the doctor today," she said, picking at the tablecloth, as if she didn't know how to continue.

Dad stood over by the sink with an empty coffee mug, looking down at the floor. My heart was struggling to beat normally.

"Have you got cancer?" I whispered.

Minda and Magnus stared at me in shock.

"Huh? Cancer?"

"No no no," said Mum. "I haven't got cancer. And it's not the menopause either."

Dad made a strange sniffling noise over by the sink. Mum turned towards him. Then she started sniffling too, and suddenly they broke down and started laughing so hard the whole kitchen echoed. They looked at each other, gasping for air as they laughed and laughed and laughed.

Minda, Magnus, Krølla and I sat motionless on our chairs. Our parents had gone completely bonkers. Who was going to look after us now? Grandpa?

"Mum…" I squeaked.

Then Mum pulled herself together and shouted: "You're going to have a brother!" She poked a finger at her soft tummy. "For Christmas. No wonder I'm fat! He's been in there almost five months!"

"WHAT?" Magnus shouted. "You're kidding!"

"Oh, good grief," Minda mumbled. "Seriously? I didn't think old people like you could have babies." She put her head in her hands. "Mum, you're old enough to be a grandmother!" she moaned from under there.

Big brothers and sisters must be related to aliens. What was wrong with them? Couldn't they see that this was absolutely brilliant? Mum wasn't ill! And we were going to have a baby. I leapt up onto my chair.

"Yippee!" I shouted. "Yippee times a hundred and three!"

Krølla leapt up onto her chair too and threw her arms in the air. "Yippee times a hundred and two hundred!" she yelled.

"That's more like it," said Mum, looking sternly at Minda and Magnus.

Then they couldn't help smiling too. Still, Minda made sure to tell me it was so embarrassing, and that even a little kid like me should realize that.

"And Lena thought it was the menopause!" I said, almost shouting, dashing out the door with the news.

But I stopped midway between our houses. Lena was only going to be partially pleased about this.

She'd been asking for a little brother loudly enough to make the walls tremble over there and so far it had all been in vain. Meanwhile, at our place, the whole Change situation had transformed into a baby.

I turned back. I had to have a little think about how I was going to tell her. People should be happy when they hear news like that.

I could have spared myself the thought. Krølla went over and spilt the beans later that evening. Ylva's teaching her to knit and, while they're knitting, Krølla blabbers on about anything and everything.

When darkness fell, Lena came crashing in. She had rain in her hair and thunder in her eyes.

"Is it true, Kari?"

Mum caught Lena in an enormous hug. "It's as true as the tide, Lena Lid."

Lena wriggled loose. "But it was our turn now, Kari!"

"You can borrow him whenever you want, Lena."

"Borrow him? Is this some kind of library you're running?"

Lena wondered if we had the faintest drop

of an idea what it was like wishing for a brother as intensely as she did while children just came shooting out of the house next door.

"I understand, Lena," said Mum.

Lena doubted it. "Have you ever counted your children, Kari? We've only got me at my place! Only me!"

Mum assured her that she counted us every evening, especially now that Minda and Magnus were capable of staying out until late at night.

"But Reidar and I spent many long years together before we became parents. Not everybody can have children, and it often takes much longer than you'd like."

I looked up, astonished. Had Mum and Dad once been childless? What did they do back then?

Lena looked sceptically at Mum. "Anyway, you should leave giving birth to younger people, Kari. You've got grey hair."

Mum agreed about that last bit. But she couldn't be anything other than happy at that moment.

CHAPTER SIXTEEN

Drama in the
Lid family kitchen

*T*he next afternoon, I popped down to see
Grandpa.

"Five times a grandfather soon!" I said, smiling.

"That's right. It's great stuff, Trille. Great stuff.
Hey, look at this."

He passed me a picture across the kitchen table.

"I found it when I was sorting out my writing
desk. Do you remember it?"

I nodded. It was the one of the huge halibut. I'd
seen it many times before. I leant over and studied it
again. Grandpa was young and had blond hair, like
me. He was leaning proudly against the wall of the

boat shed. Next to him hung the enormous fish.

"Were you alone when you caught it?" I asked.

"No, I wasn't. Inger was with me. In fact I doubt I'd have landed that halibut on my own."

It was probably my grandmother who'd taken the picture, I thought, trying to imagine it like a film.

"Look here," said Grandpa, pushing another picture across the table.

I hadn't seen this one before. "Where is it?"

"On the dock in Baltimore."

I stared at the photo. Grandpa in the United States. He looked cool, sitting there with his pipe in his mouth and his sleeves rolled up.

"I sailed abroad for a couple of years before I got married."

"That must've been exciting," I said.

"It was." He took back the picture and looked at it. Then he shook his head a little. "I was so blooming homesick."

"Were you?"

"I was. Inger was around then, you see."

"Have you got a picture of her too?" I asked.

"Mmm ... yes."

Grandpa went over to his desk and came back with a small bundle of photos. I'd seen them before, but that was a long time ago. There was one of Inger, Dad and Uncle Tor out on the steps, and one of Inger wearing an apron in a kitchen full of fish. But the best one was of Granny on her own on board *Troll*. She was wearing a big pair of waterproof dungarees, her hair was standing straight up, and her mouth was open, laughing.

"What was she really like?" I asked.

"Heh," said Grandpa, resting his chin on his hand. He looked briefly at me and then at the pictures. "Well, it was Inger or nobody, put it that way."

Then he held up the picture from Baltimore again.

"I'd made a real mess of things before I left, Trille. The whole love story could just as easily have gone to pot, I'll tell you that."

"What happened?"

He gathered up the pictures. "Well, wouldn't you like to know!" He put the pictures back in the desk drawer.

"But was it all right in the end?" I asked.

"Everything turns out all right for good-looking

men like us," Grandpa nodded, shutting the drawer with a bang. "Shall we take an evening stroll to the boat shed?"

"I've got to go and see Lena. We're doing a book project."

Grandpa stuffed his hands in his pockets. "Just let me know when you've got time for a trip out on the boat, then. It's a long time since we last went out."

I promised I would, and ran off.

* * *

There was a gloomy atmosphere in the Lid kitchen. Ylva and Lena were doing maths homework.

"Congratulations on your good news," said Ylva, smiling tiredly.

I thanked her and sat down at the table.

"Kari's very happy," said Lena. "She's very happy with all her children."

"Mm-hmm," said Ylva, straightening her glasses so she could read the maths question again.

"Were you very happy when you had me?" Lena asked.

"Mm-hmm," said Ylva again, moving her finger down along the page.

Sometimes I think the house could collapse around Ylva without her noticing. Now Lena took the maths book and pushed it away across the table.

"Were you very happy when you had me, even though you had to stop going to school and Dad ran off?" she shouted.

For as long as I've known Lena, I've been able to tell when a storm is brewing. This time it was completely unexpected. Lena swung out an arm, flinging her maths book to the floor with considerable force, and started to march out.

"What kind of a question is that?" Ylva shouted.

Lena was about to shout something back, but instead she just threw out her arms, as if she couldn't be bothered explaining.

And then the shock came. Ylva took off her glasses and said, "No. I wasn't very happy."

Complete silence fell over the Lid kitchen.

"Huh?" said Lena over by the door.

"I was far too young. I was playing in a band and was halfway through a school year. Plus your dad didn't want to be a dad. I wasn't happy. I was terrified."

I'd never heard the clock ticking in Lena's kitchen before. Now it sounded like it was slicing through the air.

"You know that the first few years were difficult, Lena."

Not a sound.

"But," said Ylva, "I didn't know it was possible to care about someone as much as I care about you, either."

Lena drew a breath, and Ylva put on her glasses.

"Just tell me if you know of a mother who loves her little girl more than I do," she said, picking up the maths book.

I could see that Lena was thinking very hard, but luckily nobody came to mind. She came and sat back down at the table.

"Are you going to make me a little brother sometime soon, then?"

"Oh, good grief," Ylva moaned. "Let Trille take over. I'm going to do some knitting with Krølla."

*

When Birgit arrived, first she gazed in awe at all of the colourful art everywhere, like most people do when they come into Lena's house, and then she smiled at us as if she was really looking forward to working on our group project. She'd brought along a big bottle of home-made bilberry cordial.

Ylva uses a lot of film in her art projects, and now she'd taught Lena how to use one of her editing programs on the computer. In the office corner under the attic stairs, Lena showed us the video from the garden on the big monitor. I thought it was embarrassing to see myself, but Birgit laughed.

"This is going to be brilliant!" she said.

Lena wanted to add some music and captions. Birgit and I sat down at the kitchen table to plan the rest. I'd never worked with anybody like Birgit before. She didn't sit there complaining about being bored: quite the opposite. She talked and explained things and made everything seem easy and fun. She told me she was slightly dreading speaking Norwegian in front of the class, but she thought it would be all right as long as she wrote down what she wanted to say.

"Maybe you could tell them about the book, and I could talk about the author?" she suggested.

"Mm-hmm," I said, trying to smile while my stomach tied itself in knots.

Lena looked at me over the top of the computer screen and frowned.

Then Isak came home from work.

"Do we need any popcorn here?" he asked, as he put his bag straight down in the corridor.

What could we do but say yes to a question like that? Soon he'd made us some in a big pot.

"Thanks, Dad," Lena said quickly as he went off into the living room.

She blushed when she saw that I'd heard her, and plonked the bowl of popcorn down with a thud on top of one of my books.

We'd just finished eating when the doorbell rang.

"Not a moment's peace," Lena sighed, heading out into the corridor.

On the doorstep, she found Kai-Tommy and Halvor.

"Yes?" Lena's voice was quizzical, as if she were speaking to two senile men who had wandered off from the retirement home.

Kai-Tommy swept back his hair. "Is Birgit here?"

We couldn't exactly hide Birgit in the fridge and say no. Soon the two boys were sitting at the kitchen table too, looking in astonishment at everything around them.

"Your mum said you were here," Kai-Tommy explained to Birgit.

Birgit smiled. Couldn't she see what an insane situation this was? I thought about all the horrible things Kai-Tommy had said and done to Lena over the years. And about the things he'd said to me. Birgit had no idea of all that. It was almost as if she'd landed from space straight into our class. Was it really possible that Kai-Tommy could seem like a nice person if you didn't already know him?

"We had some popcorn, but I'm sorry to say we've run out," Lena said, although that "sorry" didn't sound particularly convincing.

Halvor and I didn't say a word. But Kai-Tommy poured himself a glass of cordial and acted as if he'd always been a frequent guest at Lena's house. I was disheartened to realize that he was probably going to be just as tall and dark-haired as his father.

"Birgit, do you want to come and see the match tomorrow?" he suddenly asked. "We're playing against the team from the islands. Our first match since the summer."

I was about to reply that Birgit wasn't interested in football, when she said that she'd be happy to go.

"Will you be playing too?" she asked Lena.

Lena glanced quickly at Halvor and nodded. I felt totally left out. Soggy shepherds, I'd been planning on carrying up a salt lick instead. Or going for a trip out to sea, or doing something else meaningful. Blasted football.

"Are you going to come, Trille?" Birgit asked.

I coughed. It would be really embarrassing to turn up to watch when I'd been part of the team until just recently. But I imagined sitting next to Birgit in the stand. That would be quite something. If she was impressed by Kai-Tommy's hard shots, I could just tell her that he had poor technical abilities. I agreed to go, very reluctantly.

*

When I was about to leave, Lena stopped me by
the door.

"Will we be all right doing that presentation, then?"

I looked at the doorbell and bit the inside of my
cheek.

"Of course."

CHAPTER SEVENTEEN

Match-day madness

"*H*i, Trille. Are you injured?"

Axel, our old coach, plopped himself down next to me in the ramshackle football stand.

"Sort of," I mumbled. "What about you?"

"No, I'm training the younger ones now," Axel said cheerily. "Ivar wanted to take on your team. He's pretty good, you know."

I was about to protest, but then I spotted Birgit. She parked her bike over by the mini-pitch, where she met Ellisiv, who had probably been working. They walked together across the school playground. When Birgit spotted me, she waved, and a rocket burst inside my chest.

"Have you got a girlfriend?" Axel asked, nudging me.

"Ehm, no." I could feel myself blushing all the way to my earlobes. "What about you? Are you spending a lot of time at the cafe these days?"

Axel laughed as he made space for Ellisiv and Birgit.

"My girlfriend dumped me, Trille. So I don't have to go to the cafe any more."

"She dumped you?"

"Like a sack of potatoes. Hi, Ellisiv."

So we sat there, Axel and I, both of us next to a girl who wasn't our girlfriend, watching the match. It was incredible. Birgit asked me questions the whole time, and every so often she laughed her soft, pretty laugh. It was brilliant not playing football any more. Lena was right. You can't keep on doing things you hate.

And as if to make things even better, Kai-Tommy missed the goal by miles a couple of times and shouted nasty words across the gravel pitch. I hoped Birgit had noticed that. But it didn't look like she cared. Maybe she didn't know enough Norwegian yet.

The warm sun shone down on us, and it would all have been perfect if it hadn't been for one thing spoiling the mood: in goal, where once there had stood a skinny girl shouting herself hoarse, there now stood Halvor, strapping and silent. The more time that passed, the more uncomfortable I felt. Was Ivar going to bring Lena on at all?

"Is Lena injured too?" Axel asked.

I shook my head and tried to push aside the bad feeling I had seeing her sitting down alone on the bench. None of the boys were sitting there.

She wasn't brought on after half-time either. Not even when Halvor let in a real howler of a goal. Eventually we were three nil down. Ivar shouted and gave the boys instructions without losing his temper. It didn't look like he cared what the result was. The boys on the pitch were struggling.

"But why isn't Lena playing?" Ellisiv asked.

Axel said something about how it was a good idea to have two goalies, and that they probably wanted to let Halvor gain some confidence between the goalposts, in case Lena got injured. I gulped. I wasn't having a good time any more, no matter how nice it was to be sitting next to Birgit. My neighbour was sitting down there on the substitutes' bench, with her cap low over her face, her goalkeeper's gloves on, and a dark cloud above her.

Lena was brought on five minutes before the end. A shot came on target, which she easily saved, and then the game was finished.

* * *

I found Lena at home down by the barn. She was kicking a ball against the wall. The seagulls jumped into the sky with every shot.

"Halvor's got to have a bit of a go too, so it wouldn't be a total disaster if you got injured," I said cautiously.

Lena stopped shooting the ball and looked at me as if I were the stupidest person in God's creation.

"Disaster? We lost the game! I'm better than him, Trille!"

Another crash against the barn.

"But—" I began.

"Halvor's in goal because his dad's the assistant coach!"

Lena gave the ball one last mad kick, sending

it flying all the way down to the beach. The barn breathed a sigh of relief through the gap in the wall.

"What are you going to do about it, then?" I asked, feeling a bit worn out by her always getting angry about everything.

"I suppose I'll have to become a boy," she muttered furiously, heading off without even picking up her gloves.

CHAPTER EIGHTEEN

Kisha

"You used to live in Africa?"

I looked around Birgit's room in amazement. The last time I visited her I'd only been in the kitchen. Today we were finishing our book presentation. Lena was at football training and was going to join us later.

I gazed at all the pictures of giraffes and elephants. On Birgit's desk was a picture of her with summer hair almost as white as chalk. She had her arm round a girl who was as dark as Birgit was fair.

"Mum and some other people started a coffee roastery in Amsterdam," Birgit said, going on to explain that the coffee beans came from small farms in Kenya. "We spent a year living there while she was arranging everything."

The very thought of all she'd experienced made me feel light-headed.

"Why didn't you say you'd lived in Kenya?" I asked, bewildered, remembering how Lena had gone on and on about a measly holiday to Crete.

Birgit shrugged. "I don't know. I haven't met many other people who've been to Kenya, so it feels a bit weird to talk about it, I suppose."

I stared in fascination at the picture on her desk. Birgit looked so happy in it.

"That's Kisha," she said. "I miss her a lot. But we chat online."

"I'd like to hear more about Kenya," I said.

"OK," Birgit replied happily, pulling out a big photo album from her shelf.

We sat down on her bed, and she showed me pictures and told me about them. Her words took me to a green and warm place that smelt of coffee. She told me about rainy mornings, about the big animals, and about the house they'd lived in. But most of all she told me about Kisha, the best friend in the world.

147

"We've decided that we'll go and study together one day," she said. "Maybe you'd like to come too?"

I suddenly felt all warm. "Mm-hmm," I nodded.

Study? I always thought I would stay in Mathildewick Cove until my dying day. I even had my eye on a piece of land down by the sea where I would build my house. And then I'd imagined that I would be a fisherman, like Grandpa. Now it was as if the world had opened up in all directions. Could people just travel around and do whatever they wanted? Could I do that too?

Then Birgit put away the album. We had to get to work. We'd finished writing the presentation, and that evening we just had to practise in front of each other. Birgit and I took turns standing by the computer and talking. I spoke about Emil, and she spoke about the author, Astrid Lindgren, in her own beautiful kind of Norwegian. When we'd done it twice each, Lena sent a message to say she wasn't coming. I pictured her sitting in the usual spot on the kitchen table, getting bandaged up again. Had the training session been as awful as the match the day before?

"That's all right," said Birgit. "We're finished anyway. I'm a bit nervous about it, you know."

I nodded and felt a little as if I couldn't breathe properly.

Before I left, Birgit's mum asked if I'd stay to have something to eat with them. She served up a hot, bright red soup that tasted pretty strong. Did they always eat dinner that late? We all sat around the table, just like at home. Birgit's parents asked me about the farm and fishing and the mountains as if I were a grown-up. They wanted to hear about all the things I thought were ordinary and boring. I did my best to explain in a mixture of English and Norwegian, but it was difficult.

I felt completely dizzy as I walked home. My head was bursting with new thoughts, and my stomach was full of new food. When I went to bed, I lay there, staring at the ceiling. What was I going to do? There was no way I could let Birgit find out I was too scared even to stand up in front of my own class. I couldn't go to school the next day. I couldn't face it.

Lena was the only person who knew I wasn't

really ill, but she didn't say a word about it.
She just gave me that raised eyebrow look she'd
started doing, and then told me about the book
presentation when she came home. It had been a
smash hit, according to her. People had, of course,
long since heard about the flagpole incident, so it
was a real highlight for the class to get to see it with
their own eyes.

"You made a good impression, Trille," she assured
me.

The next day, Birgit seemed worried when she asked
me if I felt better. I nodded and looked away. Did she
realize what a little wimp I was?

CHAPTER NINETEEN

The ruler stunt that went wrong

I was thinking more and more about Birgit. It was almost as if a gentle and gracious bird had landed in the middle of our class and was able to see beyond all the stupidity and daftness. For example, one day we were working in pairs, and Birgit was with Andreas. In the first few years at school, Kai-Tommy used to mimic Andreas every time he opened his mouth, because he stammers. When we got Ellisiv as our teacher, the bullying stopped, but it was already too late. Andreas hardly ever said another word. But the day he worked with Birgit, I was surprised to hear him chatting away. In another lesson, she might chat the same way with Kai-Tommy, as if he were a totally normal and pleasant person. Was that what he was like when he was with Birgit?

I was crestfallen every time I saw the two of them together. He liked her; there was no doubt about that. And I was nothing compared to Kai-Tommy.

I soon became an expert at finding ways to spend time with Birgit outside of school. Dad was stunned by how many salt licks I was willing to carry up the mountain, and when the sheep had been brought down for the winter, I went up with the hedge clippers instead. Birgit liked being up the mountain and thought doing the trimming along the track was great fun. The same went for her Norwegian homework: she often needed help with it, and Kai-Tommy certainly didn't have anything to offer there. A gifted child like me, on the other hand, could teach her all about grammar and sentence construction until the sheep came home, so to speak.

I didn't mean to spend less time at sea with Grandpa. That's just how things went. I didn't mean to spend less time with Lena either. That's just how things went too.

As autumn tightened its grip and I went gallivanting around Hillside with Birgit, Grandpa went out to sea alone. I would see him doing his usual rounds from the house to the boat shed, and from the boat shed to the pier. Some days I would run down to him, sit on a fish box and have a little chat, but I never stayed for long at a time. Grandpa didn't mention it. But sometimes I noticed he'd be looking for me after I'd gone.

As for Lena, she was fighting for her life on the gravel pitch. And she was all alone too. Our team played match after match, but she was only ever let on for the last five minutes. She argued and got angry, but she kept going to every single training session. Three times a week she came home covered in gravel and grazed all over. I often popped through the hedge and over to the Lid family kitchen on those evenings. It was good for Lena to have somebody to shout at: that much was clear.

Usually Isak would be sitting there, patching her

up while the rage flew around him. I would pull up a chair too and listen with half an ear. But Ylva thought things had gone too far.

"Can't you just give up football?" she asked one evening when Lena was sitting again on what had become the official medical station, the kitchen table.

"Give it up?"

"All you do is moan about it, Lena. If it's that terrible, then aren't there other things that would be better?" Ylva tried suggesting.

"What would those be? Keyboard lessons?" Lena's voice was so sharp you could cut yourself on it.

Ylva replied that she hadn't said a word about keyboard lessons, but now that Lena mentioned it, it wouldn't hurt to practise a bit more.

"Or, to put it another way," she said, correcting herself, "it wouldn't hurt to do any practice at all." Then she continued, "Look at Trille."

I felt like I'd been caught red-handed. Not only had I started hovering around Hillside all the time, but I'd also started practising the piano. I wouldn't admit it even at knifepoint, but I was only doing it to impress Birgit and her family. I didn't want to sound like an idiot at the music school's Christmas concert.

"You'll never be good at something if you don't practise," Ylva added.

After that, Lena stopped complaining. She kept going to the training sessions, looking like a shadow of her usual self, but she never said a word when she came home.

And then she broke her hand.

"How on earth can you break your hand in an English lesson?" Magnus wanted to know.

Lena explained that there was no telling what terrible things might happen if you were bored for long enough, and that our English lessons were so boring they'd been a risk to her health for some time now.

I was there when it happened. Lena was trying out one of her ruler stunts. She'd developed a technique that involved sticking a ruler into the wall like a sword, then tipping her chair in such a way that the ruler is the only thing holding her up. While Ellisiv was reading out a long text about the school day in Australia, I could see Lena was daring herself to tip even further back in her chair, until she was almost horizontal. The ruler quivered under the strain. It certainly looked impressive.

Lena was concentrating so hard that she didn't notice everybody, including Ellisiv, starting to peer in her direction. Then, just as the schoolchildren in Australia had gone home for the day and Ellisiv was about to say "Lena Lid" in the way only she can, we heard a sharp crack as the ruler broke, and a much louder crash as the chair slipped away and Lena slammed to the floor.

"Do you know what my mum said, Trille?" Lena grumbled the next day on the way to our music lessons.

"No."

"She said: 'What bad timing with the music school concert coming up.'"

Lena waved her plaster cast about in agitation. "Floundering flatfish, never mind about the concert!" she shouted. "Now I can't play in goal!"

I closed my ears. I couldn't stand to hear any more about football.

CHAPTER TWENTY

"Für Elise"

*A*nd practise I did. "Für Elise", the piece that had looked utterly impossible when I'd first seen the notes on paper, eventually turned into music. My improvement put Mr Rognstad into a kind of positive state of shock. He didn't know that I was being driven by pure fear. I might sit by the piano wishing for a drum kit until my head ached, but still I gritted my teeth and got my fingers to sweep over all the right keys. I wanted to be able to play "Für Elise" in my sleep, with my eyes closed, and even if my mind went blank. It was the only way to get through the concert. Birgit and her family had to see that I could do more than build rafts and gut fish.

"Why are you going to your music lesson today, then?"

"To show Mr Rognstad my plaster cast. He's going to be relieved, I bet."

I shuddered. The music school concert in December stood out like a dark spot on the calendar. It was exactly the same as with the book presentation. I'd have to do something in front of loads of people. But this time I wasn't going to chicken out. I couldn't. If I was ill again that day, then Birgit would work it out. So I was going to practise, practise, practise.

It was the only way to survive.

Every afternoon, I sat at the piano while Grandpa pottered about in the boat shed and Lena was down by the barn with one broken hand and a football. I could see her from the window. Sometimes she just did keepie-uppies, and other times she went down to Grandpa and fetched some fishing buoys, which she set out in the field. She'd drawn a line that was supposed to be the edge of the six-yard box. She put the ball down there, and then she aimed and took long goal kicks towards the fishing buoys.

That's how we went on all through November and half of December. Grandpa in the boat shed, Lena outside the barn, and me at the piano.

By the time the Christmas holidays and the music school concert were approaching, I could play "Für Elise" without so much as peeking at the notes. Grandpa had fixed and mended every single net he could find, and Lena's ball was slamming into the fishing buoys with ever growing precision. She'd managed a dizzying one thousand and eleven keepie-uppies in a row too. Strangely enough, she didn't boast about this to anybody – not even to the boys in our class. She'd stopped talking about football.

"I'll come and listen," Lena came to say through the window, the day before the concert. "I'll clap even if it's a complete racket."

"It's not going to be a complete racket," I said.

"No, but if it is. You've got to squeeze out the whole of 'Für Elise' on that thing."

In any case, she promised to drum her plaster cast on the back of the chair in front and whistle along. She also wanted to savour all the other performers' nerves. Especially Kai-Tommy's.

"Although … I almost hope it goes well for him."

"What?" I'd never heard Lena say anything nice about Kai-Tommy before, and deep down I didn't like it.

"Well, it's just … Ivar's not fair to him," Lena mumbled.

I thought she was going to start whingeing about her goalkeeping career again, but instead she said that the person who got yelled at the most at training was Kai-Tommy.

"The other boys are just as bad, you know,

except perhaps Andreas. He's good at reading the game…"

She didn't say any more after that. It was as if she'd forgotten herself for a moment.

"Are you looking forward to Christmas?" she asked instead, resting her chin on the windowsill.

"Mm-hmm," I said. "What about you?"

"Yup. Birgit's going to the Netherlands, isn't she?"

I nodded. Why was Lena asking that? Was she pleased? She was smiling anyway.

"We're going to set a new record with our haul of sweets when we go carolling this year, Trille. Mark my words."

Then she pulled her head out of the window without so much as saying bye.

I started playing "Für Elise" again, even though Magnus had said that he was going to be hospitalized if I played that piece one more time. From the corner of my eye, I saw Lena crossing the frosty fields in the low December sunlight. She met Grandpa down by the boat shed. I wondered what they were talking about as they strolled out onto the breakwater together. Suddenly I felt such a longing to be down there with them, it was like something slicing through my chest. But I'd agreed with Birgit that I'd go up to Hillside so we could revise for our Norwegian test.

CHAPTER TWENTY-ONE

The Christmas present

The music school concert was a blur. I can't even remember going up when it was my turn. But my plan worked. I knew "Für Elise" so well that I played it even though I was sitting on stage like a dead monkey. In any case, Mum, with her huge tummy, said it had gone well. And Mr Rognstad clapped, clearly pleased.

I came back to my senses when it was Kai-Tommy's turn. He started off well but then ground to a complete halt halfway through, and had to start again. A nasty little feeling of satisfaction grew inside me. I glanced over at Lena. Her brows were knitted, and when Kai-Tommy finished, she burst into thunderous applause.

I tried to spot Birgit, but I couldn't see her slender frame until she took her seat on stage. People probably thought they were about to hear something ordinary and halfway decent, like when the rest of us played, but then Birgit started blazing away, playing something by Grieg that sent chills and waves of warmth down my spine.

There was total silence when she finished. Then the deafening applause began. I could see that Mum was extremely impressed. Only Lena seemed unenthusiastic, slapping her good hand half-heartedly against her thigh. She seriously doesn't have a clue about music.

Just as I was getting into Mum's car at the end, somebody grabbed on to my jacket.

"Here," said Birgit. "A Christmas present." She pushed a parcel into my lap.

"Oh, thank you!"

"I'll see you in the new year," she said softly, giving me a quick hug. Then off she ran.

Neither Lena nor Mum said anything on the way home. Mum just smiled in a very irritating way, while Lena looked out the window. The parcel on my lap felt like it was smouldering.

* * *

Back at home, I ran straight up to my room. There was no way I was going to open Birgit's present in front of everyone else down in the living room at Christmas.

It was a picture. I recognized all the mountaintops. She'd painted the view from the cairn in shades of a summer's evening. You could see Kobbholmen out at sea in the evening sun, and just next to it she'd painted a black dot. That was probably *Troll*.

If anybody had seen me there in my room, they would've thought I'd gone completely bonkers. I jumped around like a fool, bumping into the shelves so hard that the ice-cream tub holding the broken bottle Lena had given me leapt off and landed on the floor. Birgit had given me a Christmas present!

Part Three

Winter and waiting

CHAPTER TWENTY-TWO

"Away in a Manger"

*B*irgit went to the Netherlands to spend Christmas with her brothers, and suddenly I had all the time in the world. The same went for my little brother in Mum's tummy. It seemed he wasn't planning on coming out any time soon, even if Mum was so pregnant that the walls were buckling around us. She even said that Lena was right: she was too old to have a baby.

The weather outside was really miserable, so the whole family was pretty much stuck indoors, but we did all we could to pull ourselves together to make things as comfortable as possible for Mum. For instance, I would come into the kitchen and suddenly find Magnus making dinner, or Minda playing animal bingo with Krølla instead of staring at her phone and being grumpy. As for Dad, he put up decorations, ironed tablecloths, sorted out clothes and goodness knows what else. If we absolutely had to argue, we did it in the attic, and as quietly as possible.

"Could Mum burst?" Krølla whispered while we were loading the dishwasher one evening.

She was holding a fork in her hand and looking worriedly at Mum's enormous bump.

"*Pfft,*" I said dismissively.

But, secretly, I was watching Mum anxiously too. Didn't that baby realize he had to come out soon before she keeled over?

I saw unusually little of Lena. Ylva was probably keeping her at home so there would be as much peace and quiet as possible in our house. But when Boxing Day arrived and there was still no sign of our new brother, she came stomping into our kitchen in her familiar style. Outside, the wind was blowing the cold December rain sideways.

"Today we're going to go carolling, and we're going to dress up as guerrilla soldiers," she declared, wiping the worst of the rain from her face.

There was already a large puddle on the kitchen floor around where she was standing.

"Are we?" I asked sceptically.

"It's a genius idea, Trille. We'll wear Magnus's military gear and camouflage our faces. And we can borrow his hunting knife too!"

I could see several problems with what she'd said, including the fact that my big brother's name had come up twice. But I needn't have worried.

"Over my dead body!" said Mum, leaning heavily on the kitchen worktop. "There's no way you and Lena are going round wearing military gear and singing 'Away in a Manger' while brandishing a hunting knife."

She told us that Christmas was a time of peace and that we should dress up as angels or Father Christmas and behave ourselves.

We went up to my room. The wind and the rain were even louder up there. Lena scanned the walls. I could see that she'd spotted the picture from Birgit.

"Kai-Tommy got one too," she muttered.

"Got what?"

"A Christmas present from Birgit."

"Oh." My voice was indifferent, but inside it felt as if the blood had stopped in my veins.

Was it true? I'd had such a happy and warm feeling all Christmas every time I'd looked at the picture! Had Birgit given Christmas presents to everybody? Or just to Kai-Tommy and me? Why did Lena have to come here and tell me this, anyway?

Angrily, I rested my chin on my palms and peered through the rain-spattered windowpane. The wind was doing its best to shake the lights off the cedar tree out in the garden. Two crooked figures were coming up the track. Grandpa and Dad. They'd been down to see to the boats.

"I can't be bothered to go carolling in this rubbish weather," I mumbled.

I'd grown so used to Lena just shrugging and leaving me to do my own thing recently that I was really taken aback by her reaction.

She stood right in front of me. "There's no such thing as bad weather, you wimp, only bad clothes.

How many of your Christmas sweets have you got left, anyway?"

"Wimp?" I asked in disbelief. Lena had hit where it hurt most. "Only snotty little brats go carolling, Lena. I'm not coming!"

Lena's eyes narrowed and she focused on something behind me instead of looking straight at me. If I wanted to stay inside playing the piano and staring at art, that was fine by her, she said coldly. It was my life. But she was going out carolling before every Tom, Didrik and Harald went out and the sweet supplies ran dry. Then she left.

I stood there, feeling regret and anger at the same time. Eventually I pulled the sheet off my bed and stormed after her.

"OK," I said, wrapping the sheet around my shoulders.

Lena looked at me crossly. It was almost dark now.

"Are you seriously going as an angel?"

"I'm going to disguise myself as an angel," I said. "When we get up to the main road, I'm going to turn into a ghost."

I fetched a sheet for her too.

*

Down in the kitchen, two new puddles had appeared next to the one Lena had made when she arrived. Dad and Grandpa were shivering after their walk down to the sea.

"'God rest you merry, gentlemen'," Lena said in greeting, curtseying in her angel costume.

"You can forget that," said Dad. "Nobody's going out this evening."

The wind was supposed to be getting stronger, he told us. On the radio, they'd been telling people to avoid going outside unless it was really urgent.

"I know one thing that's really urgent," said Lena when Grandpa and Dad had gone to get changed. "And that's my supply of goodies."

Silently, I went to fetch the waterproof cool bag from the larder, and then we crept out.

CHAPTER TWENTY-THREE

Hurricane angels

We realized straight away that we'd have to forget our ghost plan. If we wanted to keep the sheets over our heads, we'd have needed to tie them to the ground. The only solution was to wrap them round ourselves tightly and do our best to look like angels.

"Gales and bucketing rain," Lena shouted. "It feels so Christmassy."

I was still mulling over what she'd said about Kai-Tommy. I shielded my angry face from the rain and stomped through the wind.

*

Our first carolling stop was Uncle Tor's place.

"Are you two completely crackers? Get home, for crying out loud!" he said when he opened the door, only to be met by a faceful of wind, rain and "Away in a Manger".

"We'll go home soon," said Lena, opening the cool bag. "We've just got to get enough to cover the bottom."

My uncle grunted as he threw in some assorted sweets and fled back indoors.

We probably should have gone home, but I didn't want to. What would I do there anyway? Sit looking at the picture Birgit had given me and tiptoe around Mum? We took shelter round the back of the hay barn so we could discuss our next move. Down by the ferry landing there was a whole bunch of houses sure to be full of sweets. It was only a quarter of an hour's walk, and there could hardly be any competition from other carollers wandering around on an evening like that.

"Imagine if we knocked on Kai-Tommy's door," said Lena. "I'd like to see his face when he realizes that we've snapped up the whole area while he's been inside waiting for snow and robins flying around."

I tightened my grip on the cool bag handle. "Let's go," I said firmly.

* * *

Blinking barnacles, it was so good to get out and about! We practically flew along with the wind behind us. The lamp posts waved in the wind, and the shadows of the tall spruce trees on the uphill side of the road danced wildly in the changing light. When we got to Ellisiv's house, I was all ready to sing a carol, but Lena thought we should press on and get these houses done first.

"We can do her on the way back!" she shouted.

We came round the headland before the ferry landing and could hear the sea roaring. The water droplets landing on our faces were salty. The storm was really picking up now. Sometimes it felt as if the wind had taken hold of me by the waist and was carrying me along the road.

"Let's do 'Joy to the World'. It's one of the shortest!" Lena shouted. She started running up towards the houses. Her sheet flapped over her shoulders like a load of confused washing.

*

Generally speaking, people were quite alarmed
when they opened their doors. Lena thought their
bewilderment meant they were giving us more
sweets. We were raking in the goodies!

"I knew it had to be some of you hardy folk from
Mathildewick Cove," said Thunderclap Kåre. Clearly
impressed, he gave us each an enormous bar of
milk chocolate. "Say hello to Lars from me, and get
yourselves home!"

But we couldn't go home until we'd knocked on
Kai-Tommy's door.

* * *

The house where Kai-Tommy and his family live
looks kind of American. They even have columns
by the front door. In their garden, a thousand
Christmas lights danced in the wind.

It was his brother who opened the door, the one
who's a budding football talent. He was wearing
a light blue shirt that fitted him tightly across the
chest, and he flicked his fringe back in just the
same way Kai-Tommy does. I could imagine him
wearing a football strip. Minda would probably have

swooned. Was this what Kai-Tommy was going to look like in a couple of years? Was that why Birgit liked him? Dispirited, I stared down at my boots, which were sticking out from under my sheet, but Lena looked straight at Kai-Tommy's brother and started singing "Joy to the World", the song echoing through the roomy hallway.

Halfway through the verse, Kai-Tommy popped up behind his brother. For a split-second, he looked at us in shock and awe, but then he put on his usual sneering face, as if we were the two greatest idiots in the world. Then the boys' parents appeared. Their mother was wearing a red Christmas dress, and Ivar looked like an English football manager, wearing a suit.

Lena's last "heaven and nature sing" was a little quieter under the gaze of her football coach. But when Kai-Tommy's mum brought us two large chocolate Father Christmases, Lena opened the lid of the cool bag ever so slightly and said, "We'll have to take them in our pockets, Trille. It's full up in here."

As we closed the door, I was pleased to hear Kai-Tommy inside, shouting, "How come they're allowed out and I'm not?"

"You'd think they had no parents," his mother replied.

"I think we should go home now, Lena," I said.

*   *   *

The wind and rain had crept all the way through to our skin, and now the cold had more of a bite to it. I wasn't angry any more, just fed up and worn out. It was quite different walking against the wind. It felt like walking straight into a living wall, and sometimes it was almost hard to breathe. The best thing we could do was to lean forward and walk kind of sideways, each with an arm in front of our faces.

The way home suddenly seemed endless. A little worry started gnawing away at my stomach. What had we got ourselves into this time?

But it was only when we arrived back at the ferry landing that we really understood the seriousness of the situation. Lena was blown off her feet like a paper angel. Then the ice-cold sea spray came washing right up onto the road, making me lose my footing too. By the time we got up, we were both without our sheets. As if on command, we scrambled down into the ditch on the uphill side of the road.

"We have to get to the other side of the headland," I yelled.

We half walked, half crept along the wet ditch, Lena dragging the cool bag behind her like an anchor. I remembered that her hand was still in plaster, and I turned round to take the bag. At that moment, a huge wave came roaring over the road where we'd just been, washing away stones, snow poles and anything else that wasn't tied down. A storm surge! The fear struck me like a hammer blow. I didn't know the wind could get so much stronger so quickly!

Another gust forced us to get down almost flat in the ditch. I hardly dared look at the lamp posts any more. What if they snapped?!

"Trille! Over there!"

I lifted my head. One of the spruce trees further up the road was about to come down. The wind pulled and tore at the tree's winter-green branches, and it started to give way in slow motion. It rocked and swayed, and eventually fell right over in the stormy light, like a wounded giant. We sat in the ditch, speechless, as we stared at the enormous tree lying right across the road. We were out in tree-toppling storm winds!

Then it got dark. I don't mean dark like it normally gets at night. I mean pitch-dark like in a dark wardrobe in a dark room with a dark corridor outside. The street lights went out, the dots of light on the other side of the fjord disappeared, and the moon fled as far away as it could. I fumbled my way over to Lena.

If we kept crawling onwards, we might get mashed underneath a tree. If we crawled back to the houses where we'd been, we might get washed out to sea.

We were trapped!

CHAPTER TWENTY-FOUR

Ellisiv, Axel and the big question

"Ellisiv's house!" Lena shouted in my ear.

We knew our teacher's red-painted house was all there was between the headland and the trees, but we couldn't see a thing, and it felt dangerous to crawl out of the ditch. Another blast of wind came thundering in from the sea. Then it let up slightly, so I wiped the rain from my eyes and spun my head to try and find some kind of landmark. Was this what it was like being blind?

Then something pierced the darkness like a nail.

"There!" shouted Lena.

It had to be one of Ellisiv's windows. Had she lit a candle or something? We started to fumble our way forward again. We lay down flat in the ditch every time a gust of wind came, but we dragged ourselves onwards in the small gaps between the gusts. Lena went in front, while I followed behind with the cool bag. Eventually the house was right above us. Now we just had to climb up out of the ditch and into the garden.

We waited until the wind calmed, and then we legged it. We tripped over several times. It was impossible to see where we were putting our feet, and the wind shook and ripped at us with enormous power. When we reached the house, I tripped on the bottom step and fell down flat. It hurt so much that I howled with pain, and I could taste warm blood as it trickled down from my nose and into my mouth. Another gust almost blew us back down into the garden, but finally I managed to claw my way to the door handle. I had to use all my strength to stop the door from blowing off its hinges. Then we plunged into the hallway, the door slamming behind us with a loud bang.

The sight that met Ellisiv would probably have scared most people stiff. Two soaking wet and bloodstained children lying amidst piles of chocolate and clementines. She let out a scream and put her hand to her mouth in shock. Luckily she wasn't alone. Axel, our old football coach, popped up from behind her. Lena and I dragged ourselves up until we were sitting.

"What are you doing here?" said Lena, looking at Axel in surprise.

"You're one to talk!" Ellisiv shouted. "What on earth are you doing, Trille and Lena?"

"Well, we were going to sing you a Christmas carol, but…" Lena couldn't go on.

Then I felt it too. I was overcome with cold and fear, and my whole body was shivering.

I'm not sure I'll ever be able to explain what it was like to take that steaming hot cup of warm squash in my hands. The wind was roaring against the walls outside, but Lena and I were sitting close together on an old sofa, propped up with cushions and wrapped in blankets. Our wet clothes were hanging over by the stove, making the windows steam up. The lovely squash sent waves of warmth through my body.

"Thanks," I mumbled, which was the first word I had been able to say. "We need to phone home," I added.

"The signal's down," said Axel.

Oh no! Dad was going to be worried to death! And Mum! This was the last thing she needed.

"I just managed to send a message before the network blacked out," said Ellisiv when she saw how panicked I was. "They know you're safe."

I've been through stormy nights before. Not every year, but often enough to know what it's like at home. Dad paces anxiously, wondering if the barn, the boats and everything else are all right, while Mum keeps on saying that there's nothing they can do but wait. As a rule, when the wind's really strong – when the storms are big enough to have names – then we're ordered to go down to Grandpa's flat in the basement. That's where it's safest. It's not like my bedroom in the attic, where you can hear the roof tiles rattling above your head. Were my family down in Grandpa's flat now? Were they able to relax now they knew Lena and I were here? Were they really, really angry?

Axel put more wood on the fire. He clearly knew what he was doing with that massive stove. More gusts of wind shook and tore at the house. Lena had been blue with cold when we arrived there, but the warm squash put life back in her. Now her cheeks were as red as Father Christmas's. She looked at Ellisiv, then at Axel, and then back at Ellisiv again.

"So, Axel. Haven't you got a girlfriend in town?" she asked eventually.

I'd forgotten to tell her! Ellisiv went bright red, and Axel cleared his throat.

"She dumped him," I whispered to Lena, hoping that she might start talking about the weather instead. That would give her plenty to talk about today of all days. But no.

"So are you two boyfriend and girlfriend now?"

I looked down at my squash in embarrassment.

"Well, I don't know about that," Ellisiv mumbled.

Axel stopped poking the fire. "What?" he said. "Aren't we boyfriend and girlfriend? What are we, then?"

"Well…" said Ellisiv, her face turning redder than

that time when we were nine and Lena had punched Kai-Tommy in the middle of the classroom.

A very awkward silence spread through the room. Luckily, the wind was really raging outside.

Lena took a swig of her squash.

"You two would make a good couple, anyway," she said eventually, just to settle the matter. "Can we offer you a few kilos of chocolate?"

We swept up our haul from the hallway floor and laid it out on the table. While we were doing that, Axel spotted Lena's soggy plaster cast.

"I think it might be best if we took that cast off," he said.

"Yes." Lena nodded. "It was supposed to be coming off on the third of January, anyway."

Ellisiv fetched some scissors and a knife. Soon Lena was stretching out her fingers in a way she hadn't been able to for some time.

"Now you're ready to stand in goal again," said Axel, giving her a pat on the back.

That was enough to make Lena fall silent. She closed her lips tightly, as if she hadn't heard what he'd said.

"It's mainly Halvor who stands in goal now," I said.

Axel looked at Lena, confused. "Aren't you the goalie any more?"

Lena took one of the chocolate bars that Thunderclap Kåre had given us and broke it up into pieces with short, sharp snaps.

"Lena?" Axel wasn't giving up.

"You bet your cod liver oil I'm a goalie. I just don't have a goal to stand in," she said.

Lena had been grumbling and moaning about football practice to everybody back in Mathildewick Cove, and we'd all listened with half an ear, waiting for it to blow over. Now I saw two grown adults get almost as worked up about the situation as Lena herself. Axel leant over the table and asked her all about the training sessions with Ivar and the boys, and Lena reluctantly told him how life had been on the gravel pitch over the last few months.

"But that's not fair, Lena," said Ellisiv. "Even I know you're a good goalie."

Axel nodded. "It's not right, Lena."

He seemed genuinely angry about how Lena had

been treated. I felt a pang of guilt. Why hadn't I been angry?

"What would you think about starting to play in town?" Axel asked.

"Huh?" said Lena.

"I know Lash, the man who trains the girls two years older than you. They've been struggling to find a decent goalie this season. Would you like to try out with them?"

"On a girls' team?" said Lena, as if he'd suggested that she should play with a team of camels.

"Well, you are a girl, Lena," Ellisiv said drily. "If you're going to carry on playing football, sooner or later you'll have to join a girls' team."

I was sure Lena would say no. No way would she dare to change teams! Deep in thought, she wolfed down five pieces of chocolate.

"Which days do they train on, then?" she asked eventually.

I glanced at her sideways, surprised. Was she really that brave? I wasn't sure if it was a pang of envy I was feeling, or something else.

*

As the night wore on, the weather worsened. There was no longer any doubt that this was a hurricane. Axel paced around the small living room nervously, and at one point he went out onto the doorstep, but he quickly came back indoors.

"This house has stood here since the eighteen hundreds," said Ellisiv, "so I'm sure it'll last tonight too."

She drew Lena close in the crook of her arm, in the way only Ellisiv can, and they fell asleep there on the sofa.

CHAPTER TWENTY-FIVE

After the storm

The wind dropped early the next morning. At daybreak, we went outside and stood on the doorstep, speechless. It was as if the world had been through the fight of its life and was now gasping for breath. Ellisiv's plum tree had snapped right the way through, leaving sharp, white splinters. Further towards Mathildewick Cove, fallen spruce trees littered the road, and in some spots, pieces of the asphalt surface had been washed away. One of the lamp posts down below the house was clumsily curtseying to us. Behind all of this was the sea, a grey, seasick mass.

The thought of Lena and me having been out

in all this made me feel very queasy. Down at the shore, big, restless breakers rolled onto the land, throwing up branches and debris between the rocks.

"I wonder what it was like on Kobbholmen last night," Lena said, full of thought. "Do you think the house is still standing?"

Before I could answer, we heard the sound of a tractor. It stopped a bit up the road, unable to get any further. Somebody leapt out and started scrambling over the fallen spruce trees. It was Dad.

"Trille!"

When he finally reached the house I was captured in a bear hug. After a moment, he swept Lena into the same hug. Wasn't he angry?

"Is it safe to be out in the tractor before they've cleared the road?" Lena asked.

Dad let go of her. "Safe?" he shouted. "You've got some nerve asking that, after you went strolling around carolling in the middle of Armageddon!"

He was angry. Extremely angry.

"Where's Isak?" Lena asked meekly.

I could hear in her voice that she would have

liked him to be the one to come along in the tractor and give us a bear hug.

"Isak?" Dad clasped his hands together. "Isak's with Kari, Lena! Trille became a big brother again overnight!"

*   *   *

My brother had chosen the stormiest night in living memory to be born. A night when huge trees had blocked the road so no ambulance could get through. A night when the ferry couldn't sail. And a night when the phones and emergency networks were down, so nobody could call anyone.

While the hurricane winds blasted our cove again and again, Mum had given birth to a whole new person down in Grandpa's flat. The storm had made Isak the midwife and Ylva the nurse. Minda and Magnus had run round the flat like mad, fetching towels and water, stoking the fires and keeping an eye on the candles. And Grandpa, who rarely got worked up about anything, had been wandering round like a nervous wreck, ranting and raving, puzzling over who on earth had the great idea that women should go through so much pain when they were having children. Krølla was the only one who'd slept through the whole drama.

"And it wasn't a brother after all, Trille," said Dad, his voice all puffed up, when we'd clambered carefully over the fallen trees and got into the tractor.

He turned the key very energetically. "It's a sister, folks! A big, strong, round bundle of a sister!"

Grandpa had weighed her at once on his fishing scale: four thousand, seven hundred and ninety grams!

"Do you realize what a mother you've got?" Dad shouted wildly, pinching my cheek so hard it hurt. "Do you realize?!"

* * *

Did I realize what a mother I'd got? I stood there, peeping round the corner of the bedroom door. She was as peaceful as Dad was half mad. Her grey fringe curled delicately over her forehead. She looked like she was resting after some kind of hurricane too. Krølla was sitting next to the bed, sparkling like the sun. You could see from her glow that she was now a big sister.

"Trille dear," Mum said softly when I went in, stroking my cheek. "What on earth were you thinking?"

I was about to answer, but she clearly wasn't that upset.

"Look," she just said, nodding towards the cradle. "Feel free to pick her up."

"She hardly weighs anything," Krølla said from the other side of the cradle.

"Well, I don't know about that," Mum mumbled, clearly worn out, laying her head back on the pillow.

I carefully picked up this little person. I was a fair bit younger when Krølla was born, and I don't remember all that much about it, so I was quite unprepared for what it would feel like to hold my new little sister in my arms. She more or less just crawled into my heart and made herself comfortable. If she'd ordered me to do a book presentation, I would've done it. That's how it felt. Outside, the wind had turned everything upside down, but here she lay, peaceful and safe, and new to the world. It was incredible!

I'll always look after you, I thought, looking at

her round, red face and half-open mouth.

Lena came in silently behind me. She looked at the little girl with a serious expression and shook her head slightly when I asked if she wanted to hold her. Instead she gently stroked one of her strong, stringy fingers over the top of the baby's nose. Then she sighed, and left.

*   *   *

It was strange having no electricity or Internet connection, but quite good too. Later in the day, Ylva and Dad warmed up some Christmas leftovers on the living-room stove, and managed to throw together a meal for everybody. Magnus was the only one who interrogated Lena and me about our carolling expedition. I was pleased it was lost in all the fuss, although we'd probably hear more about it when things calmed down.

"Has she got a name?" I asked when we were all gathered around the table, and Mum was feeding my little sister in the armchair by the stove.

I'd been a little worried about this aspect. Neither Krølla nor I think we've been especially lucky with our names. There's a reason we're known by our nicknames, put it that way. Mum and Dad exchanged looks.

"We're thinking about calling her something to do with wind and hurricanes," said Mum.

"Such as?" Magnus asked sceptically.

"Stormetta," said Dad. "Do you like it?"

Minda stopped chewing and looked at Magnus. He coughed slightly. Stormetta. It was certainly unusual, but we could probably get used to it. In a way, it's a good thing to have a name that not so many people have. We nodded and shrugged. Stormetta. It would do.

"If I were you, I'd call her something else," said Lena from the other end of the table.

"Lena!" said Ylva angrily.

Sometimes I think Lena forgets that she's not one of my siblings too.

Mum chuckled quietly over in her chair. "What do you think she should be called, then?"

Lena swallowed what she was eating and looked at Grandpa.

"I think Inger would be better."

CHAPTER TWENTY-SIX

Flotsam and jetsam

*H*urricanes like the one we'd just had don't only wash up plastic drums and those scoops you use for bailing out boats. After a quick search down by the water, we'd found an escaped part of a pier, Thunderclap Kåre's plastic-hulled boat, half a playhouse and a dead deer. The storm surge had also made a mess of the rocks from the breakwater and smashed the door of our boat shed to smithereens. Luckily, *Troll* only had some minor hull damage. All in all, it wasn't that bad in Mathildewick Cove. It was worse elsewhere.

When the electricity came back on and we were connected to the rest of the world again, messages started to stream in about all the destruction. Forests had been flattened like freshly mown grass on several mountainsides, boats and boat sheds had been battered all along the coast, and some people's houses had even been destroyed.

"When you think about it, the most incredible thing isn't that our sister arrived last night," said Magnus when we were down having a look at the breakwater. "The most epic event of the whole hurricane has to be you and Lena going out carolling. It's so insanely typical of you two."

"*Pssshh,*" I said.

As usual after a storm, we trawled the beaches for storm treasure. We could've built an entire armada with all the driftwood. Lena was well on the way to designing a new, improved raft.

"The one we made last time was a piece of junk. This time we can pick the proper materials," she said, examining the rubbish on the foreshore with a critical eye.

I nodded. I could feel in my chest my enthusiasm starting to grow a tiny bit. We might actually make something incredibly good out of all this. Lena hopped happily from stone to stone.

"Huh? Trille, look!" she suddenly shouted, picking up something shiny from an enormous tangle of seaweed.

But I was no longer looking or listening, as a sight had appeared back up by our houses that made my heart skip a beat. Birgit and Haas. They came strolling down the track under the rowan trees. The sun shot orange wintry rays across the fields, making everything glitter around them. She was back!

"Happy New Year."

Birgit looked warmly at me and at the chaos on the foreshore. I just smiled. How good it was to see her, and how much I had to tell her! Haas bounded headlong into my stomach, and then he ran down to Lena, who was still standing by the clump of seaweed and didn't look like she was planning to move from there any time soon.

"Lena thinks we should build another raft," I said, shrugging in exasperation.

Birgit laughed and said that she'd prefer not to.

"Me neither, really," I said, glancing down at Lena, who had just heaved half a boat-shed door up onto the grass, dropping it with a soggy smack.

Haas barked as he leapt around her.

"He's pleased to be back," said Birgit. "Mathildewick Cove is better than Amsterdam for a dog."

I wanted to ask her whether she was also pleased to be back, but I couldn't. Instead, we set off together and ambled on down to Lena.

"What was it you found?" I asked, remembering that she'd shouted something to me.

"Oh, nothing special," she grumbled without looking at me.

Then she carried on searching. I could see that she'd hidden something under her jacket, but I thought no more of it.

CHAPTER TWENTY-SEVEN

Lena resorts to violence

"Wh-why weren't you at training yesterday?"

We were back at school again. It was almost time for PE and we were sitting outside the changing rooms, freezing cold. Andreas was looking at Lena with questioning eyes.

"I'm transferring," she said curtly.

All the boys stopped talking.

"Transferring? Where are you going to play then?" Halvor asked in surprise.

"With some girls in town."

"Oh," said Andreas. "That's a sh-shame."

"Sh-sh-shame," said Kai-Tommy, imitating him. He and Halvor sniggered.

Lena put her feet up on her gym bag and gave them a scowl of contempt.

"I'm not going to waste my life sitting on the bench," she muttered.

Kai-Tommy smiled. "Good idea to join the girls' team, in that case," he said. "It's more at your level."

That was it. Finally the old Lena awoke.

"There's no problem with the level, you circus llama!"

"What did you say?" Kai-Tommy leant forward.

"I said: there's no problem with the level, you circus llama!"

Birgit looked at them in astonishment. Was she finally going to see how things worked in our class?

"What is the problem, then?" Kai-Tommy asked.

Lena didn't answer. Kai-Tommy repeated the question. He was determined to have an answer.

"The coach," said Lena eventually, looking straight at him.

Kai-Tommy started laughing. "The coach? You really don't get it, Lena!"

"What is there to get, you amoeba? I'm just as good as Halvor, and yet that father of yours has kept me on the bench the whole season. It's not fair."

"You're not as good as you think," Kai-Tommy said in mock despair. "You haven't got a chance of keeping up any more."

"That's a load of rubbish!" Lena shouted, rising to her feet.

"A load of rubbish?"

Kai-Tommy was on his feet too. I remembered the time Lena punched him. They had been more or less the same size then. Now Kai-Tommy was much bigger.

"We're building up the team," he said. "Halvor's in goal because he's got a future as a goalie. We can't bring you on just to be nice to girls."

And so it happened again. Lena lashed out.

A gasp spread through the whole group. Kai-Tommy staggered backwards, but it wasn't a knockout this time like three years earlier. He blinked a little, touched his jaw, and then he launched himself furiously at Lena. For a second, the rest of us stood there, paralysed, while they beat each other up. Big Kai-Tommy and little Lena.

"No!" I shouted, diving into the fight.

Halvor and Abdulahi grabbed Kai-Tommy.

Andreas and I got hold of Lena. We managed to separate them before the teacher came.

"You're a berk, Kai-Tommy!" Lena shouted. Tears were running down her cheeks, and she was bleeding from a cut above her eye. "You're a bunch of little berks, the whole herd of you."

Then she ran off.

Birgit stood outside the girls' changing rooms, pale and speechless. Kai-Tommy glanced over at her and wiped some grit from his cheek.

"That girl's a total nutcase," he mumbled, holding up his hands half apologetically.

But what was wrong with me? I just stood there feeling pleased that finally Birgit had seen what Kai-Tommy could be like. By the time I turned to run after Lena, I realized that Andreas had already followed her.

Lena's desk was deserted for the rest of the day. There was a strangely charged atmosphere in class. Ellisiv, who didn't know what had happened, watched us with a furrowed brow. I knew that whatever she did, Lena would never, ever tell anybody what had happened. Should I tell? I decided to leave it.

When I got home, Lena had gone to her training session. Some days she'd have to leave straight after school to catch the ferry now.

I sat down in our empty kitchen and picked at some crumbs on the table.

"Isn't Lena here?" asked Mum, who was feeding Inger in the living room.

I shook my head.

As dusk came, I stood behind the cedar tree and watched her cycling home. Should I go over to the Lids' kitchen? Was she cross with me? Blasted football! I wished it had never been invented.

Before I could decide what to do, her door opened again. Lena ran across the fields and down to the boat shed. I peered through the dark. There were lights on down there. Grandpa was doing some work on *Troll*. What did they talk about when they were together, Lena and Grandpa?

I turned around and went back inside.

CHAPTER TWENTY-EIGHT

My grandfather hands

*A*s the end of winter approached, Grandpa was always showing up wearing a dirty boiler suit. He was working on *Troll* and was keen to get his boat ready for the next fishing season.

"Can't you wait until spring comes?" Dad asked him. "What are you going out in the cold for now?"

Grandpa pretended not to hear him. He just looked across at me and said, "I think we'll be ready in time for the cod, Trille."

I nodded and felt a guilty conscience simmering in my stomach. It was ages since I'd last been with him to the boat shed.

When he went out, Grandpa didn't stay out for

very long at a time, though. My new little sister often had wind, and she couldn't whimper more than a smidgen without Grandpa dropping whatever he had in his hands and rushing to her aid.

"We need expertise here," he'd say, turning Inger so that he was holding her round belly in the palm of his hand.

Then they'd walk round the house, Grandpa and Inger, while he gently rocked her and stroked his other big hand over her little back.

"Listen to that!" he'd shout proudly at each fart and burp that came out.

He usually called her his "wee dumpling", but every now and then he'd say her name. When he did so, he said it quickly and in a slightly embarrassed voice, more or less like when Lena called Isak "Dad".

One day, I realized to my astonishment that I'd started carrying Inger like Grandpa did. My hands were smaller, but just like before in the boat shed, they were starting to act like his, even though I wasn't really doing it on purpose.

"Listen to that!" I said to Mum one day, grinning

as Inger let rip with an explosive fart while I was carrying her, Grandpa-style.

"Mini-Lars," Mum said, ruffling my hair.

It was a long time since anybody had called me that.

Suddenly I had a burning need to get down to the boat shed. I leapt into my boots and ran across the fields. *Troll* was laid up ashore, and Grandpa was painting the bottom of the hull.

"Would you like any help?"

"No, you'll only get dirty," said Grandpa, looking at my clothes.

"*Pssshh,*" I said. "I can put on some oilskins."

I took the orange oilskins from the hook in the boat shed. It was ages since I'd last worn them. A faint and familiar smell of fish and seawater stuck to my body.

"Is it time to put her back in the water tomorrow?" I asked, crawling all the way underneath the boat to the hardest to reach part.

"Looks like it, lad," said Grandpa, looking happily at me. "Tor's promised to lend a hand."

It was so good to be lying under the boat there

with Grandpa, just working away. I wished we could carry on all afternoon, but he had almost finished. The job was done in half an hour. I hung the oilskins back up, and we strolled off along the track home.

"Thanks for your help," said Grandpa, with a nod.

"No problem," I said. I was just about to follow him inside when I spotted Birgit.

She was coming down from Hillside on her bike, at top speed. I felt a pang of excitement in my stomach. Was she coming to see me? I was about to hurry and meet her, but then I was stunned to see her turn the other way.

I felt completely dismayed. I knew where she was going. It was getting clearer from conversations I overheard between Birgit and Kai-Tommy that they'd been hanging out at the ferry landing after school. I gulped.

"See you later, then," I mumbled to Grandpa, heading up to the garage to find my bike.

Soon I was sitting there at the ferry landing, outside the shop, dangling my legs. Mopeds roared around me, while Kai-Tommy, Halvor and a couple of high school pupils sat over on another table. There was no sign of Birgit. Was this not where she'd been heading after all? I'd been into the shop to look for her. Now I was sitting with a Coke in my hand, feeling like a fool.

Then Lena came along on her bike, with her football bag on the carrier rack and wearing a tracksuit in the unfamiliar red colour of the team in town. She spotted me as she parked her bike and tilted her head as if examining a rare orchid.

"You're sitting here?"

I nodded. As if to prove the point that I was now one of the kids who sat around on the ferry landing, I leant to one side and casually spat on the pier. Lena bit her lip. I knew her. She was trying not to laugh.

"What?" I said, holding out my arms in protest.

Lena hopped up onto the table and sat down next to me.

"You look like a moron, Trille. You've gone completely coo coo ca choo."

Oh, couldn't she just keep her trap shut?

"Hey hey! It's the two turtle doves of Mathildewick Cove!" Kai-Tommy shouted at us from the other side of the car park.

At that very moment, Birgit arrived on her bike. I was ready to shove Lena off the table. What if Birgit got the wrong idea? But Lena just sat there firmly, looking tiredly at Kai-Tommy.

"I really hope he gets washed away in a flood one day," she grumbled.

I waved to Birgit as she went into the shop.

Kai-Tommy kept gawping in our direction, and I could feel the tension growing. Ever since the fight, he'd been rotten to Lena. He'd arrogantly declared that she had serious problems with her temper – although he did have a point there – as well as saying that it wasn't normal to beat people up like she did. And to prove that he was right, he'd taken every opportunity to get her fired up again. He'd come pretty close to succeeding a few times, but amazingly Lena had managed not to explode.

Now she unzipped her tracksuit top and looked at me, eyes sparkling. She looked like she might burst at any moment.

"What is it?" I asked.

Lena smiled wide.

"What is it? Have you won a million or something?"

"We're going to have a baby," she said, her voice bursting with pent-up joy.

"Really? Is that true?"

Lena nodded with the happiest of grins on her face.

"Congratulations!"

"Congratulations for what?" Kai-Tommy had ridden his bike over to us and was now propping himself up against the table with one foot.

"Nothing," said Lena.

Kai-Tommy calmly opened his fizzy drink bottle and took a swig from it. He was only wearing a hoodie, even though it was freezing cold.

"Dressed like a pro, I see," he said sarcastically, pointing at Lena's tracksuit.

Lena didn't respond. Instead she looked at the ferry, which was just docking.

"How's it going in town, then?" Kai-Tommy asked after a pause.

"Fine, thank you," Lena replied, still not taking

her eyes off the ferry. "I'm getting on well at my own level."

"Played any matches yet?"

"No."

Kai-Tommy rocked a little on his bike. He seemed annoyed that he wasn't managing to wind her up.

"What was he congratulating you about, then?

"I was congratulating her because she's going to be a big sister," I said in exasperation.

"Oh," he said, surprised. "Congrats, then."

Without thanking him, Lena stood up, ready to board the ferry. I don't know whether that was what Kai-Tommy couldn't stand, or whether it was the fact he hadn't managed to make her explode. Something snapped, anyway.

He flicked back his fringe and shouted after Lena, "Lucky Isak, getting his own kid. It can't have been easy for him with you thrown into the bargain, knowing what you're like."

I felt myself turning all cold inside. Lena didn't answer. She just went on board the ferry. Hadn't she heard? I looked furiously at Kai-Tommy, but I didn't say anything, as Birgit was coming now.

She'd bought some chocolate, which she opened and shared with us, all smiles.

"Is something wrong?" she asked hesitantly.

I looked nervously at the ferry. Didn't Lena care about what Kai-Tommy had just said? She was Isak's child too! She knew that, didn't she? Kai-Tommy peered at me from beneath his fringe, and then he suddenly started sniffing the air.

"Something smells of flipping fish here."

All the blood drained to my feet. I quickly glanced at Birgit. She cautiously sniffed the air too.

"Seriously, Trille, is that you?" Kai-Tommy looked at me as if I were the most repulsive person in the world.

"No," I said, pulling back.

I quickly downed the rest of my drink and leapt onto my bike. My whole body felt like it was burning and throbbing with shame.

When I got home, I threw my bike in the garage and almost walked straight into Grandpa. He was outside the house, with a bucket of frozen herring, on his way to the boat shed.

"Are you coming, Trille?" he asked.

"No," I grumbled, running indoors with my heart pounding.

I hurled all my clothes in with the rest of the laundry and got into the shower, devastated.

CHAPTER TWENTY-NINE

The death of a chicken

The next day, I kept my distance from Birgit. I was too embarrassed to talk to her ever again, fish-face that I was. Kai-Tommy smirked and held his nose when I walked past him. If I hadn't been so deep in my own misery, I would probably have noticed that things weren't right with Lena either. But I didn't.

When evening came and Lena started sobbing because of a deceased hen, I still didn't see that there was really something else going on. I should have noticed, but what happened with the chicken led to such enormous complications that Lena completely fell off my radar.

*

It started when Birgit popped by. In astonishment, I let her into the kitchen, ashamed that the dirty dishes from dinner were still on the table.

"You can bring Haas in too," I mumbled, but she left him outside.

"I won't stay long," she said, glancing at me.

No, and I can understand why, I thought.

Birgit looked at me with her kind eyes and was just about to say something, when Haas suddenly started barking.

"Oh no, it must be the fox!"

I charged out of the kitchen. We'd already lost two hens over the past month. Dad kept saying that he was going to keep watch one morning and shoot the sneaky creature when it ventured down to the farm, but so far he'd only talked about it. When the first hen, Number Two B, disappeared we didn't get too worked up about it. Nor did we when Number Five vanished, leaving just a few feathers and some drops of blood. But that evening was different. I knew that much as soon as I came rushing out into the garden. Lena was already there, and she was absolutely raging.

Number Seven, her favourite hen, was lying on her back right up by the chicken-wire fence. Her head was wounded, but she was still alive. The fox had probably been scared off in the middle of the massacre when Haas started barking. Lena bent down, and when she stood up with the hen in her arms, she was sobbing so hard I was shocked. What on earth? It was only a chicken!

"Lena," I said gently, "she's too badly injured to survive. You can't…"

"I know. I'm not an idiot!"

She turned round, walked straight over to the door to Grandpa's flat and rang the bell. I could hear her sniffing as she tried to pull herself together. Grandpa turned on the outside light and opened the door.

"Can you help me see this one off, Lars?" Lena asked, holding the hen out in the light.

I should probably have realized then that this wasn't an everyday occurrence for Birgit. If I'd turned round, I would've seen that she was twice as pale as when we had the shipwreck on the raft. But at that moment I was mostly thinking about Lena and the hen.

Grandpa gave Number Seven a quick and clean end, as only he can.

"Now, why don't we see if Reidar can make some chicken fricassee this weekend?" he consoled us, holding the hen up to the outside light to check she was definitely dead.

I heard a gasp behind me and finally turned towards Birgit.

"What's chicken fricassee?" she whispered, her eyes still fixed on the hen beneath the light.

I explained it like I explained all new words to her.

"It's a meal. Pieces of chicken in a white sauce. Very tasty."

Birgit's eyes shone wide in the dark. "But … Lena's crying," she spluttered, looking over at Lena, who was carrying the chicken's bloodstained carcass up the stairs to Mum in the kitchen.

It's good to make food out of the animals we have to put down: that's what Dad had always said, and that's what I told Birgit now. She gaped at me as if I came from another solar system.

"Is it better to eat animals you don't know?" I asked, confused.

"I don't eat animals," Birgit whispered.

"Huh?"

"We're vegetarians, you know…"

"Oh," I said, gobsmacked. I hadn't picked up on that. "So you never eat meat?"

Birgit shook her head.

"What about fish?"

She shook her head again.

"But what do you eat, then?" I asked in confusion, as all the dinners I'd ever eaten in my life had involved either fish or meat.

"Other things!" Birgit said angrily, and then she ran off home with Haas.

I stood there in the garden, my whole body feeling powerless. With heavy footsteps, I followed the trail of blood indoors.

The scene in the kitchen was chaos. Lena was crying her eyes out, and Mum was doing her best to comfort her while she warmed up some water in a large pot on the stove.

"Is Reidar going to shoot that fox soon, or is he just bragging?" Lena shouted. I'd never seen anybody so upset before.

"Oh, Lena dear," said Mum, trying to get hold of her.

Lena tore herself away. "It's Number Seven!"

Mum knew that. She took the hen and dipped her in the hot water for a moment.

"Do you two want to help me pluck the feathers?" she asked.

"No!" Lena howled.

I looked sadly at the hen. Chicken fricassee with potatoes and boiled carrots is one of the best meals I know of. It was one of Granny's dishes. It's something really special. Did Birgit think it was disgusting?

"That fox needs to be shot," Lena shouted again.

I was relieved that Dad's firearms were safely locked away. No fox between here and Pluto would have been safe if the gun cabinet had been open.

"Smoking haddocks, I know what I'm going to do," Lena mumbled, wiping her eyes with the sleeve of her jumper. "Come on, Trille."

*

I should've cycled up to Hillside and spoken with Birgit, but I couldn't face it. Instead I took my bike and followed Lena. I'd been eating animals I loved all my life. The same bottle lambs I fed in the summer, I ate at Christmas. The rabbits that lived under Grandpa's kitchen window had been turned into soup, one by one. We ate our goat, and we'd had frequent banquets from our chickens. And fish! I'd eaten enough fish to fill a whole swimming pool. Never in my life had I thought that there might be anything wrong with it. Now Birgit, dear, kind Birgit, had stormed off home in horror and disgust. I remembered the beautiful vegetable garden they had up at Hillside. And the sourdough bread with chanterelle mushrooms I'd been given. She thought I was horrible. I smelt of fish, ate animals, and was an utterly revolting person.

As this merry-go-round of thoughts spun in my head, I pedalled on hard to keep up with Lena. Soon we were at the houses by the ferry landing.

"What are we doing?" I asked with a sigh when Lena came skidding to a halt by Halvor's house.

She didn't answer. She just threw her bike into

the hedge and rang the doorbell without mercy. Halvor opened the door.

"I need to borrow your air rifle," said Lena. "You'll get it back at school tomorrow."

Halvor held his lips tightly closed and looked like he was focusing on something slightly behind her. Once again I had the impression he was a little scared of her.

When we cycled home, Lena had the rifle over her shoulder.

CHAPTER THIRTY

Lena shoots Dad in the bum

"Hello, I'm talking to you! Have you had a brain anaesthetic or something?" Lena asked.

"Huh?"

"I said: can you bring Reidar's mountain poncho so we've got something to camouflage ourselves with?"

"You can't kill foxes with air rifles," I replied, annoyed.

Lena wasn't planning on killing it, she told me. She just wanted to scare it. The fox couldn't be allowed to keep swaggering around and killing innocent civilian hens who'd never done anything except lay eggs and go tobogganing.

"When it hears the bang of the air rifle, it'll realize."

"Lena, I don't think that—"

"You'll see!" she roared.

It had started raining, but Lena used a tarpaulin to make a little hunting shelter behind the corner of the hay barn. When I arrived with the poncho, she was sitting astride a folding chair, her face locked in concentration and daubed with camouflage paint. The rifle was lying on her leg, and on a small table beside her was a towering stack of chocolate spread sandwiches and a pair of binoculars. She looked totally crazy. Normally I would've laughed, but not that day.

I plonked myself down next to her and laid the green and brown poncho over our legs. Neither of us said a word. We just stared sombrely at the chicken run.

Suddenly, after only half an hour, we heard sounds coming from over there. Lena lifted the air rifle and fired off a shot at the moving shape.

"*Aaaaargh!* What the—?"

A large shadow stood up inside the chicken run.

"Smoking haddocks, I've shot Reidar," Lena whispered.

"Lena?! Trille?!"

We sprinted off across the twilit fields, sending slush splattering around us.

"Let's hide in the boat," Lena said, panting. "We can lock it from inside."

She was already heading out onto the floating pier inside the breakwater, where *Troll* was afloat for the first time since the hurricane. We clambered aboard and slammed the cabin hatch shut.

For a while, we stayed frozen in the darkness and listened. We heard Dad calling angrily a couple of times, and then there was silence. I felt tired, so I crawled along to the innermost bunk and lay down, dead beat and exhausted. The smells and sounds in the cabin reminded me of the summer, of Grandpa, of the sea and peaceful times. It was like returning to an old country we'd left behind.

I heard Lena rummaging around in the cupboards, and she soon appeared in the darkness, bringing some biscuits.

"These were probably well past their sell-by date before we were even born," she muttered, stuffing one in her mouth. "Are there any blankets here?"

I thought of all the times Lena and I had sat like that, talking about all sorts of things. Now we were both completely silent. We listened to the waves lapping beneath the boat as we wrestled with our own thoughts, while the dark slowly swallowed all that was left of the day.

"I've got to go now," Lena said eventually, her teeth chattering. "I can't catch a chill with all the season's games still to play."

She got the air rifle ready and opened the cabin hatch. Was she going to shoot Dad again?

"I'll stay here a bit longer," I mumbled.

Maybe I could catch a chill? I thought hopefully, tucking myself into the blankets Lena had warmed up.

With the rain drumming down outside and the waves lapping against the side of the boat, I fell asleep.

CHAPTER THIRTY-ONE

Grandpa, the sea and me

I could've been offended that neither Mum nor Dad noticed I was gone until the next morning. But there are so many of us in the Danielsen Yttergård family, it can be hard to keep track of everyone. Dad's bum hurt, and Inger had been screaming all evening. Each of my parents thought that the other had said goodnight to me.

But they hadn't, because I was lying asleep in Grandpa's boat, with a woollen blanket over my head. When I woke up, *Troll* was swaying in a different way from the night before, and the engine was running. I sat up in a daze. The grey morning light was seeping through the cabin hatch, and I

caught a few glimpses of Grandpa's blue boiler suit
out on deck. Was it morning? Grandpa was talking
on his phone. That was what had woken me. He
always holds his mobile a short distance away from
his head, as if it's a crab that he's worried might bite
his ear.

"Eh?" he was shouting. "No, Trille's not on board…"

I was about to creep out, but Grandpa was busy.

"Half the line's in the water, Reidar. I've got to go!
Call me back if you can't find him."

Then he hung up and tossed the phone into the
cabin. It landed right next to me. I felt a lump in my
stomach straight away. I remembered Birgit's face
when Grandpa had killed the hen. And Kai-Tommy
mockingly turning up his nose. The very thought of
going to school made me feel queasy. With my stiff
fingers, I picked up Grandpa's phone and wrote a
message to Dad. *I'm in the boat. Sorry that you
got shot.*

Then I turned it off and plunged back under the
blankets. I felt like a little jellyfish. I could imagine
Dad going berserk when he read the message, but I
couldn't summon the energy to care. They could go

231

ahead and shout at me. I couldn't take any more. The throbbing of *Troll*'s engine mixed with my pounding heart. I quietly tucked myself in more tightly and drifted off to sleep again. I didn't want to think any more about anything.

* * *

Several hours had passed when I suddenly awoke. Somebody was yelling!

I've heard lots of yelling in my life. Lena frequently yells, and so do the rest of my family sometimes. Every one of them. But I'd never heard Grandpa yell before. That's why I couldn't immediately work out what I was hearing. And when I did realize, it was as if a rockslide had slammed straight into me.

I threw the blankets aside and leapt out through the cabin hatch. The grey daylight blinded me. The deck was covered in fish blood, and Grandpa was leaning over the winch. He yelled again. And then I saw it: his hand was stuck, and the blood on the deck had nothing to do with any fish.

"Grandpa!" I shouted.

I saw him jump when he heard my voice.

"Trille?"

He couldn't turn round. I reached up and switched off the winch.

"The knife…" Grandpa stuttered. "On the deck… You've got to cut … the line."

The knife, the knife. Where was it? My hands scrabbled around in my grandfather's blood and the rainwater. I eventually found it in the shadow of the fish tub.

"Got it!" I shouted.

Grandpa didn't answer. I was afraid he'd black out, but he nodded at the line. It was drawn taut straight down into the sea. Something was pulling at it with immense force.

When I got to the railing, I saw something I'll never forget: there was a monster next to the boat. A white body, almost as long as *Troll* herself, shone at me from the water below. The halibut was writhing about on the hook, using its enormous strength to try and free itself. The whole boat shook.

"Grandpa…" I whispered.

The giant fish was pulling and pulling as it tried

to swim back down into the dark waters. Were there really such big creatures down there?

I turned towards Grandpa. His face was grey, and he just gave me a brief nod.

Then I cut the line with the knife. All the strain was gone. The huge, beautiful fish vanished into the depths below, and Grandpa sank down onto the deck.

CHAPTER THIRTY-TWO

A heroic deed

*J*t was as if life had all been a game up until that day. Whatever mess I got myself into, there was always an adult who would sort things out. But that day on *Troll*, the only adult was lying lifeless in his own blood. We were surrounded by rough seas. I could've shouted my lungs out and nobody would've heard. It was just me, Trille Danielsen Yttergård, and the sea.

I don't know how long I stood there with the knife in my hand, as if I'd been switched off. But, eventually, something inside me gave me a kick up the backside. I had to get Grandpa ashore!

I whipped off my jumper and wound my white

T-shirt round Grandpa's shattered arm. Then I rushed into the cabin and found an old sheet that I wrapped around it again. His arm now looked like a ball. I didn't risk moving Grandpa into the cabin. Instead, I dragged all the blankets out and managed to put two down beneath him and two covering him. As I unfolded the last blanket, Grandpa's mobile phone suddenly slipped out onto the deck, then under the railing, and into the sea with a plop.

"No!"

I ran to the side of the boat, but I could only see bubbles where the phone had disappeared.

Troll danced and drifted over the grey sea swell. The shore was endlessly distant, wrapped in clouds of mist and squalls of rain. There were no other boats to be seen. I gritted my teeth and started the engine. I couldn't head to Mathildewick Cove. We were closer to town – where the hospital was.

* * *

I'd been out with Grandpa on *Troll* a billion times, but he'd never taught me how to make emergency calls on the radio. Why had he never done that? And

236

why didn't he have an emergency stop button on the winch? Why didn't he even wear a life jacket? I beat my fist on the wheel.

"Grandpa, the radio. How does it work?" I shouted.

He moaned a few words, but it was just a muddle. The ball of fabric around his arm was starting to turn red.

The sea was getting rougher. I kept having to get up and adjust our course, and I was drenched by the rain. Then I found Grandpa's oilskins in the cabin. Shivering, I spread out the oilskin jacket on top of all the blankets. When I'd finished, Grandpa looked like a mummy. Only the centre of his face was visible, but he was still shaking. I put my ear right down by his mouth. He was whispering something. I leant closer.

"Inger," he murmured, and then it was as if he drifted away again.

I started to cry. Why was he saying Granny's name? Couldn't he see me? Was he dying?

"I'm here, Grandpa," I cried. "I'm here."

Then I had to go back up to the wheel. A prayer pounded away inside me, over and over again. Let

Grandpa live. Let Grandpa stay with me. Make
Grandpa wake up. Make Grandpa better. Let him
stay with me.

The town emerged above the misty sea now
and then. It was getting closer and closer, but we
didn't meet a single other boat. Nobody could help
me. *Troll* was pummelling against the waves and
struggling through the sea, Grandpa was breathing
and bleeding, and I was praying and crying. Oh, if
only the engine had that extra horsepower Lena had
talked about! It was so slow that it hurt.

* * *

It's hard to say what he made of it all, that sun
tanned man in the white sailing boat who was the
first to see us. He probably thought about his own
boat first, as here came a fishing boat roaring into
the town harbour with a half-crazed boy as the only
skipper.

"Help!" I shouted, waving my arms. "You've got to
call an ambulance. Grandpa's hurt!"

Then I did what made Grandpa proudest of all.
I docked the boat. I didn't smash any sailing boats.
I didn't give *Troll* so much as a single scratch either,

which clearly surpassed everything else I'd done that day.

"Old *Troll* is no easy boat to manoeuvre and berth, you know," Grandpa said later, as if that was what made me the hero of the day.

"Pure luck," was what Lena had to say about the docking. "Pure, sheer luck."

Part Four

Spring is sprung

CHAPTER THIRTY-THREE

After the accident

*I*t was so strange to be somebody else all of a sudden. I was no longer that snotty brat from Mathildewick Cove. Now I was the boy who'd saved his grandfather's life.

Magnus stopped making fun of me, Mum cried at the very sight of me, and the old men at the shop said hello to me as if I were a grown man.

"I always thought that Mini-Lars had the right stuff," I caught the hard-of-hearing Thunderclap Kåre telling Pitt one day as I was going past.

They even wrote about me in the newspaper.

But I don't think I really understood what a big thing I'd done until I heard Dad talk about it. The

Sunday after the accident, he invited Uncle Tor to dinner, as well as everybody from next door. I was in the kitchen with him while he was preparing the meal. He was stirring the pot of chicken fricassee and scurrying about in an apron that was far too small for his stomach.

"Trille," he suddenly said, nodding in the direction of the sea, "what you did for Grandpa..."

I looked up in shock. Dad never normally gives me praise. Now he was staring at me as he searched for words, emotion written all over his face.

"I've always been proud of you, but what you did... You're a good lad, Trille."

"Do you think so?" I said, stunned.

Dad nodded and fumbled with the whisk, without saying another word. I ran off happily to put out the napkins on the kitchen table. In my confusion, I laid a place for Grandpa too.

He'd been moved from the hospital to the nursing home now. I'd ridden my bike over there after breakfast. All the blood loss had made him feel weak and miserable, and his arm was never going to be quite the same again. When I'd got there, he was asleep in bed. For as long as I could remember, Grandpa had looked after me. With him I'd always been as safe as a seagull chick. Now it almost felt as if I had to look after him. I sat down quietly on the chair next to the bed. After a while, he woke up a little. A frail smile appeared.

"To think you docked *Troll* all on your own, Trille lad."

And then he fell asleep again.

And now I'd laid him a place at the kitchen table out of habit. I just left it like that. He wasn't dead, after all. I looked at the table, which was all set. At each end, bottles of redcurrant squash sparkled in the low February sunlight, and from the middle of the table, wisps of steam curled up from our biggest cast-iron pot. Dad and I looked proudly at each other.

"I would like to propose a toast to Number Seven," Lena said with a cough when everybody had arrived. "Mathildewick Cove's Formula One chicken, who sadly had to die far too young..."

"She wasn't all that young," Dad muttered, but he raised his glass anyway.

"And to Trille," said Minda. "The world's littlest lifesaver."

Then we ate the chicken fricassee, the one just like Granny used to make. And just like her parents had surely made for her out on Kobbholmen. Oh, how I wished Birgit could've been there to see it. How could I explain to her that it wasn't just any old dead chicken that had dropped out of mid-air? And had she heard about Grandpa? I knew I had to go up to Hillside later that evening.

"Can we put some chicken fricassee in a box and take it to the nursing home?" Lena asked when we'd finished tucking in to our dessert and people were about to leave. "It was Lars who provided the main ingredient, after all."

Dad said he'd been about to suggest the same thing, and he poured the leftovers into a huge plastic tub.

Lena and I fetched our bikes. When we got up to the main road, I strapped the tub onto Lena's carrier rack.

"You go," I said. "I went this morning."

Lena frowned and was about to say something, but I was already on my way up the hill.

And so it was that we each went our own way that evening. Lena cycled to the nursing home, and I pedalled all the way up to Birgit at Hillside. The same thing would happen a number of times over the next few months.

* * *

Spring was sprouting. Bristly yellow dandelions shot up like stars on the edge of ditches. The sea glittered, and even a few shining wood anemones popped out amidst all the dead grass on a slope halfway up to Hillside. I saw more and more of them as the days went by, as I was always going to see Birgit and her family. I was almost starting to get used to vegetarian food. After the accident, I could finally talk with her normally again. The episode with the hen hardly mattered any more once we'd even had a little laugh about it.

Things were different at school too. The day after the rescue, I'd turned up in my wellies. I didn't mind if I looked stupid. I was fed up with having wet feet. In any case, I couldn't give a shark's tail what Kai-Tommy thought. He could just go ahead and stare.

Everything seemed to be going a bit better, except in one place: back home in Mathildewick Cove.

I don't really know what I'd expected to happen when Grandpa finally came home. I suppose I'd imagined we'd sit down in his flat and talk about the accident, shaking our heads as we thought about the giant halibut and those dramatic few hours. At the least I thought Grandpa would look at me warmly and thank me, like Dad had done. But he didn't say anything. It was as if everything with the halibut and the winch hadn't even happened. Instead, Grandpa walked around like a shadow, holding his arm and hunched over in a way I hadn't seen before. Was he angry?

On the very first day of warm sunshine, I asked if he wanted to come along down to the boat shed again. He quickly backed away with his hand over his face, mumbling something about not quite feeling up to it.

"Maybe another day," he added, without looking straight at me.

"All right," I said, trying not to sound downhearted.

So then I asked another day, but Grandpa said the same thing. I felt a strange emptiness in my stomach. Why didn't he want to spend time with me?

Lena wasn't trampling all over our doormat any more either. To start with I thought that might be a good thing, but actually it made me sad. She was going to her blasted training sessions all the time, and when we did meet, she was quiet and morose, not really her usual self.

And then, early one Saturday morning, a few weeks after Grandpa had come home, everything became twice as difficult as before. From my window, I saw Grandpa and Lena walking down to the boat shed together. He was wearing his boiler suit for the first time since the accident, and she was carrying his toolbox. I could feel tears of anger welling up behind my eyes. Why hadn't they asked if I wanted to come too? I swallowed hard and turned away from the window. Soon I was on my way up to Hillside. They were welcome to have a nice time without me!

I didn't ask Grandpa if he wanted to come along down to the boat shed any more. But I did discover, to my despair, that many of the times I'd been to Hillside or other places, he and Lena had been down there without me.

CHAPTER THIRTY-FOUR

Rhumba ruin

"*I*t's so wonderful this is happening, especially since we couldn't come to the concert at Christmas!" Ylva said happily.

It was May, and some totally barmy person at school, probably the music teacher, had got it into their head that the ones in our class who had music school lessons should provide the entertainment at a class party for our parents. I'd actually been unusually angry when Mr Rognstad told us. I wasn't about to start practising like I'd done before Christmas. No way, José.

"It's 'Für Elise' or nothing," I'd said, surprised to find that I was able to put my foot down this time.

Ylva, who had been feeling sick for the first few months with the baby in her stomach, was sparkling as she sat next to me. I've always thought Lena has the prettiest mum. She has long, dark hair, and a silver nose stud. Now she was prettier than ever: she was shining. She was holding Isak's hand, and her other hand was lying over her baby bump. Imagine being so happy just about going to a concert.

I peered over at Lena. She was sitting there, gloomily staring straight ahead. I knew that she'd been practising. I'd heard the booming rhythms of the keyboard through the walls of her house many times over the past week. The question was whether it had helped.

The lights had been dimmed in the school hall, which was full of parents, brothers and sisters. I'd finished "Für Elise", and Krølla had clapped with great gusto. Now it was Lena's turn. She was wearing a dress, and her hair was smartly plaited. I hadn't seen her in a dress since Isak and Ylva got married. For the first time, it struck me that she looked a bit like Ylva.

Then my neighbour hurled the keyboard volume

up to full and switched on some absurd rhumba rhythm. It was clear that she'd decided to go down fighting. But she made it all the way through the piece, in her own way, with a lot of pauses and strange noises. I could see how much she hated every single note. When she'd finished, she rushed straight off stage and sat down next to Andreas instead of us. I glanced cautiously at Ylva. She tried to wave to Lena to get her to come and join us, but it was no use. Lena sat there, staring angrily at her shoes, while Birgit dazzled her way through a kind of jazz piece that left most people's mouths open in admiration.

After the concert, we waited for our parents in the car park.

"That wasn't too bad, really," I said.

Lena pulled uncomfortably at her dress and gave me a sullen look.

"I've got a match tomorrow. Two o'clock. Are you coming to watch, or what?" she said, a little irritably.

"Your first match in town?" I asked.

She nodded. It was a long time since I'd last seen Lena in goal. And it was a long time since she'd invited me to anything. I felt confused and happy in an unexpected way. I was about to say "yes" when Birgit suddenly appeared.

"Hi," she said. "It's my birthday tomorrow. Would you two like to come to mine at around three o'clock?"

"Ehm … sure," I said.

Lena looked at me more or less in the same way as she had that time I spilt the beans to Birgit about the raft.

"What about you, Lena?" Birgit asked.

Lena didn't say a word in reply. She just turned round and left. That's when I became angry. Railing rams, there's a limit. I ran after her.

"What's your problem, Lena?"

She didn't answer.

"Do you think I should miss a birthday party just to see a totally normal football match?"

Lena stopped. "I couldn't care less what you do! It's your life!" she said.

"Yes, it is, actually!" I shouted. "And I'm absolutely sick and tired of you being grumpy all the time."

"Grumpy?" said Lena in disbelief. "I'll tell you one thing, Trille Danielsen Yttergård: it's better to be grumpy than to be an idiot."

She threw her keyboard book into the ditch, sending mud splashing out, and ran off home.

"Kai-Tommy's right," I yelled after her. "You've got serious problems with your temper!"

* * *

Back at home, I went straight up to my room. I was furious. For a moment I thought about going down to Grandpa in the boat shed. But then I saw that Lena was already there. That made me even angrier. What were they doing together? Couldn't she get her own grandpa? I spotted the ice-cream tub with the broken bottle and ship in it on my shelf. I tore it down in rage and emptied all the contents into the bin by the toilet.

CHAPTER THIRTY-FIVE

My boat is so small

*B*irgit's family had set out a long table in their barn. The walls were decorated with paper lanterns, and there were bunches of spring flowers everywhere. The table was teeming with colourful foods, not bread and sausages like we were used to. It was like stepping into a film. All the boys from class were being polite and trying to behave maturely.

Birgit was wearing a light blue dress and a necklace of polished wooden beads. Her curls softly touched my face as she gave me a hug.

"Happy birthday," I murmured dizzily. "Nice necklace."

"Kisha gave it to me." Birgit put her hand on the beads, clearly pleased with it. "She sent it for my birthday."

Andreas and Abdulahi came in after me. They got hugs too. Kai-Tommy was already on the ramp at the entrance to the barn, chatting confidently with Birgit's father, the author. He was wearing a shirt like the one his brother had been wearing at Christmas.

"Wh-where's Lena?" Andreas asked. He was looking nervously at a tray of stuffed mushrooms.

"She's playing a match in town," I grumbled. The very thought of Lena made my stomach boil with rage.

From the corner of my eye, I spotted Birgit sitting down on the bottom step of the barn and talking with Kai-Tommy. They sat there for quite a while. She laughed several times. I'd managed to eat a whole load of those mushrooms before they got up. I suddenly felt that I just wanted to go home. All the small talk and all the people – I just couldn't cope. I quietly told Birgit that I had a headache, and shuffled off down the hill.

Down at the bend with the wood anemones, I stopped and looked out across the fjord. It was still and light blue in the afternoon sun. A small plastic-hulled boat was on its way out. "My boat is so small and your sea is so wide." We'd learnt that song at Sunday school. I watched the boat and the lone wake behind it. That was exactly how I felt.

I lay in my room, looking at the picture I'd been given for Christmas. Birgit had painted Kobbholmen and *Troll* and the beautiful summer colours with her own hands. What did I normally think about before Birgit came along with her curls?

I don't know how long I'd been lying there, when there was a knock at my door.

"Trille?" Mum stuck her head round. "Ylva's downstairs. She's wondering if you know where Lena is."

"Isn't she at the football match?" I asked.

No, the match had finished several hours ago, Mum told me. Nobody had seen Lena all day.

I went down to the kitchen.

"Weren't you at the game either?" I asked, looking at Ylva, who was reading a message on her phone.

"No, I couldn't face it, Trille. I felt so nauseous, and..."

"What about Isak?" asked Mum, bobbing up and down a little to calm Inger.

"Isak's on call today. I can't get hold of him either," said Ylva.

A painful feeling crept into my chest. "Did nobody go to watch her play?"

Ylva looked at me. She was forlorn, and I knew a painful feeling had crept into her chest too. Lena's first match, and nobody to cheer her on.

"I'll check with Grandpa," I said, heading out.

What nonsense was Lena up to now? Couldn't she see that people were getting fed up of everything having to be about football all the time? She hadn't even replied to Birgit when she'd invited her to her party. Actually, now I thought about it properly, she was being really selfish. I stuck my hands in my pockets as I strode across the fields.

Grandpa was standing at the door when I arrived at the boat shed. I peered over his shoulder. There were all sorts of odds and ends in there, and it struck me that Lena must have been gathering bits of flotsam and jetsam for a new raft all spring.

"Have you seen Lena?" I asked.

"No."

I explained what Mum had said. From the corner of my eye, I noticed Isak's car turning into the farmyard back up by the house.

Grandpa scratched his head a little. "Then it must be Lena who's taken it," he said. "But how on earth did she manage that?"

He disappeared into the old boat shed.

"Manage what?"

"The boat's gone," said Grandpa.

What did he mean? Both *Troll* and Dad's blue plastic-hulled boat were at the floating pier inside the breakwater. They certainly weren't gone.

"Which boat?"

Grandpa glanced at me. "Your boat."

"I haven't got a boat, Grandpa," I said quietly.

Was that why he'd been so strange recently? Had he started getting confused?

"Grandpa, I haven't got a boat," I said again, in despair.

Grandpa turned towards me. "No, you haven't, Trille, but you were going to get one."

He drummed his fingers pensively against the wall of the boat shed.

"Lena and I have been doing up an old Silver Viking for you, here in the old boat shed. It was supposed to be a surprise for your birthday."

What?

Grandpa pushed open the doors that led out to the water.

"Lena and I thought it was about time you had your own boat. You deserved it after... Well, you know."

He patted his injured arm, and gave me a sheepish look.

A boat for me? From Grandpa and Lena? Was that what they'd been doing during all those hours together down by the boat sheds? Doing up a boat? For me?

Overwhelmed, I stared across the rocks by the shore. There were clear traces of somebody having taken out a boat. The rollers for moving it were strewn all the way down to the water's edge. I knew how strong Lena could be when she was angry and upset. She would've needed a lot of strength for this.

"Grandpa, we've got to find her!" I shouted.

At that very moment, Isak came bounding down across the fields.

"Do you know where she is?" There was an unusual quiver in his normally calm voice.

"No, but we'll soon find out," said Grandpa. "Fetch your life jacket, Trille, then..."

He took a deep breath.

"Then we'll launch *Troll*."

CHAPTER THIRTY-SIX

A desperate dad

I held my breath as I stood on deck, watching Grandpa turn on the boat's ignition for the first time since the accident. It had been a while, and *Troll* coughed and shook a few times, but soon the engine was throbbing in its happy, familiar way. Isak untied the last mooring line and leapt on board, and then we put out to sea.

To begin with, Grandpa looked as stiff as a statue, but gradually it was as if the shuddering engine shook out the old Grandpa. He checked a little bit, adjusted a little bit, squinted a little bit. But mostly he stood there with his arm firmly and calmly on the wheel, peering out to sea with blue eyes.

Suddenly, I realized how quiet it had been the last few months. I leant against the railing and felt the engine throbbing throughout my body. It was as if my pulse were back.

Isak was peering all around. "I didn't manage to talk to her after the match. I had an emergency call..."

"Were you at the game?"

Isak nodded. He'd seen almost the whole thing, he said, but then he'd had to leave a short while before the end.

"I don't think Lena could see me, though, as I had to stay up by the car in case I got a call."

He was staring everywhere.

"Was she good?" I asked.

Isak turned to look at me. "Good? She was outstanding, Trille. I had no idea that she was so good. Did you know?"

I gulped. Lena, Lena. Where was she?

Grandpa had set course towards the mouth of the fjord. Neither Isak nor I had objected. We knew Lena. She wasn't the sort to nip over to town when she was upset. It was more her style to point straight out to sea.

"She's probably on her way to Crete or something," said Grandpa, trying to get us to smile. It didn't work. Isak's face was completely grey. I'd never seen him like that.

We sailed on for a while without saying anything.

"Are you sure that she's gone this way?" Isak asked eventually. He was so restless now that he couldn't stand still.

Grandpa shook his head.

"Maybe we should turn round and look…"

Isak didn't get any further. All three of us saw it at the same moment. A small boat floating in the sea. Bright white in the afternoon light, with freshly painted green boards to sit on. My boat.

Totally empty.

* * *

Now I know what a terrified dad calling out for his child sounds like. Isak was shouting so much that I thought his heart would tear.

"Lena!" he yelled out across the still waters. *"Lena!"*

I didn't call her name. I couldn't even look at the

white boat. Feeling powerless, I sat down on deck and stared at Grandpa's boots.

"We've got to alert… We've got to…" Isak stammered, fumbling with his phone. "Lena!" he called out again.

"Just hold on a moment there, Isak," said Grandpa, pointing at the horizon. "Lena might be all right."

A thin plume of smoke was rising up from Kobbholmen.

* * *

We could see her from some distance. She was standing motionless on the old pier, still wearing her football boots and tracksuit. Her black hair was hanging over her face, and her fists were clenched. Isak jumped ashore when we still had a metre to go. He reached her in two quick bounds and lifted her up like a feather. Nothing happened at first, but then Lena started crying. She cried and cried, and Isak held on to her tightly until the crying faded.

Then Grandpa turned off the engine and nodded at the bonfire. "Are you cooking hot dogs?"

Lena wiped her eyes with her sleeve and nodded.

"Are there any left?"

Lena nodded again.

I realized she must've had some kind of plan to live on Kobbholmen. She'd packed food and a sleeping bag. She told us that she'd pushed the boat away herself so she wouldn't be tempted to go home immediately.

"But why don't you want to go home?" Isak asked quietly.

Lena didn't answer. She just poked at her beautiful bonfire and was as silent as a dead crab.

"Lena?"

"Because nobody likes me," she said eventually.

Grandpa, Isak and I all stared at her in shock. Nobody liked her?

"But, Lena…" Isak looked at her, broken-hearted. "How can you say that?"

"Because it's true," she muttered.

"No, it's not true," said Isak.

Lena turned one of the logs on the fire, sending smoke and embers hissing into the sky.

"Well, I'm not the way you want me to be. So I might as well live out here."

"You're exactly the way we want you to be—"
Isak began.

But Lena became enraged. "No, I'm not," she said.
"There's not a soul who cares about what I can do.
But as for music and maths and all that rubbish I
can't do… You all think those things are a matter of
life and death."

She raked the fire angrily.

"Shrieking sharks, I don't want to be stuck
hanging around in Mathildewick Cove like some
kind of keyboard-playing Christmas decoration."

Isak was about to answer, but before he could,
Lena started crying again.

"You and Mum haven't been to see a single
flipping football match in all my life, and Trille…"

She didn't say any more.

I looked at her sadly. Isak put his arm round Lena
and told her he had been at the match. He'd seen
that penalty she'd saved. He'd heard Lena taking
charge of the backline, directing them and keeping
them in order even though it was her first match.
And he'd seen how quick and focused she was right
from the start of the game. He'd heard the other

girls, who were two years older than she was, calling to her and singing her praises. And he'd had to leave five minutes before the end, because there was a young man on the other side of town who'd had a heart attack.

Lena wiped her hand across her eyes and looked at him in disbelief.

"You saw the penalty?" she asked breathlessly.

Isak nodded.

"Did you see how she tried to make it look like she was going to shoot to the left, but I threw myself to the right anyway because…"

"I saw," said Isak.

Lena sat up straight. She had a strange expression on her face.

"But Isak, did you see…"

"I saw everything," Isak smiled. "I was the proudest dad of the whole match."

* * *

On the way home, we picked up the little white boat and towed it along. Lena was behind my back, but I could tell she was looking at me. I hadn't managed to say a word the whole time.

When we were on our way back up from the boat sheds, and I was dragging my feet under the rowan trees, she stopped and waited for me.

"Trille?"

I gulped.

"Shall we try out your boat tomorrow?"

I nodded.

CHAPTER THIRTY-SEVEN

A serious talk – and a few mackerel too

*I*t's a funny thing with Lena. As we pushed off from shore on my boat at the crack of dawn the next morning, it was as if there'd never been any problem at all.

"Isn't it a top-notch boat, Trille? It was Lars who fixed the outboard motor."

I leant over and pulled the cord. The engine started on the first pull, and soon we were speeding along. It was a brilliant boat. But I just couldn't cheer myself up. I felt a great lump in my throat at the very thought that this was my boat. I didn't deserve it.

When we stopped the boat and Lena wanted to start fishing, I took a deep breath.

"Lena, I'm sorry that…"

Lena just waved her hand. "I'm sorry too, and all that stuff."

I smiled slightly, but I felt I wasn't finished. It wasn't that simple.

"It's just that I like to be with other people too sometimes," I began.

Lena sighed. "Well, obviously. You just don't get it, do you?"

Clearly not, I thought, surprised to see that she was already managing to get on my nerves again.

"I don't want to spend all my time with you either," she said. "Smoking haddocks, that would be quite a burden," she added.

Oh, she was so…! I started to prepare my fishing line. We didn't say anything for a long while, and then it was Lena who took a deep breath.

"The thing is, Trille, it must be possible to fall in love without turning into a blinking idiot while you're at it."

"Fall in love?" I said. "I'm not in love."

"Just an idiot?"

"Huh?"

"Who knows, maybe I could even have helped you."

"Helped me?"

"Yes. Can't you see how hopeless it is to go on playing the piano when you hate it? Or to sit at the ferry landing like a nitwit? For cod's sake. Do you think that's going to entice any ladies?"

"But…"

"If Birgit has *any* sense in that head of hers – and we may very well wonder if she has, actually – then she'll see that you're the best one of all."

"Huh?"

Lena didn't say any more for a while. She brushed some dirt off her dungarees and sighed.

"I also think it would be good for your mental health if you took up playing the drums," she said in conclusion.

"You're deranged," I said.

"Thanks, you too," Lena grumbled, giving me one of her smiles that would make the greyest of rocks glitter.

I felt something melt inside me, and I started

laughing. Lena sat there for a while, looking at me with a cheery glint in her eye, and then she broke down too. We laughed and laughed. We almost laughed our way to Davy Jones's locker, both of us.

When we'd finally calmed down, we cast our lines and started fishing. The mackerel had arrived now, and it wasn't long before the lines were twitching and thrashing about on both sides of the boat.

After we'd got back from Kobbholmen the day before, I'd been down to the water all by myself. Nets and fishing lines were hung throughout the boat shed in meticulous order. None of them had been in the water since Grandpa hurt his hand. Up in the boat shed loft, I'd found the box with the damaged halibut line in it. I'd taken it down, lit the lamp above Grandpa's stool and sat there, unravelling and mending it until late in the evening. Now it was in the wooden box, ready to be used. The only thing missing was some decent bait.

Lena and I sorted that out. The tub between us was soon full of mackerel. Enough to bait plenty of lines.

"Do you think we'll get Grandpa out line fishing next weekend?" I asked.

Lena shrugged and suddenly looked serious.

"After all, we finally got him back at sea yesterday, didn't we?" I said, feeling a little uncertain.

Lena glanced at me.

"What is it?" I eventually asked.

"I think maybe Lars is worried he won't manage all this fishing any more, Trille, what with his hand and everything," Lena said. "He's starting to get old, you know," she added.

It felt like a wall had crumbled inside me. Grandpa didn't have anything to be worried about, did he? Images of the giant halibut and all the blood flickered past my eyes. I looked back to shore. Grandpa was up in the farmyard. He was pulling Inger's pram back and forth with his good arm, while looking out at Lena and me.

CHAPTER THIRTY-EIGHT

"Who do you like best?"

"I was thinking about maybe going to the match this afternoon," I said to Lena when we'd moored the boat and sorted out the fish.

The boys from our class were playing their first match of the summer season. Kai-Tommy had been talking about it for ages. They were playing against the team from town, which had won the league by a mile the year before. But the boys at school had been training hard all winter. Kai-Tommy thought they were going to win. The league title too! I knew that Birgit would be there, watching.

"Sounds good," said Lena, grabbing hold of her side of the fish tub. "But I've got training to go to."

And so it was. Lena sped off on her bike, and I went to the match. I watched her as she cycled away, feeling a warmth in my chest that hadn't been there for a long time. Lena Lid, my best friend and neighbour. There wasn't another person in the world like her.

When I arrived at the pitch, I saw Axel and Ellisiv sitting in the stand, so I went and joined them.

"Now I can safely say that I've got a girlfriend," said Axel.

Ellisiv rolled her eyes and made space for me. Down on the gravel pitch, my classmates ran back and forth as they warmed up. I looked around anxiously for Birgit. It took me a while to spot her sitting alone at the far end of the stand.

She looked up in surprise when I reached her.

"Hi, Trille! Are you feeling better?"

"Huh? Oh, you mean... Yes, it passed quickly. Was it a good party?"

Birgit nodded and looked out across the pitch. Was she watching Kai-Tommy?

"It was a bit sad too."

"Sad?"

"Yes, we're going back home to Amsterdam soon, you know."

She said she'd known the whole time that they were only here for a year, but she'd thought it would be all right.

"I remembered what it felt like leaving Kisha in Kenya, so I'd really decided not to make such good friends here."

I sat down.

"It's very difficult not to grow fond of people," she said. "Do you know what I mean?"

I nodded. Who understood that better than me? I was about to say something when a shadow fell over us.

It was Kai-Tommy, slightly out of breath, with his dark fringe and bright blue strip.

"Hi, so good you made it," he said to Birgit.

He looked at me nervously, and it suddenly dawned on me that Kai-Tommy felt just as worked up seeing me talking with Birgit as I did when he talked with her.

"Where did you leave Lena, then?" he asked me.

"She's training in town."

He sighed in annoyance. "She never gives up. Somebody should tell her that she hasn't exactly got a goalkeeper's body, the skinny sardine that she is."

I was about to say something back, but I couldn't be bothered. It was better just to leave it.

"Talk to you later, then!" he said, running off.

"Do you like Kai-Tommy, really?" I blurted out. I needed to know.

Birgit looked at me in confusion. "Yes, quite a lot."

"But…" I flung out my arms, baffled.

"He's nice deep down, Trille."

It had to be pretty deep down, I thought.

"I like you a lot too, you know," she added.

A warm feeling ran through my body. "Who do you like best, then?" I tried to make it sound like a silly question.

Birgit laughed. She looked at the boys, who'd formed two huddles out on the pitch. Then she became serious.

"Well, probably Kisha," she said quietly, with a lopsided smile.

I didn't know what else to say. Birgit was going to leave soon. The thought was unbearable, but it was good to sit there with her, for the moment.

"I'll miss you," I finally managed to say.

"I'll miss you too, Trille."

And then the game started.

CHAPTER THIRTY-NINE

The guys on the gravel pitch

*T*he match turned out to be one nobody would forget in a hurry. The red team from town put the pressure on from the start, but our local team stayed solid at the back, blocking all their attacks. It was clear that a lot had changed over the winter. Ivar obviously knew what he was doing, whatever Lena thought about him.

It was no more than a couple of minutes into the match when Andreas made a long pass to Abdulahi, who brought the ball down and shot it at the other team's goal. The goalie from town barely managed to throw himself down in time and smack the ball away.

Then it was the team from town on the offensive.

Halvor punched the ball just off the pitch, and a corner was awarded. He stopped the ball again, and reluctantly I had to admit that he was starting to turn into a good keeper. I was seriously impressed with my classmates. They managed to get past midfield time after time. The red team's defence had their hands full stopping the attacks. Several times it was only their goalie, dressed in black, who saved them from going a goal down.

Birgit was on her feet. "Come on!" she shouted.

When the ball went off for a throw-in, I cast my eyes over the spectators. Minda and Magnus and their friends were sitting at the top of the stand. Ellisiv and Axel were both on their feet, cheering. There were people I knew all the way along the touchline. And what in heaven's name? Ylva! She was standing down by the other team's corner post, looking totally confused. I sighed in despair. This was so typical of her! After the previous day's drama, she'd probably decided that she was finally going to start coming to Lena's matches, but hadn't remembered that Lena had moved teams! Was it possible? I slapped my forehead.

The goalie from town, in his black shirt, put the ball down at the edge of the goal area, took aim and kicked it in a precise arc. The ball crossed the whole pitch and landed smack bang at the feet of an unmarked player just over the centre line. Before we knew it, the boy in red had fended off two defenders and shot the ball into the back of the net. We were one–nil down!

The audience sighed and booed. The away team clapped, of course, but I could hear one person above all the rest, screaming with joy down by the corner post. It was Ylva. She was cheering on the wrong team! Lena would've had a fit.

"Sorry, I'll be back in a bit," I said to Birgit, hurrying down to the touchline. I couldn't let Ylva carry on making a fool of herself like that!

I'd almost reached Ylva when I looked again at the little goalie from town in his black shirt. He was standing there calmly, a short distance out into the penalty box, waiting for the game to get started again. He had his cap pulled down low, as he was facing straight into the sun. Every now and then he pointed and shouted something to the red team's defenders, with a slightly delicate but determined voice. I opened my mouth, and then closed it again. No ... it couldn't be!

The game was back on, and the little goalie bobbed up and down on his toes, full of concentration. He moved to the side, keeping an eagle eye on the ball. Then he brought one of his gloves up to his mouth and yelled at two of the players in red:

"Hello! Time to wake up and smell the waffles over there! Keep an eye on number ten!"

I practically collapsed there and then.

Lena!

And what happened next was something I'll never forget. While I was still standing there, slightly in shock, the player in the blue number ten shirt, Kai-Tommy, snatched the ball from the attacking town side. He turned with it and ran. Two red players behind him tried to catch up, but they were too slow. Kai-Tommy was storming forward at a furious speed. It was him against the keeper.

The player in black, with the cap on her head,

moved back closer and closer to the goal. Then, just when everybody was sure it was about to turn one–all, the little sardine suddenly started to run forward.

"Come on!" Ylva shouted behind me.

With great precision, Lena fearlessly threw herself down onto the gravel just inside the penalty area, grabbing the ball from under the feet of the lone striker. Kai-Tommy fell forward, and Lena rolled a couple of times as she held the ball tightly, as if it were a precious egg. It was a textbook tackle. And it was pretty impressively done.

An enraged Kai-Tommy got back on his feet. He was about to yell something when he saw the same thing I'd seen. If only I could describe the look on his face. It was like he'd been run over by a UFO.

"So good to get to play at the right level now and then," Lena said drily, courteously doffing her cap.

Then she turned back to the game as if nothing had happened.

* * *

The team from town completely dominated the rest of the match and took three well-deserved points home with them on the ferry. But the player of the match stayed behind, waving at them as they left.

People talked about that game for a long time afterwards. When they realized what had happened – that Ivar and the boys had more or less forced Lena out of their team – many were angry. But Lena wasn't angry any more. Moving teams was one of the best things that had ever happened to her. She liked playing with the girls, and since the coach in town had quickly spotted her talent, she was constantly being asked if the boys' team could borrow her too.

But she didn't always say yes.

"I can't play football every day," she explained. "I've got quite a lot to be getting on with at home too, after all."

I knew she was thinking about that raft.

CHAPTER FORTY

Grandpa and Thunderclap Kåre

"*I*'ve ordered an emergency stop button for the winch," Dad said softly as he cut a couple of thick slices of bread.

"Oh," I said.

We were eating breakfast at the kitchen worktop. It was Saturday, and the sun was shining. The boat traffic was in full swing out on the fjord, but through the window I could see Grandpa sitting marooned at the table in the garden, drinking his coffee.

Terrible images of the halibut and the blood flew through my head again. Was it the same for Grandpa? I peered at him out in the garden. He looked so lonely. I suddenly realized it was even worse for him.

Dad chewed his bread next to me. "We've got to get the old man out fishing again, Trille. We can't go on like this."

* * *

"Is that Thunderclap Kåre out off the headland?" I asked, plonking myself down next to Grandpa.

He nodded, turning his coffee cup round and round in his good hand. Grandpa had always made fun of Thunderclap Kåre for not going out to catch the big fish. Now we could clearly see him hauling up a load of small coalfish.

"Do you know that I once struck him down?" Grandpa said.

"You hit Thunderclap Kåre? Why?"

"He was dancing with Inger." Grandpa shook his head and chuckled. "I was seventeen and just about to go to sea for the first time."

He squinted at Thunderclap Kåre's boat. "It's the most foolish thing I've ever done in my life."

"Were you and Granny already boyfriend and girl-friend when you were seventeen?" I asked, surprised.

"No, we were friends. But that summer, she suddenly came along one day to tell me that she was going to miss me when I left. She even said that she'd gladly wait for me."

Grandpa smiled.

"And what did I do, the idiot that I am? I cheekily turned her down, just like I'd turned down all the others. I didn't want any girl waiting at home for me. I wanted to be footloose and fancy-free."

But the day before Grandpa was due to leave, something happened. There was a dock dance where the ferry landing is now, Grandpa told me. All the young people in the area were gathered there that summer's evening. When he arrived, he saw Inger among all the others. And as if by magic, it dawned on him what he'd done. Holy mackerel, she was the one he really liked!

"And so you hit him?" I asked, shocked.

"You bet I did."

I realized it had been a close call: my grandparents almost hadn't got together at all. Granny had been furious. Not only had Grandpa jilted her and made her unhappier than she'd ever been before, he then had the nerve to assault a totally innocent bloke who actually liked her. Could anybody be more of a fool? Grandpa had to sail off to Baltimore with a broken heart and a guilty conscience.

I glanced in astonishment at my calm and peaceful grandfather.

"I never would've thought you could punch somebody," I said.

"Oh?" He laughed. "I'm so old now that I know we all do foolish things. It doesn't matter that much, really."

He peered out at Thunderclap Kåre again. "What matters is what we do afterwards."

From the corner of my eye, I saw Lena come out onto her doorstep with her football in her hands. Grandpa spotted her too.

"This world's so well put together, Trille, that most things we mess up can be sorted out again. But sometimes it's a tough job," he added.

Thunderclap Kåre got his outboard motor started and chugged back towards the shore. Lena was already down in the field with her ball.

"Grandpa, today we're going line fishing," I said, making it clear that he had no choice.

CHAPTER FORTY-ONE

The message in a bottle

*T*he day Birgit left, it was summer again.
Grandpa and I were going fishing almost every day. Back on dry land, Ylva was walking around with a bump as big as the one Mum had been carrying at Christmas. And in the old boat shed, Lena's raft was ready to be launched.

The whole family from Hillside came down to Mathildewick Cove before they left. They had to drop off Haas. Birgit had decided. I knew how fond she was of her dog, and yet she wanted him to stay with Lena. She thought he would be happier here. That's what she was like – and that was why I liked her. Lena had been a bit shocked to receive such a generous gift. I didn't really know what she'd said to Birgit, but I hoped it was thank you.

"Maybe we'll go and study together one day, right?" Birgit said to me before they left.

Maybe we will, I thought. Who knows, anyway?

Then I got one last curly-haired hug, before the Dutch family drove off between the forest and the sea. I stood there, feeling weak and empty, staring at the car in the distance. Grandpa came and stood next to me. After a while, Lena stuck her head between us and put one hand on my shoulder and one on Grandpa's.

"Well, lads," she said with a smirk. "Now it's just the three of us again."

I could've hit her.

* * *

Later that day, we were back down by the shore. Lena was lying on her stomach among the clumps of seaweed, attaching a tow hook to the raft, while Haas sat calmly in the sun, watching.

"Do you seriously think we're going to tow you all the way out to Kobbholmen?" I asked despairingly, looking at the enormous raft on the pebbles by the shore. "It'll take all day."

"I've got plenty of time," said Lena, her mouth full of screws. "I've got to check this thing's sea-ready, after all."

I knew it was pointless arguing, so I went into the old boat shed to find a suitable rope. As I scanned all the hooks and shelves, I suddenly spotted a bottle with a piece of paper in it. It was hidden up on a rafter right inside the shed.

"It's a message in a bottle," said Lena from behind me. "I found it that day back in the winter when we were looking for wreckage. When Birgit came back, you remember?"

Just her name gave me a wistful sinking feeling.

"Who is it from, then?"

"Who do you think?" Lena asked drily.

I opened the bottle and unrolled the sheet of paper. It was from us, of course, and yet it felt like it was from somebody else. Childish writing careened across the paper.

Deer whoever finds this messidge in a botl we are too frends from mathildewik cove and our fone number is . . .

"This is ancient," I said, stunned.

I read it again. My heart beat warmly but painfully in my chest. I pictured Lena and me as we'd been when we were young. Two good friends in our welly boots, throwing out messages in bottles just a few metres from shore, thinking they'd travel the world.

"I wasn't very good at spelling then," I mumbled, so Lena wouldn't see that I was almost crying.

Lena could see it anyway. She tilted her head and gave me a kind look.

"I know. Imagine that, Trille. A gifted child like you."

Then she started waving a coil of rope impatiently. "Are we going outside, then?"

* * *

We put out to sea. Grandpa stood calmly and slightly stoop-shouldered, squinting as usual. He had his injured hand in his boiler-suit pocket, and his good hand on the wheel. Now and then, he glanced back and chuckled. A giant raft, made from the wreckage of one of the worst hurricanes of all time, was heavily pounding through the sea behind us, its happy owner and ship's dog on board.

"If she bumped into the ferry with that thing, I truly don't know who would sink first," Grandpa grumbled. Then he raised his shoulders slightly and turned towards me.

"Well, time for an old man to have some coffee. Do you want to take over here, Trille?"

He let go of the wheel and stepped aside. A fresh breeze ruffled my hair as I took control. I could still feel the warmth of Grandpa's hand in the wood. Birgit was in the Netherlands, but the ocean lay ahead of me, wide and blue. Far out there, by Kobbholmen, was a fishing line in the sea, exactly where my grandmother had once shown it was a good place to put it. And towed behind us, using the most solid rope in Mathildewick Cove, was my best friend and neighbour on her raft.

"Hey, Trille!" Lena yelled from back there.

She'd got to her feet and raised her hand to her mouth, like she does when she calls to the backline in her team. Her voice carried like an earthquake in all directions. I looked quizzically at

her, an old feeling of joy bubbling in my stomach.
Lena waved and laughed, and then she shouted
with all her might:

"Do you think we can speed this convoy up a bit?"

For more books by Maria Parr...

Whether it's putting a cow in a boat or advertising for a dad, no day is ordinary with a best friend like Lena.

Trille loves to share everything with her, even Auntie Granny's waffles. But when Lena faces a secret she can't share, will their friendship end?

"A wonderful life-affirming book."
Books for Keeps

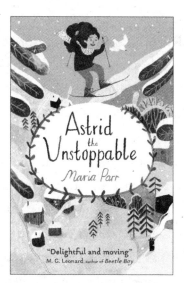

Astrid Glimmerdal loves to spend her days
racing down the mountainside on her sledge and
skis – the faster the better! She just wishes there
were other children to share her adventures.

She is thrilled when a new family comes to stay for
the holidays, but things don't get off to a good start.
Then Astrid discovers that Gunnvald, her grumpy
best friend, has been keeping a big secret from her.

"Delightful and moving"
M.G. Leonard

MARIA PARR is an outstanding Norwegian author for children. She has twice won the prestigious Brage Prize for best children's book, as well as the Sult Prize, the Norwegian Critics' Prize, France's Prix Sorcières and the Dutch Zilveren Griffel. Her debut novel, *Waffle Hearts*, was also shortlisted for the Marsh Award for Children's Literature in Translation. It was made into a popular children's television series in Norway and adapted for the stage, while her second novel, *Astrid the Unstoppable*, has also been made into a theatre production. Her books have been published in more than 30 countries worldwide. Maria lives in Norway.

GUY PUZEY grew up in the Highlands of Scotland, just a short swim away from Norway. He began translating Norwegian literature in 2006 after studying the language at the University of Edinburgh. In 2011 he went on to complete a doctorate on Italian and Norwegian language policy. He now works at the university as a lecturer in Scandinavian studies. In 2015 he was shortlisted for the Marsh Award for Children's Literature in Translation for his work on Maria Parr's first novel, *Waffle Hearts*.

ALL TOGETHER NOW!

MATTHEW QUICK

HEADLINE

First published as *Sorta Like a Rock Star* by Little, Brown and Company in the USA

First published in Great Britain as *Sorta Like a Rock Star* in 2013 by Headline Publishing Group

Published in this paperback edition in 2020 by Headline Publishing Group

1

Cataloguing in Publication Data is available from the British Library

ISBN 978 1 4722 8141 8

Typeset in Granjon by Palimpsest Book Production Limited, Falkirk, Stirlingshire

Printed and bound in Great Britain by Clays Ltd, Elcograf S.p.A.

MIX
Paper from
responsible sources
FSC® C104740

Headline's policy is to use papers that are natural, renewable and recyclable products and made from wood grown in well-managed forests and other controlled sources. The logging and manufacturing processes are expected to conform to the environmental regulations of the country of origin.

HEADLINE PUBLISHING GROUP
An Hachette UK Company
Carmelite House
50 Victoria Embankment
London EC4Y 0DZ

www.headline.co.uk
www.hachette.co.uk

FOR MR SCOTT FLEMING,
HERO OF TEENAGERS,
HERO OF MINE

PART ONE

Feel the Pain

ONE

Lying down, shivering on the last seat of school bus 161, pinned by his teensy doggie gaze, which is completely 100% cute – I'm such a girl, I know – I say, 'You won't believe the bull I had to endure today.'

My legs are propped up against the window, toes pointing toward the roof so that the poodle skirt I made in Life Skills class settles around my midsection. Yeah, it's the twenty-first century and I wear poodle skirts. I like dogs. I'm a freak. So what? And before anybody reading along gets too jazzed up thinking about my skirt flipped up around my waist, my lovely getaway sticks exposed, allow me to say there's no teenage flesh to be seen here.

I have on two pairs of sweatpants, three pairs of wool socks, two pairs of gloves, a big old hat that covers my freakishly little ears, and three jackets – because I don't own a proper winter coat and it's extremely cold sleeping on Hello Yellow through the dismal January nights.

I can see my breath.

Ice sheets form on the windows.

My teeth chatter.

Sometimes I wake up because my lungs hurt so bad from taking in so much freezing air. It's like gargling chips of dry ice.

My water bottle freezes if I take it out of my inner coat pocket.

Forget about peeing, unless you want to shiver your butt off – literally.

And it's pretty lonely too.

Because I am holding him up above my head, Bobby Big Boy (Triple B) looks down at me, panting with his perfect pink tongue hanging out of his mouth. His breath stinks like the butts he's always trying to sniff whenever he's around any dog women – BBB's an awful flirt even though he is totally monogamous and loyal to Ms Jenny – but I want to kiss him anyway, because he is a sexy mutt and the most dependable man I know. He'll never leave me – ever – which is why I don't mind the smelly doggie kisses. Plus he's wearing his dapper plaid coat, which I also made in Life Skills class, and his doggie jacket makes him look beautiful. His hair is mussed around the ears like Brad Pitt, or maybe like he needs a bath, but his eyes are loyal and kind.

As I finish my confession, I keep him waiting, suspended above me, his little legs running like he thinks he's on a treadmill or something. There's no rush. We are alone, we have all night, and Bobby Big Boy digs air-running above my face.

I've been sleeping with Triple B for somewhere around a year now. I found him in a shoebox half starved – no tags. No lie. He looked like a sock that had been flushed down the toilet – having traveled through all those gross pipes – only to be spit out of some sewer grate into a wet orange Nike box set up sideways like some elementary school kid's diorama. PATHETIC ALMOST DEAD MUTT, the exhibition would have been labeled, had some little tyke taken it into the science fair. Needless to say, I rescued his butt from the curb and nursed him back to health, mostly with scraps of meat I initially stole from Donna's dinner table until she caught me and started buying BBB dog food.

Did I put up Lost-Dog-Found posters?

I'll put it to you this way – if I ever meet the people who let Triple B get so skinny, watch out.

Bobby Big Boy is still air-running like a champ, and will keep at it until I lower him.

Regarding time, the parking-lot streetlights go out around eleven, and then there is no reading or writing – because I can't risk some curious passerby seeing me using a flashlight. That would blow our cover. With no lights – all alone – things can get quite weird, which is why I like to keep Bobby Big Boy around. But it's only nine-something now, so I'll have plenty of time to do my homework, after I'm done confessing to Triple B, who doubles as my at-home priest, of course, because Father Chee is only God's servant and not God, so therefore, not omnipresent. I have priorities, and keeping my soul white with a nightly confession

5

is high up on the list. I'm a pretty good Catholic; I'm still the big V. Momma Mary and me are, like, five-by-five; I'm a holy teenager of God, sucka! And Mom won't be back until after the bar closes, and maybe not even then. She's gone a fishin' for men, as Jesus says.

'Today, I kicked Lex Pinkston in the shin,' I tell 3B, his legs still going like mad, 'which I know is a sin, especially since God made man in his own image, so He probably does have sympathetic (divine) shins prone to the unmerciful ache of a swift kick to the holy shin bone, and those Roman thugs probably kicked good old JC in the shins a few times before they nailed Our Lord and Savior to a tree, making Him equally sympathetic to the plaintiff's case, but before you go telling God all about my sin of punting teenage-boy shin, Father Big Boy, let me stress that there were extenuating circumstances. Lex made Ricky echo something filthy again – and I warned that plebian, Lex, like fifty times – so I let him have it. I kicked him square in the shin, and he started hopping on one leg – his friends laughing like hyenas, or maybe apes. Scratch that. Primates are cute, and way smarter than Childress Public High School football players, who suck and never win any games, because they are too busy being morons.'

I could be wrong but – with his legs still running – Father BBB sorta smiles at my story, like he might even appreciate a good shin-kicking inflicted on an exceptionally evil classmate – which makes Father Thrice B seem almost human for a second. Or maybe I just want him to be human.

So anyway, what happened was … while I was throwing away my trash, Lex told Ricky to tell Ryan Gold that her 'boobies are lovely', which Ricky did, of course – not because he is one of God's special children but because he is a guy who can get away with such things because he is special – and Ryan Gold turned bright red before she started to cry, because she's still a prudish virgin pre-woman, like me, and Ricky just started robot laughing – 'Hi! Hi! Hi! Hi!' – like he does whenever he is upset and confused, and boy, did it make me mad. Especially since Ricky knows better, and is trying to earn the right to take me to prom. Donna would be devastated if I told her what her only son said today in the cafeteria.

I lower Bobby Big Boy down to my chest. He stops running and licks my under-chin in an effort to console me. The weight of him on my chest makes me feel less alone – sorta loved – which I realize might be whack, but we get love wherever we can, right? At least that's what Mom says anyway.

'So am I forgiven, Father B3? Off the divine hook? Bark once for yes.'

'Rew!' BBB says, just like I taught him. He's a good little doggie. Truly.

AA, 2009

When I finish writing the above essay, I rip it up and sigh. It kicked apple bottom, and yet I had to rip it up.

Bobby Big Boy runs south, ducks his little head, and

burrows up under my jackets and shirts, snuggling up against my barely bumpy pre-woman chest and keeping me quite warm without scratching up my belly so much, because he is a frickin' gentleman.

Maybe you think I had to rip up the essay because it was sorta a confession, and therefore private, but the truth is that I trust Mr Doolin, my English teacher, the guy who asked our class to write a slice-of-life story. He's pretty hip and lets us express the truths of our lives in our writing, gaining our trust so that our words can be more authentic, which is cool of him, because I'm sure our writing honestly – the truth – pisses off some teachers and parents, even though all freaky teenagers keep it real when we can.

Maybe you think I ripped up my essay because I didn't want to narc out my friend Ricky or those moronic football players, but I don't really care about narcing them out, because when you say or do repellent stuff in the lunch-room, that's public knowledge as far as I'm concerned. True? True.

I wouldn't want to turn in an essay that made Ryan Gold look bad, because she is a nice person, but I would have turned this essay in if Ryan was the only thing stopping me, because sometimes – when it comes to writing – you have to sacrifice the feelings of other people to make a statement. Serve the greater good and all, which Mr Doolin says almost every day.

But the truth is that I don't want anyone to know that

I am living out of Hello Yellow – that my mom's last boyfriend, A-hole Oliver, threw us the hell out of his apartment, and that my mom has to save up some dough before we can get four walls of our own. I mean, it's a pretty pathetic story, and I'm not really all that proud to be my mom's daughter right now. Homelessness reflects badly on both of us. True? True.

I'm sure there are people who would let us crash at their houses, because the town of Childress is full of good-hearted dudes and dudettes. Word. But charity is for cripples and old people and Mom is sure to come through one of these days. I still have Bobby Big Boy, and Mom still has her job driving Hello Yellow, all of our clothes and stuff fit in the two storage bins between the wheels, below the bus windows, so it's all good in the hood.

Except that sitting here with my legs up and BBB on my chest, I can't think of anything else to write about – especially since my original essay was so killer.

The quiet of an empty Hello Yellow can drive you a little nuts.

Bobby Big Boy and I just cuddle until the streetlight blinks out and everything goes black.

I can rest my eyes, but I can't really sleep until Mom gets back from fishing, because I worry about her.

She's still pretty.

Bad things happen to pretty women who have daughters like me and can't afford to do jack crap for 'em, which makes said pretty women desperate for a Prince Charming

– only Prince Charmings marry hot young chicks my age, or maybe a little older. Mom's almost forty, so she's pretty screwed when it comes to men. Sometimes I like to think about her marrying an old rich dude, who would act all grandfatherly and leave Mom tons of money when he croaked. That would be cool, but it ain't gonna happen. Truth.

Another thing: Mom's taste in men is akin to a crack-head's taste in crack cocaine. Any old hit will do. And it sucks for all nearby loved ones (me) when mi madre is hitting the man-pipe again, because she sorta loses her frickin' mind – to put it bluntly.

All alone on Hello Yellow, I think about Mom for a long time.

She sucks at being a mom. Emphatically.

She's so ridiculously irresponsible and socially dumber than Ricky – who is diagnosed with autism – but I still love her. I'm a sucker for love and having a mom in my life. Call me old fashioned, maudlin, or mawkish.

When I hear Hello Yellow's front door being keyed into, I freeze and hold my breath.

Should be Mom.

Must be Mom.

What if it's not Mom?

I'm in a creepy parking lot outside of town; it's full of eerily similar school buses parked in perfect lines. Too much symmetry can be daunting. There are train tracks on one side of the parking lot and creepy woods on the other. Bad stuff happens by train tracks and in woods, because some men are inherently evil, and left unchecked, these dudes will do bad hooey – at least according to such cool cats as Herman Melville, who illustrated this exact point through that evil Claggart character from *Billy Budd*, which we just read in my Accelerated American Lit class. The Handsome Sailor. Budd Boy spilling his soup on Claggart in the mess hall – when Billy does that, it's a metaphor for accidental homosexual ejaculation according to Mr Doolin, who has coitus on the brain 24/7, and sees a sexual metaphor in just about any old sentence. 'Handsome is as handsome did it too.' Herman Melville. Funny stuff. Truly. But being in a bus alone at night near train tracks and woods ain't so ha-ha, believe me.

Plus there have been a few rape-murders on the outskirts of town lately and the cops haven't caught the bad guy yet, which has lots of people freaked out and for good reason.

Madman nearby – beware!

Finally, I cannot take it and completely blow any chance I have of surviving an encounter with the local psychopath, mostly because I am only seventeen, and a chick, even if I am a junior now. 'Mom?' I say.

'Amber? Did I wake you up?'

Whew. It's Mom. 'No. Some crazy lumberjack train conductor was just about to abduct me and make me his slave, but you scared him off. Thanks.'

'That's not even remotely funny.'

'How was fishin' fo' men, any bites?'

'Nope. Nothing.'

'A good man is hard to find.'

'Damn skippy,' my mother says, like a used-up chippie who will never find her Prince Charming, but you can tell – by the tone of her voice – that Mom is faking something, trying to sound hopeful enough to make her daughter feel as though she will not be sleeping on a school bus forever, so I give her a little credit. She's had a harrowing life.

'Always tomorrow,' I say through the darkness, as my mom pats my forehead like I am Bobby Big Boy. I like dogs, so I do not take offense.

'Does your puppy need to go out before I hit the hay?'

'Bob probably could squirt a few drops.'

'Please don't call him Bob.'

'That's his name.'

'Your father was – best to forget him, and—'

'Well, Bob here has to take a squirt, and I have school tomorrow, so can we skip the broken-record talk and get doggie duty over with, please? I can't sleep without my pup.'

'Come on, little dog,' Mom says, clapping her hands. And Bob bursts forth from my pre-woman chest, widening the neck holes of – like – four shirts, and scratching the hell out of my neck. He loves to piss. It's his favorite.

'Use his leash!' I yell, because I don't want 3B to get lost in the dark.

'Okay,' Mom says, but I know she doesn't use the leash, because I'm on it – it's under my butt.

My mom lies to me all the time. She sorta has a problem. She is a fabricator of falsehoods. Or maybe she is just drunk again, which is no excuse.

Sometimes when I am losing faith in Mom – which is, like, all the time lately – I like to think about one of the top-seven all-time Amber-and-her-mom moments. These are little videos I have stored in my brain – all documenting the mom I knew before she sorta gave up on life, before Oliver broke Mom's spirit and got her drinking so heavily. Here's the number-seven all-time Amber-and-her-mom moment:

Back in the 80s – when Mom was in high school – she was a big-time softball player who helped her team win a state championship, which was the highlight of her entire life. She used to talk about softball all the time, and even used to play on a local bar team in a beer league. I used to go and watch Mom play softball against fat men with huge beer bellies and foul mouths. There were only a few other women who played in the league, and Mom was a million times better than all of them. Mom was better than most of the men too, for the record. She couldn't hit the ball that far, but she knew how to hit through the holes in the infield, and she was one hell of a second-base woman – never making any errors.

Anyway, when I was a little girl, Mom got it in her head that she would train me and make me into a killer softball player just like her, so she took me to the sports store and bought me a glove and a bat and a ball and a hat and cleats and even a pair of batting gloves, even though I hadn't asked for any of these things. This was well after my dad took off on us, and we never had all that much money, so this purchase was sorta a big deal, which I understood even as a little girl, so I just went along with the idea, even though I really didn't want to play softball.

The next day, Mom took me and all of my new gear to the park. She showed me how to swing a bat and throw and catch a ball, but – even though she was a really good coach – I just couldn't get the hang of any of it, and trying made me feel like a complete idiot. For weeks I swung the bat and never hit any of the balls Mom threw me; all of the balls she hit went over my head, through my legs, and occasionally nailed me in the face or stomach, and all of my throws went to the right or left of Mom or hit her feet. Mom never yelled at me or anything like that, but after a few weeks of steady failure, after swinging the bat and missing for the bazillionth time, standing at home plate, I burst into tears.

Mom ran off the mound and toward me. She picked me up and kissed me on the cheek. 'Amber, this doesn't happen overnight – you have to work at it if you want to be a good softball player. It takes lots of practice. It took me years!'

'But I don't *want* to be a good softball player. I hate softball. I really do.'

Mom looked me in the eye, and I could tell that she was surprised by this news – I could tell she had never even once thought that maybe I wouldn't want to play softball.

'I never want to play softball ever again!' I yelled. 'Never again. I hate this! All of it!'

'Okay,' Mom said.

'What?' I said, shocked, because I thought that Mom would make me keep trying, because that's what adults usually do.

'Amber, it's just a game. I thought you might like it, but if you don't want to play, well then, you don't have to play softball.'

'You won't be mad at me?'

'Why would I be mad at you?' Mom said, and then laughed.

'Because you spent all that money on equipment, and now I don't want to play softball.'

'If you don't want to play, you don't want to play. It's okay.'

'Really?'

'Really.'

We left the field, got some Italian hoagies at the local deli, and ate by the lake sitting on a park bench. We fed parts of our rolls to ducks, and it was really nice to just sit with my mom after telling her how I felt. It was good to know that I could tell my mom what I truly felt inside and still be able to feed ducks with her afterward. I really

15

love ducks. I like watching them waddle around on land, and their quacking noises crack me up. True.

I remember the sun reflected in the lake so brightly, it hurt to look at the orange water.

'Thanks for not forcing me to keep playing softball,' I said.

Mom put her arm around me.

She never ever again tried to make me play sports, although we ate many more hoagies on that bench and fed flocks of ducks for years to come – and the feeding-ducks memories are something I truly treasure.

Quack, quack.

Ducks.

Pretty killer.

Back in the present moment, when Mom and BBB don't return to Hello Yellow right away, I'm just about to get up and take care of business myself, making sure my best friend doesn't get eaten by a rogue coyote or some other dastardly carnivorous mammal, but then Bobby Big Boy is tearing through Hello Yellow, jumping up into my shirts again, warming my belly and chest, and all is well under the comforter Mom had thrown over me before she left the bus, even though I had left it out on the adjacent seat for her, because we have only one comforter.

Bobby Big Boy's pretty warm from running around and a little lighter without a bladder full of pee. I hear my mom lock up Hello Yellow and then walk toward me.

'This is only temporary, Amber,' Mom says.

'I like it. It's like camping, only on a school bus, and without fattening marshmallows, a cancer-causing campfire, or the pesky Kum-Ba-Yah singing.'

'Did you get enough food today?'

This question pisses me off, especially since she probably blew what little dough she makes on cigarettes and vodka tonight, providing no dinner whatsoever for me or B Thrice. Mom only works four hours a day at nine dollars an hour, and she'd happily buy you a drink at some crappy bar before she'd buy a meal for herself or me. So depressing.

'Watching my figure,' I say, stealing Franks' joke, 'but Bobby Big Boy had a steak I swiped from Donna's dinner table.'

'Ms Roberts,' Mom corrects me, because the drunk has some sardonic notion of proper etiquette when it comes to surnames.

'Right,' I say, like a total bitch, because I can be a cat.

My mother kisses me on the forehead real nice, says, 'Sweet dreams, my love,' and so I let go of the day's frustrations, push my palms together into prayer position, and I silently hold up all the people and dogs in this world who I absolutely positively know need me to pray for them: Mom, 3B, Ricky, Donna, Franks, Chad, Jared, Ty, Door Woman Lucy, Old Man Linder (my manager), Old Man Thompson, Joan of Old and all of the old people down in the Methodist home, Father Chee, The Korean Divas for Christ, Mr Doolin, Private Jackson, Ms Jenny, Prince Tony, the Childress Public High School faculty, and the whole damn town of Childress, even the football team, even Lex Pinkston, EVEN my absentee biological father, Bob, who may or may not even be alive for all I know – I hold them all up to JC in my prayers, asking God to help everyone be who they need to be, and then I simply listen to Mom breathe across the aisle until Triple B and I find sleepy land together, and I dream of the real bed on which Bobby Big Boy and I will rest one day. My future bed's going to be an ocean of mattress, maybe even a queen-size, sucka! Word.

TWO

Waking up at a normal time in Hello Yellow isn't all that bad, because of the many windows – warm sunlight cubes reach everywhere. This happens on the weekends. True. But on school days, we have to rise before the sun comes up so that none of the other early-rising bus drivers will catch us sleeping on Hello Yellow, which would surely cost Mom her job. So we get up super early – way before dawn. I've been doing this for a while; I usually wake up automatically sometime between four thirty and five. But no matter how much she drinks, Mom is always up before Triple B and me.

Today, Mom's inhaling a Newport just outside of Hello Yellow, her dyed blond hair full of fading moonlight. (I keep my hair naturally black and I do dig the way it sometimes shines iridescent like crow feathers. True. I'm an inch or two shorter than Mom when she stands up tall, which is like never. While my skin is freakishly white, her skin is sort of yellow from smoking so much.) Mom's orange cherry glows brighter with each pull.

Like always, she's shivering mentholated smoke out of her nose and mouth.

BBB runs right past her, off the leash in the morning newness where there are no coyotes, local rapist-killers, or other unnamed monsters. He lifts his tiny leg and merrily pisses on the front driver's side tire of school bus 260, marking his all-time favorite wheel.

'Hey, Mom,' I say.

'Good morning, sweetheart,' she says from within her dark smoky shadow.

Mom looks really thin.

Skeletal.

True?

True.

When did you last eat? I think but do not ask, because I don't really want to know the answer, nor do I want to hear another one of Mom's stupid lies.

She won't even eat the food I bring her from Donna's house.

Bobby Big Boy pushes out a few grape-size pellets of poo, squatting somehow regally with a seriously determined look on his face, as if he were a mini sphinx thinking up some kick-ass riddle. I learned all about sphinxes freshman year, when we read *Oedipus Rex*. If you don't know this already, Oedipus had sex with his mom, which is very very whack – even more so than Billy Budd spilling soup on Claggart. We have to read crazy books in high school, let me tell you.

I walk to the storage bin under the windows of the passenger side of Hello Yellow, open up her underbelly, and pull out my trash bag of clothes. I sniff armpits and crotches until I find my purple scoop-neck sweater and a basic pair of jeans. Bra and underwear were changed yesterday, so no worries there. Changing outside sucks because of the cold and the snowy slush underfoot, making your socks wet no matter how hard you try to balance on your boots when changing pants.

Dressed for school, still wearing three jackets instead of one winter coat, I walk back into Hello Yellow, BBB trailing in his dapper plaid coat; I grab my backpack, exit Hello Yellow, BBB trailing, and say, 'Will you eat something today, Mom?'

'Oh, sure,' she says, lighting up a fresh cancer stick. She forces a smile, but she is looking at something just above my hair and will not make eye contact. I'm afraid she might start crying, so I kiss her on the cheek, walk away, lift BBB over the fence and then hop my way out of the school bus compound.

Mom's not-eating started at an exact moment, which I can pinpoint. It's a good moment gone bad. Here is the all-time Amber-and-her-mom moment number six:

Two Thanksgivings ago, when A-hole Oliver was just beginning to show his true colors and Mom was just beginning to slip, she decided that she was going to make this killer traditional Thanksgiving meal with a real turkey and stuffing and cranberry sauce and gravy and wine and candles and everything else that most people have on Thanksgiving. This might not sound like a big deal to you, but Mom and I had never had a real Thanksgiving dinner before, and buying all the ingredients wiped out what little savings Mom had. True.

We got up very early on Thanksgiving morning to get the bird into Oliver's oven. And then we began preparing all of the side dishes while listening to this CD of Frank Sinatra doing Christmas music, which Mom had bought at the grocery store when she was splurging, because she is a big Sinatra fan.

This very morning – cooking with Mom – is one of my all-time favorite memories, because I had never seen her so happy, the two of us listening to Old Blue Eyes, as Mom calls Frank Sinatra.

Oliver got out of bed around ten and immediately went down the hall of the apartment building to drink with his friend and watch football, which was fine with Mom and me, because we were having such a great mom-and-daughter moment and I hated Oliver from the get-go.

I set the table really nicely, even making origami-swan place cards, and got the candles going so that Oliver's dingy small apartment actually felt sorta festive and alive.

When the turkey was ready mid-afternoon, Mom had me go down the hall to get Oliver while she cut the meat, but when I knocked on the door of his friend's apartment, no one answered.

We waited an hour for Oliver to come home before we started eating without him.

I knew that Mom was really sad that Oliver blew off her big meal – what she had spent all of her hard-earned savings on and spent so much time preparing – so I tried to make a big deal about everything and ate until I felt I was going to puke.

Mom hardly touched any of her food and just sorta stared at her plate while I shot so many compliments at her.

Oliver still wasn't home by the time we had put the leftovers into Tupperware and washed the dishes.

So Mom and I sat down on the couch and watched TV.

Jurassic Park was playing on one of the few channels we got, and I was all snuggled up in a blanket with my head in Mom's lap, taking in all the awesome dinosaurs, when she started to cry. So I sat up and held my mom for a long time while she cried and cried.

When she finished crying, she wiped her eyes and said, 'Amber, you're the best thing about my life.'

Oliver walked in all drunk right then, and Mom hustled herself into the kitchen to fix him a plate of food. I watched her dote on him, pretending not to care about his blowing off her meal, while he stuffed his drunken face. From the couch, as I watched them, I knew that I would never allow a man to treat me how Oliver treated my mother. And I began to believe that Mom knew this too – that I really wasn't going to be like her – and maybe knowing that I would not have an Oliver in my future somehow made her life a little bit better.

I liked being the best thing in my mother's life, even if I did wish that her life was a whole lot better than it actually was. Her telling me that on the couch as we watched *Jurassic Park*, it was sorta like a moment for me.

Back in the present, as I walk the cold mile to Ricky's house, B Thrice circles my heels like a maniac, and sometimes he runs through my legs when I take a long stride. Because I'm a chick, I like to pretend I'm Dorothy, BBB is Toto, and we're walking on the frickin' Yellow Brick Road, just about to meet some interesting friends who will help us melt the Wicked Witch. It's a pretty dumb fantasy, especially since Judy Garland was so super-mega beautiful and most boys would rather kiss the Tin Man – or even a flying butt-monkey – than swap spit with yours truly.

But I like skipping and singing.

It's maybe even my favorite.

There is no one out on the streets at the crack of ass, so I let loose with a couple of verses and suddenly I'm off to see the wizard in my mind. I'm a freak. True. But it ain't like I'm hurting anybody, and Bobby Big Boy gets a big bang out of the fantasy too, I know because the very second I start singing and skipping he goes mad, jumping like some tiny furry ballerina. And BBB can JUMP – like

– three feet into the air, which is pretty good considering that he is only maybe twelve little inches tall.

And then I'm at Ricky's, so I key into the back door, using my very own key that Donna made for me a while back.

By the refrigerator, BBB has a little setup – two bowls that are Phillies red, because Ricky likes the Philadelphia Phillies and so does Donna. Donna spoils B3 with the wet stuff in cans. No dry crap for him. I feed my pup and he eats merrily, his little tail going like a frickin' windshield wiper.

Next I unload the dishwasher, which doesn't take all that long.

Today is omelet day, so I crack a half-dozen or so eggs into a big old silver bowl, add milk, and then whisk the hell out of it all. I find tomatoes and mushrooms and a red pepper in the vegetable drawer, so I chop that hooey up like a pro, using one of Donna's super expensive knives and a thick-ass chopping board.

All those sliced veggies go into my silver bowl.

I add pepper, salt, a dash of hot sauce, and a shot of tequila from the liquor cabinet, which is my newest secret omelet ingredient. When it comes to cooking, I can get quite loopy. The alcohol will get cooked out, and it's only a single shot split between three servings, so no worries about getting drunk before school or anything like that.

I spray the frying pan with Pam, and then let it get good and hot, while I halve oranges and put Donna's automatic juicer to use.

Bobby Big Boy has finished his breakfast and is lying on his back in the middle of the kitchen floor so that his tiny legs are in the air and I can see he has a stiffy, which is gross. But I don't want him to feel self-conscious, especially since lying on his back with a full belly is his second favorite, next to pissing, so I pretend I do not notice.

It takes three to four oranges to make a tiny glass of juice, and I end up using twelve, just so Ricky, Donna, and I will get all the vitamin C we need to fight frickin' colds and whatnot.

The pan is not quite hot enough yet, so I retrieve the newspaper from the driveway, remove the plastic wrapper, and put the paper on Donna's seat.

I set the table and put on coffee.

The pan is popping now so I pour some omelet jizz onto the metal and let it spread out into a perfect O.

When it gets hard enough, I fold over the yellow O into a D and flip it a few times, until the outside gets golden brown.

'Amber, someday you really have to let me cook for you. I'm getting to feel like Thomas Jefferson every time I come down into my kitchen and see you slaving away. You're robbing me of all my Mom-ness and making me feel like writing some sort of proclamation or something.'

I just smile dumbly at Donna and shake my head – spatula in hand – like a moron.

Donna is my hero – plain and simple.

Sometimes, when she is being extra cool, I can do little more than marvel at her.

I admire Donna more than anyone.

I want to be Donna.

She grew up on the other side of the tracks, as they say. Her father was a truck driver, her mother died of cancer when she was seven, but she kicked butt in school and got a scholarship to Bryn Mawr College, which is a school for women who do not need a man to take care of them. She kicked butt at Bryn Mawr, earning a scholarship to Harvard Law School, where she became a lawyer. She wanted to have a child but not a husband, so she purchased some sperm and had Ricky, who turned out to be autistic, which did not freak her out at all, even though the sperm was supposedly screened for potential birth defects or something like that. She loves the hooey out of Ricky, and will kick your butt if you mess with her boy.

Donna is model tall with naturally blond shoulder-length hair. She wears these very cool business suits that are sexy in a serious womanly way, and she sports these killer heels every day. Men must seriously dig her, I'm sure. She drives a black Mercedes SUV that can fit all five members of the Franks Freak Force Federation – which is one of the awesome team names me and my closest friends, my boys, call ourselves – we all fit in the SUV if we put Chad on someone's lap, and Donna is always carting us around, because she digs freaky teenagers like me and the rest of The Five.

Ever since I first made friends with Ricky back in elementary school, she has let me call her Donna, and she is always doing cool things for me, like buying Bobby Big Boy food and letting him crash in her home when I am at school, even after he ripped up her leather couch, because he gets separation anxiety when I'm not around.

Plus, I used to steal her makeup, when I first went through puberty and started feeling the need to look pretty, and Donna wears – like – only the most expensive department store hooey too. I'm not proud of stealing her stuff, but one day when I was – like – fourteen, I went into her bathroom looking to score some makeup, and when I opened the medicine cabinet, there was a little sign that read 'Amber's Shelf', and on it were all the top makeup brands that she wears. Brand-new gear everywhere. I felt so guilty, I started sobbing in the bathroom, and when Donna heard me, she actually came in and hugged me. I held on to her for at least ten minutes, I felt so shameful. When I stopped crying, she looked me in the eyes and said, 'If you ever need something, just ask. Okay?'

That was it.

No reprimand.

No threats to tell my mother.

No guilt trip.

I've never stolen anything since – not even a piece of paper from school – and never will ever again, no matter how bad things get. Word.

As I finish cooking the last omelet, Donna scans

through the business section of the paper and mumbles stuff about all her stocks shitting the bed.

I marvel at her – a woman with stocks and business suits and her own house. And then, I'm secretly wishing that she were my mother, which I realize is a terrible thing to wish, but I can't help it.

'Amber Appleton uses hot sauce in her omelet. Yes. She likes to cook omelets on Tuesday mornings. Yes. Amber Appleton is very pretty and I would like to kiss her under the apple tree because she is Amber Apple-TON! Yes.'

'Good morning, Ricky,' I say to my friend, who is wearing his Tuesday Chase Utley home jersey – number 26.

'Amber Appleton is going to take Ricky Roberts out of Ricky Roberts' house tonight but he doesn't know where and Mommy Roberts will not tell him. Mommy Roberts will not tell him where. Yes!'

'We're going to do a mission tonight. Remember?' I say to the now-seated Ricky while placing an omelet in front of him. 'And when the Franks Freak Force Federation does a mission, how does Ricky Roberts receive information?'

'Ricky Roberts receives information on a need-to-know basis. Need to know. Yes,' Ricky says, and then begins eating his omelet. 'Need-to-know basis.'

We can't tell Ricky secret hooey, because he says whatever he thinks, and therefore can't keep a secret to save his life.

I remove a plate from the oven and place it in front of Donna. 'Can you still make it tonight?' I ask her.

From behind the business section, she says, 'As your attorney, I advise you to videotape the proceedings.'

'But we don't have a—'

'As your attorney, I have taken the liberty of securing a video camera and will be personally documenting everything that takes place tonight.' She drops the paper and looks into my eyes. 'Just make sure your boys know their lines. I'm counting on you to make this mission successful, because you're the leader of The Five, right?'

Donna winks at me and I almost crap my pants as she samples my omelet.

'Does this have tequila in it?' Donna asks.

I nod once and swallow.

'Nice. Coffee?'

I all but run to the coffeemaker and pour Donna a large cup. She drinks it black.

'Thanks,' she says. 'Are you not eating?'

'Can I use your bathroom first?'

Donna nods once and disappears behind the business section again.

Upstairs, in the bathroom, I strip down quickly, brush my teeth with the toothbrush stored permanently on Amber's Shelf, floss, use mouthwash, and then I'm in the shower washing my hair, using Donna's expensive conditioner, trying to keep my long black hair shiny. I do this all super quickly, so I don't use too much of Donna's hot

30

water, because hot water costs money. I towel off, use the deodorant and perfume and makeup that Donna buys for me, redress, and then return to the kitchen, where BBB has fallen asleep on the little braided mat in front of the sink.

My hair is soaking wet, but neither Ricky nor Donna say a word about my needing to use their shower. Ricky is used to my using his place as a second home, and Donna is too classy to bring up the sore subject of my needing to freeload off her.

I wolf down my omelet and then do all the dishes and clean up the kitchen while Donna reads the rest of the paper and Ricky does math equations in his workbook. He is a frickin' math genius. I take BBB out for one last pee, and then I kiss him goodbye just before I lock him up in his room, which is an unused first-floor bedroom with a doggie bed, tons of chew toys, a water dish, and even a radio, which we keep on the classical station to calm B Thrice's nerves. (B3 loves Chopin. I know because my pup starts jumping in the air like a maniac every time some Chopin-playing dude tickles that piano.) Just like every other morning, BBB starts crying and scratching at the door as soon as it's shut, which breaks my heart and makes me feel bad about Donna's door getting all clawed up, even though she says she doesn't give a crap about that room and has tons of money for buying new doors or whatever.

We hop into her Mercedes – heated leather seats, which are pretty killer. True? True. We rock out to

Dinosaur Jr, which is an obscure indie band of olden days. Donna digs unheard-of bands like Dinosaur Jr. She even has cool taste in music. We listen to 'Feel The Pain' three times, because Ricky likes that one, and then we are at Childress Public High School, so Donna shuts off the tunes.

'Amber, what do you have after school today?'

'The Korean Divas for Christ at three thirty.'

'You can get Ricky home first?'

'No worries.'

'Ricky, are you going to be good today?'

'Yeah-ssssss,' Ricky says in his goofiest robot voice.

'Are you going to repeat dirty words?' Donna asks.

'Nooooooooooooooo!'

'What happens if you do?'

'Amber Appleton will not go to prom with Ricky Roberts. Yes.'

'That's right. So behave your little behind. Be the gentleman I know you are.' To me, Donna says, 'Tell Franks Freak Force Federation that we meet at my house at seven sharp. I'm not picking all of their little butts up individually, because I'm in court all day – murder trial. But if they pull off the mission without screwing up too badly, we're going to Friendly's afterward.'

'Yes, ma'am,' I say, like a moron.

'Friendly's. Reese's Pieces Sundae. Yes,' Ricky says.

'All right. I have to get to the courthouse. Kisses and then out.'

Ricky kisses his mother as I hop out of the backseat and onto the sidewalk. Ricky gets out of the Mercedes, slams the door too hard, and then says, 'Going to play Halo 3 with Mr Jonathan Franks! Yes! Halo 3.'

THREE

Maybe you want to know how The Five came to exist?
True?

History of The Five.

It all began when Jared and I failed fifth grade.

Well, neither of us technically failed, but we were both
held back, dropped into Chad's, Ricky's, and Ty's class.
Jared – because he used to have this awful stutter back in
the day and could hardly complete a frickin' sentence
without repeating just about every syllable a bazillion
times. Word. And me – I was held back because I missed
too many days of school, even though I technically passed
all of my tests when I eventually took them. If you miss
so many days, you automatically get held back, or at least
that's what I was told. The reason I missed so many days
of school was because we were living with Good Boyfriend
Gerald at the time, who was Mom's best pick by far, if
you ask me.

GBG was a truck driver and used to make these long

hauls across the country, and Mom used to go nuts for road trips, so whenever she didn't want to be left alone without GBG, she'd have one of the bus driving subs cover her route for a week or so and she'd let me skip school to ride across the country with GBG in his big old red tractor-trailer truck, which he called Melissa. Since GBG was making these trips all the time, I missed tons of school.

When we'd head west, we would drive right through the night, hardly ever stopping, because Good Boyfriend Gerald got paid more if he got the load there early. We'd all sit in his truck, Mom in the middle, holding both of our hands, and it was fun to drive on the highways of America like that, sorta like a family. GBG was pretty damn old and didn't ever say much, but he had a kind, wrinkly face – he loved to smile, and even though he was really big and was rough-looking with a gray bushy beard, he was the type of guy you trust right away, sorta like Santa Claus or something like that.

After he'd drop his load off, we'd drive back east a little more leisurely, and GBG used to take us to see cool stuff too. The best thing he ever showed us was the Grand Canyon. Word. We went there in December when there was snow all around the edge, and looking down into that big beautiful gap in the earth was sorta like a spiritual experience for me. I remember that there were so many shades of brown and tan inside that majestic hole that it didn't even look real. And the clouds – those were like looking at something too beautiful, like it actually hurt your eyes to see something so gorgeous. I wanted to hike down into that canyon, and will one day – word – but Mom was against it, saying that it wasn't safe in the winter, even though tons of other people were doing it with huge back-packs and spikes strapped onto their boots. Hard-core.

GBG paid for a hotel in Arizona, and after eating dinner at this little greasy diner of sorts, Mom and I went for a walk while GBG took a shower in the hotel room, because he never could shower if I was in the room, saying it wasn't proper, which was sorta noble of him, like he was a knight from olden times. I remember walking, holding hands with my mom in this dumpy little town, and once we got away from the main drag, once we walked far enough down this empty road, my mom told me to look up.

Holding her hand, I tilted my head back and then watched my gray breath climb up toward a billion stars. Tiny blue diamonds the color of gas flames were every-where. It was *so* beautiful. My mom and I just stood there in the road looking up for – like – forever. And looking up at winter stars in Arizona – this is Amber-and-her-mom moment number five. It was very cold, but I didn't care. I had never seen so many stars – and out in the open, with no one else around, I remember praying to JC, thanking him for the stars and my mom and that moment and for sending us GBG so that we could see things like the Grand Canyon, which is one of God's masterpieces if you ask me. It was a nice moment. Word.

That winter we took a lot of trips like that with GBG, who never said much but seemed to like having us around. I really thought he was going to be the one for Mom – the one who would make her an honest woman. But then one day at the end of the school year, GBG went on one of his trucking runs and simply didn't come home. Mom held out hope for weeks, saying he would be back, but then the landlord visited us, saying that the rent hadn't been paid for two months, and soon after that Mom and I moved in with yet another one of her boyfriends – Crazy Craig, whom I don't even want to talk about, that's how crazy he was – and GBG was nothing but a memory.

I often wonder what happened to GBG, the silent abandoning one who got away.

The second week of fifth grade, take two, I was removed from class by a strange woman who wore a frilly blouse. In the hallway, the woman said, 'I'm Mrs Pohlson. I'm not a teacher, but a social skills coach, and I'd like to invite you to join a very special club.'

'Am I in trouble?' I asked her, because it seemed like Mrs Pohlson might be lying to me.

'No. Why would you think that? Did you do something wrong?'

'You don't have to do something wrong to be in trouble,' I told her.

She nodded appreciatively and led me to a small room at the end of the hall that had no windows and sorta reminded me of a big closet. Inside the room was a round table that took up almost all of the space, and seated around the table were four boys, the very boys that would eventually become *my* boys – Franks Freak Force Federation.

None of them said anything to me when I sat down at the table and said, 'Hello.'

'Boys, this is your classmate, Amber Appleton. Don't you want to say hello to her?' Mrs Pohlson said.

'Ricky Roberts says hello to Amber Appleton. Hello. Yes.'

'H-h-h-h-el-el-o.'

'Hi, Amber,' said the boy in the wheelchair.

'Hey,' said the black kid.

'This is Ty, Jared, Chad, and Ricky. All classmates of yours, although they are in the other two fifth grade classes. We'd like you to join our club,' Mrs Pohlson said.

The only black kid in town. The kid who couldn't speak properly. The tiny wheelchair kid with a big head. The retarded kid (I didn't know what autism was back then). And suddenly me. I wasn't so smart back in the day, but even I knew that I'd landed squarely in Club Freak. I wasn't all that upset about being admitted into Club Freak, because I was a freak too, and I sorta knew it – word – but I was worried that there would be punishments, like extra homework.

'What sorta club is this?' I asked.

'We play board games twice a week in this room,' Mrs Pohlson answered.

'Why?' I asked, and then looked around at the boys

who were all looking at their laps. 'Won't we get in trouble for missing class?'

'Don't you like board games? We can play Monopoly, Scrabble, Life.'

'Why would you take us out of class just so we can play games?' I asked.

'Well,' Mrs Pohlson said, 'we also practice speaking properly and interacting appropriately with our friends.'

'Interacting?'

'Playing.'

'So this is a club where we learn to play games with each other?'

'Kind of,' Mrs Pohlson said. 'Yes.'

All through elementary and junior high school Mrs Pohlson took the five of us out of class twice a week. Sometimes we played board games, sometimes we read books aloud, and sometimes we just practiced having conversations with each other.

I began to notice that The Five hardly talked outside of Mrs Pohlson's room – but when we were there, we sorta talked a lot, or at least more than we did in the lunchroom or gym or in the schoolyard, maybe because there weren't so many other people to compete with for talking time. I began to really like going to Mrs Pohlson's room, and it wasn't long before our parents were scheduling after-school and weekend events for The Five. Soon I was over at my boys' houses, like, all the time, and it was like we had been friends since birth. We got tight quick. Word. Suddenly I sorta had four brothers and all these extra parents looking after me. Suddenly, I had Donna too.

Eventually, Jared stopped stuttering, but nothing else major happened through Mrs Pohlson's intervention – except that we all became best friends.

FOUR

Almost magically, just when we had to leave Mrs Pohlson, our group social sessions, and the elementary/junior high building behind, Franks was hired to teach marketing at CPHS, so he was sorta like a freshman too (only a teacher freshman) when we started high school, which is exactly when me and The Five first started hanging with Franks. Jared and I were in his marketing class, and because Franks was so cool, allowing us to play video games during class and whatnot, we were soon bringing the rest of The Five to his classroom before school and during lunch. The rest is history, as they say.

Franks' windowless classroom is in the basement of our high school, and you can access his room from outside by descending down into the earth via a set of old concrete stairs, and then knocking on a metal door seven times. Three quick knocks. Two slow, and then two fast. This lets Franks or whoever is inside know that a Marketing Club member is on the other side of the door. There are only five Childress Public High School MC members, and all five just happen to belong to Franks Freak Force Federation as well.

After Ricky knocks, we back up two stairs. Two seconds later, Jared kicks open the door, which doesn't have a knob, but a silver bar that opens it, and then he sprints back to his seat behind one of the six televisions set up high on roller stands – every one of them connected to an Xbox and each Xbox connected to the rest via a crazy web of chords. Ty and Jared are both seated behind the television closest to the outside door – eyes glued to the ass-kicking alien action on the screen. On the other side of the room Franks is sitting next to Chad's super robotic wheelchair, which we call Das Boot, even though we don't even know what the hell *Das Boot* means exactly. All four of them are holding controllers and are trying to kill each other's spacemen in a virtual world that the televisions bring to their brains.

Ricky sits down at a third television set and turns on a third Xbox. 'Ricky Roberts wants Ty Hendrix and Jared Fox to die so that Ricky Roberts can enter into the Halo 3 game and join Mr Jonathan Franks' team, because Mr Jonathan Franks is Ricky Roberts' very favorite teacher. Yes.'

'Your wish is my command,' Franks says. And then something happens in the virtual world that makes Jared and Ty moan and hold their heads.

Chad and Franks are high-fiving now, and Ricky is

clicking buttons on his controller, entering into the virtual world.

I know my window is tiny, because once the game starts my boys are gone, so I say, 'Franks, we doing a Marketing Club announcement today?'

Marketing Club is basically an extension of Franks' marketing classes. Only once a year we compete against other schools in these debates about marketing strategies and also we do these marketing presentations in front of judges for points. My boys and even Franks wear suits to the competitions and I usually wear one of Donna's killer business skirt suits. Pretty wild stuff. If you get enough points, you can win and go on to the national competition. We've never made it past regionals.

Franks is always trying to get more people to join MC, because his job is always on the line when it comes to district budget cuts. His marketing classes are electives, and while they are usually full – because he teaches classes like Marketing Video Games, Make and Market Your Own Movie, and my personal favorite, The Business End of the Rap Game – he's not exactly a PTA favorite, nor do many of the Childress parents take him all that seriously.

Franks is maybe only five-six, he weighs close to three hundred pounds, and he hasn't cut his hair in years – sporting the gray ponytail look. To make matters worse, he wears these little photosensitive glasses that make him look sorta like a cross between Buddha and Lennon.

(John – like, of The Beatles – not to be confused with that Russian dude, Vlad.)

'You write it, and I'll read it,' Franks says, his eyes locked onto the screen ready to do space battle with teenage boys.

'Cool,' I say, sitting down at Franks' teacher desk near the whiteboard.

'You can have half of my Sausage Egg McMuffin. It's in drawer number two,' Franks says to me. 'I'm watching my figure. And the top drawer is filled with peanut M&Ms, as always.'

'Donna fed me,' I tell Franks.

'Cool,' he says.

Aside from the occasional curse words muttered and the post-killing taunting, it's easy to write when the boys are playing Halo 3, because the game distracts them and keeps them all pretty quiet.

Ricky never kills anyone in the game, and no one kills him, because he is diagnosed with autism and just likes running around in the virtual world, stimming out. And I have to say I love that my boys are cool with this – I love their letting Ricky play Halo 3 in his own pacifistic way. My boys are good people. Word.

So I write up the ad for Marketing Club, trying to make Franks sound hip, but also trying to write something that he won't read over the morning announcements, because I've never stumped him yet. There is an art to this, because I know he isn't going to read curse words or anything like that, so writing profanity into the ad would just be cheap and pointless and the opposite of urbane.

I'm halfway through the writing of the ad when I look up at the big-framed picture on Franks' desk. His little mean-looking redheaded wife is on the beach surrounded by Franks' six little redheaded children. Franks' head is sticking out of the sand by their feet – big head, little glasses. They buried him to the neck and then had someone snap the photo. I think about what would happen to Franks' kids – who are all less than ten years old – if he got canned.

'Yo, Franks!' I say, but he doesn't answer me, because he is playing the dumb video game, but I know he hears me, so I say, 'You going to the school board meeting tonight?'

Silence.

'Franks?'

The sound of buttons being pushed rapidly by boy thumbs.

'FRANKS!'

'It's of this world,' Franks says, which is what he says about everything. He means that he only worries about what will happen after this world, when God takes him to heaven, because he's a Catholic like me, and he has a super faith in JC.

Now I have faith in JC too, but I also know what it's like to live on a school bus.

'Maybe you should go, Franks. Think of your children,

bro,' I say, because tonight's when they are deciding whether to cut the marketing department's funding and if they do that, Franks will lose his job at the end of the year. But no worries. Me and The Five are not going to let that happen. We have a killer plan. We're doing a mission.

My boys, all except Ricky, shoot me nervous glances, because they don't want Franks to know what we are doing for him – they prefer to be anonymous do-gooders. So I flash them a thumbs-up to reassure them I know what the hell I'm doing.

'My family's never missed a meal,' Franks says, like a man who has never missed a meal, because he doesn't know what it's like to be homeless. But it's all good in the hood, because I'm not going to let any bad hooey happen to Franks or his redheaded kids.

'Can I give you a hug today, Franks?' I say, because I've always wanted to hug Franks ever since we met in his The Art of Marketing Junk Food class.

'Against school policy,' he says.

'Someday, I'm going to give you a big old hug. Teddy bear-style.'

'Maybe when you graduate,' he says just as Ty and Jared start moaning again. 'Undefeated Halo 3 champs! Our streak is still alive, brother!'

From his wheelchair, Chad says, 'Who's your poppa?'

Chad and Franks slap hands and then touch elbows before slapping hands again. Man stuff.

Just as I finish the last line of the MC ad, the five-minute warning bell sounds, so I stand by the door and, as they exit, I hand each one of my boys a piece of paper folded into a swan – origami style. Inside all of the swans are coded instructions regarding where to meet and at what time, plus their individual speeches for tonight, written by yours truly. Jared made up our code two years back and we all have it memorized. (It's just each letter plus 1, so that *A*s are written as *B*s and *B*s are written as *C*s and so forth. Not overly secure, but it stumps most of the morons in our school. True.) And as they walk through Franks' door, I give each of my boys a pat on the butt too, like I am a football coach or something. The pat on the butt makes my boys blush and smile. I have to pinch Chad on the cheek because he's in a motorized wheelchair and all, but I get him blushing too.

'Ricky Roberts wants a paper swan-coded message like everyone else in the—'

'How does Ricky Roberts receive information?' I ask him.

'On a need-to-know basis. Yes.'

'You only have five minutes to get to homeroom,' I say, and then Ricky is off.

Back inside of his lair, I hand Franks the Marketing Club ad and say, 'Read that over the loudspeaker – if you dare.'

'Cool,' Franks says with a smile.

'Hug?'

'Homeroom,' Franks says, raising his chubby hand.

I slap his red palm, and then I'm on my way to homeroom.

'Rub-a-dub-dub, it's Marketing Club! What's the rub, bub? Nada. MC for real, with plenty of zeal – and that's the appeal! Do you have what it takes – to slake – the growing desire for marketing and advertising fo' hire? We meet in the basement every day, hey, so what do you say? Drop on down, give Franks a pound. Become a Marketing Club man or woman today. Peace out, homies! And keep hope alive!'

Sitting in homeroom, I smile to myself. Franks read my announcement verbatim, just like he promised. He's an honorable man, a man of his word, which is rare in this world, or at least that's what I've observed after seventeen trips around the flaming ball in the sky. (That's the sun, sucka!) Everyone around me is talking and totally not paying any attention to the announcements; not even my homeroom teacher, Mrs Lindsay, listens or gives a crap, but I know that there are at least four teenage boys sitting in homerooms hysterically laughing at my advertisement and Franks' awesome delivery – and I know that it might be the only laugh they get today. Franks Freak Force Federation will get a little fuel from this, and maybe that will be enough for them to make it through the school day. 'Keep hope alive.' I'm pretty sure Jesse Jackson said that when he was running for president back in the 80s.

Yeah, we learned that hip catchphrase in my US History II class a few months ago.

The day passes uneventfully – boring Spanish III, lame-ass gym, boring pre-calc, boring chemistry – and since Mondays and Tuesdays are Ricky's socialization days, we don't eat our lunch in Franks' room, but in the cafeteria, because the special education department thinks that Ricky should interact with the student body more. Great idea, special education people who have no idea how evil the student body can be to special people like Ricky Roberts.

When I'm in the lunch line, watching over Ricky, protecting my boy, Lex Pinkston elbows me in the back and coughs out a disgusting single syllable word for a woman, which I'm not even going to repeat. He pretends to cover his mouth and cough, because he is a moron, but it is clear that he is calling me this worst of all words, so I say, 'Like you'd even know what one was.'

'I've seen your mom's,' Lex says, five moronic football players standing behind him. 'Everyone in this town has.'

I slap his face hard enough to turn his head – *SLAP!* – and it makes me smile, even though I'm a Catholic and JC is not down with violence.

And then Lex's hand is on his face. He cannot believe that I frickin' slapped him.

The football morons are shocked as hooey – their pieholes wide open, like their eyes.

Ricky is screaming, 'Hi! Hi! Hi! Hi!'

The lunchroom monitors show up, get between us, and

the next thing I know I'm in Prince Tony's office, waiting for him to finish some stupid phone conversation. When he finishes, he looks at me from across his battleship-size desk and says, 'What now?'

'Your quarterback called me a disgusting single-syllable word for a woman – which I'm not even going to repeat – and then implied that he had sex with my mother, so I slapped his kisser,' I say, and then add, 'Prince Tony.'

'It's Principal Fiorilli to you, young lady.'

'Come on, Prince, we're behind closed doors. Just us here,' I say to the tiny man, because he is weak and can be swayed if you flirt with him the right way – not in a sexy way, but in a father-daughter sorta way.

He turns red, and I know I have him.

'I heard you kicked him in the shin yesterday. His father called to complain and—'

'Lex Pinkston is an evil boy who—'

'I know exactly who Lex Pinkston is and his father—'

'I prayed for you last night, Prince Tony.'

'You did?' He doesn't know how to react to this one. Church and state and all. This is a public school. 'Why did you *pray* for me?'

'I pray for you every night. True.'

'Thank you,' he says, blushing again.

'When are you going to start protecting the good people of Childress Public High School?'

'What would you have me do?'

'Expel Lex Pinkston.'

'For what?'

'For being evil.'

'It's not that easy.'

'So you are admitting Lex Pinkston is evil?'

'*I said* it's not that easy.'

'Yeah, it is.'

'First, Mr Pinkston is a school board member and we have to be delicate when – *why am I explaining myself to a seventeen-year-old girl?*'

'I'm going to say one thing to you, Prince Tony, and then I'm going to walk out that door.'

I stare into his eyes, and I see him swallow once. He digs me, and he knows that Lex Pinkston needs to be kicked in the shin and slapped every so often, if only to maintain the balance of power within the student body so that evil doesn't get out of control; the boss man sees this because deep down, Prince Tony is a good man – even if he is a wimp who plays both sides of the political fence – and like Billy Budd, Prince Tony needs a Captain Vere to protect him from the evil people in the world. I fancy myself a more adroit and less dreamy, less starry Captain Vere. Captainess Appleton, at your service. Word, all you lime-suckers.

'You're a good man, Prince Tony,' I say, 'and I believe that you will eventually clean up this school and protect the common students from the selfish interests of school board members like Mr Pinkston. My money's on you, Prince Tony. *My money is on you.*'

I get up and start walking out of his office.

'You simply cannot assault students in my building, Ms Appleton. I will not endure your vigilante approach to—'

'Search your heart, Prince Tony. You know what's the right thing to do. I believe in you. And I'm praying for you. Every night.'

I walk out of his office, and his ancient wrinkly secretary Mrs Baxter – who wears the reddest lipstick I have ever seen on any woman, and looks like a patriot with blue hair and white skin – asks me, 'How'd it go in there?'

Mrs Baxter is pretty nice, and I think it's safe to say she's an Amber Appleton fan.

'I'm praying for your boss,' I tell her. 'He has the ability to turn this school around.'

'If he only had the chutzpah,' she whispers, with her hand shielding her ancient lips so that only I can see.

'Viva la revolution, Mrs Baxter,' I say as she writes me a pass, and then I jog up two flights of stairs so I can check out Doolin's Accelerated American Lit class, where I learn all about civil disobedience and that cool cat Henry David Thoreau, whom I admire a whole bunch, because he represented hard-core and even went to jail for his beliefs, which is saying something. True? True.

FIVE

Practical Life Skills class, where I work on my prom dress.

Semi-boring history, and then I'm at Ricky's locker.

'Amber Appleton slapped Lex Pinkston in THE FACE. Bad girl! Bad girl! Bad girl!'

'If you don't stop saying bad girl, I'm going to tickle you.'

'No! Ricky Roberts does NOT like to be tickled. No tickle-tickle.'

This is as close as Ricky gets to making a joke, because tickling is his favorite. I get him good under his armpits, and he doubles over and yells 'Hi! Hi! Hi!' until some bearded teacher I don't know comes out of his classroom and asks if everything is okay.

'Beautiful,' I say to the beard.

'Amber Appleton is my best friend. She makes omelets with tequila and takes me on missions and I am taking her to prom in a limousine! Yes,' Ricky says.

The beard nods once, real serious – as if Ricky told

the beard that he needed to donate a kidney to the president because it was the beard's civic duty or something – and then the beard walks back into his classroom.

Truth be told, there are a lot of teachers who are scared of Ricky, because he flips out sometimes and punches himself in the head, which can get a little intense.

As we walk to Donna's house together, Ricky counts aloud, and I enjoy the afternoon winter sun on my face.

Bobby Big Boy always pisses himself whenever we are reunited, so I pull a few paper towels from the roll, and then let him out of his room. In the tiled hallway, he circles me seven times, like he has been snorting cocaine all day, and then he pees on the floor, so I wipe up the yellow puddle and give Thrice B a kiss. He tries to slip me the tongue, but he doesn't make it into my mouth or anything.

I give Ricky a sleeve of Fig Newtons and a blue Gatorade.

He's already doing his math homework, because he frickin' loves math.

'I have to go see The KDFCs,' I tell him, but he doesn't look up from his math. 'I'll be back to cook dinner. Okay?'

'Ricky Roberts is doing math. Do not talk to Ricky Roberts when Ricky Roberts is doing math!'

'Cool,' I say, and then lock the door behind BBB and me. Ricky will do math problems forever if you let him, so no worries leaving him alone.

I take Donna's ten-speed bike from the garage and put

B3 in the little basket Donna bought for him that is attached to the handlebars. He fits perfect so that just his head sticks out. It's pretty frickin' adorable.

We are flying through the cold January air, out of town, across the tracks, and into the ghetto. There are a lot of down-and-out people in this town, and they usually stare at me when I ride my bike through.

The first time this happened, it scared me a lot, because it sorta looked like these people wanted to kill me, but I have since learned a trick.

Whenever someone looks at me like they want to stomp my face in, I now look the person in the eyes, smile really huge, wave, and say, 'Hope you're havin' a great day!' It's pretty wild, because doing this really works. If you don't believe me, try it yourself. Even the meanest-looking people will get this really stunned look on their faces, but then the smile blooms, and they usually wave back and say something nice like 'God bless you!' or 'Same to you!' It's a pretty cool trick, and maybe even a pretty killer way of life, if you are a crazy spiritual ho like me. True? True.

Today I yell, 'Hope you're havin' a great day!' eight times, and I get two 'Thanks!', one 'Jesus loves you!', two 'You go girl!'s, two 'Same to you!'s, and one 'You a sexy bike girl! Ride on, girl, ride on,' which made me laugh, because the man who yelled this had to be at least ninety-seven.

And then I'm at the Korean Catholic Church, which

is an old shoe store turned house of God, and sits nestled between a McDonald's and a liquor store. In his penguin suit, Father Chee is waiting outside for me, because the men in front of the liquor store sometimes say bad things to me, and the 'Hope you're havin' a great day!' trick doesn't always work on them so well.

Technically, I got hooked up with Father Chee through my high school guidance counselor, who says I have to do a load of community service if I want to get into Bryn Mawr College, which is where I want to study English, because you can go to law school if you major in English and do really well at Bryn Mawr College. That's what Donna did anyway. But to tell you the truth, I don't really give a crap anymore about fulfilling the community service requirements, which are of this world, as Franks likes to say. I still want to go to Bryn Mawr and all, but doing what I do with Father Chee has become part of my religious practice, which I realize might sound truly whack to some, but I believe in what FC and I do, like – for real. Word. And I had been praying for a chance to make a difference in the lives of people who needed it most, because that's really all I want to do with my life – help people who need it, just like JC told us to do.

About a year back, Father Chee contacted the high school looking for someone to teach English to the women in his church who wanted to learn. At first, I tried to simply straight-up teach them vocab and grammar and whatnot, but it was so boring and depressing for the women that I had to think up a killer alternative or quit. Lucky for FC's church members, I'm pretty good at thinking up killer hooey. Also, Father Chee and I work well together – we're an awesome team – and ever since I implemented my new teaching technique, my enrollment has more than doubled.

Father Chee holds open the front door and I ride Donna's bike right into the church.

My Man of God locks the door behind us, which is sorta weird since it's a church and all.

'Hello, Bobby Big Boy,' Father Chee says, patting 3B on the head. Triple B licks Father's hand, because they are boys, and then FC is pulling BBB out of the basket so that they can get a man hug in, which is cool, because B Thrice loves to hug Men of God.

My dog is Catholic. And if you say dogs don't have a soul and therefore don't go to heaven, I will slap your face silly. Word.

Maybe – before I get into the story of The Korean Divas for Christ and Father Chee – you might want to know how I became a Catholic and a crazy-serious religious person?

Well, the only thing my father, Bob, left behind for me when he took off was this series of children's books called Jesus Was a Rock Star. They were these big picture books for kids – twelve in the series – and each was about one of the killer adventures Jesus had on earth, how Jesus rocked the world and then got crucified for being so cool.

These books were pretty awesome because Jesus was always doing miracles like turning water to wine and walking on water and even bringing people back from the dead, which is definitely a pretty killer thing to do. Also, in the pictures, Jesus was very handsome (sorta like Jack White of the White Stripes) with His long rock-star hair. JC always had an entourage around Him, He never freaked out when people let Him down or things went wrong – JC was always so very cool – and He loved everyone and went around saving people like Mom and me, people everyone else had already given up on.

My favorite Jesus adventure was when He stopped the crowd from stoning a hooker. You probably know that one already, but all these mean men were actually going to throw rocks at the woman's head until her skull caved in and she was dead, but Jesus did this Jedi-mind-trick thing and just wrote words in the sand until the mean men noticed and asked what the hell JC was doing. Then – so cool, like a rock star – Jesus says that the person without any sin can throw the first rock at the woman. And then the men start to feel guilty and freak out and leave – which is the best part. Jesus didn't even have to raise His voice, let alone throw any fists. Who would have thought that writing words in the sand would work? And then JC doesn't even yell at the woman for having too much sex. He just saves her and tells her to live a good life, which is pretty cool of Jesus. No guilt trip or anything.

I still have my Jesus Was a Rock Star books, and the

pages are all worn out from my reading them so many times. True.

My mom never really dug Jesus too much, maybe because my dad was big on JC and he broke Mom's heart – shattered it – leaving her all alone with newborn me and an endless train of loser boyfriends.

So Mom never took me to church or anything like that.

But when I was in eighth grade, Ty was always complaining about his mom making him attend these religious classes about Jesus so that he could join the Catholic Church and avoid getting sent to hell. I asked if I could go with him, and this excited Mrs Hendrix very much. So I started attending Jesus class with Ty at St Dymphna's, which is this big old church with killer stained-glass windows, ancient wooden pews full of comfy red cushions, and a massive organ that can blast your eardrums until you go deaf – St Dymphna's pretty much has the works.

Only the priest there – Father Johns – told the Jesus stories all wrong. Father Johns was always going on and on about how Jesus was going to be disappointed in us if we sinned or didn't do enough charity, and the way he talked about JC made the Son of God seem more like a mean, pissy old lady than a rock star. But the one thing that really hit home with me was Father Johns telling us that we would go to hell if we didn't join the Catholic Church, do enough charity work, and live a good life.

That bit sorta scared me and made me want to join for real.

Needless to say, I was baptized, did the confession thing, had my First Communion with all of these little kids whose parents were good Catholics and therefore didn't let their sons and daughters get to middle school before they have their First Communion, and then Ty and I joined the church as his parents watched all proud. Mrs Hendrix was my sponsor – and she even bought me a white dress and white shoes for the big day. I took Mary for my confirmation name – not too original, I admit – and then I went to a big party at the Hendrix house, where Ty's relatives actually gave me presents simply because I was an official Catholic now.

Mom didn't come to see me baptized, nor when I became a member of the church – probably because of my religious dad leaving her.

For a year or so, I went to church with the Hendrix family every week, but then I just stopped going for some reason. I think it was because the priest kept on messing up the Jesus stories – talking about Jesus as if he were this boring arrogant person who didn't rock, which we all know is not the case. I didn't feel anything when I went to church, and I could read about Jesus at home and pray anywhere, so I just stopped going to Mass. I think I really let Ty's mom down, but religion and JC aren't for impressing people's moms. True.

I was going to try another church to see if they talked

about Jesus any differently, but then I met Father Chee – and instantly, I knew that I had found my priest for life. Word. FC rocks, just like JC.

Inside Father Chee's church, there is a small room where you can hang your coat, which is where I park Donna's bike, and then there is the sanctuary. A big crucifix hangs front and center over a little altar and a simple podium. The walls are cinder blocks painted puke yellow, and there are no windows and no pews, but only long white lightbulbs in the ceiling – the kind that look like lightsabers – and rows of flesh-colored fold-up chairs, which are currently occupied by a dozen or so Korean women, all of whom jump up and start smiling just as soon as I walk into the church.

I don't want to brag, but I'm sorta like a rock star to these people.

The first thing that happens whenever I enter The Korean Catholic Church:

Every single one of The KDFCs gives me a big old hug and then they speak their homework sentence in English. I give them a prompt at the end of each class, which I copy down a dozen or so times because I don't have access to a photocopy machine. Father Chee usually explains the prompt in Korean, which is sorta like cheating, but it's also good because we want The KDFCs to do the assignment so that their English will improve and they can start branching out into America and whatnot.

Last week they all failed to do the assignment correctly.

I had asked them to state what they would most like to do in the world and to describe how doing it would make them feel, using one killer adjective. But all of these kind-hearted women – every single one – said what they would like to do for their husband or their children or their parents.

'I would like to buy a big house for my son or daughter.'

'I would like to buy my husband an expensive car.'

'I would like to send my nice parents to Hawaii.'

So I failed them all and told The KDFCs that they had to use better adjectives and say what they wanted for *themselves*, because having dreams for yourself is totally American, and if they were going to live in America, they needed to think like American women.

So I say, 'Na Yung, did you do your homework?'

'Yes, Amber,' Na Yung says.

'And?'

Na Yung, who is old enough to be my mom, gets all nervous whenever she is speaking English around me, which is why I called on her first, so she can get it over with and relax.

'I would like see live handsome movie star in Hollywood – like *delicious* men I see in photo American magazine.'

'Nice job,' I tell Na Yung. 'Very American! Good pronunciation and delicious is truly a killer adjective! A-plus. How about you, Sun?'

'I dream to fly in beautiful fat *rotund* air balloon so hair will blow warmest behind my ear.'

'That's *damn* good, Sun. Rotund is *very* good. I'd like to fly in a beautiful fat rotund air balloon too. That would be truly killer.'

As I listen to the dreams of all the Korean women present, Father Chee smiles at me so that I can see every one of his teeth. I can tell he really really digs me, in a non-sexual good-guy priest sorta way. Maybe he wishes I were his daughter, because he's not allowed to make a daughter for himself. He would be a cool dad.

The KDFCs love it when I praise their English, and you can tell that they really dig expressing themselves in my class too, which is pretty cool. I'm having a good time listening to their dreams, but then suddenly everyone has spoken and The Korean Divas for Christ are lining up in two rows by the altar – songbooks in hand – so eagerly, because they pretty much come for the soul singing. FC and I know that they like singing better than learning English, which is why we invented this awesome alternative class in the first place.

'Shall we?' Father Chee says, offering his arm like a frickin' gentleman.

Just like always, he walks me arm-in-arm to the front of the church, as if he were about to give me away on my wedding day.

When I am in position, Father Chee bows to me once, and then takes his place at the old beat-up piano to my left, opening his songbook to the number we always start with.

'Okay, ladies,' I say. 'What do we need to work on this week?'

Back when I first started teaching, I let each one of The Korean Divas for Christ choose an English language name the way my Spanish teacher let us pick Spanish names back in Spanish I. (I went with Juanita.) After I started English the fun way, I had each one of The KDFCs take the name of a famous R & B singer.

Hye Min – who goes by Tina – raises her hand, so I nod in her direction. She says, 'A selling the word.'

'That's right, Tina. You need to sell the frickin' words. And how do we do that, ladies?'

Front-and-center Kyung Ah – aka Diana – raises her hand, and when I nod at her, she says, 'Hips and the hands.'

'It's all about the hips and hands. And?'

A back row exceptionally tall woman named Sueng Hee – we call her Beyoncé – yells out, 'Shoulder dips!' without my calling on her, which sorta pisses me off, because I find her outburst threatening to my authority, but I appreciate the unbridled enthusiasm, so I let it slide.

'Shoulder dips. *And*?'

The oldest KDFC, a wrinkly grandmother we know as Ella, waves at me, so I point at her.

'The souls clap,' she says.

'The super-duper soul clap. That's right,' I say, and then start clapping slowly, soulfully.

All of The KDFCs follow suit, because they are all frickin' pros.

So I add a shoulder dip and a step to the right – clap!

The KDFCs don't miss a beat and move with me.

Shoulder dip, and a step to the left – clap!

We repeat this for a few times, and then I yell, 'Work those hips, ladies! Work what God gave you – meaning yo' apple-bottom booties!'

So we all let our booties snap with our heads.

Left – slide – clap!

Right – slide – clap!

When we are nice and warmed up, I yell, 'Hit those keys, Chee!'

Father starts playing piano, and then The KDFCs are rocking 'You Can't Hurry Love' by The Supremes. The way they sing sounds very staccato, because they are Korean and don't know English all that well, but they sell the song with the moves I gave them, and I have to say that I am proud of these chippies today, because they are sorta rocking my socks off.

Before we all got so damn good at soul singing, Father had the church buy us twenty copies of *The Supremes Complete Songbook* and then – using Korean-English dictionaries – the Korean Divas for Christ and I translated all the songs, writing the Korean under the English, so that my students would know what the hell they were singing. Then we worked on pronunciation, and then finally, selling the songs onstage.

I didn't know that Father Chee could play piano when I thought up the singing-to-learn-English idea, but on the day that we were first going to start singing, the piano magically showed up in the church. When I asked him where the piano came from, Father Chee said that God had put it there. When I asked him who was going to play the piano, Chee said God would play through Father Chee's fingers. Maybe some corny hooey to you, but I like the way Chee keeps God magical, sorta like Santa Claus when you are a kid. More priests should take this approach, because there is a frickin' reason why Santa is more popular than Jesus nowadays.

I take The KDFCs through 'I Hear a Symphony', 'Stop! In the Name of Love', 'Baby Love', 'You Keep Me Hangin' On', and a few other classics, before we make the power circle, which is when all the women put arms around each other's shoulders so that we are all linked up in a super-powerful woman circle, and then I yell some empowering hooey I made up a while back.

'What are we?' I yell.

'Strong!' The KDFCs yell back.

'Who are we?'

'The Korean Divas for Christ!'

'Who loves us?'

'JC!'

'Who wants us to be happy?'

'God!'

'Who rocks?'

'The Korean Divas for Christ!'

'Who are the best Korean soul singers in the world?'

'The Korean Divas for Christ!'

'Hell yeah?'

'Hell yeah!'

'HELL YEAH?'

'HELL YEAH!'

And then I break off and run around the inside of the power circle giving each Korean Diva a super high five, which is a two-handed slap above the head. The KDFCs go crazy for this sorta pumped-up ending. They like to hug me before I go, and since I really dig hugs, I go wild with the hugging too. Every KDFC gets a big old hug from me, which takes like ten frickin' minutes.

When it's time to go, it's usually dark, so – in his penguin suit – Father Chee jogs next to me and BBB as I ride my bike through the ghetto. He likes to make sure I get home okay. I smile at damn near everyone in his neighborhood and do the 'Hope you are having a great day!' trick, which makes Father Chee laugh and glow in a fatherly proud sorta way.

While I'm riding, I usually confess my sins.

'Forgive me, Father, for I have sinned,' I say to Father Chee.

'Confess your sins and Jesus will forgive you,' FC says.

'I kicked Lex Pinkston in the shin yesterday and slapped his face today. But he called me a disgusting single-syllable word for a woman – which I'm not even going to repeat – said he had sex with my mother, and made Ricky say something sexual to a classmate.'

Still running, Father Chee nods wisely – like – a million frickin' times. 'Jesus offered us an example. Turn the other cheek, He told us.'

'That's why I'm confessing. Do you think I haven't read the Bible?'

'You are forgiven.'

'No penance?' I ask.

'You've done it already. Teaching English to my church members.'

'But I *enjoy* doing that.'

'God wants us to be happy!' FC says, which makes me smile.

When we get pretty deep into my neighborhood, he says, 'I'm going to return to the church now.'

I stop riding my bike and we look at each other, smiling face-to-face, both knowing that we kicked butt for God today – making The KDFCs happy and hopeful.

I pretend that Father Chee is my dad, and maybe he pretends I am his daughter.

'Can I get a hug, Chee,' I say.

'Of course,' he replies, and then he hugs me like any good father would.

'How 'bout some love for B3?'

Father Chee pats BBB's head, so lovingly, and I say, 'You're a good man, Chee,' just before I pedal away.

I look back, and – as always – Chee is there watching, making sure I get to Donna's okay, and that makes me smile and feel like there is so much good in the world.

SIX

When I arrive home, Ricky is still doing math problems at the kitchen table, so I feed Bobby Big Boy some wet canned stuff and start cooking Donna's dinner. I decide to go with rice, red peppers, and chicken. So I defrost the chicken in the microwave, chop up two red peppers, boil some rice, and dig out the wok.

After I cut up the chicken and the red peppers into thin strips, I put it all in a big old silver bowl and douse it in a load of soy sauce and sesame seeds.

Next, I get a shot of Jack Daniels from the liquor cabinet and dump that onto the chicken and red pepper.

'What the hell,' I say, and then pour some Jack onto the now-hot wok, which makes a sizzling noise and produces a good warm wheat smell.

I stir-fry it all up, and it smells pretty delectable.

Ricky is STILL doing math problems, and BBB is chillin' on the kitchen mat, looking up at me, watching my every move, because the dashing mutt's totally in love with me.

Donna comes home at exactly six thirty; she is one regimented woman.

'Like I've told you a million times before, you don't have to cook for us, Amber. But it sure smells good,' she says as she tosses her keys into an old crystal ashtray that she keeps on a stand by the kitchen door, and sets down her bags and hangs up her overcoat.

She runs her hands through Ricky's hair and kisses him on the forehead, and I get a little jealous, I must admit, because my mom is so uncool compared to Ricky's.

'How's my boy?'

'Doing math problems. Do not talk to—'

'What time is it?'

Ricky looks at the clock on the wall and then shuts his workbook. 'Time for Ricky Roberts to eat his dinner with Mommy Roberts and Amber Appleton.'

'That's my boy,' Donna says to Ricky. To me she says, 'How was your day, Amber?'

I nod and then shrug, like a tool.

'Okay,' Donna says. 'Can we eat?'

I serve everyone, and we begin to eat.

'Is there Jack Daniels in this?' Donna says after tasting my newest dish.

'Yep,' I say.

'Tastes divine,' Donna says. 'Got you a present, Ricky.'

'Mommy Roberts got Ricky Roberts a present!'

'See that bag by my briefcase? Over there by the door?'

'Ricky Roberts sees a bag!'

'Why don't you go see what's in that bag.'

Ricky stands and walks over to the bag. He picks it up and shakes it like a Christmas present. He even holds it to his ear. A hand finally goes in and comes out full of camouflage. 'Ricky Roberts gets a shirt.'

'What does it say on the shirt?' Donna says, fork in hand.

Ricky holds the shirt above his head and reads the words written in hunter orange. 'Franks Freak Force Federation!'

It is the coolest shirt I have ever seen.

'How many are in that bag, Ricky?' Donna says.

Ricky counts. 'Seven!'

'One for every member involved in the mission.'

I swallow hard; I love Donna so much. She was in court all day – a murder case – but she still got us team shirts for the mission. She rocks!

'There are *FIVE* members of Franks Freak Force Federation. Mommy Roberts brought *SEVEN* shirts. Seven.'

'Well, your attorney needs to dress the part. And I thought Franks might want one, so I had my assistant make up seven. What the hell, right, Amber?'

I nod dumbly. I want to have an assistant someday who will make freaky teens cool T-shirts so that they can do good things in style. I want to be Donna. So frickin' much.

Donna winks at me, and then eats some more of my stir-fry.

Ricky strips off his Utley jersey and puts on some camo. 'Franks Freak Force Federation!'

'You like?' Donna says.

'Ricky Roberts likes very much!'

'Amber?'

I nod fifty times, like a moron.

'There's one in there for you,' Donna says.

I sprint to the bag and find that there is a fitted girly tee in there for me, so I go into the other room and put it on, checking myself out in the hallway mirror. The cut makes my boobs look perky, and the coloring makes me look dangerous – sorta like Sarah Michelle Gellar playing Buffy the Vampire Slayer or maybe Uma Thurman in *Kill Bill: Vol. 2*. I feel so ready to fight for good tonight.

I walk back into the kitchen and Donna says, 'You look like a knockout. How am I going to wear a fitted tee if I need to stand next to young sexy you?'

'Amber Appleton is sexy!' Ricky says.

'True?' I ask, and then blush like a moron.

'True,' Donna says, and nods in this killer gangsta way that makes me believe her.

BBB barks once in agreement. 'Rew!'

'Cool,' I say, smiling.

I eat my dinner, and then Ricky and I clean up the dishes while Donna answers a bazillion e-mails on her Blackberry. Her thumbs move at the speed of light, and

I dig how she mouths the words she is typing, like a little kid would.

Jared shows up with his brother Chad strapped to his back like a toddler in a baby backpack. Chad never really grew, and his head is almost as big as his body. We told him to leave Das Boot at home for dramatic effect. Ty is right behind the Fox brothers, and all are totally psyched to put on their new shirts.

The boys talk about Halo 3 while I take BBB out to pee and Donna gets changed.

After I have B Thrice locked up in his room and listening to classical music, I hear Donna calling my name so I walk upstairs and into her bedroom.

She has a frickin' king-size bed even though she is thin and single. It is very kick-ass. When I enter, she's checking her makeup in the mirror and wearing her fitted camo tee with a black skirt and knee-high leather boots with blocky two-inch heels.

'Sit,' she says to me, so I sit on the edge of her bed. 'Those boys downstairs, would they be doing what we are about to do tonight if you weren't around to lead them?'

I shrug. My heart is beating like mad.

Donna looks me in the eye. She is a goddess.

'They wouldn't be doing anything tonight if they didn't know you. They'd be playing video games or jerking off or doing whatever teenage boys do when left to their own devices.'

I don't know what to say, so I say nothing.

'I see something in you that I like very much, Amber. You're not like most people. You are going to do something very special with your life. You're going to do something very special tonight, because it's what you were born to do.'

I almost crap myself, and I can feel myself shaking a little.

'Here's a little secret between old friends,' Donna says, and then bends down to whisper into my ear. 'Most people – even adults, even grown men – are like teenage boys, only they pretend they are not.' Donna stands up and winks at me. 'People like you and me need to tell them what to do, so that the world won't get too messed up. They want you to give them instructions. They need you to do this. And you know what needs to be done, because you have a good heart – and you have courage. I've seen your good heart at work time and time again over the years. You're all good. One hundred percent. So trust your instincts, and speak your mind tonight. Be brave. Those boys look up to you. You're the shepherd. Herd the sheep. Understand?'

I nod thirty times in ten seconds and blink back a few tears, because no one really talks like this to me ever, and I think I understand what Donna is saying, because I get this feeling in my chest sometimes, and I'm not really like other people.

'Let's do this,' Donna says, and I follow her out of the bedroom.

When we get to the living room, the boys stop talking and take in Donna's hotness. It mutes them instantly. Donna lets them take in her presence. I study Donna, and this is one of her tricks. She waits for people to take in her hotness before she speaks – always. She is the greatest person I know, and if she weren't an atheist, I'd say she was perfect, or maybe even God incarnate.

On the way to the school board meeting, I can tell my boys are tense. I'm in the back with Ty, Jared, and Chad – and their collective nervous quietness is freaking me out a little. Also, Donna is not rocking any music, nor is she saying anything, which is strange, because she always seems to be talking or listening to music when we drive, which is how I know she is now testing my leadership abilities. Ricky is quietly counting the streetlights we pass – oblivious.

I start to wonder if my boys need a pep talk, so I say, 'How does everyone feel?'

'Cool,' Ty says.

Jared and Chad nod. Chad is sitting on his brother's lap.

'Did you memorize the speeches?' I ask.

'Yeah,' Chad says.

'Can we nail them tonight?' I ask.

'No worries,' Jared says.

'This is Franks' livelihood we're talking about. If Franks gets canned, no Halo 3 next year,' I say.

'Yeah,' Ty says, 'we get that.'

'And Franks' six kids,' I add. 'Think of them tonight. We don't want them living on the streets, right? Use them as motivation. Picture them in your mind.'

'We got it,' Jared says.

'Have we ever let you down before?' Chad asks.

They aren't nervous at all, maybe because they are teenage boys and therefore do not know how much is at stake. None of them has ever been homeless either. None of them has ever missed a meal. Their lawyer and banker fathers are around to provide houses and clothes and food and all the other good stuff. These boys don't understand what I understand.

Following my own advice, I think about Franks' redheaded kids as we park, and my chest starts to burn – my eyes start to water.

'Leave your coats in the car, boys,' Donna says. 'I want everyone to see your shirts.'

We take off our coats, get Chad into the babypack on Jared's back, and then Donna says, 'We bust in. I make a brief introduction, and then you boys follow Amber's lead. Understood?'

My boys nod. They understand.

'Ready to start filming?' Donna says.

'Wait,' I say. 'We should pray first. Before we go in.'

'If you must,' Donna says, and then walks toward the door, Ricky following his mother, because Ricky is also an atheist, just like his mom.

We are all shivering in our T-shirts, because it is cold out, but we are also geared up for the mission.

Chad, Ty, and Jared don't really dig on JC as much as I do, but they all believe in God, so they bow their heads and close their eyes as I grab Ty's and Jared's hands, and say, 'Dear God, we are gathered here tonight for a good cause. Franks' job is on the line. We believe that CPHS needs Franks, that he does much more good than harm in that building, which is cool and important. If our cause be just, give us the strength to use the talents with which you have already blessed us. Help us rock the worlds of those board members. Peace out, God. And peace be with you.'

We all drop hands and open eyes.

'Ready?' I ask.

'Hell, yeah!' Chad says from behind his brother's head.

We walk toward Donna, who has the video camera out and recording now, which makes me realize that she videoed my prayer. I'm not sure I like her videoing my prayer, but I don't say anything about that.

Donna says, 'Introduce yourself, boys.'

'Chad Fox, aka the Desert Fox, ready and willin' and chillin'.'

'Ty Hendrix. Tower of Power even if I am only five-ten.'

'Jared Fox. Just Jared.'

'My name is Ricky Roberts. The macking

mathematician,' Ricky says, which makes me smile because I made up that name for Ricky.

'Amber Appleton. Just a girl with God on her side.'

Donna holds the video camera at arm's length and films herself saying, 'Donna Roberts, attorney at law. We're at the Childress Public High School board meeting. The time is 7:46 PM Tuesday, January 27, 2009. The rest will be self-explanatory.'

Keeping the camera on herself, Donna walks into the converted-into-offices house next to the elementary school, and into the boardroom where the school board meets.

There are community members and one or two local reporters seated in folding chairs; Prince Tony is in the front row with a few other administrators, and the school board is seated behind this long table front and center. Pretty standard adult stuff abounds.

We're all in camo, hunter orange letters proclaiming who we are quite loudly. But wearing a three-piece suit that actually has a pocket watch chain draped like an evil gold smile across the man's belly, as if he is stepping out of some old corny movie about waiting for trains to show up, Mr Pinkston stands, removes his pocket watch from his vest, and – while reading the time – he says, 'Who are you and what the hell do you think you are doing?'

Donna just stands there in front of Mr Pinkston, front and center, wearing camo, filming herself, confidently letting all present take in her hotness.

'Sit,' Donna says, as if she were talking to Bobby Big Boy.

Amazingly, Mr Pinkston looks up, surprised, and then sits.

The room is dead quiet.

'Ms Roberts,' Prince Tony says in a calm, soothing voice. 'What's going on here? We don't allow these meetings to be videotaped. Surely you can understand why.'

Donna completely ignores Prince Tony and addresses the room. 'Boys and ladies. I'm with Roberts, Bradley, and Wong. If you haven't heard of our law firm, I guarantee your lawyers have, and those boys will want to know what has been said tonight, so take notes. It's come to our attention that you are considering cutting funding for Mr Jonathan Franks' marketing classes. I'll be representing Mr Franks and all five of the students who will be speaking tonight. All pro bono, for as long as it takes. You need to know two things before we begin. One. Roberts, Bradley, and Wong. That's not alphabetical order. Two. Name one. The one in charge. Roberts. That's me. Amber?'

Donna starts filming me.

I'm in total frickin' awe.

'Amber?' Donna says.

Ty elbows me in the back.

'You're up,' Donna says.

I look at all of the school board members. With such freaks as us in front of them – represented by one of the most feared lawyers in the tri-state area – they are in total panic mode. I can see it plainly all over their faces. All of them are impressed with Donna, except Mr Pinkston who looks sorta like Dick Cheney and is glaring at me like he might want to roast my carcass alive and eat me for dinner. Like father, like son. Suddenly, I find my swagger.

'As my colleague clearly stated.' *I called Donna my colleague. Was that a mistake? Too much?* 'We are here on behalf of Mr Jonathan Franks. You may—'

'Okay. Enough foolishness. This school board is within its legal rights here tonight,' Mr Pinkston says, completely interrupting me. 'It's perfectly legal to consider—'

'Don't you ever interrupt my client again, Mr Pinkston.' Donna locks eyes with Mr Pinkston. She is unflinching. 'And I think my client knows a little bit more about the law than you or anyone else in this room, because I've informed Ms Appleton of her rights. As a taxpayer and a concerned citizen, I'm trying to help you avoid making yet another classic and extremely costly blunder.'

Donna turns the video camera on Mr Pinkston.

'Don't you dare film me!' he yells.

Donna smiles, keeps the camera on Mr Pinkston until he turns red, and then she turns it back on me.

I clear my throat and then say, 'You may think Mr Jonathan Franks is expendable, but he serves at least two great purposes, one of which is to protect you from lawsuits. Lawsuits? I can hear you asking. Lawsuits. I'm the poorest girl in the high school. I haven't been to the doctor or dentist for a decade because my mother cannot afford health insurance. For all I know, I may have cancer or may be in need of a lung transplant. But I'd never know it, because we cannot afford to go to the doctor. Maybe if she worked for a good employer, I'd have health insurance. But she works for your school district – for fifteen years now – driving buses, which doesn't pay so hot. No benefits either. So I don't have money for the sorta fitting-in clothes your sons and daughters wear, nor do I have money to fix my messed-up teeth, and this has led to some serious self-esteem problems. But can I see one of the quality therapists some of my classmates get to see? No. Because I don't have health insurance. Word. This high school is a daily hell for me, let me tell you, but there is one place where I am always welcome – where I don't feel like going on a freaking rampage – and that is Mr Franks' room. I am the Marketing Club team leader, and I oversee the Childress MC chapter. I personally won second place in the marketing fast food competition last year at the regionals. Mr Franks runs this club for little to no pay when you break down the hours and the costs of the trophies, ribbons, and pizza parties he throws to boost MC morale. And it is the only thing in this school that gives me any sense of self-esteem. So don't take away the one good thing in my school day – or I might just snap, and start needing all that therapy you don't provide the children of your employees. Ty?'

I take a step back. I survey the school board and catch a few sympathetic eyes. One large woman even nods at me and gives me a wink, like she is my mom or something and is proud. Cool, I think. We're moving people tonight.

Ty steps forward and says, 'I have a dream. I dream that some day in the near future Childress Public High School will diversify the faculty and recognize Martin Luther King Day. I'm the only black kid in the school, and the only place I feel comfortable is in Mr Franks' room. If Mr Franks lost his job, there would be no refuge left for me in this school, and I think I might have to start writing letters to the local papers about how hard it is to be black at Childress High School, a place that does absolutely nothing to celebrate my heritage. A place that inadvertently says to me every day that white is right. No black authors in the English curriculum. Coaches always asking me to join the basketball team. Mrs Watts always trying to get me to sing Negro spirituals in her all-white choir. I'm sick of it, yo. The only thing I've ever done through CPHS in celebration of my heritage was to raise money for the United Negro College Fund, because a mind is a terrible thing to waste. I ran a charity Ping-Pong tournament last year and do you know who was the faculty member that helped me market and chaperone that tournament? Mr Franks. He also made the biggest faculty donation too. Don't fire Franks, or you'll be sorry when MLK day rolls around and you don't observe the holiday again! Because I'm speaking up this year if Franks gets cut.'

Ty steps back, looks over at me, and I nod at him,

which makes him smile, so I give him a wink, Donna style, and say, 'Jared and Chad.'

'I'm just a regular white kid – I love Franks and all, but you probably noticed that I'm carrying around my younger brother in a backpack,' Jared says. I worry that he is going to forget the *Scarface* line, but then he remembers and says, 'So say hello to my little friend!'

'Hello,' Chad says over Jared's shoulder. 'Maybe I would have driven my electronic wheelchair in here if the building was wheelchair accessible. But it's not. Nor are the gym locker rooms, really. And Das Boot – my two-wheeled ride – don't fit through the library aisles, so I can't browse the books or anything like that. If I want to pick out a book to read, I have to be carried through the library, which is humiliating. No one – besides the kids in this room – really talks to me at school. I'm late for every class because I have to take the elevator and all the kids push the buttons on every floor when they walk by – ha-ha – so I have to wait forever. You people suck at accommodating the special-needs people of the world. But you know who makes me feel like I am wanted, every day? Mr Franks. Yeah, we play video games, but you know what? In the video games I have normal legs and arms. I can run around and jump and walk in a virtual world that Franks sets up for me using his own equipment that he buys with his own money because you people do nothing to fund his program. Try not walking for seventeen years, and then tell me that video games are stupid.

If Franks goes, there will be no more Xbox in school and therefore no place in the high school where I can socialize or interact normally with other teens doing something age appropriate.'

'We don't have Xbox at home,' Jared adds, and then the brothers step back.

I give them each a nod and a wink when they look at me. My boys are rocking tonight. I'm so proud. 'Ricky?'

Donna hands Ricky a prepared statement, and tells him to read it, which he does. 'My name is Ricky Roberts. I am the only Childress Public High School student diagnosed with autism, and I do not like the special education teachers very much. Also, school board member Mr Pinkston's son Alexander Pinkston torments me on a daily basis, which makes me sad and angry sometimes. But I love Mr Franks, because he always lets me into his room and makes me feel like I am wanted and that I have many friends, and that my friends are also wanted in the school. I do not like eating in the lunchroom, because Alexander Pinkston torments me. I like eating my lunch with Mr Franks. Mr Franks is my favorite teacher. Please do not fire him. Please. Thank you. Yes.'

Donna steps forward and says, 'And I am a tax-paying community member. Mr Pinkston's son likes to trick my son into making sexual overtures to female classmates. My son will repeat almost anything he is told, especially when encouraged by the captain of the football team, so this is quite an easy task to accomplish. On Monday, Mr

Pinkston's son told my son to tell sophomore Ryan Gold that her *quote* boobies were lovely *unquote*. So Ricky did, which resulted in Ryan Gold's bursting into tears in the middle of the lunchroom.'

Mr Pinkston stands and says, 'How dare you burst into our meeting and accuse my son with unfounded—'

'Sit down, Mr Pinkston!' Donna says.

Mr Pinkston scans the crowd for support, finds none, and then sits.

'We visited with Ryan Gold and her parents yesterday,' Donna says. 'Ryan Gold is a member of the National Honor Society. She goes to church every week. She is the nicest, most well-spoken girl you have ever met. And she is willing to testify in a court of law. Now I have talked with Principal Fiorilli several times and have even sent him letters regarding the harassment Mr Pinkston's son has inflicted on my son and other students. These letters are documented, of course. I have responses. So if you fire Franks, or if this man's son with malicious intent comes within thirty feet of my son or Ryan Gold or any of these good kids here tonight, I will launch a lawsuit on this school that will drain your budget so fast, you'll have to fire every damn teacher in the district to get it passed. Am I clear?' Donna's eyes scan the crowd. She lets them take in her hotness. 'And if any of these children have any sort of uncomfortable experience during the next few school days, this digital document gets copied and sent to every newspaper and television station in the area. Have a good meeting, boys and ladies. Keep Franks. Avoid legal trouble. It's a win-win.'

When Donna strides out of the room, we follow, and when we are outside, Donna distributes the celebratory high fives, and my boys are all smiles.

'What do you think, Amber?' Chad says.

'Did we deliver the speeches okay?' Ty says.

'Do you think it will work?' Jared says.

For some crazy reason, instead of answering, I smile and give each one of my boys a big old hug, which makes Ricky say, 'Hi! Hi! Hi!'

And Donna says, 'Let's go to Friendly's!'

So we all pile into her Mercedes.

When we arrive at Friendly's we get a big booth and Donna orders one of every sundae on the menu and six spoons, and we eat ice cream as a team, sword fighting with long ice cream spoons, laughing our butts off, getting chocolate sauce and whipped cream and caramel all over our teenage chins as we shuffle around the sundaes and sample all of the delicious concoctions – replaying the night, talking about how cool we all were, and how Franks is sure to keep his job now, and how Franks Freak Force Federation rocks hard-core, especially in our new camo shirts, which we all agree to wear to school tomorrow like the sports teams do before big games. But when people ask us what the shirts are about, we won't tell them, because it's our secret. True? True.

So I try not to get any sundae on my new shirt and

catch myself looking at Donna a lot. She's not really saying anything, and she doesn't eat very much ice cream, but she's smiling in this very satisfied way, and every so often she runs her nails through Ricky's hair, which makes me jealous again. God, I really wish she were my mom. I'd be so much cooler and smarter and – but then I remember to be thankful for what JC sent my way today, and I smile and run my nails through all of my boys' heads of hair, which makes them say, 'Stop! Ice cream hands! You sticky ho-bag!' So I laugh at them and keep on trying to run my hands through their hair, pretending to go for one, and then at the last second, going for another boy's hair, which results in a lot of grabbing wrists and screaming.

The waitress comes over when we almost knock over Chad's high chair. She's a teen from another high school, who says, 'You must chill, or Kevin is going to – like – freak.'

'School night, kids,' Donna says, and then pays the bill while we all try to mess up each other's hair on the lawn outside of Friendly's. As we wrestle, I think about how much I love these boys. They are good people. I really really love these boys. All of them equally. My boys. My friends. Franks Freak Force Federation.

After Donna drops off Ty, Jared, and Chad, I say, 'How did you know that Lex made Ricky say that stuff to Ryan Gold?'

'Lex Pinkston is a bad boy!' Ricky says. 'Bad boy! Bad boy! BAD BOY!'

'Hello?' Donna says. 'Son diagnosed with autism. No secrets in the Roberts household.'

'Did you really talk to Ryan Gold and her parents?'

'Yep.'

'But you had a murder trial today and—'

'I sent Jessica to represent our interests regarding the Golds.'

Jessica is Donna's young and pretty and extremely smart assistant, whom I hate, because Donna is always going on and on about what a great future Jessica has.

'Cool,' I say, totally wanting a Jessica of my own someday, who will help me do even more killer good for deserving people.

'You're not really self-conscious about your teeth, are you?' Donna asks.

'No. I just made that up on the fly. I'm cool with my teeth.'

'Good, because they really do look white and straight.'

'Thanks.'

'Will I be driving you home, Amber?'

'Got to pick up Bobby Big Boy, because I can't sleep without my pup,' I say.

'How about I drive you and Bobby Big Boy home after that?'

'No, thanks.'

'It's pretty cold outside,' Donna says.

'Yeah, but I have to stop by Franks' house.'

'Mr Jonathan Franks!' Ricky says.

'Oh?' Donna says, because she knows I'm totally lying. I'm pretty sure Donna knows I'm living out of Hello Yellow. She's super smart. When I don't say anything, Donna says, 'Amber, I know how you feel about taking help from me, but I *can* help you and your mom if you need it. I know people who can—'

'We don't need your help,' I say, and am surprised that I sounded like a cat saying what I did. I feel badly about this – especially after all Donna has done for me – but I can't help adding, 'Not everyone needs your help, you know.'

I am such a bitch.

But Mom is going to come through one of these days. I've got my money on mi madre, and mi madre on my mind, sucka!

'Pride is not pretty,' Donna says.

'I'm not a pretty girl,' I say, because I can't help myself, and I dig Ani DiFranco.

'You're gorgeous,' Donna says, 'you shine, only you don't know it yet.'

This is a weird thing for Donna to say, so I clam up and listen to Ricky counting aloud and wonder about what he could possibly be counting.

SEVEN

When we get to Donna's house, I let B3 out of his room, mop up his welcome-home puddle, put his plaid coat on him, and then find Donna in her room changing.

'Donna,' I say.

'Yeah?'

'I'm sorry I was a bitch in the car.'

'You weren't a bitch in the car.'

'You rocked the school board meeting pretty hard,' I say.

'No, *you* rocked the school board meeting pretty hard,' she says.

'I couldn't have done it without you.'

'Yeah, you could have. You just don't know it yet.'

'I'm going to leave now,' I say, because I don't want Donna to patronize me, even if she is trying to be kind. I could never do what she does. I sleep on a school bus. I'm a freak. I couldn't even take first place at the Marketing Club regionals.

'Okay,' Donna says. 'See you tomorrow morning?'

'True,' I say, and then leave without saying goodbye to Ricky, because – all of a sudden – I'm feeling sorta down for some reason.

It's cold outside. North Pole cold. And I don't have a proper winter coat.

As I'm walking toward the school bus compound, I remember what I said about visiting Franks' house, and since I don't want JC to think I am a damn liar, I make a detour. Franks lives in the neighborhood, in a grass-hopper green rancher with a big old addition on the back – bedrooms for all of his redheaded kids.

It's kind of late for a school night, but B Thrice and I walk up his driveway and knock on his basement window. Franks is playing Halo 3 in his basement, probably against Ty of the Franks Freak Force Federation and people all over the world, which boys and men do through something called Xbox Live. He looks up at me, then points to his watch and shakes his head. But before I can knock again, I hear Franks' mean redheaded wife say, 'I'm calling the cops if you don't get off our property! I know who you are, Amber Appleton. Go home and leave my husband alone! He's not working now!'

'I'm totally in love with your man,' I say to Franks' wife, just to get her riled up. 'He's going to leave you and marry me as soon as I'm of age!'

'I'll kill you with my own bare hands!' she yells, step-ping out of the kitchen and into the cold night. She's wearing a depressing bathrobe and slippers, which makes her look really sad and homely.

'Just kidding, Red. Your husband is an honorable man, and he loves you to death and would never leave you or the kids. Not for a million bucks. That's why I want to hug him so much. I don't expect you to understand, but please know that I'm praying for you and your family every night.'

'What are you talking about?' Mrs Franks says.

'You're a lucky woman,' I tell her, and then BBB and me walk away.

B3 is a little lackluster at night. He's a morning dog. So I usually talk to JC on my long walk home to Hello Yellow.

'JC,' I pray. 'You see us at the school board meeting? Whatcha know about that, sucka?' I laugh because it's sorta fun to call JC sucka when I'm praying. 'Were you proud of me, Heavenly Father? Did your daughter do you proud?'

I look up into the sky and there are no stars. Just streetlights and blackness.

I don't really feel like JC is listening tonight, so I stop praying and start to cry.

I cry a lot when I am alone, probably because I am a chick and all, but maybe because I'm not strong like Donna, and I think about stuff too much – like, for example, some-times I get this idea that my dad has really been watching over me the past seventeen years sorta like a guardian angel or something, only he's really alive and waiting for me to earn the right to have a dad, and once he sees me doing enough good, he's going to run up behind me and surprise me with a big old fatherly hug, picking me up off the ground and spinning me around like in the damn movies. Sometimes, after I have done something pretty kick-ass, I turn around really quickly, because I sorta believe that he might be there ready to hug me. But he never is.

I don't want to turn around tonight, because I'm seventeen, so I realize that the fantasy is silly and even delusional maybe, but as I'm walking home tonight, I think about how I protected Ricky from Lex Pinkston today, and how happy The KDFCs looked when we were performing 'You Can't Hurry Love', and I know that Father Chee is definitely proud of me, and I got my boys to save Franks' job, which is something that any good father would be proud of, and as I'm walking down the street, I start to feel like my father is really behind me – I even think I hear his footsteps.

I don't want to turn around and be disappointed once again, but I also still believe in hope and the possibility of beautiful things happening in this world. I still believe that JC and God have a kick-ass plan for every one of us, so I say, 'Dad?'

With so much hope in my heart, I spin around in the middle of the sidewalk and there is no one there – like always.

And so I cry – so hard that BBB gets scared and starts

barking, so I pick him up and carry his butt back to Hello Yellow.

Mom's asleep under the comforter, so I let her be.

I don't do my homework.

I sit in the quiet darkness for a long time.

For some reason I start thinking about the time I asked my mom for a tent, which is all-time Amber-and-her-mom moment number four:

When I was maybe seven or so, I saw this sitcom on television where the mom and daughter spend the night in the backyard. The little girl gets a tent for her birthday and then she wants to sleep outside instead of her room, so the mom sets up the tent for her, and they have these great times pretending that they are explorers pioneering across America back when it was inhabited by Native Americans, back in the day. It looked like fun, so I begged my mom for a tent.

Mom didn't get me a tent, but she made me one out of blankets and broom handles one summer night and we attempted to camp behind the apartment complex we were living in at the time, back when Mom was with a different boyfriend, Trevor, who was only around for a few months or so.

By flashlight, Mom and I read books I had checked out of the library, and then she told me silly ghost stories before we went to sleep.

I woke up in the middle of the night feeling some sorta slime on my face.

'Mom?' I whispered. 'Mom?'

'What's wrong?' she said.

'I think there's something on my face.'

'Go back to sleep,' Mom said.

'I really *really* think there is something on my face. Can you check?'

Mom turned on the flashlight and started to scream.

I sat up and started to scream.

There were slugs all over the inside of the blanket tent, all over our sheets, and a few were even on us.

Both of us ran out of the tent, and we couldn't stop screaming.

Eventually, the cops showed up with their guns drawn, because someone reported a disturbance.

We were so freaked that we couldn't even talk.

Mom just pointed to the tent.

The cops actually aimed their guns at the tent and started to talk very mean to the slugs. 'You're surrounded. Come out with your hands up. We can resolve this peacefully.'

It was pretty funny to hear the cops talking to slugs like that, so I started to laugh.

The cops didn't like that, and started questioning us, and soon they understood that they had drawn their guns on a tent full of slugs, so they had to laugh too.

After Mom had explained the situation, she offered to buy the cops a cup of coffee to make up for the misunderstanding, and when they agreed, we got to ride in the cop car. I asked the officers if they would put on the lights and sirens, and they said, 'Sure.'

We rode super fast to the all-night doughnut shop, where Mom flirted with the cops and I got to eat doughnuts in the middle of the night, which was pretty killer.

When the cops dropped us off back at the apartment building, we went inside and, since Trevor had to work in the morning, Mom slept in my bed with me, which was really nice, especially since the bed felt so comfortable after trying to sleep outside on the grass for a night.

What I wouldn't do to be in a bed tonight.

In the present moment, after taking BBB out for one last pee worrying the whole time that the local rapist murderer will get me, back on Hello Yellow – even though I really don't feel like it – I force myself to pray for everyone on my list, asking God to help us all be who we need to be. And I pray really hard, even though I can't feel God tonight, and I wonder if He is mad at me or something, which makes me feel as though maybe my day wasn't so kick-ass after all.

I'm cold without the comforter, but BBB keeps me warm – his little body inhaling and exhaling against my chest – and I eventually fall asleep.

When I wake, I cannot remember my dreams – but Mom is outside smoking a Newport, and everything begins once again.

PART TWO

Freak Scene

EIGHT

After another frickin' freezing night in Hello Yellow, my
butt has finally thawed and is now all nice and toasty. I'm
singing in the back of Donna's Mercedes. Again, heated
leather seats. So nice.

We're listening to Dinosaur Jr's 'Freak Scene', which
is my favorite D. Jr song, pretty much because it is also
Donna's favorite, and I like watching her sing it like a
teenager.

Donna is driving too fast, bobbing her head to the beat,
singing all of the lyrics at the top of her lungs, her hands
pounding out the beat on the steering wheel as Ricky
counts inaudibly.

I think it's funny that Donna listens to songs about freaks,
because she is so cool and hip and stylish and smart and
together and she is definitely what every woman wants to
be as far as I'm concerned – certainly not a freak like me.

Maybe she just listens to music like this so she can
relate to her son Ricky and The Five.

Maybe.

But she is rocking pretty damn hard this morning – so much that she even blows through a stop sign, but I don't say anything, because I don't want to kill the mood, which is totally rocking, and how often does one truly get to rock out hard-core? Let alone a high-powered attorney who has a murder case to worry about. Sometimes you just have to let crap slide when it comes to adults acting like kids, because that can be a beautiful thing. True? True.

When we arrive alive at the high school, Donna kills the music, kisses Ricky, and tosses me the XXL camo shirt for Franks.

'Your boy Franks should be proud today,' Donna says, and then winks at me before she turns up the tunes again and pulls away.

'Going to play Halo 3 with Mr Jonathan Franks!' Ricky says, and then we're knocking on the outside basement door.

Ty kicks open the door this morning, and then Franks and Chad kill off Ty's and Jared's spacemen so that Ricky can join the action – just like every other morning.

Before I lose my boys to video games, I say, 'Franks, check this out,' and then hold up the camo shirt.

'For me?' Franks says.

'Mommy Roberts made a shirt for Mr Jonathan Franks and all five members of Franks Freak Force Federation!'

'Cool,' Franks says, taking the shirt from me, admiring

the orange lettering and rubbing the material between his thumb and forefinger as if the shirt were made of precious fabric – like it's the original American flag sewn by frickin' Betsy Ross or something. '*Very* cool,' Franks says.

'You do see that we are all wearing the same shirt?' I say.

'Also cool,' Franks says.

'We playing a game, or what?' Ty says, and then all of the boys are logging into the virtual world.

Did my boys forget all about last night, or did they already discuss the school board meeting with Franks?

Before I can bring up the subject, just before their minds are sucked into the various Xboxes positioned around the room, Lex Pinkston knocks on the hallway door and sticks his head in. 'Um, Mr Franks, may I come in and say something?'

'Mr Pinkston, all students are welcome in my room. Enter.'

Lex enters slowly. He is tall and full of muscles and dumb-looking, but today he has this very sincere look on his face. 'Listen,' he says to the room. 'Sometimes I say dumb things because I like feel I have to in front of people or something because there's a lot of pressure on me, being that I'm the QB and all, and well, I know that what I've been telling Ricky to say is well, um – not cool.'

'Are you trying to apologize?' I say.

'I'm sorry that I said those things to you, Amber.'

'I'm praying for you every night,' I say.

'Why?'

'Because you need it.'

'Well, I'm also sorry for telling Ricky to say those things to Ryan. I'm sorry, and it won't happen again. Okay?'

'Did your daddy make you come down here this morning?' I ask – like a total cat.

'Listen, I said I was sorry. It won't happen again. Okay?'

'No. It's not okay, because you can't just erase—'

'Do you like playing Xbox, Lex?' Franks says.

'What?' Lex says.

'Are you a gamer?' Franks says. 'Do you like video games?'

'Yeah. Who doesn't?'

'Are you any good at Halo 3?' Franks asks.

'Beat anyone in this room,' Lex says.

My boys all exchange glances and restrain smiles.

'Why don't you play a game with us,' Franks says.

'Right now?'

'Homeroom doesn't start for fifteen minutes.'

'Are you serious?' Lex says.

'You're on Ricky's team,' Franks says. 'Amber, why don't you pull up a chair?'

I pull up a chair next to Franks and for the next ten minutes I watch my boys' virtual spacemen kick the crap out of Lex's virtual spaceman in every way imaginable. If I had to guesstimate, I'd say Lex gets killed an average of five times per minute, and never even records one kill.

My boys are unmerciful.

My boys are triumphant.

My boys are beautiful.

'You guys are really good,' Lex says when the game is over.

'Bring your friends next time,' Franks tells him. 'We play every day before school and at lunch. All are welcome.'

When the warning bell rings, my boys skedaddle like someone yelled fire or something – the lab rats – but I hang back.

'Why did you tell Lex he could hang in *our* room?' I ask Franks.

'This is everyone's room. All are welcome,' Franks says.

'*Lex Pinkston?* Do you know that just yesterday he called me a disgusting single-syllable word for a woman, which I'm not even going to repeat?'

'Maybe if he were in this room more, he wouldn't have called you that name. Maybe you'd become friends?'

'Are you for real, Franks?'

'No, I'm an illusion,' he says, and then laughs at his own joke – like a moron.

'Have you heard how the school board voted last night?'

'No.'

He doesn't bring up our saving his job, so I assume my boys didn't tell him.

'Aren't you worried about the vote?' I ask.

'It's of this world.'

'Your wife was pretty pissed when I came to your house last night.'

'You shouldn't come to my house, Amber.'

'She doesn't really think I'm in love with you, does she? Why can't I hug you, Franks? Just once.'

'Why do you do that? Why do you insist on making me feel uncomfortable whenever we are alone?'

'A hug is a good thing, Franks.'

'Not always.'

'Like – when is *a hug* not a good thing?'

'When it makes someone uncomfortable.'

'I'm down with hugging,' I say. 'I hug everyone indiscriminately.'

'Not everyone wants to be hugged.'

'Well, that's just dumb.'

'Why, because you say so?' Franks says. 'Would you hug Lex Pinkston?'

I'm sorta getting pissed at Franks, especially after everything I did for him last night – not to mention how he invited Lex and his buddies into The Franks Lair – but the second bell rings, which means I'm late, so I just leave without answering and go to homeroom, where there is a pink slip waiting for me, so I about-face and walk my little behind down to Prince Tony's office.

All of my boys are on the bad-boy bench, except Chad who is in Das Boot.

'Amber,' the red-lipped Mrs Baxter says to me just before I address my boys, 'can you come over here?'

So I walk over to Prince Tony's secretary's desk.

'I heard about last night,' she whispers. 'You certainly have chutzpah.'

'Thanks,' I say, and then join my boys, who are more than a little bit fidgety sitting on the bench of discipline.

'We better not get in trouble,' Ty says.

'Ricky Roberts needs to go to calculus in how many minutes?'

'This don't seem so good,' Chad says from Das Boot.

'Beats going to gym,' says Jared.

'Guys, it's Prince Tony,' I say. 'Just let me do the talking. No sweat.'

'What if he calls us in one at a time?' Ty asks.

'No chance,' I retort.

'How do you know?' asks Jared.

'How many minutes until math?'

'I know Prince Tony. He'll want to save time. He's efficient to a fault.'

The door opens. Prince Tony says, 'The lot of you. Inside.'

I give my boys a knowing glance, as if to say *Told ya!*

Inside we all take seats in the various corners of the office, Chad motorizes Das Boot front and center, and Prince Tony sits behind his huge desk.

'The school board voted to keep the business department.'

We all clap and cheer!

'You'll be pleased to hear that Mr Franks will be getting an increased budget.'

I smile and nod my head confidently. Score!

'Now, all of those other things you were complaining about last night,' Prince Tony says, 'were you serious? Do you really feel strongly about those other issues, or was it just a collective front to save Mr Franks?'

'Pretty much just a front,' says Ty.

'We just really like Franks,' Jared says.

'How many minutes until math?'

'Halo 3 during lunch and before school. Is that too much to ask?' Chad adds.

'So this matter is resolved?' Prince Tony says. 'No more busting into school board meetings? You're satisfied?'

'Pretty much,' Ty says when no one else speaks up.

'Good,' Prince Tony says, and then adds, 'you kids were impressive last night. Truly. Now off to class.'

All of my boys jump up and happily follow Das Boot and Chad out of Prince Tony's office, but I stay seated and shake my head sadly.

Even after all the slaying they have done in their virtual Xbox world, my boys just don't have the killer instinct.

'Ms Appleton?'

'Is that how it works with adults?' I say.

'I'm not sure I follow.'

'It takes a bunch of threats to get what you want, but

no one really cares about anything that doesn't concern them? No one cares about doing what's right for the sake of doing what's right?'

'What are you talking about? Mr Franks' program is secure for at least another year – through your graduation. You've accomplished your goal. You should be happy.'

'Maybe.'

'What's wrong?'

'I don't know.'

'You can talk to me, Amber,' he says, like any old adult would.

'Don't you think that we should recognize MLK day and diversify the faculty? Don't you think we should make the entire school handicap accessible and friendly? Don't you think that kids shouldn't have to endure harassment from people like Lex Pinkston?'

'Of course. Yes to all of those.'

'Then why don't you make all that stuff happen?'

Prince Tony leans forward, looks me in the eye all fatherly, and says, 'Don't you think I would if I could?'

'But you're the principal of the school. You can do anything you want.'

Prince Tony smiles sorta sadly, and says, 'You're a good kid, Amber. And you are going to be a great woman someday.'

'Why does everyone say that to me? Like I'm a bottle of wine or something.'

'Someday you'll understand.'

'That's such a BS answer.'

'And someday you'll give that same answer to someone younger than yourself.'

'No, I won't.'

'Better get to class, Ms Appleton,' Prince Tony says, and then he starts opening his mail, like I'm not even there anymore, and I wonder if anything we did last night meant anything at all.

NINE

Lex Pinkston actually brings his football buddies down to The Franks Lair during lunch, my boys merrily play Halo 3 with the enemy, and – to make matters even worse – under Franks' supervision, everyone seems to get along, which pisses me off, so I go back into the lunchroom and read *The Crucible* by Arthur Miller.

Now, John Proctor was a man I can admire. Going to the gallows instead of giving up his friends to the witch hunt. Proctor was a man of principles, unlike Prince Tony and my boys, who jumped at the first chance they got to play video games with the cool kids – the same kids who called me a disgusting single-syllable word for a woman and made Ryan Gold cry less than forty-eight hours ago.

It's all so depressing.

Confusing.

Messed up.

* * *

After school I collect Ricky at his locker and go to Franks' room. Franks usually has to pick up his kids after school – because his wife isn't a teacher and works regular adult hours – so Franks doesn't stick around too long after the last bell, but I catch him in the hallway just before he is about to leave for the day.

'Did you even hear about what we did for you last night?' I ask him.

'Yeah,' Franks says, his hands full of folders. 'Principal Fiorilli filled me in.'

'And?'

'*And?*'

I try to shrug off his lack of gratitude, but I can't control the shocked expression on my face, which says, *Aren't you even going to say thanks?*

'I appreciate your speaking on my behalf, Amber. And you too, Ricky.'

'Mr Jonathan Franks is Ricky Roberts' favorite teacher.'

Franks gives Ricky a quick but heartfelt high five.

'So why aren't you like – more touched by our gesture?' I ask.

'Well – I'd like to think I'm keeping my job because I'm a good sales and advertising teacher, and not because you threatened the school board without bothering to ask how I felt about your doing so. Maybe the school board voted the way they did simply because they think I am a good teacher.'

I can't even believe that he isn't thanking me properly and freaking out with happiness. I thought Franks would hug me for sure. I really thought this was going to be our moment.

Something inside me snaps.

'What?' I say. '*We* saved your job, Franks. *We did it*. Us. Franks Freak Force Federation. Are you even serious with that good teacher crap? You play video games all day and offer kids easy electives so they can pad their GPAs. We saved your butt. Don't you understand that? They would have fired you if it weren't for us.'

As soon as the words come out of my mouth, I am sorry.

'Why did you *really* go to the school board meeting, Amber? For me, or for you? I don't need saving. *Do you?*' Franks says very coolly. Then he adds, 'If you need help, I'm willing to help you here at school. Anytime between 6:30 AM and 3:15 PM. Just ask. My door will always be open to you. But stop coming to my house. It crosses the line, Amber. *It crosses the line.*'

And then Franks walks away from us.

'Amber Appleton is crying. Why is Amber Appleton crying? Where is Amber Appleton going? Why is Amber Appleton crying? Why is Amber Appleton crying?'

I cry raging tears all the way to Donna's house with Ricky trailing me.

'Why is Amber Appleton crying? Why is Amber Appleton crying? Why is Amber Appleton crying?'

He only stops repeating the question when he opens his math workbook and sits down at the kitchen table.

I let BBB out of his room; he pisses for a full minute – making a yellow river – and then jumps up into my arms.

I give him a long squeeze before I mop up the river with paper towels.

Before I leave, I give Ricky a bowl of pretzels and a can of mandarin orange seltzer, and then I'm on Donna's bike, BBB in the basket.

'Stop crying,' I say to myself. 'You have old people to cheer up. They believe in your ability to keep the tears at bay. They are depressed enough already about being old. Buck up, Amber! Buck up! You can't battle when you're crying. You need to defend your title. Stop crying!'

At the last second I remember to stop at Alan's Newsstand and buy a large cup of hot cocoa and a Snickers bar, and when Alan asks if I have been crying, I say, 'What?' and laugh crazily, so he won't ask me again. Then I finally pull it together as I pedal the last few blocks to the Methodist Retirement Home.

I got this Wednesday gig here after I saw an ad stapled to one of the big old trees in front of the retirement home. I was walking by after work and the hot pink paper of the ad caught my eye, so I took a closer look. The ad read something like this: 'Today is the perfect time to make a new friend. Seniors have wonderful stories to tell and are always ready to share their grand array of life experiences. If you want to be a senior pal, if you want to be regaled by stories of olden times, please inquire within. Make a new friend today.' I'm totally down with making friends, I'm a very good pal, and I absolutely love being regaled, so I inquired within and signed up for the program. I became a regular at the Methodist Home once Rita's closed for the season and I stopped scooping water ice after school.

When I first went to the old folks home, I was told by the staff that I was simply to talk with the old people in the common room – do puzzles, listen to stories about grandchildren, the Depression, the cost of milk seventy years ago, all of which started to make me feel really depressed. These people didn't need someone to listen to their crappy stories; they needed a spark, something to remind them that they were still alive. And it was pretty obvious that the staff paid them little to no attention, especially since people die here, like every day. Every week I come back someone's missing. But for the longest time, I wasn't sure what I could do to liven up the joint.

Then I met Joan of Old, who – on the outside – is the meanest person you ever met, but on the inside, she's actually pretty philosophical, which you have to discover by breaking through the meanness by being mean yourself, so she will respect you. I discovered this by accident one day when I told her I wanted to go to Bryn Mawr College and she said I'd never get in because I wasn't smart enough.

Her rudeness surprised me because old women are supposed to be really grandmotherly and nice, so I lost my cool and cursed her out really badly, calling her some pretty nasty things, which made her smile, which was weird, but led to my having a kick-ass idea: turn the common room into a word-battle arena where hope dukes it out with despair once a week, which sounded crazy loopy at first, but I've always trusted my visions, so I pitched my idea to some of the older men – who were always putting their arms around me and squeezing my shoulders – and they ate the plan up and made it happen.

Because she loves being evil, Joan of Old agreed to play her part right away, and it has really improved morale at the home very much – or at least that's what the residents tell me anyway.

The front of the Methodist Retirement Home has these huge slavery-times plantation columns and a porch with wooden rocking chairs that look out over a big old rolling lawn, but I use the back entrance, where you have to sign in and pass through security, which – on Wednesday afternoons – is pretty much Door Woman Lucy.

So I park Donna's bike behind a bush – hiding my ride, so it won't get stolen – grab BBB, and then walk into the visitor's entrance with my pup in one hand and the hot chocolate in the other.

'Ain't no dogs allowed in this building,' Door Woman Lucy says from behind her desk, shaking her head slowly, staring into my eyes. 'You know the rules, Ms Appleton. I don't make 'em, and I need to get paid, so that funky little rat's gonna have to stay outside.'

'DWL.' That's what I call Door Woman Lucy to her

face, and I think she likes the nickname, because she always smiles when I say it. 'It's cold out.'

'Sure is.'

'Too cold for a dog to be outside.'

'Wouldn't know.'

'Bet it gets cold every time that door opens.'

'Sure does,' Door Woman Lucy says, lifting one eyebrow.

'I just bought this hot chocolate here, but I'm not really feeling much like drinking a delicious wintertime beverage right now. But it would be a shame to throw it away. I'd really hate to chuck a fresh cup of hot chocolate.'

'Ms Appleton, as you know, I'm not allowed to accept bribes from visitors, but if you left that drink on my desk, knowing that it won't change the fact that that dog of yours must stay outside the building, I'd maybe see it don't go to waste.'

Very slowly, I place the cup on her desk, lay the Snickers across the lid as an added bonus, sweetening the deal – because I really do dig Door Woman Lucy – sign the clipboard with all the lines and names of people who have visited today, record the time of my visit, and then I step away slowly, making my way into the building, BBB under my arm.

'Thanks for leaving that dog outside, Ms Appleton. I'm sure you understand that rules are rules,' Door Woman Lucy says.

'Oh, I understand,' I say.

BBB barks once to convey that he understands as well.

And then B Thrice and I both walk through a second door and into the home.

We make our way through some depressing hallways with dusty fake plants in the corners, but we don't see any staff members.

There is a great cheer when I walk into the common room.

I don't want to brag or anything, but I'm sorta like a rock star to these people.

I slip BBB to Knitting Carol, who hides my pup in a lap full of yarn. B Thrice loves to sleep in yarn, so no worries. Knitting Carol loves dogs, so it's a match made in heaven. With B3 in her lap, she's smiling like a little girl on Christmas morning. True? True.

'All right, kid,' Old Man Linder says to me, massaging my shoulders from behind. 'The old broad has been mumbling nasty things about you all week. She's coming at you hard today. Don't let her rattle you with any low blows, because the wrinkly bag's brimming full of 'em, as you are well aware.'

Old Man Linder is my manager. He's something like a hundred and fifteen years old and has to drag around an oxygen bottle that pumps pure air through these clear tubes that are stuck up his nose. His breath stinks and he has spots all over his face, but he is a kick-ass manager, and he hasn't thrown in the white towel on me yet. He's tough as nails, so I trust him to manage my corner.

Big Booty Bernice has shut the common room doors,

so the staff won't hear the cheering and come break up the battle in the middle of my exchange with Joan of Old.

All of the old people are slowly pushing chairs and wheeling the wheelchair-bound into position, so that everyone can see and hear, which means that everyone has to be really super-mega close to the battle, because old people don't see and hear too well. Word.

White hair abounds, along with homemade sweaters, no-name dress sneakers, cough drops, ear-hair, yellow fingernails, shaky limbs, wrinkles, diapers, and an intense hospital smell that dries out your nasal passages in – like – ten seconds.

Joan of Old is in her wheelchair, front and center, staring me down with her wrinkly pink eyelids, trying to psyche me out. She might weigh eighty pounds if her clothes were soaking wet. She's wearing all black like always, still mourning her husband who died – like – thirty years ago. True.

Joan of Old wiggles an old pink finger at me and then shakes her head so that her black bonnet falls a little to the left, so she straightens it with her bony shaky hands.

Joan of Old has no manager, mostly because everyone in the home hates her. She is such a downer most of the time, and she likes to quote depressing Nietzsche 24/7, which, of course, wins her no friends.

I take my place by the sunniest window in the room, and Old Man Linder says, 'Remember, the crowd doesn't always get your newfangled MTV kid references, so keep your jokes age appropriate. You're battling for our happiness. This is the only thing we look forward to all week. Besides this weekly battle, our lives bore us to death. This is the one thing that's different and exciting, so don't let us down. You making that old crusty broad smile – this is something to believe in. It breaks the awful chain of days. So for us, please just keep going at her until she smiles. No mercy!'

I nod once and roll my head along my shoulders, crack my knuckles, and jab the air a little – like Cassius Clay. (Also known as Muhammad Ali, sucka!)

All of the old people are seated and waiting for the battle to begin, so Old Man Thompson – who actually wears a bowtie every Wednesday, just to play the role – stands and turns to face the audience. He's hunchbacked but sprightly.

'Welcome once again to the Wednesday Afternoon Battle between Hope and Pessimism. To my left we have the indomitably hopeful one, the girl of unyielding optimism, the teen of merriment, the fan favorite, the girl you wished were your granddaughter or maybe even your great-granddaughter, the only minor who visits the home on a non-holiday, the undisputed Wednesday Afternoon Champion, Amber the Princess of Hope Apple-Toooooooooooooooon!'

I raise my hands in the air and hop a little.

The people clap and all the old dudes with front teeth left whistle.

'And now the challenger,' Old Man Thompson says,

and everyone starts to boo. 'This woman needs no intro-duction. The woman in black. The constant mourner. The self-proclaimed nihilist. The one who says the building is too cold and forces management to keep the thermostat so high that we have to dress as though we are all back in the spring of '36 when we had that record-setting heat spell. The woman who once faked a heart attack because she thought we were having too much fun at last year's Christmas party. You know her well. You have no doubt suffered her insults at least once in the last twenty-four hours. The brittle broad you love to hate. Joan! Of! Old!'

Boos abound. Someone throws a crochet hook at Joan, but misses her head by at least four feet.

Joan's little raw bony hands swat at the many booers, whom she cannot identify – because she is blind.

'All right, ladies,' Old Man Thompson says, 'front and center.'

Joan of Old wheels herself over, and I step to her.

'Now we want a clean battle,' Old Man Thompson says, his breath smelling like he powdered his tongue with the dust found at the bottom of a Tums bottle. 'Politics and religion are off limits. This is a Methodist home, so let's keep the cursing to a minimum. You know the rules. Joan of Old smiles and the young lady wins again. Amber Appleton cries, and the old broad wins her first battle. The challenger calls the flip.'

'Tails,' Joan of Old says.

Old Man Thompson flips and catches a quarter, smacking it down on the back of his spotted and veiny hand. 'Heads!'

'How do I know you're not lying?' Joan of Old asks. 'I'm blind, you know.'

'Feel the top of the coin for all I care,' Old Man Thompson says, offering the back of his hand to Joan of Old.

She feels his hand and the coin, and then says, 'Damn it!'

'You kicking or receiving?' Old Man Thompson asks.

'Kicking,' Old Man Linder answers for me, and then slaps me on the butt before saying, 'Go get 'er, kid,' and then he sits down.

'Let the battle begin!' Old Man Thompson says, and all of the old people clap and hoot.

'The problem with women of your generation,' JOO opens with, 'is that you waste all your time doing community service, harboring dreams of a college education, when you should be trying to find a husband who will put a roof over your head and food in your refrigerator. Smarten up, chippie. Coming here is a waste of time. We'll all be dead in a few weeks anyway. The time to find a husband is now, while you're still skinny, because you'll be a heifer in less than ten years. Do you really want to end up a spinster?'

'Ooooo!' the crowd says, and Joan of Old nods confidently.

'Okay. Okay,' I say. 'Joan of Old is so ancient.'

'How ancient is she?' my manager yells, just like I taught him.

'She's so ancient her elementary school teacher had to chisel her report cards in stone, and Joan had to ride a dinosaur to school every day.'

'Hey!' the crowd says, and cheers, repeating my silly joke to each other, nodding their approval.

This joke may not be funny to you, but you have to consider my audience – old people love safe corny jokes.

No smile from Joan. Nothing.

'When I was a young woman there were no dinosaurs about, but there were lonely plain homely girls who never got asked to dance by handsome promising boys. All of these ugly girls ended up living lonely virginal lives in depressingly small government-subsidized apartments, because no man would have them. When I was your age, we usually found these dinosaur-faced girls at the old people's home, doing community service.'

'Oooo!' the crowd moans.

I swallow hard. That one sorta cut me.

Do I really have a dinosaur face? And how would she know, since she's blind? Did someone tell her *I have a dinosaur face?*

It's true that boys don't ever ask me to dance. I'm not all that jazzed up for boys or anything – why would I be after seeing what A-hole Oliver and company did to my mom – but I don't want to be alone for the rest of my life either, after all of my boys (The Five) marry stupid women, younger versions of Joan of Old.

And I really don't want to end up like my mom.

I swallow once and look over at my manager. Old Man Linder has the white towel draped over his shoulder, but he is nodding confidently, showing me his old pink palms, saying, 'Relax,' so I roll my head along my shoulders, look out into the crowd, and can see that they look very concerned.

'Joan is so old,' I retort, 'she farts dust.'

'Hey!' the crowd roars, and I lift my hands in the air.

But Joan of Old is undaunted. She's not smiling.

'Friedrich Nietzsche once wrote,' JOO says, '"The thought of suicide is a great consolation: by means of it one gets successfully through many a bad night." I offer that little tidbit to you as a form of future consolation, when we are all dead and buried and you are all alone in some federally funded box of an apartment – manless and childless – thinking about your barren womb.'

'Below the belt!' my manager yells.

'Watch yourself, Joan,' Old Man Thompson says.

'Joan, didn't you used to date Nietzsche, back in the 1800s? After your husband died,' I say, and a few old men cheer, but most of the old people moan, so I know my joke didn't go over so well. Spoofing on dead husbands is sorta off limits around here. Unwritten rule.

'Watch yourself, Amber,' Old Man Thompson says. 'Let's keep this wholesome. Good clean fun.'

'What do you know, child?' Joan of Old says. '"Life always gets harder toward the summit – the cold increases, responsibility increases." Also Nietzsche. You haven't even begun to feel pain, young woman, but you will. You will feel pain. Life is hell, and your life has only just begun.'

Joan sorta stares at me through her pink wrinkly eyelids, and suddenly, this old Nietzsche-quoting woman chills my bones. Maybe she's right. Maybe there is nothing but pain in my future. Endless pain and then you die. Can this be what's true?

The room is dead quiet, and I haven't got a joke left in my head. I feel that this might be the end, that I am about to be defeated by Joan of Old for the first time, and that hope is going to die shortly in the Methodist Retirement Home along with everything and everyone else.

But then I remember that I have God on my side, so I pray silently.

Come on, JC. Just one little joke. Let me keep hope alive for these old people who are all about to die. Let me give them a little hope – enough so that they can keep on believing until they croak.

And then I have it!

I walk over to Joan, say, 'That's okay. Be as pessimistic as you want, JOO. I'll still love you anyway,' and give her a big sloppy kiss on the cheek. Joan's mouth opens wide in this very dramatic way, and then I know I have her. Everyone howls with laughter. 'You cute little old wrinkly incredibly depressing kook – I love ya!' I give her another

125

big sloppy kiss on the other cheek, and then Joan is blushing, and –

'She smiles!' Thompson says. 'Joan of Old smiled for the briefest of seconds. Do we have a witness?'

Half of the old people in the room yell 'Aye!'

'That's my girl!' Old Man Linder says as he lifts my left hand into the air, proclaiming me victorious once again.

'Amber Appleton is the winner and your undisputed champion!'

The old people who can stand do, and all of them begin to congratulate me, which quickly yields to stories of grandchildren who never visit – these tales are accompanied by endless wallet-fold pictures that show the grandchildren at various stages of their lives and are presented (usually) in chronological order, one picture per each year the child has attended school – talk about the cost of grocery items fifty years ago, the weather over the last eight odd decades or so, homemade arthritis remedies, the inadequacy of social security checks, who died this week, and, of course, recapping the trickier jigsaw puzzles recently assembled.

Before we leave the community room, Bobby Big Boy visits the lap of almost every old person in the building, and they all smile as they pat BBB's head and scratch his belly. My dog is great with old people – so gentle, so calm – it's like he actually knows that old people are brittle and fragile and about to die.

Just before I bust out of the old folks home, I walk

over to the far corner where Joan of Old is sitting all alone facing a wall, which she thinks is a window.

'Joan?' I say.

'What do *you* want, Ms Hopeful? Come to gloat? Come to rub it in?'

'Do you want to pet my dog before I go?'

'That filthy beast? Ha!'

'You almost made me cry back there. That bit about no boys liking me. That really cut to the quick, as you old people like to say. You couldn't see it – because you are blind – but my bottom lip was quivering. True.'

'Truthfully?'

'Yeah. It was a close call. I felt the tears coming.'

'You're just saying that to make me feel better.'

'I'll probably cry about it later tonight, when I'm all alone.'

'You don't have to say that,' Joan of Old says, 'but thank you.'

'You really are pretty mean and depressing, JOO.'

'Well, I try. And I really hate to admit it,' Joan of Old says, 'but you're pretty hopeful and funny, Amber Appleton. But that kiss was a cheap trick, and I'm going to protest the battle, just so you know.'

I catch her smiling again, but I don't call her on it.

The smile vanishes like a flame in the wind, and Joan of Old says in this very sad voice, 'Do you know that you are the only person who has ever made me smile since my Lawrence died back in '82?'

This is depressing news, even though I realize it is a weird sorta compliment.

I sigh. 'I wish you were the only person who ever made me feel like crying, but I can't give you that honor, Joan of Old. Sorry.'

'"Simply by being compelled to keep constantly on his guard, a man may grow so weak as to be unable any longer to defend himself." That goes for women like us too. Remember that, Amber. Remember that.'

'Nietzsche?'

Joan of Old nods once and then says, 'I hope I don't die before I make you cry, Amber. I'm going to beat your young little hopeful butt one of these days.'

'May we have many more battles,' I say, and then go collect BBB from the lap of Agnes the Plant Talker. Agnes talks to any old plant and pretends it's her son, who lives in California and never visits.

As I put on my jackets, Old Man Linder gives me one more shoulder squeeze and says, 'You were brilliant up there, kid. You keep us feeling young with your youthful ha-has and your skylarking.'

'Can I get a hug, Old Man Linder?' I ask.

'Is the Pope Catholic?' he says, and then gives me this very long hug, his nasty breath making my neck sorta wet, which I tolerate, because he's got oxygen tubes up his nose and is probably going to die any day now, plus I really like hugs.

'See you next week, Old Man Linder.'

'If I live that long!' he says, and then gives me a wrinkly wink.

"Bye, all you crazy old people!' I yell across the common room, and then BBB and I walk the depressing hallways with the dusty fake plants in the corners.

'How'd you get that little dog in my building?' Door Woman Lucy says to me when I walk past her, which makes me laugh.

'How'd you like the hot chocolate and Snickers?' I ask her.

'I don't even know what you're talking 'bout.'

Door Woman Lucy and I share a smile. She's good people. Truly.

I retrieve Donna's bike from the bush, put BBB in the basket, and begin my ride back to Donna's house.

As I pedal, I start to get a bad feeling. I start to feel like I have everything all wrong, and that everyone – all of the many people who are not like me – everyone else is right, and all my hopefulness is just childish bullcrap.

I mean, yes, there are a few people who like to watch me do my thing – taking on the school board and Prince Tony, singing with The Korean Divas for Christ, defeating Joan of Old on a weekly basis – but it really doesn't mean anything, because there is only one of me and so many of the people who are not like me, and maybe I'm just an amusing distraction for those other people. Maybe I'm just a freak. A sideshow.

Speaking of sideshows, here's all-time Amber-and-her-mom moment number three:

When I was a little girl Mom always took me to see the circus every year, whether we could afford it or not – all through elementary school. There were years when we couldn't even afford to turn on the heat and had to go without eating meals from time to time, but Mom always came through with circus tickets for us, and when we were at the circus, she'd always buy me cotton candy, popcorn, peanuts, soda, and a souvenir – sometimes a stuffed elephant or monkey, sometimes a T-shirt or a hat or a poster of someone being shot out of a cannon or walking the tightrope or a million clowns getting out of a tiny car.

I didn't even really like the circus particularly, but I liked to look at my mother's face when we were there watching all the acts, because she always looked like a kid. She got so excited whenever the guy got in the cage with the lion, or the motorcycle guy rode around the inside of a metal ball super fast on his bike, or the trapeze artists swung and did flips. All that stuff amazed my mom – she'd be on the edge of her seat the whole time, and if you looked at the faces of all the kids around us and then looked at my mom's face, you'd see that same sense of wonderment.

I remember when I first *really* understood that my mom was a kid at heart – it was the last time Mom and me went to the circus when I was in sixth grade and was sorta outgrowing the circus and other little kid things too.

I didn't really want to go to the circus that year, but since it was a tradition, I didn't say anything to Mom. And then we were there in the middle of it all, in the big tent, seeing the same tired acts, and I was bored out of my mind until I noticed how into the circus Mom was – how much going meant to her. You could tell just by looking at her face – Mom frickin' loved the circus.

I wanted to be able to light up my mother's face like the circus did.

It was an important moment for me.

So maybe that's when I started trying to be something more than I was, but truthfully – five years later – no one really takes me all that seriously. At best, I'm just an interesting blip in people's lives – an amusing footnote. Which is probably why my dad split and my mom can't stay sober and all of her boyfriends ditch us after only a few months or so. Sometimes I wonder why I try at all. What's the point?

In an effort to prep for my battles with Joan of Old, I did some research on Nietzsche at the library. He was an atheist like Donna and Ricky. And he once wrote: 'What is it: is man only a blunder of God, or God only a blunder of man?'

That statement made me mad at first, because I am a Catholic. But it also made me think. How do we really know that we didn't just make up God? What proof do we really have of God's existence? And if God doesn't exist, is there really any reason to be hopeful at all?

I asked Father Chee these questions a few weeks ago, and he said this is what faith is all about – not knowing for sure. I would sure say that was a BS answer had it not come from FC, because my Man of God sorta has something cool going on. He seems enlightened, and not just because he's Asian. I believe in FC (and God) so I kept and keep holding on to hope for some reason, even though it does get harder and harder the higher you climb toward life's summit – like Joan of Old and Nietzsche both say. True? True.

All these thoughts have me down – so I really don't feel like cooking dinner for Donna and Ricky. I can't even think up one recipe anyway.

Maybe I should skip dinner and go to Private Jackson's house?

His pad is on the edge of town close to the ghetto. It's where I go whenever I am feeling blue.

TEN

I met Private Jackson last year when my history teacher assigned us real live local veterans. We were supposed to write these dudes on Veterans Day for homework points. We were instructed to echo this form letter that Mr Bonds had typed up and handed out. Basically, he wanted us to copy the words in our own handwriting, so it would seem like we thought up the carefully constructed sentiment. It was all about how we were proud to be Americans and were thankful for whatever our fill-in-the-blank veteran had done in whatever fill-in-the-blank war in which they had fought, and that while we would never understand what they endured for our country, we appreciated the benefits of American citizenship – what they fought to protect.

So I was assigned Private Paul Jackson and was told he fought in Vietnam. I copied my letter and filled in the blanks, but it made me feel sorta funny. I mean, how did I even know he did something good in the war? Maybe he was a crappy soldier who did more harm than good, and here I was thanking him for doing it. How would I even know? I felt sorta mad about this when I was made to write the letter, but truthfully, I forgot all about it after it was written, turned in, and sent – especially since most of the kids in my class got kick-ass thankful response letters, and I didn't get jack crap.

About a month later, after the holidays, Mr Bonds had some of the Vietnam veterans we had written come talk to our classes. Private Jackson didn't come, but the four dudes who did told us some pretty wild stories that made most of us students cry, because the vets talked about their friends being killed in horrible ways and the anti-war hippie people spitting on our soldiers when they came home to the US of A and how much every Vietnam veteran hates Jane Fonda, who is an old-lady actress and is also known as Hanoi Jane because she posed with the enemy for pictures during the war, which is *so* whack. Word. When I saw these four dad-aged men fighting back tears – in front of a bunch of teenagers – still suffering from a war that happened so many years ago, I realized that our letters were pretty damn important to them, and I started to think a lot about Private Jackson and why he never wrote me back.

So I wrote him another letter, telling him about the men who had come to speak with our classes, asking him if he knew these dudes, only I did not call them dudes in the letter. And then I told him all sorts of stuff about my life: how my dad took off on me before I could even speak, and how I sometimes get lonely, but I am very loyal and would make a good pen pal if he were interested in writing someone who appreciated the sacrifices he made for our country back in 'Nam, but understood if he didn't want to talk about all of that – I just wanted him to know that Americans like me welcome him home now, and shame on anyone who made him feel otherwise, back in the day. The letter was very formal and heartfelt, but it was also pretty kick-ass too.

When I asked Mr Bonds for Private Jackson's address, he wouldn't give it to me, but told me that he would read my letter and if it were appropriate to send, Mr Bonds would mail it for me. I told him that was unacceptable, and we sorta got into a fight about censorship and freedom of speech, which is protected by the first amendment – one of the very things Private Jackson fought to protect. Finally, Bonds agreed to listen to me read the letter aloud and then – if the letter were appropriate – I could watch him address the envelope, after which we'd drop it in the mailbox together, so I'd know that he'd mailed it, but he wouldn't be forced to reveal Mr Jackson's personal information, which was not listed in the phone book or anywhere on the Internet; I know, because I checked in the library. Word. The deal was that we students wrote the veterans introduction letters, and if they wanted to write us back, then we were free to write them whenever. Since my veteran hadn't written back, I wasn't supposed to get a second shot.

So I read Mr Bonds my second letter, and because I am a pretty kick-ass corresponder and I skipped over all of the really personal parts about my dad and whatnot,

Mr Bonds said my letter was well-written and appropriate and worthy of a postage stamp, which he applied to a Childress Public High School envelope and then stuffed my words in that white rectangle.

When we got to the mailbox outside of the school, I asked if I could put the envelope into the box, because I love mailing things, which was a lie I made up, and he said, 'Sure.'

I glanced at the address just before I dropped the letter into the mailbox, and when Mr Bonds went back into the school, I walked to Private Jackson's home.

Private Jackson lives in a very small barn-red rancher at the edge of town, near the ghetto, as I mentioned before. There is nothing particularly interesting about his house – he has some bushes out front and a young maple tree. He drives a regular car. You'd pass right by without even thinking twice if you were walking down the sidewalk and trying to guess which house belonged to a Vietnam veteran. I was sorta expecting there to be one of those black POW flags flying outside, but no dice.

So I had to look for the right number, the regular old address-finding way, and, when I found the 618, I went right up to the door and knocked.

No one answered, so I knocked again, and then again.

I was just about to leave, thinking, *Duh, the guy is probably at work*, when the door swung inward and this very normal-looking almost elderly man wearing a yellow button-down shirt, silver glasses, and tan slacks appeared. 'Can I help you?' he asked.

'Did you get a letter from some crazy high school girl named Amber Appleton?' I asked him.

'Yes. Why?'

'What did you think of her letter-writing abilities?'

'Nothing.'

'That's why you didn't write her back?'

'Are you Amber?'

'We learned about your war in school and I met some of your friends.'

'My friends?'

'Guys who fought in Vietnam like you – they came to our class and told us all sorts of things.' I didn't want to mention his friends being killed, or people spitting on him, so I brought up the part that most seemed to unite the dudes who came to speak to our class. 'Like about that bitch, Jane Fonda.'

He just looked at me like I was crazy.

'You know Hanoi Jane?'

'What do you want?'

'I wanted to apologize for writing you that crappy form letter. My teacher made me write it – but that was before your friends came and told us about what it was like to fight in the jungle. Had I known what it was really like, I would never have written you such a lousy form letter. I wrote you a better letter today – more interesting and personable. But my teacher made me mail it, so you won't get that letter for like – three days or so, I would guess.'

Private Jackson just looked at me for a second, and then said, 'Is this some sort of joke?'

'Hell, no! Seriously. I just thought that maybe you'd want to – like – get to know me?'

'Why?'

'Why not?'

'I'm not going to tell you war stories, if that's what you're after. I don't talk about the war anymore. I've let go.'

'No. I'm totally not after Vietnam stories at all. I couldn't believe all of the things your friends told us when they visited our classroom, and it was really hard to listen to them, especially since they all cried at least once, and it's really hard to watch grown men cry. I've heard enough. True. Do you have any kids?'

'No.'

'Can I come in?'

'I don't think that would be a very good idea.'

'Do you want to – like – maybe take a walk with me?' I asked him.

'Why would I want to take a walk with you?'

'I don't know – I'm interested in learning more about the you of today.'

'Why?'

'Because I don't like writing strangers, so since I was forced to write to you, I figure I should at least know something about you, so we can keep writing letters and maybe even hang out from time to time.'

'I'm sorry,' Private Jackson told me, and then shut the

door in my face, which made me feel really sad – and like a peon.

So I pounded on his door with my fists and yelled, 'That was mean!' even though he wouldn't open the door a second time. 'You'll regret slamming the door in my face when you read my next letter, especially since it took me hours to write and is therefore very moving! And if you hadn't fought for our country in Vietnam, if you hadn't been in the jungle for a year or whatever, I'd call you a bad name right now! Goodbye!'

About a week or so later, when I had all but forgotten about Private Jackson, at the end of Mr Bonds' class, when all of the kids were lined up at the door, my history teacher said, 'Ms Appleton. You got mail.'

He handed me this envelope that was addressed to me C/O Mr Bonds via Childress Public High School.

I opened the envelope and the sheet of paper inside had eleven handwritten words on it:

WALKING MS JENNY
FIVE O'CLOCK P.M. TODAY
SHE RUNS THE DIAMOND
        –JACKSON

I instantly recognized that Private Jackson had written me a haiku – which is a form of Japanese poetry that has three lines and seventeen syllables. I learned all about haikus in – like – third grade, back in the day. But I had no idea why Private Jackson had written me a haiku, nor what the hell his haiku meant. But I *did* know that I'd be going to his house later that day.

I realized that this was highly irregular activity – receiving haikus from a strange man – but I chalked it up to Jackson's being in Vietnam. A lot of men didn't come back right, but they're still our men, damn it! I felt it was my civic duty to check out what the hell Private Jackson's haiku was all about. As a citizen of the free world, I owed him this much.

So at five PM I stood outside of Private Jackson's house and waited to see what would happen.

Private Jackson emerged on schedule wearing a brown coat and one of those Irish hats that old people wear forwards and black people wear backwards. PJ wore his the old-man way.

But the coolest detail about this moment was that PJ had this tiny little funny-looking gray dog on a leash. When I saw the dog, I ran over to it – all girly of me, I know – and I bent down to give the pup a big kiss and a pat on the head.

As you know, I go frickin' nuts for dogs.

'You pass the test,' Private Jackson said to me from above. 'She likes you. And she's a very hard judge of character.'

'So this is Ms Jenny?' I said, rubbing the crap out the little dog's head.

'Yes.'

'What breed is she?'

'Italian greyhound.'

'What did you mean by writing *she runs the diamond*?'

'You'll see if you take a walk with me.'

We started walking down his street, following Ms Jenny.

'So you dig haikus?' I asked him.

'Yes.'

'Kind of interesting for a dude your age to be writing haikus.'

'Why?'

'Aren't they for children?'

'Why would you think that?'

'Elementary kids write haikus when they study Japan. I had to read one while wearing a homemade bedsheet kimono at the Cultures of the World Festival, back in the day, when I was only a wee one.'

'Do you remember the haiku you read?'

'No.'

Private Jackson didn't say anything in response.

'Why did you write me back this time?' I asked him. 'Why did you send me a haiku?'

'I don't know. I didn't want to. If we're going to be honest, I now wish I hadn't.'

'Why?'

'I don't really like people.'

'Why?'

'Dogs are better than people. I have a dog. That's all I need. Dogs are easy. People are complicated.'

'Tell me about it. Dogs are way better than people.'

'It was rude of me to slam the door in your face. My actions troubled me for days. It was rude. Unkind. I feel as though I have accrued bad karma.'

'No worries. People are rude to me all the time. I'm totally used to it. My mom's boyfriend slams the door in my face all the time. At least you didn't call me a bitch, right? Oliver's a grade-A a-hole.'

PJ didn't laugh at that joke but said, 'You looked like the type of person who likes dogs.'

'How can you tell?'

'You have a kind dog-loving look about you.'

'Thanks.'

'I wasn't complimenting you. I was just stating a fact.'

'Un-thanks.'

He laughed slightly at that one, covering his mouth, as if he had burped, and then said, 'I thought maybe if I sent you a haiku, and you understood what it meant, that would prove that you'd like to see my dog run, and then – after you saw Ms Jenny run the bases – we'd be even.'

'That's a pretty elaborate plan, Jackson.'

'Please don't make fun of me.'

'I wasn't making fun of you. I was just stating a fact,' I said, because I love a running joke.

'I'm not going to write you any more letters. This is a one-shot deal. I want to be upfront about that. I'm not looking to make a friend. I just wanted to erase the bad karma I created when I slammed the door in your face. I didn't ask you to come to my door, but the universe sent you and I acted poorly, so I have to reverse that before I go back into my house where I can be alone with Ms Jenny.'

'Cool. Letters suck,' I said, even though I really dig letters. I was sorta figuring out that PJ was a little nuts by this point, but I still dug him. He didn't seem mean, and he was trying to make up for slamming the door in my face. People don't often make stuff up to me. 'So why did you write me a haiku?'

'I write haikus all day long. That's what I do. All I do.'

'What do you mean that's what you do?'

'I mean, I get up in the morning, walk and feed Ms Jenny, write haikus until five PM – keeping my thoughts concentrated and pure – walk and feed Ms Jenny, read the haikus of other more talented poetry masters at night – keeping my thoughts pure and concentrated – and then I go to bed at eight PM.'

'Every day?'

'Yes.'

'No bull?'

'It's what I do. Not very interesting, I'm afraid.'

'Are you kidding me? That's the most interesting hooey I've heard in – like *weeks*.'

PJ smiled at that one, but in a confused sorta way – like he maybe had to pass gas. 'You're teasing me.'

'No way. I really dig haikus. Five. Seven. Five. Seventeen syllables. That's the bomb.'

'You're making fun of me.'

'Why would I make fun of you?' I asked PJ.

'I'm not used to taking walks with people.'

'Neither am I.'

'We're here,' PJ said to me, and when I looked up and around, I realized that we were on the town baseball field. *She runs the diamond.* 'Watch this. It's beautiful. The opposite of a door slammed in your face.'

When he let Ms Jenny off the leash, the little thing started sprinting around the baseball diamond. She ran really fast and hard, but her legs were so little that it took her quite a long time to make it all the way around, which was so frickin' cute that I had to follow her on her second lap, which made her bark and start to run circles around me as we made our way around the bases. When I hit home plate, I looked over at Private Jackson and he was smiling at me in this very strange and almost eerie way, so I picked up his dog and held her to my face, giving her a kiss, before we walked back to PJ.

'So do you forgive me for slamming the door in your face? Are we even now?' he asked me.

'You bet. That was great!'

He kinda smiled in this really sad way, and then I couldn't think of anything else to say.

On the walk back to his house, Ms Jenny peed on a tree and pooped by a bush, but neither of us said anything.

When we arrived at his house, I said, 'If you ever feel like writing me another haiku, I'd love to read more of your work.'

'Don't make fun of me,' he said.

'I'm not. Can I send you some of my haikus? Maybe you could critique one or two for me,' I said, even though I hadn't written a haiku since third grade. True.

'I just wanted to make up for slamming the door in your face, and now that I have erased the bad karma, I'd like you to leave me alone. Please. It's what I most want.'

That bit muted me.

He turned and started walking toward his door, and I kept waiting for him to look back over his shoulder and say something nice, or give me some sorta sign that he really wanted to see me again and be my friend, but he didn't look back or anything, which made me feel sorta mad at first, but then that madness turned into a sadness that stuck with me for many days, until I got this crazy idea: I would send Private Jackson a hopeful haiku every day, and every one of the haikus would be about dogs, because that was the only thing I knew he liked.

I washed and waxed Donna's Mercedes for twenty bucks – she lets me do that sometimes – and then I used the money to buy a box of envelopes and two books of stamps.

I started sending Private Jackson one doggie haiku a day.

According to Private Jackson, here are my all-time top three doggie haikus (out of more than a crapload):

> Pooping anywhere
> You like outside, anytime
> A dog's life rocks hard

> A pup will never
> Forget to kiss you goodnight
> Even when you smell

> Dogs have lots of fur
> Does that count as wearing clothes
> Or are they naked?

Okay, I suck at writing haikus, but I was faithful and wrote Private Jackson every day for more than a month.

He never wrote back even once.

Then one day I found this little wet furry thing in a Nike box, who I named Bobby Big Boy and nursed back to health, as you know.

> I found a doggie
> In a designer shoebox
> He was very sad

(I actually sent that haiku to Private Jackson but got no response.)

What you don't know is that BBB was all traumatized from his stint on the streets, living in a bright designer shoebox, and after I rescued him from the clutches of starvation, B Thrice was very sad for a time, even after we got him back up to his fighting weight.

I used to sing to BBB, give him extra spoonfuls of peanut butter, bathe him in Donna's tub, give him full body rubdowns, read him happy books, and I even made him a dapper coat. Donna bought him all sorts of toys and gourmet doggie food and Phillies dishes, but nothing seemed to cheer him up. I just couldn't figure out what would make BBB happy.

Then I saw these two goth kids making out hard-core in the A-building stairwell of our high school – they looked so happy and in love when they paused the spit-swapping and let me pass through, and for some reason right then and there I knew I needed to get Bobby Big Boy a girlfriend.

When I thought about the size and weight of BBB's perfect companion, Ms Jenny came to mind, so I took B Thrice to the baseball diamond at five o'clock and introduced him to Private Jackson and Ms Jenny.

We arrived when Ms Jenny was already off the leash and doing laps, so she didn't notice us at first.

'Who's this?' Private Jackson asked, saying nothing about all the haikus I had sent him, which bummed me out a little.

'This is Bobby Big Boy.'

Private Jackson bent down and patted BBB on the head. 'Where did you get him?'

'I found him on the street in a shoe box,' I said, wondering whether PJ had not received and read any of the haikus I had sent him about BBB.

'You rescued him,' PJ said.

'Yes, sir.'

'That's good karma.'

That's when Ms Jenny saw Bobby Big Boy and Cupid's arrow stuck. She came tearing ass off the baseball field and began sniffing BBB's butt. I had him on the leash, so he started crying.

'Let him off the leash,' PJ said.

'What if they fight?'

'They won't. Ms Jenny's a lover.'

So I let BBB off the leash and the two little dogs began to wrestle and run around in circles and roll all about for at least a half hour as PJ and I just watched and smiled.

'This is the happiest I've seen B Thrice since I picked him up off the streets,' I told Private Jackson.

'I think Ms Jenny is in love,' PJ said to me.

And then we both agreed that for the sake of our dogs' happiness, we would meet at the field at least once a week, for doggie playtime.

But when it was time to say goodbye, I couldn't help asking whether PJ liked the doggie haikus I had been sending him.

'Ms Jenny will be looking forward to seeing Bobby Big Boy again,' PJ said. He leashed Ms Jenny and walked away.

I was pretty proud of BBB for not trying to hump Ms Jenny on the first date, so I chalked the experience up as a victory, and left it at that.

We started visiting the baseball diamond pretty regularly, and after a few weeks or so we were walking Ms Jenny and PJ back to their house, and then one day we went inside for tea, and I saw that Private Jackson had been hanging up my haikus on his living-room walls, and that he had completely covered one of four walls with *my* haikus!

'Why do you put my haikus up on the wall?' I asked him.

'Do you like green tea?' he replied.

'Yes,' I said, even though I had never before even had green tea, and then we drank tea together silently, while BBB and Ms Jenny took a nap, spooning on the rug under a glass coffee table.

A bit later on – after many house visits – Private Jackson started allowing me to read through his haiku notebooks, which impressed me very much, because he writes beautiful poetry.

Here's Private Jackson's best haiku, as far as I'm concerned:

> TOGETHER PLAYING
> GRAY AND WHITE-BROWN DOGS OF OURS
> WE WATCH QUIETLY

Simple and true. Like a frickin' snapshot. Jackson wrote that one for me and gave it to me on this really nice piece of paper for my birthday last year. I carry that haiku around in my backpack and I read it whenever I am feeling really down. I have it memorized, of course, but I like looking at Private Jackson's handwriting, because it is so meticulous – like a little kid's. It's as if he was trying so hard to remember how to spell each syllable, or maybe like he was giving each syllable so much importance, that every single letter had to wait an extra second to be born and is therefore spaced just a little too far apart. You've never seen anything like it, and his kick-ass handwriting makes the haiku even better.

To this day, if I ask Jackson any questions about his past or his family or anything like that he'll usually say some Zen bullcrap like 'There is no past', or 'I am here in the present', or 'Like our dogs playing in the grass, I am'. It used to piss me off a lot, before I got used to the Zen hooey. But now, I sorta like it. True.

And that's all I ever do with Private Jackson – run the dogs, drink tea, and read his haikus. I still write him haikus, only I hand deliver the poems to save money, because postage adds up and I'm living in Hello Yellow as of late.

Something cool: I've covered three and a half of his living room walls with doggie haikus. I'm going to cover all four before junior year ends. Word.

As we are riding Donna's bike back to her house from the old folks home I ask BBB if he needs some good lovin' and he barks once, so I make a detour and we ride toward the ghetto, toward Private Jackson's house.

It's past five, so no diamond running for BBB today, as we've missed Ms Jenny's daily sprint around the bases, but B Thrice can still get some kissing and spooning in, so when we arrive, we stash the bike around back and then knock on PJ's front door.

When Private Jackson opens up, BBB sprints into the house in search of Ms Jenny and disappears into the hallway that leads to the bedrooms. My dog can get quite randy from time to time. He needs a release every once in a while.

'I'll put on tea,' PJ says to me as I enter his house and sit down on his old-ass couch.

I listen to PJ preparing tea in the other room – the sound of water running into a metal kettle, the clicking sound of the electric gas stovetop starter, the ignition of gas – I imagine the blue flames and the bubbles rising in the kettle, and I start to feel better.

Time sorta stops when I'm in PJ's house – it's sorta like stepping into a real church, not like Father Chee's converted-store-strip-mall church, but like some ancient holy stone church that smells of centuries worth of praying and hoping and believing, sorta like in the Catholic church where I was confirmed, St Dymphna's, and PJ's house feeling holy is strange, because – after reading so much of Private Jackson's poetry – I've sorta gathered that he's in the Nietzsche-Donna-Ricky camp. I'm pretty sure PJ's an atheist.

Here is the saddest haiku I have ever read:

CUNNINGHAM PRAYS WHILE
BAGGING OUR CASUALTIES AND
I AM SO ALONE

Private Jackson wrote that one back in 'Nam. He doesn't know that I read it, because I flipped through the back section of one of his haiku notebooks when he was making tea.

He had said I could read any poem in the sections segmented by the blue and red and black plastic dividers, but he didn't want me to look at the pages between the green dividers. Of course, I turned to the green section just as soon as PJ was out of the room, and he seemed to stay in the kitchen for a very long time – way longer than it takes to make tea – so maybe he wanted me to read the Vietnam haikus, I don't know. But from what I have gathered from reading his haikus – because he doesn't tell me squat about his life – it seems like Private Jackson started writing haikus in the jungle, maybe as a means of staying sane, and he just never stopped writing haikus when he came home.

ELEVEN

'So what is bothering you today?' PJ says as he hands me a steaming hot cup of green tea.

'What? Can't I just visit you for no reason at all?'

'You only come when you're sad.'

'Joan of Old hit me with a whole bunch of new depressing Nietzsche quotes, but I eventually made her smile,' I say, and then sip my tea, which tastes like mown grass. Green tea is an acquired taste that I have not yet acquired, but I drink it like a woman for Private Jackson, mostly because it's all he keeps in his house other than water. He mostly eats rice and roots, so no snacking here either.

'How'd you get her to smile this week?' he asks, which makes me pause, because he usually never asks me any questions about anything. This is as lively as PJ gets when it comes to conversation. This is Private Jackson on speed.

'I kissed her. And I said a bunch of funny stuff too.

Hey, do you think I have a dinosaur face? You can be honest with me. If you were seventeen would you want to get all hot and heavy with me, or no? And if no, is it because I have a dinosaur face? You can be totally honest with me.'

'I think you are exactly as you should be. You are perfect for this moment.'

'More Zen hooey.'

'Do you have any poems for me?'

I reach into my pocket and hand him a sheet of paper housing eight doggie haikus written by yours truly.

Private Jackson reads my poetry very slowly as he slurps his tea with this very determined look on his face – almost like he is taking a dump or something.

'Which is your favorite,' I say after – like five minutes. He's still reading, contemplating each set of seventeen syllables as if they were new constellations that suddenly appeared in the sky one night. He's a crazy serious cat sometimes.

'They are all perfect,' he says without looking up.

'No Zen bullcrap. Which one is your favorite?'

'I cherish them all equally and will hang them on the wall just as soon as you leave, finding the perfect spot for your words.'

'Which do you think is the funniest then?'

Private Jackson reads them all over again and then a little smile blooms on his face. He reads number four very dramatically, saying, 'Dogs go into the bedroom and get funky wild – humans drink green tea.'

'Tried to capture the present moment,' I say.

'You certainly have.'

'You want to meet Donna?' I say, because I've been telling Private Jackson that I could hook him up with the sexiest woman he has ever seen in his life – and she's rich ta boot!

'No.'

'You don't know what you're missing out on, and—'

'How do you like your tea?' he asks politely.

'Tastes like grass.'

'Grass is natural. Grass is good.'

And then we sip tea in silence until Ms Jenny and BBB come out of the bedroom, walking like they are a little drunk or something, with this crazy look in their eyes.

'Only dogs can truly love,' Private Jackson says.

'You could know love, my friend,' I say. 'Donna is a catch. She is – like – very hot.'

'I will wash your teacup now,' Private Jackson says.

I hand him the teacup and say, 'Can I give you a hug before I leave?'

'I would be honored to shake the hand of such an accomplished poet,' he says like always, so when he extends his hand, I hold it with both of mine for as long as Jackson will let me.

'You're a good man, Jackson,' I say, looking him in the eyes, 'and a great poet.'

'I will wash the teacups now,' he says, and then he

drops my hand, turns his back, and walks into the kitchen.

And so BBB and I hop on Donna's bike again and ride it back to her house.

When we arrive, I don't really want to go inside for some reason, but B Thrice needs to eat, so I go in for the sake of my doggie's health.

Donna all but sprints into the kitchen when she hears the back door open and says, 'Did something happen to you, Amber?'

'No. Why?' I say without making eye contact, even though I realize she was worried because I didn't make dinner, and then I make my way over to the cabinet where BBB's cans are kept.

I pop one open and feed B Thrice.

He starts pigging out, because he's always hungry after making love to Ms Jenny.

'Did Joan of Old finally make you cry?' Donna asks, looking genuinely concerned.

'Almost, but I got her to smile with a big, sloppy sneak-attack kiss. She's protesting the battle, because she says kissing is illegal, but it's pretty much a bullcrap claim, and Old Man Thompson is never going to side with Joan of Old, because of that time when she called the cops and tried to get him thrown out of the home by placing a restraining order on him, because he was looking at her funny.'

'Isn't she blind?' Donna asks.

'She is. Word.'

'Then how did she know he was looking at her?'

'She didn't. He wasn't. Joan just made that hooey up.'

'Why?'

'Because she's Joan of Old, evil incarnate.'

'I have to meet this Joan of Old someday.'

'Come to the battles. Any Wednesday afternoon. Better come before she dies though, because that could be – like – any day.'

'Ricky told me that Lex Pinkston apologized to you, and then came to The Franks Lair for lunch.'

'Can you believe that bullcrap?'

I realize that I am being sorta flip toward Donna, but I need to keep being flip or else I might start crying again. I don't want to be around Donna right now, maybe because she's too perfect, and I know I'll never live up. And that's a hard reality to swallow. True? True.

'Ricky was very excited about socializing with the football team. He said they were very nice to him for once.'

'Yeah, because you threatened Mr Pinkston with a lawsuit.'

'Remember what I told you about teenage boys and men, how they need to be herded like sheep?'

'Yeah, so?'

'Are sheep evil?'

'No, they're sheep.'

'So maybe you should give Lex Pinkston and his boys a try. I hear the rest of The Five enjoyed playing Halo 3 with the football team. It's good to make new friends.'

'That's so messed up,' I say, shaking my head, feeling the tears coming.

'You know who boys like Lex tease and call names? Girls they are secretly in love with. The kid probably has a crush on you. And if he's willing to play nice, why not let bygones be— Amber, where are you going?'

I'm frickin' out of there, BBB following behind, and then we're walking through the night, down the street.

My stomach is growling because I haven't eaten anything since breakfast, but I don't give a crap.

'You're going to have to take a rain check tonight, JC,' I pray, 'because I got nothing left over for you. I just can't pray tonight. Sorry.'

I walk pretty quickly back to the school bus compound, BBB and I hop the fence, and I am surprised to find that Mom is home and awake.

'I made dinner,' Mom says when I enter Hello Yellow, and then she proudly holds up a McDonald's bag.

'I could kiss you, Mom.'

'Why?'

I hug Mom for a long time, until I start crying like a baby once again. Her body feels so skeletal, and I can actually feel her ribs through the back of her jacket, which makes me sob even harder.

'It's okay, Amber,' Mom says, alcohol on her breath. 'We won't be on this bus forever. I'm working on it.'

I want to tell Mom that I really don't give a crap about living on a school bus, but that the world is beating me down and I feel like I'm battling everyone and no one is putting any fuel back into my tank and I'm not sure I'm going to make it to adulthood unscathed and still believing in hope because JC isn't doing me any favors as of late and everything is so frickin' messed up – but I can't stop crying, so I just let my mom hold me and pat my back for a half hour or so of pathetic sobbing.

When I finish crying, I open the McDonald's bag and find an ice-cold child-size Happy Meal: small Coke, a handful of fries, four chicken McNuggets, and some stupid toy promoting some stupid kid's movie.

'Did you eat?' I ask Mom.

'Oh, sure,' she says, and then takes a sip from a Coke can, which I know is filled with vodka, because I can smell it.

'Mom, if you love me,' I say, my stomach growling with hunger, 'will you please, please, please eat this meal while I watch?'

'I bought it for you, Amber. You're a growing girl and—'

'Please, Mom,' I say, tears suddenly streaming down my face again. I hold a chicken McNugget up to her face and say, 'Please eat this. Please. For me, Mom. Please. I want to see you eat.'

Bobby Big Boy is watching me from an adjacent seat, wanting to eat the chicken nugget himself, but he's too good of a dog to go for it, so I don't worry.

Finally, my mother takes the piece of chicken from me, bites off a tiny bit, and then chews.

Mom swallows, and then says, 'There. Are you happy? Now you should really eat—'

'Eat the rest. The whole meal, Mom. For me. Please.'

'Amber, you have to eat something yourself and we only have—'

'I ate like – ten pounds of hamburgers at Donna's. Please let me watch you eat the rest. I've had a bad day, Mom. Please eat. Try. For me.'

Slowly, my mom nibbles at the food, sorta like a suspicious mouse might nibble on rat poison, as I watch.

Mom really does try to eat, which makes me proud of her.

After ten minutes or so, she gets down two and a half chicken McNuggets – and then she starts to throw up.

By the time I get her off Hello Yellow, she has puked three times. After another bout of puking in the bus yard – which scares me a lot – finally Mom stops vomiting.

When she asks for her cigarettes, I get them for her and let her smoke. I even bring her the Coke can of vodka, because I'm terrified now, thinking my mom might die right here and now, and I know that vodka is what she most needs.

There are paper towels and some sorta blue spray cleaning stuff under the driver's seat, so I clean up Mom's throw-up, which is full of blood and tiny shredded pieces of chicken.

I gag all the way through.

I try to think of something nice to take my mind off the present reality, so I think about all-time Amber-and-her-mom moment number two:

I'm tiny.

I cannot talk.

My arms and legs are wrapped up in a sheet – like a mummy.

I'm in a baby stroller and it's late summer.

I'm shaded by one of those baby awnings above me – that rounded half dome that covers half of the baby stroller.

Bob is pushing the stroller and Mom has her elbow linked to my father's and I hear the cry of a seagull, so maybe we are near the beach.

Suddenly – we stop moving.

Bob leans down and kisses Mom.

Baby me watches Bob and Mom kiss – baby me smiles.

Now, I know that there is no way I could remember this moment because I was only a few months old when my dad took off, and he probably wasn't so in love with Mom before he took off, because why would he take off if they were actually in love?

So maybe I made the memory up?

It's still my number two – regardless.

Back in the present moment, while I was trying to remember, while I was cleaning up puke, BBB has been hiding on one of the back seats, because I have been sobbing the whole time, and that scares him.

By the time I am finished, I reek of throw-up, and since there is no sink or anything around, I'm going to smell like puke for the night unless I wash with the dirty black slushy snow in the bus parking lot, which would make me smell like gas and bus emissions. I don't even have a water bottle tonight. Nothing.

When I go back outside to throw the puke towels into the woods, BBB follows and starts his jumping routine – and I just can't take it right now, so I scream, 'Stop jumping!'

He stops.

He looks up at me with his little ears pointing straight up – like I hit him or something.

And then he starts whining, as if he is crying too.

So I throw the puke towels over the fence, into the woods – erasing Mom's mess – and then I pick up BBB and give him a kiss on the lips.

'I'm scared, Bobby Big Boy. I'm scared. I can't keep doing this.'

'Rew!' he says in agreement before we walk back to my mom.

'I have to go out,' Mom says, exhaling mentholated smoke.

'Where?'

'I'm going to get medicine for my stomach.'

'Where?'

'At the drugstore.'

'The Childress Rite Aid?'

'Yes.'

'Let me come with you,' I say. 'It's late.'

'You have school tomorrow. I'll be fine.'

'Mom. Are you going to get more vodka? You can tell me the truth. I won't try to stop you. I just want to know the truth.'

Mom will not look me in the eyes. 'Going to the drug-store. I just need some Pepto-Bismol. I'll be back in a few minutes. You just go to sleep,' she says before she starts walking away from me, staggering a little.

I know that I should stop her, that I should maybe follow her to make sure she is okay, but I'm only seventeen – I'm still a girl, just a stupid confused chick – this is nothing new, and I have nothing left in my tank. I'm on empty, and so I go back into Hello Yellow and cry myself to sleep without even praying first. Sorry, JC.

TWELVE

When I wake up, the streetlights are off. 'Mom?' I say.

Silence.

'Mom?'

Somehow I know she is gone.

My heart is pounding.

I stand.

Slowly, as my eyes adjust to the darkness, I feel every seat in the bus with my hands and keep on saying, 'Mom? Mom? Mom? Mom?'

BBB sniffs the entire bus floor.

Mom is not on Hello Yellow.

I know it is after eleven, because there are no street-lights on, but I have no idea how late it is. Mom goes out to the bars all the time, but for some reason, I have this very bad feeling that something horrible has happened. I can't really explain it – I just instantly know, or maybe I just feel it in my gut.

'Come on, B Thrice,' I say, and then we leave Hello Yellow.

I know Mom went one of two places: Charlie's Pad, which is the bar on the edge of town, the first bar in the ghetto; or the liquor store next to Father Chee's church, where they sell big plastic bottles of vodka for very cheap – less than half the prices charged in Childress, plus the store in the ghetto is open later.

I'm not thinking too clearly right now – granted. I just know that something bad might have happened to my mom, so I'm sorta on autopilot – walking super fast.

I go right by Private Jackson's house, walk a few more blocks, and then I am in the ghetto, trying to open the metal front door to Charlie's Pad. The neon beer signs behind the high windows – which are covered with mesh wire to keep out burglars – those signs are off and the door is locked. 'Hello?' I yell. 'Hello?'

No one answers.

'Hello! Anyone in there? Mom? Mom!'

'Shut up, bitch!' someone yells, but when I turn around no one is there.

I don't see anyone on the streets.

Just trash swirling in the wind.

If the bar is closed, it must be well after midnight – I know this much. And since the bar is closed, the liquor store is definitely closed, but for some stupid reason, BBB and I start walking toward the liquor store very quickly, as if we might actually find my mom there.

I'm desperate.

I'm a little loopy tonight.

I'm alone.

I'm scared.

I'm stupid.

I pass a crazily bearded insane-looking homeless man who throws an empty beer can at me and yells, 'Catch a cat by the tail 'till you spin around and drown! Catch a cat by the tail—'

BBB and I start running.

The icy wind cuts my face.

I hear car alarms going off in the distance.

When I get to the liquor store it is closed and the doors are chained shut. No one is around.

For some stupid reason I bang on the doors, yell, 'Mom?' and then I bang on the doors of the Korean Catholic Church, and yell up to Father Chee who lives above the church, but no lights go on.

Then I remember where I am and what time it is.

I start to get really scared, especially when this crappy-looking car – with silver rims and tinted windows and booming bass and neon-pink lights that make the road under the car glow – this crazy car pulls up and idles right next to me.

I start to walk down the street, back toward the town of Childress.

The car follows, going only as fast as I can walk.

It follows me for an entire block – rap music blasting – before BBB and I start to run.

When I get halfway down the next block, the car speeds up and turns, and then screeches to a stop, cutting me off at the corner.

The door opens and this tough-looking white dude with a blond spiky haircut and too many gold chains gets out.

'Where's the fire? Where you going so fast, little girl?' he says, smiling at me.

He's wearing a white tracksuit that is very baggy.

Because I am so tired and confused and worried, I start to cry again – like a wimp.

'Don't cry. It's okay,' he says, taking a step toward me, moving very slowly. 'What's wrong?'

BBB is now barking at this man skeptically. Like Ms Jenny, B Thrice is a good judge of character, but for some reason I want to believe that this guy is not evil – that maybe JC is sending me some help.

Blondie's actually kind of handsome, if I'm being truthful, and almost innocent looking – like Billy Budd.

'I'm trying to find my mom,' I say, because it's the truth, and I'm so very tired.

'Get in – I'll help you look,' he says. 'You're very pretty, you know.'

When he calls me pretty, something in my stomach begins to churn, and the man begins to look more like

Claggart than Billy Budd. 'I think I'll just walk, thanks for the offer, though.'

'Bad things happen to girls like you when they stray out of their neighborhoods in the middle of the night,' he says. 'You should come with me.'

'Amber!' a voice yells, and when I look over my shoulder, Father Chee is running toward me in slippers through the cold night and wearing only his black pajamas, making him look sorta like some crazy martial arts ninja or something.

'Who are you supposed to be?' the blond man asks FC when he reaches us. 'Jackie Chan?'

'Amber, come,' FC says, and then takes my hand.

'Is he your pimp or something?'

'He's my priest,' I say.

'Well, maybe another time then,' the blond man says, smiling kind of funny, chuckling. He gets into his car and drives away.

'Come,' Father Chee says, and then we sorta jog back to The Korean Catholic Church.

'Please tell me what are you doing here in this neighborhood at night?' Father Chee asks when we are inside with the doors locked.

I'm scared for my mom, so I come clean.

As I tell him everything about Mom and our living on Hello Yellow and Mom's not coming home tonight, the adrenaline rush wears off, and I start to get seriously nervous and upset and worried.

My voice becomes all tiny and whiny, which makes me feel like I'll never be as brave and strong as Donna – like I'll never get into Bryn Mawr College.

When I finish, I am crying again, so FC gives me a fatherly hug, patting my back very gently, which is cool of him. He's a good man.

'We should call the police so they will start looking for your mother,' Father Chee says.

'Do you think I should consult my attorney first?' I ask.

'You have an attorney?'

So I tell him all about Donna, and then we wake her with a phone call, using the pay phone in Father's Chee's church, after which FC puts on his penguin suit.

We take a cab to Ricky's house, where I tell Donna the whole story as Father Chee makes coffee.

I can tell that Donna is mad at me for not telling her how bad things were with my mom and my living on Hello Yellow for months, because, very loudly, she says, *Months?*

And when I nod, she asks me why I didn't tell her earlier, and I start to cry again because I am so weak and stupid – even though I'm sorta mad at her for not figuring it all out earlier. *Why else would I need to take a shower at her house every morning?*

Father Chee serves us coffee, and then Donna makes a few phone calls.

I hear her talking to the police, and then to some sorta private detective.

At one point I hear her say, 'Money is not an issue.'

Donna's young assistant shows up without makeup and without her hair done, making her look less intimidating.

'You're getting a raise,' Donna says to her assistant.

'Are you okay?' Jessica says to me, and I can tell that she is sincere. I remember thinking how much I hated Jessica in the past, so I start crying even harder now because I'm such a little girl.

'If we're not back, don't tell Ricky anything when he gets up in the morning,' Donna says to Jessica. 'Tell him I had to go to trial early, let him eat whatever he wants for breakfast, and then take him to school. Oh, yeah. Feed the dog a can, and then let him out. Okay?'

Jessica nods, and then FC, me, and Donna are in her Mercedes driving back to Hello Yellow.

We call Mom's name and search the parking lot with flashlights.

Mom's not in the parking lot.

Mom's not on Hello Yellow.

'Grab your things,' Donna tells me, so I get my trash bags from under Hello Yellow and Father Chee takes them to Donna's car. 'Where else might she have gone?'

'She might have met a man?' I say hopefully, because it's better than any alternative of which I can think. 'She was always trying to find a man with an apartment so we'd have a home.'

'Did she ever leave you alone for an entire night before?' Donna asks.

'No,' I say, but then feel like I shouldn't be lying now. 'Well, not very often. Sometimes. But tonight is different. I feel like something very bad might have happened. I sorta just know it somehow. You have to trust me on this. Seriously, Donna, I'm really scared.'

'Okay,' Donna says, and I can see in her eyes that she is worried – that this is bad. Very bad. So terribly messed up.

The three of us drive around aimlessly looking for Mom.

We cruise the ghetto, all of the major Childress streets slide past the passenger-side window; we pass all the bars and liquor stores of which we can think and then go back to the bus lot when it is time for the bus drivers to pick up schoolchildren.

Mom's boss confirms that my mother did not show up for work today, and none of the other bus drivers have seen her. Mom didn't call out sick either.

I start to feel as though I am very alone in the world.

When we get back to Donna's house, Ricky is gone, and BBB has shredded the arm of Donna's leather recliner.

When Jessica comes back from dropping off Ricky, she apologizes for the mess, and Donna says, 'My fault. I forgot to tell you to lock up Bobby Big Boy whenever you leave the house.'

Even though Donna doesn't say anything about my dog ruining her expensive furniture, seeing the damage makes me cry again for some reason.

I'm so tired.

After a few phone calls, Donna convinces the local police to come interview me. She leaves Father Chee in charge, and then the lawyers shower and dress and get ready to go to Donna's ongoing murder trial.

Father Chee just sits next to me on the leather couch BBB ripped earlier, and we take turns petting B Thrice.

FC doesn't say anything stupid, like most adults would, but just sits with me, which I appreciate.

Right after Donna and Jessica leave, two nice uniformed officers come and ask me a bunch of questions about where Mom and I were living, Mom's drinking problem, and her long list of past boyfriends, all of whom I describe in great detail, while the cops write it all down.

Donna told me to tell the truth, and so I do.

I give all of the same answers to the private detective Donna hired, who shows up seconds after the police leave. He's a twitchy man with a big yellow mustache and acne scars all over his face. He also writes down my answers – all the secrets I have been keeping for months now.

When we finish, it's almost noon, which means that – besides the hour or so of sleep I got on the bus – I have been up for thirty-some hours straight.

'Are you okay?' Father Chee asks me.

'I'm so tired,' I say, and then because I really need to, I snuggle up to my Man of God, resting my head on his shoulder, and cry some more.

Somehow I fall asleep.

PART THREE

Puke and Cry

THIRTEEN

It takes them nine days to find my mother's body, but when they do, the story is the lead on every TV news station and is on the front page of every local paper, especially since my mother's killer is immediately linked to the other rape-murders that had happened in the area, so I'm sure you know all of the gruesome, unreal, sadistic, and childhood-ending details. I'm not going to list these details here, because I don't want to give the facts any more credence than they already have.

I'm pretty numb now.

Maybe even numb enough to be an official nihilist like Joan of Old.

For some things there are no explanations – no reasons, and so, when these things happen, there is nothing to talk about really. And it is best not to dwell on said things for too long, because you will find that life has no real meaning if you do.

Maybe you think I am only saying this because I am

in a state of denial or shock, but that's just not the case.
I'm being honest, maybe for the first time.

With Father Chee and Donna, I go to identify the body,
even though Donna says I don't have to.

For some reason, I need to see.

I insist.

I'm a real cat about it.

Maybe I want to know, just so I won't be wondering
for the rest of my life – like I do with Dad. And as selfish
as it might seem, knowing that my mother is definitely
dead is better than thinking she might be out there somewhere having abandoned me in an effort to live an easier
life without her stupid daughter to worry about.

I go to the morgue.

I see the facts.

It's worse than anything I could have ever imagined.

My howling stops them from uncovering more than
Mom's head and shoulders.

I don't want to see any more.

I crumble.

I melt.

I evaporate.

They cover what's left of my naked mother back up
with a sheet and push her into a wall, which is when I
realize that she is in some sorta freezer.

I do not talk for three days.

I sit.

I stare.

I see my mother's naked dead body in a dark freezer.

Sometimes I shake.

It seems like I am in a constant nightmare.

Donna brings me soup and crackers and toast – and takes care of BBB's needs.

At my request, Donna pays to have my mother cremated.

Fire. Warmth. It's better this way.

I promise to pay Donna back, and she says it's not necessary.

The very next day, at my request, Father Chee performs a private ceremony at the bench where Mom and I used to feed ducks.

BBB is the only other person invited to the ceremony, because this special childhood place is mine alone – it's what I have left, so I don't want to share it with anyone except FC and BBB. Not even Donna and Ricky are invited.

Father Chee does a very good job eulogizing my mom, especially since he never met her. He says a lot of things about Mom going to heaven and my seeing her again, which is pretty nice, especially since Mom was never baptized or confirmed as a member of the Catholic Church – and I'm pretty sure she never went to confession – so I know FC is supposed to say Mom was going to hell and all.

Maybe the Pope is pissed?

I don't care.

FC says he doesn't care either.

I'm not going to tell you exactly what Father Chee says at Mom's funeral, but it was very beautiful – as beautiful as Private Jackson's best haiku, which is saying something. True.

We spread Mom's ashes on the water and grass around the bench – and I pray flowers will bloom there in the spring, which is a girly and maybe silly sentiment, but a nice thought too.

FOURTEEN

Donna takes me in, buys me a bed, gives me my own room, and begins sorting through the legal red tape involved for her to become my legal guardian, which is complicated since no one knows if my father is still alive or where he might be – and I don't know of any living family I may or may not have since my mom left her home out west early on in life, hitchhiked east at the age of thirteen, and never told me anything about her parents whom she hated and refused to even name. I never even knew my own mother's maiden name.

Donna says she knows enough people to keep me out of the foster care system at least until I turn eighteen this summer, provided that I will state before a judge that I want to stay with Donna and Ricky, which I do.

The police arrest a man with huge brown glasses and strange hair.

I am sure you read all about him in the papers or see him on television.

His face is everywhere.

He becomes famous.

He admits to doing what he did, but his lawyer stresses that the whole thing was random, an accident even, because my mother's killer went off his medications, but is now back on meds, as if that matters at all to anyone.

Along with the families of the other victims, the prosecution contacts me and says I will be made to testify, which I will hate doing, even though I have Donna to help me out – and I'm not going to tell you about the trial, because it will prove to be too horrible.

My mother's killer uses my name whenever he talks to the press.

Through the media he apologizes to all of his victims' family members, but the only name I really hear him say is Amber Appleton.

He says he is sick.

He says he deserves whatever he gets – and his unfeeling mechanical voice makes me shiver.

He has a long criminal history.

He is a registered sex offender.

Looking into his eyes makes you believe that life can be absolutely meaningless.

He is like every other man who makes people disappear in horrible unimaginable ways.

He reminds me of a Nietzsche quote I found while

doing Joan of Old research: 'A casual stroll through the lunatic asylum shows that faith does not prove anything.'

Donna tells me this man will go to jail for life, that he will be punished in terrible ways over and over again by the other inmates – and I tell her I don't really care about any of that – in fact, I never want to talk about that man ever again, and I do not really care what happens to him.

FIFTEEN

I do not go back to school.

I lose fifteen pounds.

I am always cold.

I become very jumpy; any old noise will scare me horribly.

Donna tries to get me to see a therapist, but I refuse.

I cannot stand listening to Ricky's autistic nonsense, and I yell at him a lot – until he finally gets the message and just leaves me alone in my room.

I decide to quit being Amber Appleton, which isn't to say that I change my name or anything. I just decide that I can't keep living the way I used to live – swinging for the fences, believing that things are going to work out, that everything is worth fighting for, and that I am brave and strong enough to change my reality, because I'm not and I can't.

Joan of Old was right.

I get her now, and what she said about life being a hell that I was only beginning to experience – that makes sense suddenly.

SIXTEEN

I'm not a kid anymore.

SEVENTEEN

Ty, Jared, and Chad-in-a-backpack come over to Donna's and – in my new bedroom – they say a lot of dumb things.

At first, they say they are sorry, and ask what they can do, and when I don't say anything, they get sorta fidgety, and start talking about the recent Halo 3 games they have played in The Franks Lair, and how they are organizing an all-night video game tournament to help the football team raise money for new safer pads and helmets and other sundry equipment.

This seems important to them.

Back in the day, that news would have pissed me off, because Lex and company are obviously just using my boys – but listening to Ty, Jared, and Chad go on and on, I can't even shrug.

I just stare at my boys with what I suppose is a very blank look on my face until they leave.

That night I tell Donna I don't want to see Ty, Jared, and Chad anymore – but she doesn't respond to my request.

EIGHTEEN

Father Chee jogs to my house every single morning and comes up into my bedroom – even on Sundays, before he presides over Mass.

He never fails to show up.

If I am up, he'll ask if I want to talk.

For weeks, I do not want to talk, so FC just sits next to me for an hour, and we sorta breathe together.

We just sit on the edge of my bed breathing, occupying the same space, which is okay with me, because I really like my Man of God, even if I am mad at God Himself.

If I'm not up, or if I am pretending to sleep, or if I am just lying there like usual, staring at the ceiling, Father Chee will kneel by my bed and bow his head.

If I ask him what he is doing, he'll say he is lifting me up to God, asking God to help me be whoever I need to be at this moment of my life.

He comes every day, and I don't mind his coming.

NINETEEN

Franks sends me a card that reads:

> Dear Amber,
> We were very shaken by the news.
> I am always here if you need me.
> We miss you down in The Franks Lair.
> I'm praying for you, and will be
> looking forward to your return.
> Be well,
> Franks

I throw his card away.

I throw away all of the flowers and cards from classmates and community members.

I don't even sniff or open any of those.

I do not want any of these flower arrangements or sympathy cards to exist, so I ask Donna to burn them in the backyard, but I never see any smoke rising past my window, so I don't think she is honoring my request.

TWENTY

This zombie-type mom in need of extra cash starts coming to 'tutor' me, since I'm not going to school right now.

She's large.

She smells like mothballs.

She never laughs or smiles or tells a joke.

She reminds me of a robot caked in meat.

Her name is Mrs Redman.

My real teachers give her assignments that I am supposed to complete. At first, there are little hand-written notes on the assignments – encouraging words from my real teachers – but these notes disappear after a few weeks or so, which is when I realize that my teachers have given up on me. It didn't take them very long.

Because I still want to go to Bryn Mawr, I do all of my assignments and show Mrs Redman my work three times a week when she comes to visit me.

She gives me all A's, even when I answer incorrectly on purpose.

I think she is afraid of me, or something.

TWENTY-ONE

'Father Chee?'

   'Yes, Amber?'

   'Why does God allow men to go mentally insane?'

   'I don't know.'

   'You'll never lie to me, will you?'

   'No.'

   'Promise me. That you won't tell me lies like everyone else. That you won't BS me.'

   'I promise – I will never lie to you.'

TWENTY-TWO

Prince Tony calls me on the phone from time to time, but I don't really listen to what he says to me. It's all crap about the seasons of life and the ebb and flow and other blah-blah stuff adults tell you when they don't know what the hell to say. 'Do you understand?' he always asks me at the end of the conversations, and I always say yes.

TWENTY-THREE

'Father Chee?'
    'Yes, Amber?'
    'Why are dogs more humane than humans?'
    'I don't know.'

TWENTY-FOUR

Right about the same time my mom's name starts showing up in the news, Private Jackson begins sending me one haiku a day in the mail.

He doesn't write a letter stating that he is sorry for my loss, nor does he ask how I am doing or any of that other crap that doesn't help. He just sends poems. And his haikus are not aimed at inspiring me or making me feel better or helping me deal with the loss. With words, he simply takes snapshots of simple things for me – like a leaf, a bottle cap, a snowflake, a bird in flight, an ant, a single breath – and when I read these haikus I sorta trip out on the image that is never good or bad, happy or sad, exciting or boring.

These images just are.

I begin to really look forward to reading PJ's haikus, and going to check the mail is the only time I leave my new bedroom other than to use the bathroom.

Covering the four walls with Private Jackson's

haikus – one page a day – I slowly make my room into a cocoon of poetry.

Here is the first one he sends me:

> I WAKE AND SIT UP
> SQUIRRELS SCRATCHING FROM INSIDE
> MY WALLS ARE ALIVE

At first, I read it – like a million times, wondering if Private Jackson was trying to communicate with me through metaphor.

I puzzled out all sorts of interpretations too.

Maybe it was a metaphor for the madness – or the chaos I was feeling as of late, which is sorta hidden in my chest and mind, but real?

I had been in my new room for days now.

Maybe it was a metaphor for the madness of the man who killed my mother?

Maybe PJ was telling me that I needed to wake up and see that things were still alive and moving around me, even though my mom was gone and I felt so all alone?

Maybe he meant something else, and I was just too dumb to understand?

But then I remembered what Private Jackson stood for, what he was all about – all of the Zen stuff.

I instantly understood that PJ woke up in the middle of the night and heard squirrels in his bedroom walls, so he took a mental snapshot of the moment and wrote me a haiku.

Nothing more.

The moment just was – free of the emotions and judgments or any of the other illusionary things we humans feel the need to attach to everything we encounter.

Reading Private Jackson's haikus after my mother's murder – I totally got why he had been writing haikus all this time, ever since 'Nam, training his mind to allow things to exist without all of the complicated emotional baggage.

Everything simply is – always and forever.

THE FALLEN LEAF FLIES
LIKE A YOUNG ICARUS AND
THEN DISINTEGRATES

I totally get haikus now. True.

And Private Jackson is my favorite writer.

TWENTY-FIVE

'Father Chee?'

'Yes, Amber?'

'Why does God allow horrible things to happen to good people?'

'I don't know.'

TWENTY-SIX

One day – on Donna's iPod – I listen to Dinosaur Jr's 'Puke and Cry' a million times in a row. I just set it to repeat the one song over and over again, and then I listen for several hours – tripping out.

I pretend that the lead singer – J Mascis – is singing me the song over and over again from Donna's living room downstairs. Mascis – who has long silver hair, because he is old now – keeps on singing, 'Come on down. Come on down. Come on down', like he really wants me to come down from my little cocoon of haikus and misery.

I don't come down, but I like pretending there is an obscure rock star who wants me to.

The battery finally runs out, and when I take the headphones off, my ears are ringing, J Mascis is gone, and Donna is calling to me, asking me if I want some soup.

TWENTY-SEVEN

'Father Chee?'
'Yes, Amber?'
'When will it stop hurting so badly?'
'I don't know.'

TWENTY-EIGHT

GRASS TEA BOILED AND DRUNK
MY DOG ROLLS THROUGH TOMORROW'S
CUP - THERE'S ENDLESS TEA

TWENTY-NINE

After a month or so, Old Man Linder pays me a visit on behalf of the entire Methodist Home.

Donna comes into my room and says that I have to come down to see Old Man Linder because he can't walk up steps. Donna's murder trial ended a week or so ago and she has taken some time off from work to care for me, which I told her not to do. She dotes on me now, even though I hardly talk to her.

'I only go down once a day to check the mail,' I tell Donna. 'Tell Old Man Linder he'll have to come up here if he wants to talk to me.'

'The man has tubes running up his nose and is attached to an oxygen—'

'Yeah, I know him,' I say, like a total cat.

'He can't walk stairs. He said it could kill him, but he really wants to talk to you, Amber. I don't think he leaves the home much. Please just come down. He's an old man and I think it might be good for you to—'

'No,' I say. 'Tell him he can come back tomorrow around one fifteen when I'll be checking the mail. That's when I will next come downstairs.'

'Amber, what's happening to you?' Donna says in this really dramatic fashion that pisses me off.

When I don't answer, she leaves.

Ten minutes later, Donna returns and hands me a cup of hot cocoa and a Snickers bar, and then shakes her head at me before exiting my poetry cocoon.

I hear Old Man Linder breathing really hard on the steps.

One footstep, clunk, heavy breathing.

One footstep, clunk, heavy breathing.

One footstep, clunk, heavy breathing.

His oxygen tank makes an awful clunk each time he sets it on a higher step.

'Mr Linder,' Donna says, 'perhaps – you really shouldn't—'

'Don't tell me what I can and can't do! I'm old enough to be your grandfather, thank you very much!' Old Man Linder says, and then sucks in an awful breath like he has been underwater for the last two hours or something.

He and Donna fight about whether he should be walking up the steps for another few minutes before I yell, 'Donna, your making him yell isn't helping!'

And then I only hear footsteps, clunking, and heavy breathing.

When Old Man Linder reaches the top of the stairs,

he looks like he might fall backward and die. His face is completely white, which makes me feel like a total cat, so I walk into the hallway, grab his arm, and escort him into my room.

When he squeezes my shoulder football coach-style, I know that he is going to be okay – that he probably won't die in my room.

He points to the Snickers and cocoa on my dresser. 'Compliments of Door Woman Lucy.'

I nod.

'How you holdin' up?' he asks me, and then sits down on the wooden chair that goes with the desk Donna bought for me.

I shrug.

I can see that his clear air tubes look sorta fogged up, and I wonder if that is bad.

'What are all those papers on your wall?'

'Haikus.'

'Hi-whats?'

'Short Japanese poems.'

'You can read Japanese?' he says.

'They're written in English,' I say.

'By you?'

'No, by Private Jackson.'

'Who's Private Jackson?'

'He was in 'Nam back in the day. Now he writes haikus. He's my favorite poet.'

'I'm not going to get into all that, kid,' Old Man

Linder says, adjusting the nozzle on his oxygen bottle, which produces a hissing sound. 'I know you've suffered a horrific, senseless, and cruel loss, and while I won't pretend to know what that must feel like – I will say that I'm old enough to know that life throws you a few nasty blows before she's done with you, but each time you're knocked down, you have to pull yourself up by the bootstraps, and—'

'Please don't,' I say to Old Man Linder. 'Please.'

He looks confused.

He's wringing his hands.

He's so old school.

He's so out of his league.

'I was nineteen years old when I lost my best friend in World War Two. I never did feel the same—'

'Please stop.'

He shakes off my request, smiles knowingly, and says, 'We miss you down at the home. Joan of Old wants a rematch. She's still contesting your last battle. Stating that the kiss was a violation of the damn rules, not that Old Man Thompson will ever side with her.' Old Man Linder forces a laugh. 'But some of the older feeble-minded broads have taken Old Joan's point of view. If we don't make some sort of public statement quickly, the fans will think—'

'It was just a stupid game. It wasn't real.'

'The Wednesday Afternoon Battles are something to look forward to and—'

'I'm retired. Joan of Old can have the title by forfeit.'

'Forfeit? Retired? *Are you kidding me?* You haven't even begun to peak and you—'

'I'm done making old people smile. It's over.'

He pauses for a second, gathers his thoughts.

So softly, Old Man Linder says, 'Amber.'

When I look into his eyes they are moist, and I can tell that he loves me like I am his own granddaughter, but I can't play that game anymore for him, so I look away.

'Life goes on,' he says. 'Whether we choose to enjoy it or not. So you might as well find a way to enjoy the parts you can. You can't just give up on life, Amber.'

'Why not? Everyone else does. Everyone. Why don't *you* get up there this Wednesday and tell jokes? Why don't any of you take on Joan of Old yourselves? I'm tired of carrying all you people. I can't do it anymore. I can't be the Princess of Hope for you, because I've got no hope left! Didn't you read the papers? Don't you remember what happened to my mom? How can anyone have hope after something like that? And yet you expect me to snap out of it and carry on for you? Give you a laugh once a week? Get well just so I can play some stupid game with old people every Wednesday afternoon? For what? Why should I?'

And then I break out in tears.

I sob for minutes.

'I shouldn't have come,' Old Man Linder says. 'I was just trying to—'

'Just leave, okay?' I scream.

It takes Old Man Linder a long time to stand, and from the sounds he is making, I think he is crying now too, which makes me feel even worse, but I don't try to stop him from leaving and I don't say I'm sorry.

I just want him to leave.

I can't be what he needs me to be anymore.

In fact, I was never really who he wanted me to be – I was a fake.

For the next few minutes or so, I listen to him take one step at a time, setting down his oxygen tank with heavy clunks – Old Man Linder sucking air like a madman.

I hear Donna apologizing for me downstairs, and Old Man Linder says he shouldn't have come again, which is when I realize that I crushed him – that I kicked him square in the metaphorical balls and knocked what little hope he had right out of him, the lightweight. It's so easy to crush men like him. I pity Old Man Linder. How did he ever make it to old age?

After I hear the front door open and close, Donna comes up to my room and says, 'You should be ashamed of yourself. This isn't you, Amber. You're better than this.'

'Fuck you,' I say – still sobbing – shocking myself.

Donna looks at me for a second or two – like I had slapped her – and then her bottom lips starts to quiver, which is something I never even thought was possible.

I see a tear slide down her cheek, and then she is gone.

So even the mighty Donna can be crushed, I think.

THIRTY

WRITING HAIKUS ONE
AFTER THE OTHER, KNOWING
ONLY THE MOMENT

THIRTY-ONE

'Father Chee?'

'Amber?'

'What is it: is man only a blunder of God, or God only a blunder of man?'

'So you are quoting Nietzsche now?'

'You know his work?'

'Yes.'

'Does reading Nietzsche ever make you doubt your faith?'

'Yes.'

'But you still believe in God?'

'Yes.'

'How do you keep believing?'

'I have faith.'

'Why?'

'Because when I asked Him for help, God sent me a young, hopeful girl who was able to convince a group of shy Korean women to sing The Supremes – making ordinary women into divas – doubling my church's membership. This was a great miracle that I saw with my own eyes. It boosted my faith much.'

'What if that young, hopeful girl never recovered from the blow God sent her way? What if she never sang with those Korean women ever again, and people stopped coming to your church and the Pope fired you and then you got sick and were about to die all alone feeling like your life meant nothing – and then some mentally insane man appeared and killed you in a strange and bizarre and terrifying manner? Would you still have faith in God then?'

'I don't know.'

THIRTY-TWO

THE SUN IS NOT A
BALL—IT'S AN ENDLESS WHITE STREAK
TIME'S AN ILLUSION

THIRTY-THREE

'Father Chee?'

'Yes, Amber?'

'If I had followed my mom on the night she was killed, do you think I might have been able to stop that man from doing what he did?'

'I don't know.'

THIRTY-FOUR

Four-leaf clover: A
miracle, mutation, or
happy accident?

THIRTY-FIVE

'Father Chee?'

'Yes, Amber?'

'Why do some people go through life never knowing a single major tragedy, and then others have horrible things happen to them over and over again?'

'I don't know.'

THIRTY-SIX

BITING INTO MY
YELLOW-GREEN APPLE - LIPS AND
FINGERS GET STICKY

THIRTY-SEVEN

'Father Chee?'

'Yes, Amber?'

'Do you believe that I was a pretty good person before my mother died?'

'I know it. You still are a good person.'

'So it really doesn't matter if we are good or not – bad things will still happen to us regardless?'

'Yes.'

'Why?'

'I don't know.'

THIRTY-EIGHT

Outside my window
Sparrow makes a nest out of
What I threw away

THIRTY-NINE

'Father Chee?'

'Yes, Amber?'

'Why didn't God turn the other cheek when Adam and Eve ate the apple? Why did He have to punish all of mankind for eating a damn apple?'

'It is a metaphor for wanting to know more than what we can handle. God tried to protect us from the consequences of knowledge, but we failed to listen.'

'Do you think I ate some metaphorical apple? Do you think my mother was killed because I pissed God off somehow? Did I fail to listen or something?'

'No. I do not think this. Not at all.'

'Then why was my mother killed?'

'I don't know.'

FORTY

FORTY-ONE

'Father Chee?'

'Yes, Amber.'

'Why do you keep coming here every day?'

'Because you are worth visiting.'

'Why?'

'Because you will come through this and be stronger on the other side. You will help people again someday.'

'Do you really believe that?'

'Yes. It is inevitable.'

'So why do you need to come if it's inevitable?'

'No need. I like visiting Amber Appleton. I want to be here when you are reborn – when you finally come through this and are stronger for it.'

'Is that why bad things happen – to make us stronger?'

'Maybe, but truthfully – I don't know.'

'I miss my mom. She was a terrible mom, but I miss her. I really do.'

'I also miss my mother.'

'What are your parents like? Are they here in America or in Korea?'

'My parents were very good people. They are both dead now.'

'How did they die?'

'They were murdered.'

'Seriously?'

'Yes.'

'Why didn't you tell me this before?'

'You did not ask.'

'How were your parents murdered?'

'Many years ago. In a detention camp.'

'What's that?'

'It is a prison where people who criticize the North Korean government are taken.'

'What did your parents say about the government?'

'They said that people should be allowed to believe in Jesus and build churches.'

'That's a crime?'

'It is in North Korea.'

'And they were killed in prison?'

'Yes.'

'Why would JC let them be killed after they stuck up for Him?'

'I don't know.'

'Is that why you became a priest here in America? Because of your parents?'

'Yes.'

'Why?'

'So my parents' death would mean something.'

'How does your being a priest make your parents' death mean something?'

'They gave their lives for a good idea. Now I use my life to tell other people the good idea.'

'What's the good idea?'

'That no matter how much evidence we have to prove that life is meaningless, we should believe that life makes some sort of sense – and that the story of Jesus is a good story, simply because it teaches us that we should be kind to others. That we should do whatever it takes, that we should sing soul music if it makes the lives of others better. That we should try to be good people, and love everyone.'

'Do you love the people who killed your parents?'

'I pray for them, and all like them.'

'But do you love them?'

'I don't know.'

'You think that I'm going to be like you, don't you? That's why you come here every day?'

'I think you are going to be much better than me.'

'Why?'

'Father Chee cannot do the soul clap so well.'

For the first time in many weeks, I smile – and Father Chee laughs out a single note – *ha!*

'I'm sorry your parents were killed for believing in JC,' I say.

'I am sorry your mother was taken from you for no good reason at all, Amber. I am truly sorry for your loss.'

'But there is nothing either of us can do to bring our parents back, right?'

'There is nothing we can do to bring them back, but we can honor their memory by moving forward.'

'Why should we do that?'

'Maybe it is better than sitting in a room forever?'

'Why?'

'You know why,' FC says.

'It's not fair.'

'Life is not fair. You are correct.'

'Then why should we be fair?'

'Because we can.'

'I don't know, FC. I mean I totally dig your coming here every day. I do. True. But I don't think I can go back to being who I used to be.'

'Who were you?'

'Amber Appleton. Aka the Princess of Hope.'

'You were, are, and will always be a hopeful person, until you die.'

'Why do you say that to me? Even now, when you know I've got nothing left. Why do you put that on me?'

'Because I have faith, and it is riding on the Princess of Hope. I believe in you, Amber Appleton. I've seen your powers.'

'Don't do that to me.'

'What?'

'Put your faith on me. I can't take that kind of pressure right now, okay? I just can't take it!'

'I did not mean—'

'Just don't,' I say, and then go to the bathroom.

I stay in the bathroom for a long time – until I hear FC walk down the steps and leave Donna's house.

FORTY-TWO

THE FLY THAT DIED BY
SMASHING INTO MY WINDOW
PANE, I DISPOSE OF

FORTY-THREE

Ty visits my bedroom solo and says, 'I brought you this.' He places a clear vase with a single rose and some baby's breath on my dresser, and then adds, 'How you feeling?'

'Crappy,' I say from under my comforter; I don't even sit up.

'I've been thinking about you a lot, Amber.'

I haven't thought about Ty even once in the last few weeks, so I don't say anything.

'I don't really know what to say about what happened,' Ty continues, 'and it seems like you don't want to talk about it, so I'm just going to talk about other stuff, okay?'

With my head still on my pillow, I just look at Ty, who is leaning his butt against my new dresser.

He swallows once and says, 'The Marketing Club regionals are next week.'

'I know.'

'We've been practicing pretty hard. The team and all. Maybe Ricky told you, but Franks has us debating and practicing our pitches in the morning instead of playing Halo 3. We debate at lunch too. We're on a video game hiatus until after regionals. We're all pretty nervous and excited. We think we can place this year, no sweat.'

'Good luck.'

'You're really not going to compete this year, are you?'

'No.'

'You would take first place if you did. We'd all do better, if—'

'Well, I'm not competing, so I'm not taking any place. And The Five will just have to be The Four, because I'm out.'

Ty smiles sorta weird and then says, 'I'm going to win regionals for you. I'll even give you the red ribbon. I'm going to do it for you. Then we'll take The Five to nationals. Would you come to Vegas with us if I won?'

'No.'

'We miss you. All of us. The entire Five.'

'I'm sorry my mother's murder has inconvenienced you.'

Ty's eyes narrow as if I had sucker-punched him. 'Why you being like that?'

'Like what?'

'So mean.'

'Because I'm a cat – a real bitch.'

'No you're not. You're the coolest girl I ever met. I've always admired you, Amber. And maybe I didn't say it before, but—'

'Just leave.'

Ty looks at me for a second, and then says, 'I thought maybe sometime The Five could like maybe share a sundae at Friendly's? We could all go to the one in Hampton, so no one would know, if you are afraid of being seen outside the house. You could sneak out one night. I got my license last week. It was my birthday, remember? I sent you an invitation to my party. Did you get it? Ricky came.'

I remember throwing it out, but do not say so.

'Maybe Ricky told you my dad bought me an old Volvo station wagon. I've been driving Ricky to school and all. My ride's outside actually. So I was thinking maybe I could take you out sometime?'

'No.'

'No?'

'Hell no,' I say, and then I walk over to my desk and pretend to do my assignments.

Ty stands there for a few minutes, and then he leaves.

A week or so after Ty visits solo, I receive an envelope with a second place Marketing Club ribbon in it. A note reads:

AA,
I tried to win for you. I really did.
Franks said I was robbed by the judges.
My Friendly's offer still stands.
Ty

PS – M.C. regionals weren't as much
fun without you. Everyone else agrees.
Even Franks said it. If Ricky hasn't told
you already, no one made nationals.

FORTY-FOUR

'Amber?'

'Yes, Father Chee?'

'I am sorry.'

'For what?'

'For putting unneeded pressure on you. For putting a cross on you when you are already suffering. It was wrong of me. Selfish.'

I don't say anything.

'Unless you ask me to keep coming, I will no longer come to visit you every day. In fact, I will never come again if you do not ask me to come. I want to help you, yes, but I also have been coming here because I need to believe that you are someone I need you to be, so that my faith will be increased. This is not fair to you. You spoke this truth the last time we talked. So this is the last time I will come to your room uninvited. The Korean Divas for Christ miss you very much and would love to sing with you again, but they will be just fine if you choose never to return to us. It is your life to do with as you wish, and you should make the decisions you think are best. I will be praying that you are who you need to be, always. And for selfish reasons, I hope that I will see you again soon. But Father Chee will also be okay either way, so do not worry about him. Goodbye.'

When Father Chee turns to leave I want to hug him and tell him to stay – that I want him to keep coming every day – but for some reason, I say nothing.

FC does not come the next day, and I am equal parts surprised, angry, and sad.

FORTY-FIVE

FLOWERS ARE IN THE
GROUND, WHERE WE CANNOT SEE THE
FUTURE WONDERMENT

FORTY-SIX

Easter comes and goes.
   I do not go to church.
   I do not celebrate the resurrection.

FORTY-SEVEN

Sun streaming through the window, my carpet is warm enough for bare feet

FORTY-EIGHT

Jared and Chad-in-a-backpack visit me again for the first time in weeks.

'I know you told us not to come,' Jared says.

'But we came anyway,' says Chad.

'Did Ty really come here solo?' Jared asks.

'Yeah,' I say.

'He's growing a beard,' Chad says.

'What?' I ask.

'Ty says he's not going to shave until you come out of your room and agree to go to Friendly's with us,' Chad says.

'He's calling it a friendship beard,' Jared says. 'Says it's an outward sign of his support for the reunification of The Five.'

'And he grew a full beard in days!' Chad says. 'He's beginning to look like Bin Laden.'

'What? Why?' I ask.

'Because his beard is getting all long and pointy at the

chin,' Chad says. 'Not because he actually wants to look like a terrorist or anything like that. Ty's a patriot. Red, white, and blue – tried-and-true.'

'No, why is he growing a beard? Seriously.'

'As an outward sign of his support for you,' Jared says. 'Just like I told you. It's a friendship beard.'

'But I'm not seeing the beard, because I'm in my room, so why would he grow one?'

'He sorta sent us here today to tell you about it,' Chad says. 'Show her, brother.'

Jared flips open his cell phone, hits a few buttons, and suddenly bearded Ty is smiling through the little square screen. His beard is sort of pointy at the chin, but he looks nothing like Bin Laden.

'We wanted to see you anyway,' Jared says, 'because we miss you a lot and we feel really badly about your missing Marketing Club regionals and refusing to be a part of The Five. But Ty is really worried about you. He's really upset.'

Jared says, 'So what should we tell him?'

'Tell him?' I say.

'What's your reply?' Chad asks.

'I don't know,' I say.

'Will you – maybe go to Friendly's with us?' Chad asks.

'I'm not going anywhere right now,' I say.

'But maybe you *maybe* will – like – go to Friendly's again with us in the future?' Jared asks.

I sigh. This is ridiculous.

'Okay,' Chad says. 'We'll take that as a maybe and leave before you change your mind.'

When they leave, I sigh and shake my head.

I hear Donna ask Chad and Jared how it went, and they say 'Pretty good' just before I hear them exit through the front door.

FORTY-NINE

Air goes in and out,
Of my nose, throat, lungs, blood, heart,
Brain - and so I am

FIFTY

'Do you notice anything different?' Donna asks me. She's sitting down on the side of my bed, rubbing my back lightly with her hands. She's been doing this lately. She also has been combing my hair at night. I don't say anything to her about this – because I secretly like it when she rubs my back and combs my hair, as if I were a little girl again and she were my mom.

Donna's not my mom – my mom is dead – but it still feels good.

I don't say anything to Donna, because I'm still being a cat.

'When was the last time you saw Bobby Big Boy?' Donna asks me after rubbing my back for – like – fifteen minutes or so.

I think about it, and suddenly, my heart starts beating really fast.

It's been days – maybe weeks.

No, it can't be.

When *was* the last time I saw BBB?

I haven't thought about BBB even once for so long.

I am a terrible pet owner.

I sit up.

'Bobby Big Boy?' I yell.

'Shhh,' Donna says, 'he's sleeping downstairs.'

'Is something wrong with him?'

'Well. He's been acting a little funny,' Donna says. 'So – I'm just going to say this, Amber – I called a veterinarian today.'

'Why?'

'Bobby Big Boy has had a lot of diarrhea lately. He hasn't been eating regularly. He's been lethargic – looking sort of *unthrifty*. And today when I took him for a walk he – well – he collapsed.'

'What?'

'He recovered. He's okay now. But I'm taking him to the vet in a few minutes, and I wanted to know if you wanted to go with me.'

I run downstairs and find BBB in his room, lying on his bed.

His eyes are glassy.

He doesn't even pick up his head when I walk into the room.

I pick him up in my arms and kiss him.

'I'm sorry, B3. I'm so so sorry I've neglected you. I'm here now. I'm here.'

His eyes look so sad – defeated.

I hate myself for neglecting him, for not noticing that he was suffering – I'm such a cat, such a bad pet owner.

I finally leave the house.

FIFTY-ONE

Donna drives B Thrice and me to the veterinarian. Ricky stays home and does math problems.

'Do you think Bobby Big Boy might die?' I ask Donna in her Mercedes, with BBB curled up in my lap.

'Let's not jump to any conclusions,' she says.

'So you think this could be serious?'

'He's a relatively young dog, and pet medicine is good these days. We're taking him to the best veterinarian in the tri-state area. Dr Weissmuller at Weissmuller Pets of Childress.'

'We're taking you to the best, Bobby Big Boy. You hear that? The best.'

When we get to Weissmuller Pets of Childress, I carry BBB into the waiting room and a woman wearing black scrubs asks us if we have been there before, and when we say we haven't, she asks for BBB's medical records or anything that would prove he's had all of his shots.

'Where did you take him before you started living with us?' Donna asks me.

'Nowhere. He was never sick before,' I say.

'So you've never taken your pet to the vet before?' the lady asks me – sending me tons of attitude, cocking her head to one side and resting the end of her pen on her puffy apple-red kiss-shaped lips.

'Listen, I found him in a Nike box when I was living on a frickin' school bus. We were so poor we couldn't even afford to eat – like ever. My mom was killed a few months back by a psychopath, so I don't need any extra crap from you, okay?'

'Oh, *oh, my God*. You're *Amber Appleton*, aren't you?' the woman says, so nicely now. 'I'm so sorry. The name on the file says Roberts. I didn't know. Let me get the doctor right away. Just give me ten seconds.'

She disappears into another room.

I can see that all of the other pet owners waiting to see the doctor are staring at me now. Regular, work-weary people. A collie is barking at B3, a poodle is hiding under a chair, and this little kid with a runny nose is holding an evil-looking ferret with pink eyes.

'Ms Appleton?'

When I turn around, a man in peach-colored scrubs is smiling at me.

'Right this way,' he says.

In a room with photos of dogs taped up all over the walls, I put BBB down on a silver examination table. He lies on his side and breathes slowly.

'What is wrong with you, my friend?' Dr Weissmuller says to BBB, shaking his paw like formal men in suits do whenever they meet.

'Bobby Big Boy has been tired lately,' Donna says, 'he's not eating much, he threw up yesterday, he's had diarrhea – and today he collapsed while we were taking a walk.'

Dr Weissmuller feels BBB's belly.

'What do you feel?' I ask.

'His abdomen is distended.'

'Is that bad?' I ask.

'I don't know yet,' he says, and then removes a long needle from a drawer. 'I am going to stick this into the place where I think there is a tumor, and if blood comes out – then we'll know something.'

Dr Weissmuller inserts the needle into BBB's belly.

Blood comes out, but BBB doesn't move or even whimper.

'You see the blood?' he asks.

Donna and I both nod.

'So we should do an ultrasound to see if the tumor is on the spleen or liver.'

'What's the difference?' I ask.

'If the tumor is on the liver – there is nothing I can do for your dog. If it's on the spleen, we can operate.'

'How much is the ultrasound?' Donna asks.

'Seventy-five dollars.'

Donna nods once and says, 'Do it.'

Dr Weissmuller picks BBB up so gently and takes my doggie into another room, leaving Donna and me alone.

'I don't have any money to pay for this,' I say. 'I blew through my Rita's money back in January.'

'Don't worry about that.'

'Can I borrow the money from you?'

'I'll pay, don't worry, Amber.'

'What about the surgery?'

'If BBB needs surgery, I think I can afford it,' Donna says.

I shake my head – and I even cross my arms. I know that I mooch off Donna all the time, but taking responsibility for BBB has sort of become symbolic to me after all that has happened: it's one of the few things that I can control, and so I simply say, 'No.'

'No?'

'BBB is *my* responsibility. I'm going to pay for the surgery if he needs it,' I say.

'How?'

'I'm not sure yet.'

'Amber, you just need to worry about getting yourself together now and—'

'Stop,' I say, and then we wait in silence.

After a few long minutes, Dr Weissmuller returns and gently places BBB down on the silver table. 'The tumor is on the spleen.'

'So what now?' Donna asks.

'The tumor is bleeding into the abdomen. I will remove the spleen and we'll do a biopsy. They send me the results in less than a week. If the tumor is benign – your dog will live.'

'I can't take two deaths in one year,' I say to Donna, crying.

Dr Weissmuller says, 'I recommend surgery. Again, I will take out his spleen, and if the tumor is benign, your dog will live.'

'What if it is benign, and we do nothing?' Donna asks.

'Your dog will eventually bleed to death – internally.'

'How much is the surgery?' I ask.

'There can be complications, and maybe your dog will need blood transfusions – all told, the cost should be around two thousand dollars. Should I leave you alone to discuss this matter?'

Donna nods and Dr Weissmuller leaves the room.

'Can I borrow the money?' I ask Donna.

'I'll pay for all of it, Amber.'

'No. I just want a loan. I want to take care of this myself.'

I can see that Donna wants to help me. Her eyes are kind and her face is compassionate, but she doesn't understand that charity is for old people and cripples.

I bury my face in BBB's fur.

'Dr Weissmuller's going to get you feeling better, and then I'm going to get better too. I'm going to take you to see Ms Jenny just as soon as you are healthy. You stay alive,

BBB, and I'm going to be a better pet owner. I promise.'

I cry harder like a chick as I hold BBB close to my cheek.

'*Dr Weissmuller?*' Donna says.

Even though Donna protests, I sign all of the forms; I agree to pay for the operation in installments over the next few years, Donna co-signs, and then we leave.

As we are driving home, suddenly, I'm saying, 'Will you drop me off at Private Jackson's house?'

'Why?' she asks.

'I really need to see him.'

'So does this mean you're officially out of your room?' she asks, sorta surprised and maybe even hopefully.

'Something like that,' I say.

'Okay,' Donna says.

I give her directions and she drives me to PJ's house.

When Donna drops me off on the curb, she asks if I want her to come pick me up, and when I tell her I'll walk home, she says, 'Amber, are you sure you're okay?'

'Yeah,' I say. 'I just need to spend some time with PJ. I'm cool. Really.'

'Okay,' she says. 'But call if you want me to pick you up. Cool?'

I nod once and then walk toward PJ's house.

FIFTY-TWO

It's dark, so I know that Ms Jenny has already gone for her run.

I also know that PJ is home, so I knock on the front door.

When PJ opens the front door, he doesn't say anything about my mom or about me or why the hell I haven't visited him in months – he doesn't even ask if I liked the haikus he has been sending me every day. He only says, 'Please come in. I'll put on the tea.'

When I enter his house I see the blank spot on the last wall of his living room – the hole that I have not yet covered with doggie haikus – and it makes me feel really depressed.

I sit down on the couch as Private Jackson makes tea.

Ms Jenny comes looking for BBB, and when she doesn't find him, she jumps up on the couch and ducks her head under my hand, so that I will pet her.

I pet her with all I got.

When PJ brings me the tea, it is green – like always.

I sip it.

He sits and sips his cup.

I sip mine again – and then I start sobbing.

I sob so hard I drop my teacup and Ms Jenny jumps off the couch and hides under the coffee table.

I can't stop crying.

I can't stop shaking.

Snot is running down my nose – spit down my chin.

It all comes out.

Everything.

My dad leaving us.

Being homeless.

My mom's murder.

BBB's having a tumor.

I'm not even an adult yet.

It's not fair.

It's really not fair.

I close my eyes so hard – trying to stop the tears.

I start to cough wildly.

I feel like I might die.

And then Private Jackson is next to me on the couch.

He's moved toward me for the first time.

I throw myself at him.

He hesitates for a second or two, but then he puts his arms around me.

I bury my head in his yellow button-down shirt, and he holds me.

After a few minutes, I stop coughing, but I can't stop crying.

I soak his yellow button-down shirt with hot tears.

We stay entwined like this on his couch – father-daughter style – for a long time.

When I finally let go, Private Jackson turns his face from me quickly and says, 'I will get you more tea.'

Before he leaves the room, I see that his face is also streaked with tears.

He stays in the kitchen for a long time – longer than it takes to make green tea.

When he returns, he hands me a new steaming-hot cup.

When I sip, he says, 'I just wrote a haiku in the kitchen.'

He has a piece of paper in his hand, so I ask, 'Can I read it?'

He hands it to me.

It reads:

THE SUN SETTING THROUGH
PINE TREES AT THE EDGE OF TOWN
MAKES ME SQUINT AND SMILE

'It's good,' I say. 'But it doesn't capture the present moment.'

'Maybe sometimes – on special occasions – every so

often, it is best to capture a different moment, maybe, when the present moment is not the right moment for you. It is sometimes nice to think that more moments are always coming. Always. Like the moments when you come to visit me.'

'True,' I say, and then sip my tea, realizing that what PJ just said is like – revolutionary for him, so I don't push it. I simply enjoy the present moment – having released so much emotional baggage – as this moment bleeds into the next one.

Silence.

We sip our cups for an hour, not saying a single word, just occupying the same space.

When I finish, I stand and say, 'You're a good man, Private Jackson.'

'I will wash the teacups now,' he says.

'I'm going to bring BBB here in a week or so to visit Ms Jenny, cool?'

'Ms Jenny will be looking forward to the visit very much,' he says, and then takes our teacups into the kitchen.

I let myself out of PJ's house and then walk through the darkness, navigating the Childress streets back to Donna's house – thinking about Dr Weissmuller cutting open Bobby Big Boy and removing his spleen – and before I know it, I'm praying again, asking JC to be with Dr Weissmuller, to help him to be exactly who he needs to be, so that BBB will be okay. And then I sorta promise JC that I will try to return to my hopeful self if He spares

BBB's life – even after what happened to my mom – which is a pretty good bargain for JC, as far as I'm concerned.

I'm still sorta mad at JC, but I've missed Him too. True.

I sorta need to pray, and all.

Praying keeps me sane.

Maybe it's my true favorite?

When I get to Donna's house, I find Ricky in the kitchen eating Ritz crackers and peanut butter.

'I'm sorry, Ricky,' I say.

'Ricky Roberts is supposed to leave Amber Appleton alone because her mother was killed and it wasn't fair, so she is mad at everyone for now, but she will snap out of it in the future. Yes. In the future.'

I snap both of my fingers and then give Ricky a kiss on the cheek.

'Amber Appleton kissed Ricky Roberts! Yes!'

'I'm sorry I was mean to you, Ricky,' I say, and then I notice that Donna is in the doorway watching the apology.

So I walk over to Donna, say, 'I'm going to school tomorrow,' and then I give her a big old hug before I go up to my room and stare at the ceiling all night – wondering how in the hell I will pay for B Thrice's surgery.

PART FOUR

We're Not Alone

FIFTY-THREE

I don't sleep a wink.

Around five thirty, I get up and make omelets.

Eggs, milk, peppers, mushrooms, tequila – all whisked up in a big old silver bowl.

Omelet jizz in the pan.

Sizzle.

Sizzle.

Sizzle.

Fold over: O to D.

Flip, flip, flip.

Plates in the oven.

Oranges halved.

Donna's juicer used.

Coffee put on.

The paper I get ready for Donna.

The table I set.

'Good morning, Amber,' Donna says, big old smile on her face.

'Hope it is,' I say, and then serve the omelet.

'Amber Appleton is making omelets for Ricky Roberts, yes-ssssss! Tuesday is omelet day. Yes.'

'Is it Tuesday?' I ask as I serve Ricky, noticing the Tuesday Chase Utley jersey. 'I haven't really been keeping track of the days.'

'Tuesday – all day,' Donna says from behind the business section.

We eat omelets.

'How do you think BBB is doing?' I ask.

'I'm sure he's fine. We'll pick him up just as soon as I get home from work,' Donna says. 'Okay?'

'Okay,' I say.

I clean the table when everyone is done eating as Ricky does math problems.

After I have everything in the dishwasher, I go shower, put on makeup, and pick out a killer outfit from the new clothes Donna has been buying me for the past two months. I go with these designer jeans that make my butt look pretty good, and this crazy preppy purple v-neck sweater that makes me look like I might be going to play tennis.

When I come downstairs, Donna says, 'You look great. But are you sure you're ready to go back to school? I don't want you to feel rushed.'

'Yeah,' I say, 'I have to execute my plan.'

'What plan?' Donna asks.

'The Save Bobby Big Boy Variety Show,' I say.

'What's that all about?' Donna asks.

But then – suddenly – Ty is beeping his car horn out front.

'Have to drive to school with Ty Hendrix!' Ricky says, and is out the door, backpack in hand.

'Take this,' Donna says, and then hands me a twenty.

'I don't need your money,' I say as I put on my backpack.

'You have to eat lunch, Amber. Please.'

I take the bill, shove it in my front pocket, and then give Donna a kiss on the cheek. 'You're a good woman,' I say, and then I'm out the door.

Ty is just about to pull away when I yell, 'Wait!'

He smiles all surprised when he sees me running toward his Volvo station wagon.

I'm shocked to see his beard.

It's already three inches long.

He looks like frickin' Rip Van Winkle.

'You comin' to school today?' Ty asks as I climb into the backseat.

'Yep,' I say.

'Cool,' he says, and then turns up the radio before pulling away.

P!nk's 'God Is a DJ' is playing.

I sorta dig that song, which Ty knows, so I sing along – yelling out the curse words that the radio station bleeps out.

Ricky counts to himself – *who knows what he is counting?*

Bearded Ty keeps on looking in the rearview mirror, watching me sing – so much that I worry we might crash, but I only smile at him and sing louder.

P!nk kicks butt. Period. She's another one of my women heroes. She doesn't need a man to take care of her – no way.

We park two blocks from the school.

'Going to play Halo 3 with Mr Jonathan Franks!' Ricky says, and then we follow him toward the The Franks Lair.

'It's good to have you back in school,' Ty says.

'Are you going to shave now?' I ask.

'Not until you agree to go to Friendly's with us.'

'Why?'

'Because I made a vow,' Ty says. 'Respect the sanctity of the friendship beard.'

When we knock on Franks' outside door, Jared kicks it open and I see ten or so boys playing Halo 3. Chad, Jared, Lex Pinkston, some other meathead football players, a few guys whose names I don't know, and Franks.

'Amber?' Franks says, and then everyone turns and looks at me.

The Halo 3 game stops.

'I'm back,' I say.

'Welcome,' Franks says, and then walks over to shake my hand like I'm the president or something.

Everyone looks really nervous – I can feel the tension in the room.

No one knows what to say, because my mom was murdered.

Everyone is looking at me.

'Listen,' I say, 'I know you are all probably freaked out by what happened to my mom, but it's not contagious. *Right?*'

No one laughs at that one.

Blank faces all over the room.

'Listen. I don't want to talk about my mom. Cool?'

'Cool,' Chad says from Das Boot.

Everyone else looks like they think I have the plague or something.

'Listen, to top it all off – and this is no bullcrap story – my dog might have cancer. He had to have an operation last night, which I can't afford. Now I know a dog is not a person or anything, but I went ahead and said I'd pay for it all, and I'm broke. So I need to raise – like – two or three grand. I don't even know if BBB made it or not – I find out later today – but I have to pay regardless, and I'm assuming he did, because he's a fighter.'

'BBB has cancer?' Jared says, and sounds truly concerned.

'Damn,' Chad says.

'I'm so sorry,' Ty says.

'So I'm thinking of setting up a variety show and selling tickets to raise money to pay for my dog's operation. I can get Prince Tony to give us the auditorium, no sweat,' I say. 'I just need to find some acts. Who's with me?'

'You want us to perform?' Jared asks.

'Yeah, or find performers,' I say.

'I'll give you money,' Lex Pinkston says. 'I have some in the bank. It's yours.'

'No. I don't want anyone to give me money. I want to *raise* it for myself. I'm not a charity case.'

'What's a variety show?' one of the football players asks.

'How will we find acts?'

And then everyone is talking all at once – sounding very confused.

Until Franks loudly says, 'I'm in!'

Everyone gets quiet.

All of the boys look at Franks and he nods confidently.

'Cool,' I say.

'I'm in,' Ty says.

'Hell yeah,' Chad says.

'Why not?' Jared says.

'Ricky Roberts is in – yeah-shhhh!'

And then all of the boys present agree to help.

'First thing to do is shut off those Xboxes, because this is going to take some planning,' I say.

Lex shuts off all of them.

'Franks, you're the sales and marketing teacher, so how do we make this kind of money?' I ask.

'Well, we need to advertise all over town and include as many people as we can in the show. It's all about inclusion.

People will give because of the situation. People like dogs. Yours is a sympathetic story. But the more people we include in the show, the more parents and community members will buy tickets and make donations. I have a special folder in my car, it's red and it has a lot of ideas for advertising in it. It says "Advertising Ideas" on the front. Would you mind going and getting it for me, Amber?' Franks says, and then holds out his keys toward me.

'Sure,' I say, and then take his keys.

I leave the room and go to Franks' car – an old rusty Jeep with a hardtop – in the faculty parking lot, but when I key in, there is no red folder on the front seat. There is no folder of any color in the car at all – not on or under any seat. I check the glove compartment and the trunk, just to make sure, but there is no folder, period, so I walk back toward Franks' room feeling sorta annoyed, because I want to get this plan rolling.

When I return, Franks has the boys all fired up.

Lex tells me that the football team is going to do a secret performance.

'What are you going to do?' I ask him.

'You'll see.'

'I've got a little something planned for you,' Chad says from Das Boot.

'I'm going to do math problems on stage!' Ricky says.

'I can do the lighting and stage stuff,' Ty says, because he is the head of the theater's stage crew.

'Jared's performing with me,' Chad says.

'What?' Jared says.

'Don't be a wuss,' Chad tells his brother. 'Maybe we'll get prom dates, eh? Girls dig what we're going to do onstage.'

'Umm,' Jared says. 'I don't – I'll handle finances and incoming money.'

'And do that thing we are going to do onstage, because you are a Fox brother and not a wimp,' Chad says pretty aggressively from Das Boot.

But then the homeroom warning bell sounds and everyone scatters.

'There was no red folder in your car,' I tell Franks, and then give him back his keys.

'That's weird,' he says, and then eats a few peanut M&M's from his desk drawer.

'What did you tell the boys when I was out of the room?'

'Just brainstormed ideas for acts. That's all.'

'So will you be the faculty advisor for The Save Bobby Big Boy Variety Show?'

'Sure,' he says.

'Can we make an announcement over the loudspeaker this morning?'

'Sure,' Franks says.

'All right. Let's go tell Prince Tony.'

Franks and I go up to the main office, and Mrs Baxter goes nuts when she sees me.

'Amber, come here!' she screams, and then runs

around her desk to plant some lipstick on my cheek and give me a big old hug. 'I'm so sorry for your loss. I've been so worried about you. Did you get the flowers I sent you?'

'Yeah, thanks,' I say, even though I chucked all the flowers without even reading one damn card. 'Do you like variety shows?'

'What?' she says.

'Amber Appleton,' Prince Tony says from his office doorway. 'How the heck are you?'

'Cool,' I say, 'but I need to book the auditorium for a variety show. It's got to be a Friday night, because that's when the most people will come out. I need to raise money to pay for my dog's operation.'

'What are you talking about, Amber?'

'Can I talk to you in your office?' Franks says.

'I'm not sure I—' Prince Tony says, but Franks forces him into the office and then closes the door before I can sneak in.

I'm sorta mad at Franks for excluding me while making the Prince Tony pitch, so I decide to make my own announcement before homeroom even starts.

I walk over to the microphone Franks uses to make the morning announcements and ask Mrs Baxter how to make myself heard all over the school.

'You just push the red button, but I don't think you should be—'

I push the red button and say, 'Attention, fellow

Childress High School classmates. This is Amber Appleton. The girl whose mother was murdered. I don't want to talk to you about that, so please do not bring it up, okay? I would like to invite you to participate in The Save Bobby Big Boy Variety Show, which will raise money for my dog's operation, which he had last night. He might have cancer. I have to pay two or three grand for that, and I'm broke. So please help me do this by signing up to be in the variety show, or by buying a ticket – those will go on sale soon after I iron the details out with Prince Tony. Cool? Thanks. Peace out. Amber Appleton.'

When I finish my announcement, Prince Tony and Franks are smiling at me from Prince Tony's office.

'Are you cool with my making an announcement?' I ask.

'I think this variety show is a great idea. I'm one hundred percent behind it,' PT says, and then takes me into his office so we can discuss dates, while Franks does the morning announcements. PT shows me all of the available dates for the auditorium, I pick a Friday night three and a half weeks from today, and he tells me that Mrs Baxter will handle all ticket sales, but that we should feel free to collect donations and sell program advertisements around town; PT says that all of the advertisement checks should be made out to the high school. 'You can get Mr Valerie to do the programs. He does all of the theater programs. I'll talk to him about it today. It's good to have you back in the building, Amber. It's so good to see you.'

'Cool to all of that,' I say, and then go to my first period class.

No one – not even teachers – asks me about my mom all day, but craploads of people – many of whom I've never even met – want to be in BBB's variety show. At first I write down the names and ideas in a notebook, but after I fill seven pages, I realize that we will need to have an elimination audition, or something, and I'm sorta amazed at how well my plan is working.

During lunch Ricky and I blow off socialization time in the lunchroom and go to The Franks Lair, where kids aren't playing video games but are actually brainstorming marketing techniques for The Save Bobby Big Boy Variety Show.

When Franks sees me, he says, 'Amber, will you take a walk with me?'

'Sure. Why?' I ask.

The Five are looking at me really funny.

'Come on,' Franks says, and then leads me outside of the building, where it is pretty springlike and sunny.

'The guys want to surprise you with the acts,' Franks says. 'They want to put together the variety show for you, and then let you emcee the event.'

'What? Why?' I ask.

'They think it would be fun.'

'So they don't want me to be involved at all?'

'We want you to drum up support and enthusiasm.

We want you to emcee and to be the star, but we want the acts to be a surprise.'

'I don't understand why they would want that,' I say.

'Because they want you to be surprised.'

'How will I emcee if I don't know what acts are involved?'

'We'll make you note cards.'

'So I have to trust you?' I ask.

'Yeah,' Franks says. 'Trust your friends too.'

'Do you think we can raise enough money to pay for BBB's operation?'

'I do,' he says, and then smiles confidently. 'We will. I promise.'

Franks is a man of his word, so I start to feel better – relieved, excited. 'Okay,' I say. 'Just leave one slot open, because I got an act lined up already. As soon as I confirm the act, I'll put you in contact with the right people.'

'Cool,' Franks says.

I go back into the lunchroom and buy some food with Donna's twenty.

A billion people ask me to sit with them, which is weird, so I go outside, eat alone, and start to worry about how BBB is doing.

After I finish my turkey hoagie, I go to the pay phone by the gym, drop in some change, and dial Weissmuller Pets of Childress.

'Hello, Weissmuller Pets. How may I help you?'

'May I speak with Dr Weissmuller please?' I ask.

'He's with a patient, can I take a message?'

'It's Amber Appleton, I just want to—'

'Hold on, Amber, I'll put him on the line. Just hold for a second, okay?'

'Okay.'

I hear easy listening music for a few long moments – before Dr Weissmuller says, 'Hello?'

'This is Amber Appelton. Bobby Big Boy. My dog. Is he okay?'

'The surgery went well. Your dog's tumor was sent out for a biopsy. BBB is recovering, but he is fine.'

'Thank you so much, Dr Weissmuller. I'll be in later today.'

'Bobby Big Boy should be ready to go home by seven tonight.'

'Thank you,' I say, and hang up, trying hard not to cry like a chick, but of course, I do leak a few tears.

I say a little thank-you prayer to JC, and then I finish my school day – working on my prom dress a little in Life Skills and daydreaming through my real classes.

By the end of the day there are posters and signs hung up all over the hallways.

The Save Bobby Big Boy Variety Show
Presented by Amber Appleton
April 24 – Friday Night
Save the Date

Some have pictures of Bobby Big Boy on them and I wonder how that came to be.

Weird.

Bearded Ty drives Ricky and me home in his Volvo station wagon, and as we drive, I ask him why The Five want to keep the acts a surprise.

'Don't you like surprises?' he asks me.

'Sure,' I say.

'So?'

'Ricky Roberts is going to do Stump the Mathematician.'

'Well, I know one act, eh?' I say.

Ty looks at me in the rearview and smiles through his beard.

FIFTY-FOUR

After I get Ricky doing math problems at the kitchen table, I ride Donna's bike through the ghetto to the Korean Catholic Church for the first time without BBB, doing the 'I hope you are having a great day!' trick the whole way there, which always makes me feel good, because I dig lighting up people's faces.

When I get there, Father Chee is not out front because he is not expecting me. I haven't talked to him since I told him I couldn't be what he needed me to be anymore.

The church door is locked, so I knock, and after a few minutes, Father Chee appears.

I ride my bike inside, and Father Chee locks the door behind me.

'You left your room,' FC says to me.

'I'm out,' I say as I hop off Donna's bike. 'And I'm sorry.'

'For what?' FC says with a smile.

I give him a big old hug.

'Welcome back,' FC says as he pats my back all fatherly.

When we let go, FC asks, 'Where is BBB?'

So I tell him all about B Thrice's tumor, The Save Bobby Big Boy Variety Show, and also about how we will know whether BBB is going to live within a week.

'I will pray for BBB,' Father Chee says. 'The KDFCs have missed you. Want to say hello?'

'Hell yeah,' I say, and then we walk into the sanctuary.

The KDFCs are sitting around with English-Korean dictionaries. They are all writing Korean into what looks like new songbooks.

'Jesus sent us Aretha Franklin's Greatest Hits,' Father Chee explains, and then yells something in Korean.

The Korean Divas for Christ look up and then attack me, giving me so many long drawn-out hugs that I think I might pop!

In English, they all tell me that they are sorry about my mom, and then they say a lot of things to me in Korean, which Father Chee translates into English.

These things they say in their native language are so heartfelt, so beautiful, The KDFCs make me cry, which makes them cry and hug me even more.

Finally, I tell them about Bobby Big Boy's tumor, and The KDFCs start hugging me again and shaking their heads and talking very quickly in Korean.

So I tell them about The Bobby Big Boy Variety Show

and ask them if they will perform – if they will do a few Supremes songs to help me raise money to pay for BBB's operations.

The KDFCs look down at their feet.

'What?' I say.

Father Chee says something in Korean.

Yung Mi says something back.

Sun says something to Yung Mi.

Na Yung shakes her head, and offers her opinion.

Hye Min yells at Na Yung.

And then all of The KDFCs are bickering in Korean.

Father Chee tells me, 'Some of the women want to perform, but others think that their English is not good enough yet, and that they will embarrass you and themselves.'

'Are you kidding me?' I ask them very loudly. 'You guys are frickin' pros.'

'We good backup singers,' Sun says, 'but we need good English-speaking front woman. True diva.'

'Amber is the true diva,' Na Yung says.

'No, no. I'm emceeing,' I tell them.

'Why not sing with them?' Father Chee says.

But I don't want to sing with them. I know I should sing because I am one of The Korean Divas for Christ – even if I am not actually Korean by birth, only by association – and also I shouldn't ask people to do something that I am not willing to do, which I fully realize, but the truth is I'm not really feeling up to the task of rock-starring in front of all my classmates, especially after my mother's death, and so the bickering continues amongst The Korean Divas for Christ, until I change the subject and simply help them translate '(You Make Me Feel Like) A Natural Woman.'

While Father Chee jogs me home, he says, 'You have to realize that you are the only white person many of our church members have had any meaningful contact with. Walking into an English-speaking high school like yours terrifies them.'

'I can understand that,' I say. 'Believe me.'

'But if you would sing *with them* – behind you, a true diva – I think they would sing at the variety show.'

'I'm not a true diva,' I tell him. 'I'm just a crappy English teacher who uses R & B as a teaching tool.'

'Well then, I will pray that Jesus sends us a true diva to lead The KDFCs, so that they will feel confident enough to participate in your variety show,' Father Chee says, and then he suddenly stops running, so I stop pedaling.

I'm straddling Donna's bike.

We look at each other.

'Are you okay?' FC asks me.

'Yeah,' I say.

'Are you sure?'

'No. But I'm moving forward.'

'You are out of your room. This is good.'

'Because Bobby Big Boy needs me.'

'Many people need you, Amber.'

'One thing at a time, FC.'

'You are stronger than you think.'

'Hug?' I ask, because I can't take too many compliments right now.

'Of course,' he says, and then hugs me all fatherly.

'Will you pray for me?' I ask.

'Every day,' FC says, smiling at me. 'Almost every hour.'

And then I ride my bike back to Donna's house and cook chicken in a pan, slice that hooey up, and make a chicken salad with honey-mustard sauce and kick-ass croutons.

When Donna gets home, we eat.

'How was your first day back?' Donna asks me.

'Ricky Roberts is going to Stump the Mathematician onstage April twenty-fourth, Friday night, in the Childress High School Auditorium so that we can raise money for Amber Appleton.'

'For Bobby Big Boy,' I say. 'We're doing a variety show to pay for BBB's operation.'

'You are, eh? Prince Tony went for that?'

'Franks backed it big-time. Do you know any real-live divas?'

'Divas?'

'To be The KDFCs' front woman. They won't perform without an English-speaking front woman because they are too embarrassed of their English, even though I taught them pretty well.'

'Why don't *you* be their front woman?' Donna asks me.

'Hello? Have you ever heard me sing?'

'Something will turn up,' Donna says. 'I talked to Dr Weissmuller.'

'So did I,' I said.

'So you know that BBB is fine.'

'Yeah,' I say. 'Until we get the biopsy anyway.'

'One thing at a time,' Donna says with some honey mustard sauce dribbling down her chin.

When we pick up BBB, his belly is shaved and stitched up, and he is wearing a little lamp shade on his head.

I carry BBB to Donna's car, and we take B3 home.

Bobby Big Boy is a little sluggish at first, and doesn't dig wearing the lampshade one bit – I know because he claws the hell out of it within the first forty-eight hours – so we eventually take it off, and BBB is eating and crapping merrily in no time at all.

FIFTY-FIVE

A week later, I call Dr Weissmuller after school and he tells me that my dog is cancer free.

BBB and I celebrate by taking a bike ride over to the Methodist Retirement Home.

We hit Alan's Newsstand, and Alan says, 'I'm sorry about what happened to your mother, and I bought two tickets to The Save Bobby Big Boy Variety Show.'

'From whom?' I ask.

'Kids have been asking me for a week to buy tickets. Must have been three hundred kids asked me already. Better be a good show.'

'It's going to be the bomb,' I tell him as I pay for the Snickers and the hot chocolate with some of the lunch money Donna has been giving me.

'The what?' Alan says.

'You won't be disappointed,' I say, even though I don't even know what the hell The Five are cooking up.

And then BBB and I are stashing Donna's bike behind a bush and offering Door Woman Lucy the regular bribe to get B Thrice into the building.

'You get the Snickers and hot chocolate I sent you?' DWL says to me.

'Yeah, thanks,' I say.

'Ain't right, what's been happening to you. Ain't right at all.'

'Tell me about it.'

'Your little boyfriends been 'round here selling tickets to some show they say you puttin' on.'

'Boyfriends?' I ask.

'Tiny kid in a wheelchair. Tall funky-lookin' white kid. Cute black kid with a beard.'

'They're not my boyfriends.'

DWL sips her hot chocolate and then smiles at me sorta weird.

'Strange times, DWL. Strange times.'

'What's this show you putting on all about, anyway?'

'It's a variety show.'

'To honor your mother's passing?'

'No, it's for Bobby Big Boy here. He just had surgery. See his scar?' I hold up BBB's belly. 'It cost me almost three grand, so I have to raise money.'

'Well, you let me know if you need any help, Sister Amber.'

I nod once, smile at DWL's calling me Sister Amber for the first time, which makes me feel pretty cool, and then

BBB and I walk into the old people's home – through the depressing hallways with the dusty fake plants.

When we get to the common room, I can't believe what I see.

All of the old people are seated in two long rows.

Old Man Linder is singing a song with Old Man Thompson.

Both are wearing red sports coats.

They're singing some ancient song about makin' whoopee, and as I listen to the lyrics, I think they are actually singing about sex!

The old people are smiling and laughing and singing along so happily as Old Man Thompson sings his heart out and Old Man Linder echoes the verses in spoken word – and suddenly I realize that Old Man Linder has taken me up on my challenge.

He's gotten up in front of his peers.

He's entertaining the people.

He's giving them something to look forward to – something to break up the boring days and weeks.

He's keeping hope alive!

BBB and I watch the performance from the back of the room and laugh every time one of the old men punch the air in front of them, or try to move their ancient hips to the beat.

The performance is not all that lively.

My boys don't sing that well.

But as I look at how much fun the old people are

having – many of them singing along with the two old men in front of them – I realize that this is enough, that these old people are getting a little fuel from my manager, and I feel something warm heat up my chest.

When they finish the old-time sex song about makin' whoopee, Old Man Linder sees me standing at the back of the common room. 'Amber?' he says.

Fifty blue-haired heads turn around slowly, and then everyone is staring at me and BBB.

I walk toward my elders and say, 'Hey.'

When no one says anything, I give Old Man Linder a hug, whisper, 'I'm sorry,' into his big hairy ear, and then – to the crowd – I say, 'Who knew these old guys could sing so well?'

No one says anything, and Old Man Linder looks a little nervous.

'Listen,' I say. 'I'm okay.'

'We were really worried about you,' Old Man Thompson says.

'We didn't think you'd ever visit us again,' Big Booty Bernice says.

'I hope they fry that horrible man who killed your poor mother,' Agnes the Plant Talker says.

'Are you really okay?' Old Man Linder says.

'Where's Joan of Old?' I ask.

'She had a heart attack,' Old Man Thompson says.

'What?' I say.

'It wasn't fatal,' Old Man Linder says. 'She's in the

hospital wing. I hear she goes in and out of consciousness – but when she's awake, they say she's still with it.'

'Well, I'll have to visit her after the show,' I say, and then sit down, allowing B Thrice to curl up on my lap. 'I want to see what else you two got up there.'

Old Man Linder smiles proudly, snaps back into character, and – in an old-time radio voice – says, 'How many of you remember this gem from 1927?'

Old Man Thompson and Old Man Linder start snapping their fingers and tapping their toes, and when they sing the next song all of the old people get really excited and start to sing along in rousing unison – everyone is waving index fingers in the air, nodding out the beat, and singing their dusty old lungs out.

Because they repeat the chorus so many times I sorta figure out the song's called 'Side By Side', and it's about two people with no money who don't know what's going to happen, but at least they have each other to travel through life together. The old people love this corny old song, and I have to say – seeing them sing it so passionately makes me feel something good. True.

My old men are moving people this afternoon.

When the song is finished, Old Man Linder says, 'Thanks for coming to the Wednesday Afternoon Old-Time Sing-Along with The Red Coats – Albert Linder and Eddie Thompson. Until next week, when we will be singing more of the songs you remember and love – make sure you stay alive at least seven more days!

Because you won't want to miss what we have in store for you! Reminisce, people. Reminisce!'

All of the old people clap for a few minutes while The Red Coats bow, and then resuming once again is the endless talk of grandchildren, jigsaw puzzles, who died last week, the weather over the past eight decades, and – of course – the many family members who never visit.

I leave BBB curled up in a pile of Knitting Carol's yarn and step out into the hallway with Old Man Linder.

'You were really good up there,' I tell him. 'You had everyone into it. True.'

'Listen, I was mad at you for a week or so, kid. I could have died climbing those damn steps, and then the way you treated me,' Old Man Linder says – oxygen tubes running out of his nostrils. 'But then, I thought, you know what – the girl's got a point. I'm not dead yet, and I have to do something to keep myself alive. I can't always depend on others. So I thought up the sing-along with Eddie, who carries me up there with his golden voice – if you didn't notice. I'm the ham. He's the voice. But I always loved to sing. And the old chippies favor men who sing in public. Can't keep them off me lately.'

The old man winks at me.

I smile at Old Man Linder.

'Are you okay, Amber?'

'Truthfully, no. But I enjoyed your singing very much – and I'm out of my room, at least.'

'That's a start.'

'It's something.'

'So?'

'I would like to visit Joan of Old,' I say.

'You sure? I haven't been to see her yet, but I hear she's in bad shape.'

'Yeah, I'm sure,' I say.

I follow Old Man Linder through a bunch of depressing hallways full of mauve wallpaper and mauve carpets – finally, we arrive at the hospital wing, which is just another mauve hallway with special hospital-looking rooms.

When a nurse pops out of one of the rooms, Old Man Linder says, 'Excuse me, but do you know which room is Joan Osmond's?'

The nurse doesn't answer, but points to a door down the hall, so we walk toward it.

Joan of Old is a tiny mountain range under a sky-blue blanket – her sunken pink wrinkled face sticking out, her small head resting on a pillow.

'Can I get a few minutes alone with Joan?' I ask Old Man Linder.

My manager says, 'Sure. I'll wait out here for you.'

I walk into the room and close the door behind me.

I pull up a chair next to the bed.

'Joan?' I say.

Joan of Old doesn't move.

I can hear her struggling to breathe.

Her mouth is open slightly.

I reach under the blanket and hold her hand.

It's freezing cold.

'Squeeze if you can hear me,' I say.

Nothing.

'I guess you heard all about my mom and my depression. I've been in a room for months, pretty much being a bitch to everyone. I've been crying a lot too. True. But what you probably don't realize is that I cried a whole bunch before my mother was killed too. The Amber you saw during our battles – that was all an act. I'm not very strong. I'm not very hopeful. I'm not very much of anything. I'm just a stupid girl who can tell a few good jokes at pivotal moments and knows how to work a crowd. If you only knew how much I internalized all of your insults. Word. You really have me thinking I have a dinosaur face, which freaks me out a lot. True.'

Joan of Old doesn't squeeze my hand at all.

I can still hear her breathing.

'I'm starting to think that you are right about life, Joan. Maybe it's all meaningless? I mean – I still dig JC and all. I still pray, and I still believe in certain people. But that guy who killed my mom – he's not human, and he scares me, because he *is* human, and yet he did what he did, which will never make sense, no matter how long I think about it. It's so random. So vile. It makes me get why you are so mean and cranky. I bet you weren't like that before your husband died, right?'

Suddenly, Joan of Old squeezes my hand and scares the hell out of me.

'Why are you telling me these things?' Joan asks.

'Were you awake that whole time?'

'Yes.'

'You rotten old lady! Why didn't you say so?'

'Because I'm gathering information for our last battle – when I will finally make you cry.'

'You can't be that evil,' I say.

Joan of Old smiles up at me from her pillow, and her wrinkly pink eyelids bore through my forehead.

I shiver.

'Why'd you really come in here, Amber?'

'I don't know. I really don't. Are you going to die?'

'We all die eventually,' Joan of Old says. 'That's just about the only thing God got right.'

'Okay,' I say, 'I think I'm going to leave now.'

'When do we battle next? My doctors say I could die any day now.'

'Sorry, I'm retired,' I say.

'You have to give me one last shot at the title.'

Suddenly, Joan of Old just seems too absurd for me to handle, so I walk out of the room.

'Amber? Amber? *Amber?*' Joan of Old says as I walk down the hall with Old Man Linder.

'What did the old broad say to you?' he asks me, dragging his oxygen bottle behind him.

'She faked like she was sleeping so I would tell her personal things that she could use against me the next time we battle.'

'I wouldn't worry too much about that.'

'Because I'm retired?'

'Because she's going to die any day now. And ding dong the wicked witch will be dead.'

'You know what's the weirdest thing about that?'

'What?' Old Man Linder asks.

'I'll miss her.'

'I miss everyone from my past, Amber. I really do. It's the curse of old age.'

We walk the rest of the way in silence, and just before we reenter the common room, I say, 'Will you and Old Man Thompson sing one of your songs at The Bobby Big Boy Variety Show?'

'No one wants to hear two old men sing forgotten songs, Amber. Especially one who needs bottled oxygen to breathe. Singing's a young person's game. Who would want to hear me sing?'

'I would.'

Old Man Linder smiles at me all grandfatherly, but his eyes get misty and sad.

When he doesn't say anything, I give Old Man Linder a kiss on the cheek, and then – in the common room – I make the rounds with BBB, allowing everyone to check out his scar while they give him a pet on the head.

And then B Thrice and I are walking through the depressing hallways with the dusty plants.

'How'd it go in there today?' DWL says.

'Okay. Even though he said he didn't want to do it,

286

I'm hoping Old Man Linder will change his mind and he'll sing at The Save Bobby Big Boy Variety Show. That would be pretty cool.'

'Who asked him to sing?'

'I did.'

'Why didn't you ask *me* to sing?'

'Do you sing?'

'You kiddin' me? I'm a pro. I got me a band and everything. They're called The Hard-Working Brothers. We do weddings mostly, but we play clubs too.'

'What type of music?'

'Mostly R & B. I'm known for my Aretha Franklin impersonation – but I do The Supremes, Ella Fitzgerald, Nina Simone, all the big names.'

I cross myself, and then say, 'DWL. You're a diva?'

'Girl – I bring the roof down whenever I sing. I just work this job for the health insurance.'

Suddenly, I understand that Father Chee's prayers are being answered – that JC has sent me and the KDFCs a diva. Word.

'Are you for real?' I ask.

DWL laughs and hands me her card. It reads:

Sister Lucy and The Hard-Working Brothers

There is a phone number underneath.

I explain my relationship with The Korean Divas for Christ, our asking JC to send us a true diva front woman, and then, like a frickin' maniac, I pedal Donna's bike all the way to Father Chee's church, telling everyone I pass that I hope they're having a great day, and when I get there, I bang on the door until FC opens.

'Amber, what brings you here today on a—'

'I found us a true diva!' I say, and then hand him DWL's card.

Father Chee reads the card and then smiles knowingly. 'So Jesus has sent us a diva.'

'Hell yeah,' I say.

'I will take care of everything,' Father Chee says, and then jogs me and BBB in-a-basket back to my neighborhood, only I don't go home after FC turns around – BBB and I go to Private Jackson's house.

After so much time with people – I'm tired.

I'm not used to people.

I've been alone in a room for two months.

This is all baptism by fire.

I want to go somewhere I can just be – where I can chill and process the miracle of finding a true diva for The KDFCs.

I stash Donna's bike around the back of PJ's house and knock on PJ's door with BBB in my arms.

'Come in, please,' PJ says while scratching Bobby Big Boy's head. 'I'll put on tea.'

I put B Thrice on the floor inside of the door, and even though he had surgery not so long ago, he tears ass toward the bedroom. I'm a little worried about those stitches, but then I just sit down on the couch figuring Bobby Big Boy knows his own limitations.

A few minutes later, Private Jackson hands me a steaming cup of tea.

We sip in silence for a time.

I put my cup down on the coffee table, stand, pull an origami swan from my pocket, and hand it to PJ.

'It's beautiful,' PJ says. 'It's perfect.'

'Open it up,' I say.

'No, I want to let it be – just as it—'

'I'll fold you up another one. There's a haiku inside.'

PJ nods and then unfolds my origami swan.

He reads my latest haiku for like – an hour, nodding and rubbing his chin.

'Do you like it?' I finally ask.

He looks up at me and says, 'It is perfect. Will you do a reading for me?'

'You serious?' I ask.

'I would very much like to hear you read this haiku.'

I take the piece of paper from him, and read.

'We cry together – on the couch – for different reasons, but it helps.'

'I will hang it on the wall now,' PJ says, taking the paper from me.

'But it's not about a dog.'

PJ smiles, tapes my haiku to the blank spot on the final living room wall, and then says, 'I like you, Amber Appleton, just as much as I like dogs. And I like dogs better than people.'

'And I like you, Private Jackson, just as much as I like dogs.'

'We are very lucky then,' he says, and we both sit there smiling and sipping green tea for a half hour.

BBB and Ms Jenny come out of the bedroom all glassy-eyed and wobbly, but BBB seems to be smiling, so I laugh and say, 'You can't keep a good dog down, eh, BBB?'

I pick B3 up in my arms, kiss the furry spot between his ears, and then tell PJ I gotta go.

'I will wash the teacups,' he says.

Outside, I put BBB in Donna's bike basket, and he's asleep before I pedal one block.

FIFTY-SIX

For the next two weeks I work on my prom dress, which I am going to wear when I emcee The Save Bobby Big Boy Variety Show, so – in an effort to finish in time – I start going to the Life Skills room before and after school.

Franks and The Five hold auditions for the variety show.

Door Woman Lucy and the Hard-Working Brothers meet with Father Chee and The KDFCs.

Kids I don't even know sell tickets door-to-door.

Mrs Baxter collects money.

Mr Valerie sells advertisements and puts together the program.

And I take BBB to see Ms Jenny every single day.

I drink tea with Private Jackson – and I fill that blank spot on the last wall of his living room.

Everything is moving toward something – but I'm sorta in a daze.

Sometimes I think I see my mother.

Whenever I see a school bus – my heart leaps.

When I see a bleach-blonde in a crowd.

When I close my eyes at night.

When Donna kisses me, sometimes I pretend, and I get to feeling really badly about my wishing Donna was my mom – back when Mom was actually alive.

I wonder if Mom's death was God answering that wish.

I wonder.

I feel guilty a lot.

I sweat through the nights.

I shiver through the days.

The only thing I really like doing – believe it or not – is drinking green tea with Private Jackson. Sipping in complete silence, surrounded by my haikus.

FIFTY-SEVEN

On the day of The Save Bobby Big Boy Variety Show – before school – I finish my prom dress. It is a silver sleeveless with an empire waist and a scoop neck that shows off what little cleavage I got. When I try it on, my Life Skills teacher, Mrs Tyler, says, 'It's the best prom dress ever made in this classroom. A-plus.'

I smile at her and begin to look forward to wearing it later.

All day, students smile at me dramatically and say, 'See you tonight, Amber,' way too much.

I mean, I'm all about a good variety show, but it seems like people are really going nuts for The Save Bobby Big Boy Variety Show.

Too nuts.

I skip lunch, and go right to The Franks Lair.

When I enter, thirty students stop speaking and turn to face me.

Total frickin' silence.

'What's going on?' I say.

'We're finalizing tonight's plan,' Franks says.

'Cool,' I say.

From Das Boot, Chad says, 'If you come in right now, it's going to ruin the surprises.'

'Surprises – plural?' I ask.

'Come on, Amber,' Jared says. 'Just trust us.'

'Am I still emceeing?' I ask.

'All's you have to do is show up at the auditorium at six forty-five,' Ty says.

'What time does the show start?'

'Eight,' Franks says. 'See you then.'

'Okay,' I say, feeling quite weird and a little embarrassed by how little I have had to do with the preparation.

I chill outside for a bit, and then finish up my school day.

Ty drives Ricky and me to Donna's, and after I take BBB out – I actually take a nap. I'm always tired lately. Naps are becoming my favorite. Word.

I wake up to Donna yelling, 'We have to get you to the auditorium in less than an hour!'

So I get up and shower.

Makeup is applied.

Hair is blown dry.

Silver prom dress is put on my pre-woman body.

Red pumps are put on my nasty feet.

Prayer is said to JC – with much conviction and hope. 'Please help everyone to be who they need to be tonight! Amen!'

Ricky is wearing a tuxedo.

'You look dapper, Ricky!'

'Amber Appleton is wearing a silver dress!'

'Are you ready for this?' Donna asks, and I nod once.

Amber Appleton, Bobby Big Boy, and Ricky Roberts are driven to the CPHS auditorium in Donna's Mercedes with the heated seats on.

When we arrive, there is this huge line to get into the auditorium. There are no seat numbers, so if you want a good seat, you have to line up early.

We have to walk past this line to get to the stage.

When the crowd sees me, they actually start cheering – as if I were a rock star.

No bull.

There are hundreds of people lined up – all looking at me with these really sympathetic eyes.

We pass a section of Korean people – maybe forty of them.

We pass a group of women who look a lot like Door Woman Lucy.

And we pass a lot of Childress citizens.

Halfway up the line, some reject starts chanting, 'Amber! Amber! Amber!'

All of the morons in line start doing the chant, and I start to blush.

When I notice that Donna is also chanting, I elbow her and say, 'Stop.'

She laughs at me and keeps on chanting – like a complete dork.

When we get to the front of the line, Ricky heads into the auditorium, and I start to cry.

The first person in line is Private Jackson.

He's in a yellow button-down shirt, like always.

He has his ticket in his hand – as if he's some excited kid waiting to get into a ball game.

He's smiling at me all proud of himself.

I know this is the first time he's been out in public – besides walking Ms Jenny and getting groceries – probably since he came home from 'Nam.

'What are you doing here?' I ask.

BBB licks PJ's hand.

PJ pets BBB's head, and says, 'I wanted a front row seat, so I came early.'

'How did you even know about this?' I ask, because I never told him about The Save Bobby Big Boy Variety Show.

'A boy with a beard, he came to my house and told me that you would appreciate it if I came tonight. So I came. Why didn't you tell me about this?'

Ty. I could kiss him.

'Must have been enjoying the tea-drinking moments too much,' I say, and then I get PJ through door security, which is pretty much the bearded history teacher who asked if Ricky was okay when I was tickling him in the hallway three months back and a gym teacher I don't know who lifts a lot of weights.

Inside the auditorium, Donna and Private Jackson take center front row seats – the best seats in the house. And I can tell Donna thinks Private Jackson is handsome, because she sits sideways in her chair and leans forward a little toward him, so that PJ will get a good view of her boob crack.

I smile, and then carry BBB backstage.

There are a crapload of people backstage:

Chad in Das Boot, Jared, Ricky, and Franks are in tuxedos.

Lex Pinkston and the entire football team have greased their hair and half are wearing leather jackets and jeans and white T-shirts – so that they look like they have just stepped out of the '50s – and the other half are wearing black pants, purple button-down shirts, and pointy dress shoes.

The KDFCs are all wearing identical beautiful gold dresses.

Father Chee is in his penguin suit.

Door Woman Lucy is in a tight red dress and killer heels – she is also wearing hair extensions and much glitzy makeup, all of which makes her look like Queen Latifah, who is entirely awesome and another woman I admire.

The black men with instruments – whom I assume are The Hard-Working Brothers, since they are the only brothers backstage besides Ty – those guys are dressed in black suits and wearing white shirts, black skinny ties, and old-school sunglasses with green lenses. Whenever I look at one of The Hard-Working Brothers, they all nod at me as if they are a unit – connected or something.

Ty is at a table just offstage, punching away at a laptop that controls the mics and lights and curtain and sound system. He's dressed like every other day in jeans and a red hoodie sweatshirt. I smile at him because he got Private Jackson out tonight, but Ty's too busy with the laptop and doesn't notice me.

There are cheerleaders dressed in their uniforms.

Two hippie-looking kids with acoustic guitars.

A pimply kid in a medieval jester costume with a hat that looks like a red and yellow palm tree.

And then I see two old men in red sports jackets standing off to the side all alone, one with an oxygen bottle, so I run up to Old Man Linder and Thompson and say, 'You guys are singing tonight?'

'We're opening up the show!' Old Man Thompson says.

'You know it,' Old Man Linder says, and then pinches my cheek.

'I thought no one wanted to hear old men sing?'

'You said that?' Old Man Thompson says.

'That bearded classmate of yours over there convinced me otherwise,' Old Man Linder says, and when I look back at Ty, I smile. He looks so serious at his laptop – so loyal, so dedicated, so like a good friend should.

'You have to make power circle!' Sueng Hee of The KDFCs says to me, and then pulls me and BBB toward the middle of everyone.

'You got something to say before we take the stage?' Door Woman Lucy says.

I look around at all of the faces, some of which I love, some of which I do not even know – all of which I can plainly see need me to say something hopeful so that they will be able to rock Childress High School.

'I want to thank everyone for coming out tonight,' I say. 'It means a lot to me and Bobby Big Boy, who is cancer free, thank God.'

I pause, because I know that the night requires more of me.

I have to be more than a teenage girl.

I have to move people – get them pumped up.

I have to be a rock star.

So I say, 'Everyone form a big old circle. Arms around your neighbors' shoulders. Feel the love, people! Feel the love! Ty, you too. Get your butt over here!'

Ty looks up from the computer and then takes his place in the power circle.

Maybe more than fifty people are surrounding BBB and me – all with arms around each other, all watching me.

'Bow those heads,' I say. 'If you don't believe in JC, well then feel free to sub in whatever deity you dig! If you are an atheist like Ricky, then just humor me, okay?'

Everybody except Ricky bows his or her head.

I close my eyes and say, 'JC, you got some good people gathered together down here for a good cause. Please be with all of these good people tonight. Help them be whoever they need to be. Please let us rock. Please let us move some people – so they don't ask for their money back. Be with us tonight, JC. Amen.'

'Amen!' most of my people say, and then start to unlink their arms from their neighbors' shoulders.

'Get those arms back around those shoulders!' I yell.

Everyone does what I say.

I start stomping my left foot.

Stomp! Stomp! Stomp!

Everyone catches on.

Fifty-some feet are stomping now.

The floor below us seems to be moving.

'If the people in the house are feeling all right tonight, say "Yeah!"'

'Yeah!'

'If the people in the house are feeling all right tonight, say "Hell yeah!"'

'Hell yeah!'

'I can't hear you!'

'HELL YEAH!'

Stomp, stomp, stomp, stomp!

'If you're ready to rock Childress Public High School tonight say, "Woo! Woo!"'

'Woo! Woo!'

Stomp, stomp, stomp.

I can't think of any other cool empowering jazz to say, so I end with, 'Bring it in for some love! Everyone put a hand in the middle of the circle.'

I quickly see that Das Boot is going to mess up the unity, so I say, 'Scratch that. Everyone put a hand on Chad's head!'

We all circle Das Boot.

We all put a hand on Chad's head – well, most of us do, and the rest put hands on the shoulders of people who have their hands on Chad's head.

'Watch the hair, people,' Chad says.

'Thank you for helping me pay my vet bill,' I say. 'I love you people. All of you. On three, we say, "Go time." One, two, three!'

'Go time!' everyone yells.

And when they back away from Das Boot, they look pretty pumped up.

Suddenly, on the other side of the front curtain, the crowd is chanting, 'Amber! Amber! Amber!'

And I think, *Damn, I really am a rock star*.

'You look good in that dress,' Ty says.

'Thanks, I made it myself,' I say, and then he returns to his laptop.

'How was the prayer?' I ask Father Chee.

'God was very pleased,' FC says.

'How do you know?' I ask.

'He told me!' FC says.

'Did He tell you if tonight was going to work out?'

'Yes, He told me that too.'

'What did He say?' I ask.

'He says it's time for you to take the stage,' FC says, and then points to Franks, who is standing by the edge of the curtain waving me over. 'Better hurry.'

I carry BBB over to Franks, who says, 'Okay, Amber. Before each act, I give you a note card. You read the info on the card, and then you announce the act any way you see fit. Cool?'

'Cool,' I say.

Franks hands me a card, and then I walk out onto the stage with BBB in my arms.

A spotlight hits me.

The house lights dim.

I step up to the microphone stand.

The crowd hushes.

I see PJ and Donna smiling up at me.

I hold BBB up over my head.

'Cancer-free!'

People cheer.

'Now we have to pay the vet bill.'

The crowd laughs, but I'm not sure why.

'Thanks for coming out tonight.'

I scan the crowd. Packed house.

'Ladies and gentlemen, I have a special treat for you this evening. Backed by tonight's house band – The Hard-Working Brothers – singing the old-time classic "Makin' Whoopee", the best two men the Methodist Home has to

302

offer – let's give it up for Albert Linder and Eddie Thompson, better known as The Red Coats!'

The curtain rises, and The Red Coats start snapping their old fingers.

The Hard-Working Brothers start playing the old-time song, and Old Man Thompson starts to sing 'Makin' Whoopee' in this good but corny old-time singing voice.

With his oxygen bottle and all, Old Man Linder doesn't really sing, but in a speaking voice sorta echoes Old Man Thompson – and it works.

The Hard-Working Brothers are a pretty good band too.

From offstage, I look out into the audience and I see some old people singing along.

Cool, I think.

After The Red Coats finish their number, the crowd claps, and I announce various other acts – some fellow classmates sing and play instruments, some do dance routines, the kid in the medieval jester costume actually juggles knives and flaming tennis balls, which gets Prince Tony out of his seat. PT tries to stop the juggling act, but gets booed so badly that he eventually allows the kid to finish.

When I announce the Mackin' Mathematician, Ricky takes the stage and Franks throws a couple dozen or so cheap calculators into the audience. 'Ladies and gentlemen, I have a genius here with me tonight,' Franks says.

'Yes,' Ricky says into his microphone.

'Anyone who caught a calculator can ask Ricky to multiply any number and he will do it in his head in less than five seconds – providing you with the correct answer. You are welcome to check his math using the calculators, although I assure you this will not be necessary.'

'Yes,' Ricky says, standing center stage in his tuxedo.

Franks hops off the stage and walks the cordless microphone into the audience. 'Who's first?'

Some regular-looking dude raises his hand and says something to Franks.

'Ricky, this gentleman wants to know what is one-hundred fifty-seven times five-hundred twenty-one.'

'Eighty-one thousand, seven hundred and ninety-seven. Yes.'

'Is he right, sir?' Franks asks.

The man punches the numbers into his calculator, and then nods, looking amazed.

Fifty hands go up in the air.

'One thousand, two hundred sixty-eight times one-two-nine-six-oh, Ricky.'

'Sixteen million, four hundred and thirty-three thousand, two hundred and eighty.'

'Five times nine,' some little kid wants to know.

'Forty-five,' Ricky says. 'Forty-five.'

'Sixty-five times three-hundred thirteen thousand, one-hundred thirty-one.'

'Twenty million, three-hundred and fifty-three thousand, five-hundred and fifteen.'

'Five hundred and sixty-eight point thirteen times five-hundred sixty-seven point seventy-seven,' some wise guy wants to know, throwing decimals at Ricky.

'Three hundred and twenty-two thousand, five hundred and sixty-seven point seventeen.'

Ricky does several more math problems in his head – each time the difficulty is raised – and he answers all of the questions correctly, before he says, 'Ricky Roberts is hungry,' and then walks offstage.

The crowd claps for Ricky, and Donna looks so proud in the first row.

There are a few more singing and dancing acts before I make this announcement: 'People, it is my pleasure to introduce my good friends Chad and Jared Fox, performing The Spinners classic "Working My Way Back to You" accompanied by The Hard-Working Brothers and the Childress High School cheerleaders!'

Chad, Das Boot, Jared, and The Hard-Working Brothers take the stage.

My boys look good in their tuxedos, although Jared looks like he is about to crap his pants.

The Hard-Working Brothers' drummer starts the song and the bassist plays some funky notes.

In this really affected put-on voice, from Das Boot, Chad starts singing about how hard he's working to get back his woman.

When his brother begins to sing, Jared starts clapping and sorta moves his weight from one foot to another.

Suddenly, the cheerleading team comes flying across the stage doing cartwheels – their skirts flying up and down.

It is the strangest thing I have ever seen.

As Jared and Chad sing, the cheerleaders do all sorts of acrobatics – throwing girls up into the air, building human pyramids, and doing spirited jumping jacks with pompoms.

People in the audience actually start to get up and dance.

My boys are a hit!

Chad is doing circles around the cheerleaders with Das Boot, singing to them.

Jared is still moving his weight from one foot to the other, backing up his more confident brother – looking sorta like he is about to have a heart attack.

And I can't help but laugh.

When the song ends, the crowd goes wild, and Franks hands me the next note card.

I take the stage and say, 'And now performing selected scenes from *West Side Story*, ladies and gentlemen, I give you *the Childress High School football team*?'

Lex and a bunch of his teammates walk onto the stage wearing purple shirts and pointy dress shoes – snapping their fingers in a crouched sneaky position.

The rest of the team enters from the other side of the stage wearing the leather jackets and jeans – also snapping their fingers while in a sneaky crouched position.

What ensues is a street war orchestrated through fabulous dance moves, and set to heart-racing jazzy recorded music.

And as I watch the football team perform selected scenes from *West Side Story*, I am amazed by how good they are. They are frickin' pros.

As the quicksilver of fake knives flashes, people in the audience are on the edges of their seats!

These boys were born to do musical theater!

Suddenly I understand why our football team never wins any games.

The Jets and the Sharks get a thunderous round of applause as they link arms and take a bow center stage, and I have to say, I'm impressed.

'Ladies and gentlemen,' I say, 'we've come to the headliner, which combines two very talented groups of people – people I know well and love very much. I give you The Korean Divas for Christ, Sister Lucy, and The Hard-Working Brothers!'

People clap as the curtain rises.

The strings and brass are set up stage right, the drums are deep center, The KDFCs are lined up on risers, tiered in all their golden glory stage left, and Sister Lucy is front and center holding a microphone.

'Come on out here, Sister Amber,' Sister Lucy says.

I carry BBB out to center stage, and Sister Lucy puts her arm around me.

'You know, they say the way to a woman's heart is to

give her enough chocolate,' DWL says, and the audience laughs at that one. 'Before she knew I was a diva, when she thought I was just a door woman at the old people's home, when she was homeless herself, every week Amber brought me a hot chocolate and a Snickers bar. Might not sound like much to some, but I liked it well enough. It was something to look forward to on Wednesdays. I'm sorry about what happened to your mom, Sister Amber. It ain't right. So this one is for you.'

When Lucy lets go of me, I walk to the side of the stage, and an electric organ starts playing.

I look over by the horn section at the keyboard synthesizer and I suddenly realize that Father Chee is playing it – he's playing with the band!

Sister Lucy starts singing and her voice is deep and rich and divine.

She's singing about Mother Mary.

The KDFCs are doing these slow hand motions I didn't teach them – and then they are echoing Sister Lucy beautifully, like pros.

They're doing an R & B version of The Beatles' 'Let It Be'.

The Hard-Working Brothers kick in with the drums and the bass and guitar and then the horns too.

The people in the audience are standing now.

Their hands are swaying back and forth over their heads.

I listen to the lyrics and understand what Sister Lucy is telling me – and then I'm crying like a baby.

Jared puts his arm around me during the saxophone solo.

From Das Boot, Chad reaches up and holds my hand.

BBB licks my under-chin.

Toward the end of the song, Sister Lucy really starts to push it – showing off her vocals – and this is when I know that she is indeed a true bona fide diva.

I'm so proud of The KDFCs, who sound and look great.

Listening to Sister Lucy sing – backed up by The KDFCs – I feel like JC is there with me, and that everything is going to be okay somehow.

It's a pretty powerful moment.

Maybe even holy.

And then the song is over.

'Let it be, Sister Amber, let it be,' Sister Lucy says to me. And then, to the crowd, she says, 'Childress Public High School – you people ready to dance your butts off?'

The crowd cheers, and then Father Chee hits some funky old-time piano chords on the synthesizer, The Hard-Working Brothers start playing, and Sister Lucy is rocking 'Think' by Aretha Franklin.

The KDFCs are shoulder dipping, booty shaking, making circles with their open hands, and whenever Sister Lucy points at them, they all shout, 'Think!' or 'Freedom!' They are rocking so hard – I'm amazed.

The crowd is going frickin' nuts.

There are people dancing in the aisles.

Everyone is on his or her feet.

And when I look down at the first row, Donna is dancing with Private Jackson. PJ sucks at dancing – but he is dancing! That's a miracle!

So I start dancing with Jared and Chad and BBB – and then I even try to get Ricky dancing, but that doesn't fly so well.

Sister Lucy runs through 'Come See About Me', 'Baby Love', 'O-o-h Child', 'I Want You Back', '(Sweet Sweet Baby) Since You Been Gone', 'Freeway of Love', and when she gets to 'Respect', everyone on stage is soaked with sweat – and everyone in the audience is drenched with sweat too.

The roof is officially off the Childress High School Auditorium.

Sister Lucy rocks the Aretha Franklin signature song, and The KDFCs get to shine on this one too, as they do all kinds of hand movements, shoulder dip with tons of attitude, and sing, 'Sock-it-to-me. Just a little bit.'

When they finish the set, the crowd claps and whistles for ten minutes, and The KDFCs are beaming with pride.

JC is definitely in the house tonight.

Sister Lucy announces the names of the band members and The KDFCs, making all the Koreans in the house cheer like mad, which is when I realize that The KDFCs' families have come to support them, thanks – no doubt – to Father Chee. And I think, *Cool, we're bringing people together tonight.*

I can't believe how well The Save Bobby Big Boy Variety Show has gone.

I'm so amazed.

I'm so thankful.

But then Franks is telling me that Ty is going to post the total amount of money we raised on the big movie screen at the back of the stage, and that I'm supposed to thank the crowd for coming, so I do, with BBB in my arms.

When I turn around and point to the movie screen at the back of the stage, behind The Hard-Working Brothers' drum set, Ty does his computer thing, the $0000.00 numbers on the huge screen start to spin and 'We're Not Alone' by Dinosaur Jr starts playing very loudly, probably because Ty knows it's one of my very most favorite songs.

$375.15 flashes on the screen.

People cheer.

I nod and think, not bad.

But then the numbers start to spin again.

$657.15

Nice!

People cheer even louder.

$2,019.89

People start to cheer like mad.

$3,998.23

I've accomplished my goal!

I'm so happy.

$5,002.11

Could we have possibly raised that much?

What will we do with the extra money?

I look back behind the stage curtain and Franks and The Five are smiling at me. People are clapping like mad now. Everyone is smiling, and I notice that there are people crying in the audience, which makes me feel very strange.

$7,628.54

This can't be right.

$23,425.76

I almost crap myself.

$62,981.72

What is going on?' I yell to Franks, sorta laughing now, because there is no way we raised that much money.

He winks at me from offstage.

$121,521.09

Suddenly I notice news cameras in the aisles, camera crews and news reporters.

$215,671.87

The last number flashes on the screen several times and then the words Grand Total appear for a few seconds.

Suddenly – Bobby Big Boy and I are standing on the stage alone now, and the auditorium is completely silent.

The screen goes blank.

What the hell is going on?

These words flash up on the screen:

A Message From Amber's Nemesis

Suddenly, Joan of Old's head is on the screen, which completely shocks me for obvious reasons. The shot is a close-up, so her wrinkly face is gigantic. I can see the pillow behind her head, and it looks like she is having trouble breathing. Her wrinkly eyelids look really pink and her skin looks like wax, or maybe ancient cheese.

'I'm probably already dead by now,' Joan of Old's pink wrinkly enormous eyeless head says. 'For those of you who don't know, Amber and I used to battle every Wednesday afternoon. Her strange little boyfriends recorded this several days ago, which was fortuitous, because I am probably gone and buried by now, yes – but especially because I vowed to make Amber cry before I died, and I always keep my word, Ms Appleton, Princess of Hope. Today is the day I defeat you, once and for all. The doctors say this is the end of the road for me. It's about time. My body is going to return to dust. Good riddance! Now I understand the town is having some sort of pep rally for you because of what happened to your mother and because you were so constantly on your guard that you are no longer able to defend yourself, like Nietzsche said. I hear you've lost hope, and – regardless of my philosophical views – you're far too young for that. What will you have to look forward to in old age, if you become a nihilist before you hit eighteen?'

313

Joan of Old starts coughing very badly here, but then recovers.

'I want to say two things to you before I die. One. My Lawrence was a German philosophy professor, hence my obsession with Nietzsche. Here is a quote I never got around to sharing with you: "We should consider every day lost on which we have not danced at least once. And we should call every truth false which was not accompanied by at least one laugh." That was my Lawrence's favorite quote. He used to dance me around the house every night. Every. Single. Night. And how we would laugh. He was a beautiful man, who died far too young, but he would have absolutely loved you. Keep making people laugh, Amber. At least until you are old and gray. Laugh at yourself and others will always laugh with you. Even mean old defeated women like me.'

Joan of Old coughs again.

'Two. I've got some bucks left over – and I'm leaving my entire estate to The Amber Appleton Community Service College Fund, which is what your friends have established without your knowing it. My son Teddy hasn't come to visit me in eleven years, so screw him! Bye-bye, Amber. See you in hell.'

Joan of Old smiles the last grin of a dying woman – which is huge and beautiful – and then she says, 'I finally got you, didn't I?'

I'm crying now onstage even though I'm not exactly sure what is happening.

The film cuts to the old folk's common room at the home. My old able-legged silver-haired friends are gathered around my wheelchair-bound silver-headed friends. With his oxygen bottle by his side, Old Man Linder steps forward and says, 'Kid, you were the only one who came to visit us when we needed a good laugh. Life is a long, long race, and the finish is often lonely. Even our own flesh and blood – many of our sons and daughters – abandoned us at some point, so when we heard about what happened to your mother, we all wrote you into our wills. Some of us are giving more than others, but you should be all set covering your Bryn Mawr tuition over the next five years or so. Maybe there'll be some left over for law school too.'

The audience is clapping now, camera crews are rolling film, women are crying, and I'm still not sure what the hell is going on.

But then Franks and The Five walk out onto the stage.

Franks has a live microphone. He says, 'I've never met a person with more spirit, I've never met a person with more hope and love in her heart, I've never met a more deserving person than Amber Appleton. She never thinks of herself first. She's always thinking up some crazy scheme to help others, whether they want help or not. Well,

Amber, this time it was The Five who thought up a plan to help you in your time of need.'

Ricky, Chad on Das Boot, Jared, Ty, and Lex Pinkston dressed as a Puerto Rican gang member – they are all smiling at me.

'You are loved, Amber Appleton,' Franks says.

'So this money is for me?' I ask.

'It's your college fund.'

'What about Bobby Big Boy's operation? How will I pay for that?'

'She wants to know how she's going to pay for her dog's operation,' Franks says into his microphone, and the audience starts laughing – as if everyone is in on the joke except me.

Dr Weissmuller stands up in the third row, smiles, and yells, 'On the house!'

The audience cheers again, and then some bright loser starts yelling, 'Speech! Speech! Speech!'

The chant catches on, and then Franks is handing me the live microphone.

I'm still crying a little.

'Thank you, everyone. I'm not really sure this is real, or what it means exactly. I hope my mom is looking down on us tonight,' I say and then pause, because I start to cry a little harder.

I swallow and think about my mom.

She'd have liked to see this.

She would have crapped her pants when that last number flashed up on the screen.

'I don't know what else to say. I'm speechless. Thanks.'

I hand the live microphone back to Franks, and he says, 'Thanks for coming, everyone. You make me proud to live in Childress – the town that takes care of its own. Drive home safely!'

And before he sees me coming, I give Franks a big old teddy-bear hug right onstage – getting my arms halfway around his big belly and sinking my tear-streaked face into his chest.

Surprisingly, he hugs me back, and I smile and close my eyes – savoring the moment.

'You're a good man, Franks,' I say. 'You really are. True.'

'How about you give the rest of us some love, sweetheart?' Chad says.

But before I can answer, I'm rushed by a bunch of reporters who stick cameras in my face and ask me all sorts of personal questions about my mom.

Before I can even think, Donna is onstage, yelling, 'My client has no comment at the present moment! Boys, let's get her out of here!'

So I say a quick goodbye to PJ, FC, The KDFCs, DWL, The Hard-Working Brothers, Old Man Thompson, and—

'Get the hell out of here already before those reporters lynch you,' Old Man Linder yells at me, and then squeezes my shoulder like he always does.

The Five gets me the hell out of there, leaving Das Boot behind, because it doesn't fit into Donna's Mercedes. No worries. Mr Fox will take Das Boot home in the Fox family van.

In the car I pet BBB, hug my boys and thank them for getting everyone to participate in the show, filming Joan of Old, and raising money for my college fund, which is pretty amazing. I even thank Lex, who is still dressed as a Puerto Rican gang member and is somehow smushed in the car with us – making us The Six and no longer The Five.

Donna says, 'Sundaes at my place!'

After a quick stop at the food store, I wash my hands, make proper sundaes in Donna's kitchen for my boys, and then we celebrate the night by sharing ice cream and sword fighting with spoons. True.

After everyone is finished eating, the boys go to Ricky's room to play Halo 3, and Donna and I wash dishes in the kitchen.

'What the hell happened tonight?' I ask.

'The town of Childress came together and tried the best they could to make a wrong right. And I'm not talking about the money. They came together in the auditorium, gave their time to say that they care.'

'Why?'

'Because most people are good,' Donna says, and then passes me a rinsed bowl.

I stick it into the dishwasher and say, 'Did they make a wrong right?'

'What do you think?'

'It doesn't bring my mom back. It doesn't erase what happened – which is still messed up beyond imagination. Whack.'

'No, it doesn't. And yes, it still is.'

'So I really have access to all that money?' I ask, shoving a handful of spoons into the dishwasher utensil bin.

'No,' Donna says while rinsing the last ice cream bowl. 'You have a college fund that you can use to pay college and graduate school tuition. I drew up all of the papers.'

'What happens if I don't use the money?'

'Why wouldn't you use the money? You're still planning on going to Bryn Mawr and then Harvard, right?'

'Yeah, but maybe I'll get scholarships – like you did.'

'I thought of that.'

'You did?'

'If you get to go to school for free, you can donate the money to the charity of your choice.'

'Really?'

'Really.'

'So I could like – donate all of the money to the Childress Public High School Business Department so that Franks could maybe build a killer classroom and get out of the basement? Or maybe, at least, he could get some windows put in and he wouldn't have to buy all of his own supplies using his own personal money?'

'You could do something like that. Absolutely.'

I smile, thinking of all the good hooey I can do for others with the money.

FIFTY-EIGHT

When the junior prom rolls around, Donna rents Ricky and me a stretch limo. I wear my silver dress. Ricky wears his tuxedo. Donna has flowers for both of us. We take a crapload of pictures in the backyard, and then we go to Ty's house and pick him up. He's still got the beard, but he looks dashing in a navy blue tuxedo. Mr and Mrs Hendrix take pictures of Ricky, Ty, and me for – like – an hour, and then we jump into the limo and tell the driver to take us to Jared's and Chad's house, where they are waiting with their dates – Carla Winslow and Sally Craig – from the cheerleading squad. These girls are bimbo airheads, but for my boys, I'm super nice to both of them. Mr and Mrs Fox take pictures of all of us in various poses for another hour, and then we are in the limo again – off to the local Hilton reception room where our junior prom is held, with Mr Fox following us in the Fox van, which transports Das Boot for Chad.

When we arrive, we get Chad into Das Boot, and then we make our entrance.

Franks is a greeter, which means he has to check our breath for alcohol.

So we walk in all staggering, pretending to be hammered.

'Want some vodka?' I ask Franks.

'I'll probably need some by the end of the night,' Franks says to me, and we all laugh.

'How do I look, Franks?'

'All of you look great,' Franks says, and Carla and Sally giggle at that one.

At the prom we eat good food, we dance to the music the DJ plays, we mix in with Lex Pinkston and all of the football players and their cheerleader dates. I split the slow dances equally between Ricky and Ty. And when they play 'Always And Forever' at the end, all members of The Five and Sally and Carla dance in a big circle with our arms linked – and our teachers watching and waiting to go home. It's all pretty silly, really.

When the prom is over, we put Das Boot into the Fox van, hop into our limo, and drive to Ty's parents' beach house in Long Beach Island, or LBI. Mr Fox follows us down with Das Boot, because he is a good dad.

Ty's parents' house is actually right on the beach, so after we get Das Boot into the house and Mr Fox leaves, we put Chad in a backpack and hit the sand to do some stargazing.

Barefoot, but still in our tuxedos and dresses, we run along the edge of the ocean, the water licking our ankles – laughing and singing like the kids we are.

Somehow we decide to spend the entire night on the beach so we can see the sunrise.

We pick out a spot in front of Ty's parents' house.

We lie down on the sand making this big pile of teenagers.

We look up into the universe, and we get pretty quiet as we marvel.

Everyone falls asleep except me.

I think about my mom.

I get up and cry a little down by the ocean, so that the others won't hear.

After a few minutes, Ty appears and puts his arm around me – in a brotherly sorta way.

When I turn around surprised, he holds me, I sob into his overly starched tuxedo shirt, and his friendship beard scratches my forehead.

Hours later, the sun comes up.

Ty and I are simply sitting together on a sand dune.

When The Five finds us, I snap out of my sadness and yell, 'I'm making breakfast!'

And then in Ty's parents' beach house, I make killer omelets for everyone.

FIFTY-NINE

By doing some Internet research, I learn that you have to fill out a visitor's application and get it approved before you will be allowed to visit any prisoner in a maximum-security facility. There are these rules you have to read and agree to follow with a signature. If you are not eighteen you need to have a guardian sign the forms as well, and since I don't want Donna or anyone else to know that I am going to visit my mother's killer, I wait until my eighteenth birthday to fill out the form and send it in – which I do after the barbeque party Donna throws for me in the backyard.

My eighteenth b-day party is sorta a big thing, as Old Man Linder, Old Man Thompson, and some old people from the home come, The KDFCs bring their families along with FC, the Franks family shows, The Five are, of course, there along with many of my fellow CPHS classmates, Prince Tony, and Mrs Baxter – and even PJ and Ms Jenny show up, which is sorta cool, because in a sexy summer dress, Donna flirts with PJ and he doesn't leave early. Sister Lucy and The Hard-Working Brothers do an encore outdoor performance with The Korean Divas for Christ, which rocks hard-core, and brings the neighbors out of their houses and into our backyard. I am embarrassed by the many super-cool presents. And later that night, after everyone has left, I fill out the visiting-prison form and drop it in the mail – which is my birthday present to myself.

My mother's killer has to agree to see me as well, and I worry that he'll refuse.

I also worry about Donna getting the reply letter, so every day I sneak away from my summer job at Rita's water ice when the mail is delivered at two, just so Donna won't intercept the letter from the prison.

After a few weeks of waiting, I get a very official response.

The letter states a date and time.

I am granted a fifteen-minute non-contact visit – meaning we will be separated by Plexiglas, which is just fine with me.

I'll only need five minutes with my mother's killer, so I'm cool.

The day before the non-contact visit, I call Ty and ask him if he will ditch work at one of his dad's bank branches – where he does his summer nine-to-five as a drive-thru bank teller. I ask if he'll take me somewhere secret, and promise never to tell anyone about it for as long as he

lives, and in exchange, I'll finally go to Friendly's with
him just like old times, so he can finally shave off his
friendship beard. We still haven't been to Friendly's since
my mom died.

'What time do I pick you up?'

'Eight AM. And make sure you have a full tank of
gas.'

'Cool.'

The next morning I call my boss at Rita's and tell him
I am having woman problems so he won't ask any questions, and he doesn't.

Bearded Ty shows up right on time, I jump into his
Volvo station wagon, and he says, 'Where we headed?'

'Get on the turnpike and go north.'

'Cool,' Ty says, and then we are off.

I give him directions for almost two hours, and when
we pull into the parking lot of the maximum-security
prison, he says, 'Um, Amber. What the hell are we doing
here?'

'I have a non-contact visit scheduled with my mom's
killer.'

'What? Why?'

'Because I need to face him and then move on.'

'I'm not sure that's a good idea.'

'Trust me.'

'Amber, um—'

'Just wait here, okay? I'll be back in less than an hour.'

'I don't like this,' Ty says, and I notice that his

friendship beard is almost six inches long now. It has to go – and soon.

'Get ready to lose that beard,' I say, and then walk across the parking lot.

Ty yells my name from his car a few times, but he doesn't follow me into the prison.

Inside I have to walk through a metal detector, show my driver's license, my CPHS school ID, and my visitation permission letter – and then I am frisked and searched by a large woman in a guard uniform. She's packing heat too.

When she concludes that I have no weapons on me – that I am only a harmless girl – she leads me down a hallway and through two sets of guarded and locked doors, where she has to yell, 'Visitor coming through – searched and clean!'

At the end of the fourth hallway, she opens a door and says, 'This is it. I'll wait for you here.'

Right before I step into the room, I get really nervous, and for some reason I just can't make my legs carry me into the visitation room, so – in my mind – I conjure up my all-time Amber-and-her-mom number-one moment to give me courage.

I wasn't going to tell you this, but my mom's last boyfriend – A-hole Oliver – well, he didn't exactly throw us out of his apartment.

The whole deal went down something like this:

Mom, BBB, and I were watching the debut episode of

Buffy the Vampire Slayer from the season one DVDs, which I had borrowed from Jared and Chad. Buffy was just about to save her new friend Willow from the vamps when A-hole Oliver came home and told us that he wanted to watch the Sixers game, so I immediately turned off *Buffy* – right at the good part – and handed AO the remote, because it was his apartment and his DVD player and I really didn't feel like arguing with A-hole Oliver, because he was pretty stubborn and would cut you down in a heartbeat with one of his mean, straight-for-the-jugular insults.

He put on the Sixers, which didn't really bother me all that much because AO pretty much controlled the TV whenever he was home, so I wouldn't have expected anything different. But Mom, she was sorta into *Buffy* after watching season six – which Chad and Jared gave me for my birthday the year before, saying that season six was the best because that one has the musical episode, *Once More, With Feeling* – and it was actually Mom's idea to borrow season one from my boys so we could watch the whole series in order, together, mother-and-daughter style.

I think that maybe Mom dug the show because Buffy kicks so much apple bottom for a regular chick, even if she is a slayer. She's really like a role model for women. But Buffy keeps it real too. She may be a superchick, but she still hangs out with her dorky friends Xander and Willow, who are totally like real people even if one falls in love with a demon and the other becomes a powerful witch, so you sorta believe in Buffy – like she's real – even though she kills vampires and monsters and lives on a hellmouth. The show gives regular chicks like Mom and me hope. True? True.

We watched the Sixers for a while, nobody saying anything, and then A-hole Oliver went into the kitchen and didn't come back for a few minutes.

'Why did you make us turn off *Buffy* if you aren't even going to watch basketball?' Mom yelled to her man.

'I'm listening to it,' AO said from the kitchen, making himself a sandwich.

I was shocked when Mom got up from the couch, took back the remote, and put the *Buffy* DVD back on.

AO returned to the living room, sandwich in hand, and said, 'I'm watching the Sixers!'

'We were watching *Buffy*,' Mom said, which surprised me because my mom never stuck up for herself at all.

'When you start kicking in some more bucks for rent, you can control the TV,' AO said. 'You're responsible for two of the three people living here and you don't even cover your half of the bills. So as long as I'm picking up the *entire* cable bill, we watch the Sixers whenever they're on.'

Oliver sorta pushed Mom aside, ejected the *Buffy* DVD, and threw it at me like a Frisbee, but too hard. The disk rose up, hit the wall over my head, and then fell behind the couch. BBB began to bark.

'Hey, what the hell?' I said. 'That's not mine. You're paying for it if it's scratched.'

AO pointed to the DVD player and said, 'That machine's not yours either. Nothing in this apartment is yours. You don't own anything besides that found mutt. And if it weren't for me, you'd be out on the streets – and don't you forget it.'

'I work,' I say.

'And do I take any of your water ice money?' AO asked me as if he was a hero or something.

'No.'

'Well then,' AO said, and then sat back down.

I looked at Mom and could tell that she'd had enough of Oliver, but I wasn't ready for what she said next.

'Amber, go into your room and put all of your clothes into trash bags. Pack up all your belongings. Don't forget your comforter.'

'Why?' I said.

'Because we're moving out,' Mom said with this real determined look on her face.

'Where are you going to live?' AO said with a laugh, flashing a mouthful of half-chewed lunch meat – laughing at us. *On your school bus?*

Mom went into the kitchen; I followed her. When she grabbed the trash bags from under the sink, went to her room, and started stuffing all of her clothes into the bags, BBB and I went to my room and did the same thing. We didn't have that much stuff, so we only filled six bags.

With coats on, bags in hands, we walked past A-hole Oliver, and he said, 'You'll be back. See you in a few hours.'

We walked out of AO's apartment complex, and then my mother kissed me on both cheeks, held my head in her hands, and said, 'Oliver was an asshole. I'm sorry I made you live with him for so long. We're never going back to his apartment. I promise.'

I smiled at her, and for some reason we both began to cry right there on the sidewalk, hugging each other, as BBB watched.

'It might take me some time, Amber,' my mother whispered into my ear, 'but I'll get us into our very own apartment. We can make it without Oliver. I'll get a better job or maybe find a better man. Something will come along for us.'

'I know,' I told my mom, but the truth is that I was very scared, because Mom had a lot of alcohol on her breath and I sorta understood without Mom saying it that right then and there, we were officially homeless. But we were also free, and Mom's standing up to Oliver and taking a chance, well that was something I could respect. It kicked a little apple bottom – Buffy-style. Or at least that's what I thought at the time, three weeks before Mom asked A-hole Oliver to let us back into his apartment and he refused, even after Mom brought me to him and begged him to let us back in if only for her daughter's sake.

'Promise me something right now,' Mom said while looking me in the eyes, still holding my cheeks with her hands, five minutes after we had first left AO's apartment. 'You'll never ever let a man treat you the way Oliver treated me.'

'I won't.'

'Tell me that you won't live your life afraid, but will grow up and live a better life than your mother could ever imagine.'

'I will,' I said.

We were both crying in public, with our six trash bags of belongings circling our feet, and for some reason, right then and there, I felt like I was saying goodbye to my mother, that she was going to descend into a place that doesn't allow you to return – that this was the beginning of the end or something for her. It was like she had snapped – as if her mind had begun to turn on her and she knew it. It was like she was on her deathbed in some stupid movie and I was vowing to fulfill her last wishes. But it was also sorta like a beginning for me, because what I promised my mother – I didn't take that vow lightly then, and I sure as hell don't take it lightly now.

So standing there in the doorway of the prison visitation room, just before I face my mother's killer, I take a deep breath – remembering all that has happened, all that I have survived, how strong I've become – and once more I say, 'I won't. I will.'

When I walk into the room, another security guard – a young skinny man – shows me to a little booth that is sorta like a desk with dividing walls to separate me from the other visitors, even though there are no other visitors in the room right now.

My mother's killer – he's seated on the other side of thick Plexiglas and is staring at me.

On the desk are headphones I am supposed to put on that have a little microphone stick that hangs out over your mouth – sorta like what a helicopter pilot might wear.

My mother's killer already has his headset on.

He's staring at me – blankly.

Huge brown glasses.

Crazy hair.

Orange jumpsuit.

His wrists are handcuffed to the belt that circles his belly.

I try not to think about what he did to my mother, but I can't help it – a wave of anger rushes through my limbs.

I take a few deep breaths.

He nods toward the headset and mouths the words: PUT IT ON.

I look into his eyes and shiver.

There is nothing there.

He is not human.

He is a thing.

There is nothing left in his eyes.

Nothing.

He is a monster.

Seeing the daughter of his last victim – no emotion registers on his face.

Nothing.

So I do not put on the headset.

Instead, I pull out an origami swan from my pocket and show it to him.

No emotion registers on his face.

I unfold the swan with trembling hands.

My poem is written in huge letters.

With an open hand, I hold my words up to the glass and watch my mother's killer read what I have written to him – how I am responding to his murdering my mother.

You may exist in
This world—but I exist too
And I will not yield

The face of my mother's killer does not change.

He nods toward the headset again and yells, PUT IT ON!

He's trying to yell through the glass, he obviously wants to say something to me, but he doesn't get to call the shots today.

I see the guards behind him stiffen.

I keep my haiku up against the glass and shake my head no.

Suddenly, the man lunges toward the glass.

Attacks my haiku with his head – banging it against the glass several times before the guards come and drag him out of the visitor's room.

I don't even flinch.

Only when they have him completely out of the room do I lower my haiku from the glass.

I leave my poem there on the desk; I want it to stay in the prison.

'What the hell did you write on that piece of paper?' the young skinny guard asks me.

When I don't answer, he walks past me and picks up my haiku.

I walk out of the visitor's room, and the woman guard escorts me past security, through the metal detector, and out of the prison.

Surprisingly, I'm feeling a little better having faced my mother's killer.

He has not defeated me – and if a man like him can't beat me, I know nothing will.

There is life all around me.

Sky.

Clouds.

Trees.

Endless air.

Birds flying overhead.

There is a good bearded boy in a Volvo waiting for me.

All this, right now, is mine to experience.

I need to drink it up for Mom, for all of those who cannot – and for me too.

I'm only eighteen.

These are the days.

I'm still a kid if I want to be.

And I do.

Bearded Ty gets out of the car when he sees me walking across the parking lot, but he doesn't say anything. His face expresses concern. I can tell he cares about me – deeply. And I can tell he is still a kid too – in spite of the hideous friendship beard.

'I did what I had to do,' I tell him.

'Do you want to talk about it?'

'No.'

'Okay.'

'Do you want to open your presents?' I ask.

'Presents?'

'For driving me today.'

'I'm not sure this is the appropriate—'

'We're opening your presents. Get in the car.'

We get into his Volvo station wagon.

'Here's present number one,' I say and then hand him a small but heavy wrap job.

'This is sort of weird,' Ty says.

'What?'

'Opening presents in the parking lot of a maximum security prison.'

'We're celebrating our freedom. We're celebrating our ability to be kids when everything is trying to take that away from us. It's a choice, Ty. We can do whatever we want.'

'What are you talking about?'

'Come on, just open it already. You're going to like this present. I promise.'

Ty rips off the wrapping paper. 'Batteries?'

'Open 'em up. You'll only need two.'

'For what?'

'For present number two.'

'What?'

'Just do it.'

Ty gets two batteries ready and then opens his second present.

'An electric razor,' he says.

I grab the box, open it up, and put the batteries into the electric razor.

I flick it on and it makes a buzzing noise.

BZZZZZZZ.

I look Ty in the eyes and I say, 'I think it's time to shave off that awful beard.'

'I'm not shaving until you agree to go to Friendly's with The Five,' he says, and then laughs sorta strangely, as if he's no longer sure about his plan. 'Remember?'

But then suddenly, I want to look into his eyes – I

want to know that there is something inside of Ty. Something human. The opposite of what I saw while looking through the Plexiglas – gazing into the eyes of a monster.

I search those brown orbs.

They are innocent.

They are the color of bark.

They are alive.

They are boyish.

They are full of possibility.

They are full of hope.

They are gorgeous.

They are beautiful.

They give me fuel – they make my chest feel so warm.

'Well, then, we'll go to Friendly's,' I say. 'Just as soon as we pick up The Five. You have my word. So this is the part where I get to shave off your beard.'

BZZZZZZZZ! says the electric razor

'You have to trim it with scissors first,' Ty says.

So I show him the scissors that came with the electric razor.

'You're gonna do it in my car? Right here?'

'Yep,' I say.

He swallows once, and then says, 'Please, Amber. Not in my sweet ride.'

So we step out of the car and I carefully snip Ty's beard down to the skin with scissors – so much hair falls to the asphalt of the maximum-security prison parking lot.

338

Carefully – I shave Ty's face with the battery-operated electric razor.

A boy emerges from underneath all that facial hair.

'How's it feel to be clean-shaven?' I ask when we are back in the Volvo.

'The people at the bank are going to be pleased,' Ty says. 'My parents will probably write you a thank-you note.'

Ty and I eat a late lunch at McDonald's – cheeseburgers, salty fries, milk shakes – and then we ride the rest of the way home from the maximum-security prison listening to pop music on the radio, and when a good song comes on that we both know, we sing it loudly.

When we get back to Childress, we stop by Chad's and Jared's house.

'You shaved the beard!' Jared says. 'Does that mean we're going to Friendly's?'

When I nod, the Brothers Fox smile and Jared carries Chad into the backseat.

We pick up Ricky just as Donna is getting home from work.

In the kitchen, Ricky says, 'Ty Hendrix does not have a beard. Yes. Where did his beard go?'

'You're going back to Friendly's, eh?' Donna asks as BBB runs around our legs and licks my boys' hands when they bend down to pet B Thrice.

'You wanna come with, Donna?' I ask.

'You kids go and have your fun,' she says.

'You haven't ridden in my Volvo yet, Donna,' Ty says. 'It's a sweet ride.'

'You really want me to come?' Donna asks.

'Come on, sugar,' Chad-in-a-backpack says. 'You know you want to sit next to me in the backseat. I'll keep my hands to myself. Promise.'

We all laugh, and Donna says, 'I'm paying then.'

I put BBB in his room, put on the classical music station, and it's playing Chopin's 'Minute Waltz,' which makes BBB start jumping and dancing, so I watch him for a while – my best buddy, BBB – and then I lock B Thrice's bedroom door and we all pile into Ty's Volvo station wagon, and someone suggests that we ring and run Franks' house, so we drive there, and Jared runs up to the door, rings the doorbell, and then runs back into the car. When Franks' redheaded wife steps outside and looks around clueless, we all laugh, and Ty hits the gas.

At Friendly's Donna orders one of every sundae and some fries too. We all sword fight with the long dessert spoons, getting whipped cream and cherries and caramel and chocolate sauce and nuts all over the place. We laugh our heads off. Donna takes it all in with a wise smile. And in my head I say a little prayer to JC.

I don't get it, JC. I don't understand the plan. I miss my mom. To take her like that when I'm not yet even a woman – it's not really fair, is it? But I'm glad there are times like this.

I'm glad there are friends like this. I am glad there are Friendly's sundaes. That's all for right now.

Donna is smiling. All my boys are eating ice cream. I have a whole booth full of good friends. And I think to myself, you cannot give up, Amber. No matter what happens.

I won't. I will.

Suddenly, as I think about my mom, I feel like I might start crying.

~~Before I burst into tears,~~ in my mind, I start pumping myself up with accolades to stop the waterworks, and I'm using a super-mega sports announcer voice:

The indomitably hopeful one!
The girl of unyielding optimism!
The teen of merriment!
The fan favorite!
Your undisputed champion!

'Amber – Rock Star of Hope – Apple-TOOOOOOOOOON!' I yell across the Friendly's, and everyone in the joint turns and looks at me like my head is on fire.

'You are *such* a freak,' Jared whispers to me, and all of my boys smile and laugh.

I smile right back at them and fill my mouth with a spoonful of delicious coffee ice cream.

Maybe I am a freak – but I'm one hopeful misfit, and you could be worse things in this world. True? True.

I spread hope.

I'm a hope spreader.

I guess that's what I do – licentiously – that's why I'm still circling the big flaming ball in the sky. (That's the sun – sucka!)

ACKNOWLEDGMENTS

I would like to thank my wonderful and tenacious agent, Doug Stewart – D, you are simply amazing – and my brilliant editor, Alvina Ling, for believing in both Amber and me and for pushing me to tell the best story I possibly could. I am wildly blessed to be working with such smart and hip and kind professionals. Props to their assistants, Seth Fishman and Connie Hsu. Thanks to all at Sterling Lord Literistic and Little, Brown and Company who worked on this manuscript and/or helped to get my words out into the world. Much love to all of the friends and family members who continue to support me and my career – but an extra nod to the people who played a special role in the creation of this book (whether they know it or not) and the people who keep me feeling hopeful: my wife, Alicia Bessette; Sister Megan; Brother Micah; K-Hen; Mom; Dad; Barb & Peague; Bill, Mo, and Owen Rhoda; Flem; fellow Bardbarian, Scott Humfeld; Scott Caldwell (Mr Canada); Myfanwy Collins; Justin Dunn; K-Rob; BD; veterinarian extraordinaire, Dr Corey Shagensky; Roland Merullo; Old Man Harry and Grandmom Dink; Uncle Pete; my webmaster, Tim Rayworth; my photographer, Dave Tavani; LL; The WMs; Chris Barrett; everyone who attended the TSLP launch party; and many many more. . . .